Reunion at the Wetside

A novel

by

Alec Clayton

Cover art "Hale Bopp," painting by Penelope G. Merrell.
Cover design by ClaytonWorks.

ISBN: 978-0-9800322-7-7

DISCLAIMER

This is a work of fiction. All characters are the product of the
author's imagination. Resemblance to any person living or dead
is entirely coincidental. (Except when intentional, you know
who you are.)

ACKNOWLEDGEMENTS

I am indebted to Larry Johnson and Jack Butler for editorial help and to Linda Delayen for her constant encouragement. I want to thank Reiko Callner, a former prosecuting attorney, and Randy McCarthy, crime writer for The News Tribune in Tacoma, Washington, for their help with the crime and punishment sections of this book. If there is anything about the criminal justice system or crime reporting that seems less than believable, it is because I didn't follow their advice in every instance.

Thanks to Cheryl Robbins from the Old Neighborhood for certain inspirations and for telling me what ICH (Darling Debs) pledges were forced to wear around their necks.

Thanks to my wife, Gabi, for her meticulous editorial and graphic help.

Also by Alec Clayton

Fiction
> **Until the Dawn**
> **Imprudent Zeal**
> **The Wives of Marty Winters**
> **The Backside of Nowhere**
> **Return to Freedom**

Non-fiction
> **As If Art Matters**

Books by Alec Clayton available online at

www.alecclayton.com
www.mudflatpress.com

This may be confusing, so try to keep up.

The stories told in this book are augmented by selections from two other sources written by four different writers. They are the "Police Blotter" column in the Wetside *Daily Journal* and "Best Friends," the Internet blog written by Jim Bright and Alex Martin.

Harold Drews wrote the "Police Blotter" from 1954 to 1978. His son Harry resurrected the column in 1980 and continued it until May 4, 2010. Harry's column was published in both the print and Internet versions of the *Journal*. The columns by Harry Drews that are reprinted in this book were taken from his blog and those by Harold Drews are from early editions of the *Journal*. Thanks to the *Journal* editors for granting reprint rights.

Alex Martin and Jim Bright began collaborating on the blog called "Best Friends" in January 2010. New entries were posted two to three times a week. It is still being published. Alex and Jim's blog entries have been reorganized to fit the chronological order of the stories told, which relate to memories from their shared childhood as well as recent events beginning in October 2008. Dates and titles of blog entries have been eliminated to avoid unnecessary redundancy in chapter headings. Alex and Jim each made comments on the other's blog postings. These comments appear at the end of the posting when necessary. Some have been edited out.

Readers were allowed to post comments on both the "Police Blotter" and "Best Friends" blogs. These reader comments have been edited to eliminate the boring and irrelevant ones. Most were stupid, prejudiced, ill-informed and marked by atrocious spelling and grammar. The editors chose to leave a few of these for whatever entertainment value they may have.

Thanks to Jim and Alex for permission to lift their words from the Internet.

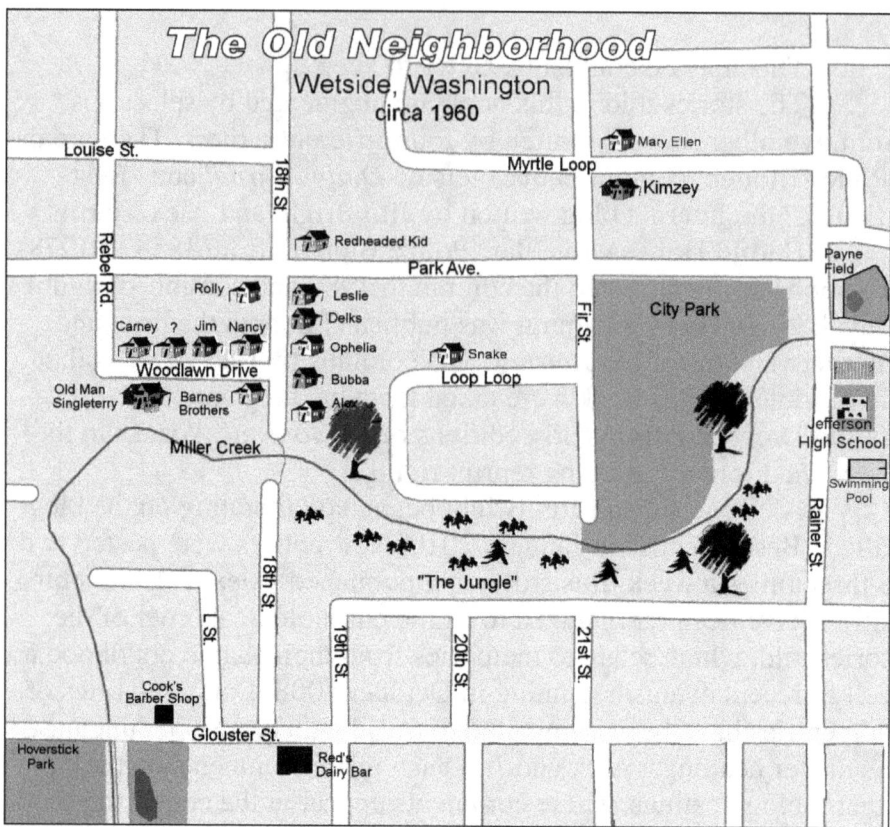

Cast of Characters

COPS

Adam Spitzer - police spokesman in the early years
Brewster Crockett - really bad cop, nickname Walrus
Christopher Hatcher - private eye in 2010
Gene Whitney - Sheriff's Office spokesperson in 1954
Fred Felts - bad cop, nickname Warthog
Rand McKnight - Police chief in the '50s-'60s
Sgt. Delk - a drunk
Snake Collins - bad boy, Wetside police spokesman in 2009

Cast of Characters (continued)
QUEENS
    Amanda Darling (Jim Bright, aka Amanda Bright)
    Anita Mann (George Newman)
    Bonnie Parker (Billy Martin)
    Honey Jewel (Raymond Craig)
    Liza Jane (Larry Butler)
    Miss Tammy Tucker (Tom Rogers)

POLICE BLOTTER REPORTERS
Harold Drews and **Harold Jr. "Harry"**

TEACHERS
    Doug Silver - history and coach
    Jesus Gomez - Spanish
    Mr. Sutter - Jefferson HS principal
    Mrs. Evans - 10th grade math teacher

IN THE NEIGHBORHOOD
    Abilene - Mr. Singleterry's strangely estranged ex-wife
    Alex Martin - our hero
    Anna Shemper - Darling Deb SWJ*
    Aunt Belinda and **Uncle Art** - they're dead
    Barney Pressman - owner of Barney's Wetside Pub
    Betty Black - Darling Deb SWJ*
    Bill and Rodney Barnes - dated Sullivan girls
    Bubba Austin - bad boy
    Buster James - frat boy
    Carney Jones - Santa Claus
    Christine Rocker - black girl
    Delks - three boys
    Donny Brooks - Alex's first husband, an actor
    Dudley Strong - big kid, judge

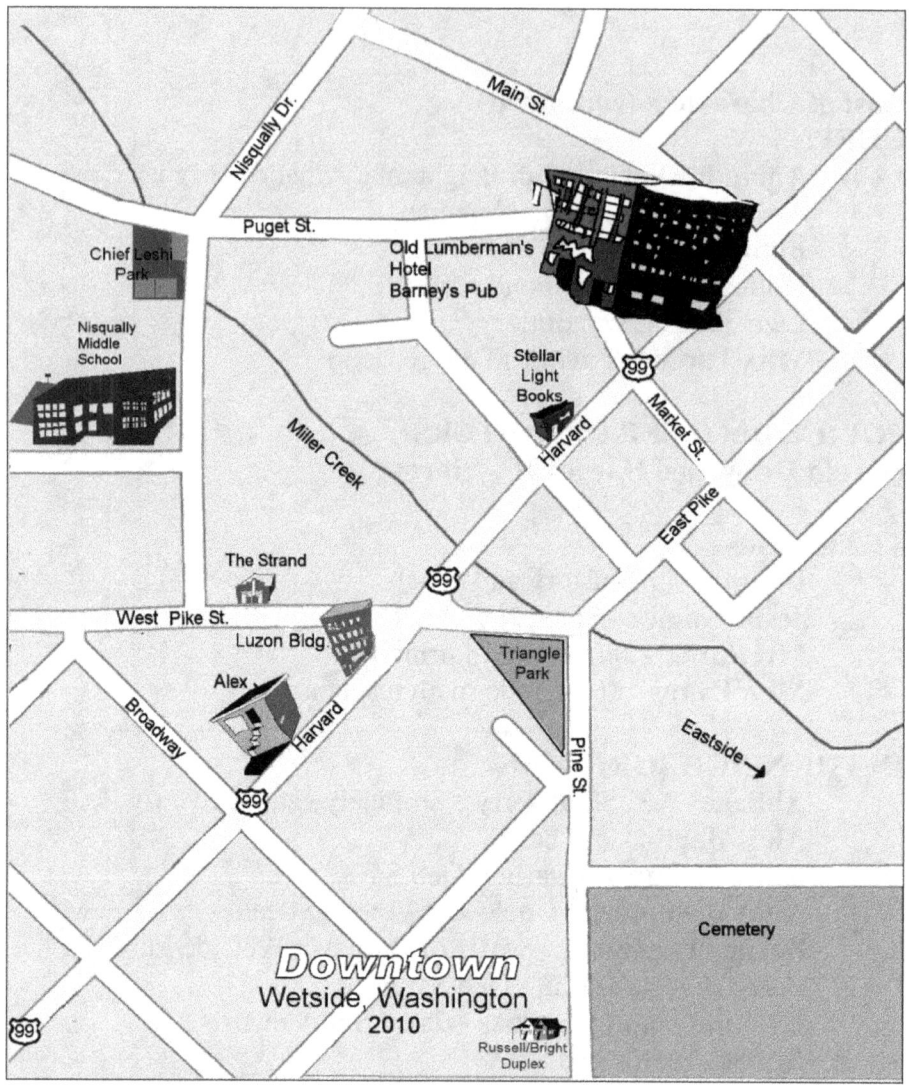

Chief Leshi Park

Nisqually Dr.

Main St.

Puget St.

Old Lumberman's Hotel

Barney's Pub

Nisqually Middle School

Stellar Light Books

99

Market St.

Miller Creek

Harvard

East Pike

The Strand

West Pike St.

99

Luzon Bldg.

Alex

Triangle Park

Broadway

Harvard

Pine St.

Eastside →

99

Cemetery

Downtown
Wetside, Washington
2010

Russell/Bright Duplex

99

Cast of Characters – In the Neighborhood (continued)
Greg and Nellie Jones - Twin boys Kyle and Doyle
Greasy Hendrix - Jim Bright's next door neighbor
Heather Cross - Darling Deb
J.B. Van - coroner
Jean Herbert - followed Wanda from Louisiana

Cast of Characters – In the Neighborhood (continued)

Jessica - Mr. Singleterry's new wife
Jim Bright - our other hero
Jimi Sue - Hendrix housekeeper, second neighborhood slut SWJ*
Johnny Delgado - nice kid
Kimzy Williams - crazy naked Kay Kay
Lara Cockburn Grant - Darling Debs officer SWJ*
Leslie Grant - shy kid, married Susan Smith SWJ*
Miriam Heart - Gender Identity Center, Seattle
Marvin Tuttle - Eastender
Mary Elizabeth Lucious - Miss Wetside 1960 SWJ*
Melody Sauer - young hooker in 1957
Mr. Singleterry - neighborhood developer
Nancy Hendrix Bright - Jim's first wife SWJ*
Nelly and Ned Turner - owners Nelly's BBQ
Ophelia Sullivan - first neighborhood slut SWJ*
Randy Glass - bartender
Ralph Johnson - managing editor *Daily Journal*, 1969
Red - the kid without a name
Red Rogers - owns Red's Dairy Bar
Reggie Sheffield - Bubba Austin's half brother
Rolly Simpson - Jim's next door neighbor, married Molly Robbins
Ross brothers - Jimmy, Roy and Stew, bad boys
Smiley Russell - black boy
Samuel Bright - minister of the Clear Water Baptist Church, Jim's father
Sam Grant- owner of Grant's dept. store (succeeded by Sam Jr.)
Trisha Sullivan - Ophelia's sister, called Pug
Uncle Bradley - Jim's gay uncle
Wanda Bright - Jim's big sister married Jean Herbert

*SWJ - slept with Jim

Raindrops, the blog of the Daily Journal, Wetside, Washington, October 30, 2008

POLICE BLOTTER
By Harry Drews

Shoplifter moons judge

Eighty-four-year-old Melody Sauer of 1428 Mercer Street was removed from County Court yesterday when she mooned the judge. County Judge Dudley Strong was hearing her case of disorderly conduct. The charge stemmed from an incident a month earlier when the octogenarian caused a ruckus in the Victoria's Secret store in Westwood Mall when she was apprehended while attempting to shoplift a package of panties. The undergarments were priced at $12.00 a set. They were thong-style panties, which came six to a set in a variety of colors—red, black, green, blue, pink and yellow, size extra large. Sauer was stopped at the door by a security guard who asked to see in her bag.

"For what?" she demanded to know, clutching her bag to her chest, according to the guard. "Taint none of your beeswax what I got in here."

The guard tried to wrestle the bag out of her hands. Sauer grabbed the package of underwear out of the bag, ripped it open and shouted, "You want these? You want these?"

The guard said "Remember how Robert De Niro said, 'You talkin' to me?' in *Taxi*. That's the way that old lady taunted me, except with different words and some of 'em you can't print in your newspaper. And then she balled the panties up one at a time, and started throwing them all over the place while screaming 'I'll give you the (expletive) panties you (expletive) big (expletive)'. See what I mean about them words."

Store manager Mary Worthington said, "I can't imagine why an old lady like that wanted thongs in the first place. They're for much younger girls."

Sauer appeared in court wearing a simple denim skirt and a T-shirt. Judge Strong fined her $100. When the fine was pronounced

Sauer turned her back to the judge and pulled her skirt and underwear down around her calves, and bent forward, thus exposing her ample derriere to the judge and the court stenographer and a police officer, the latter of whom laughed out loud and was promptly admonished by the judge. The defendant was not wearing thongs of the type she attempted to shoplift from Victoria's Secret. Rather, she was wearing men's boxer shorts, the stenographer noted.

The red-faced judge banged his gavel and shouted, "Get this harlot out of my courtroom."

Sauer was removed from the court and her fine was increased to $1,000. A good Samaritan who asked that his name not be used paid the fine.

The elderly Miss Sauer is known as a local eccentric with a long history of colorful misdemeanors. As a young woman she was repeatedly arrested on prostitution charges, including one incident involving underage boys. County records reveal that she was still operating as a street walker well into her sixties and that even after apparently retiring from the world's oldest profession she continued to have run-ins with the law in the form of various misdemeanors. In 1995 the Alpha Tau Omega fraternity at City University printed and sold T-shirts that said "I heart Melody Sauer." The shirts were very popular on campus.

Sauer's most recent run-in with police prior to this incident was in 2006 when she attacked a young man with an umbrella. The youth claimed he had grasped her elbow with the intention of helping her across the street. Sauer said she thought he was trying to steal her purse. The case was dropped.

Chapter 1

Jim Bright was the last person in the world Alex expected to see sashaying up to the bar in Barney's Pub, the most notorious gay bar in Wetside, Washington. Jim had been Mister Everything in high school almost fifty years ago—all-conference quarterback for the Jefferson High School Golden Wave, track star (holder of the state record in the mile. 4:28), class president (unopposed), voted most handsome and most likely to succeed (both in and out of bed was the popular quip at the time).

Jim and Alex kept in touch after high school, but little by little they began to drift apart. They went to City U, but started running with different crowds and then lost contact. Alex thought Jim must have dropped out after a couple of years. She thought maybe he transferred to some highbrow college that would have been more his style and went on to a high-paying job in Seattle or Miami or New York and marriage to a fashion model or an actress, or maybe a romance writer. The reason she pictured him married to a romance writer was because he looked like Michael Douglas who romanced the Kathleen Turner character, a romance author, in *Romancing the Stone.*

After half a century—could it possibly have been that long?— they renewed their friendship after a chance meeting in Barney's.

Best Friends – Jim and Alex's blog

Oh how we change
by Alex Martin

I purt-nigh pissed in my panties when I saw Jim Bright. Purt-nigh squirted beer out my nose to boot. Wouldn't that have been a fine kettle of fish? Maybe he'd of run over and done a Heimlich on me.

Meeting up with him for the first time since forever got me to thinking about how some people change and others don't. Like the very first year after high school, or more precisely the summer after most of us finished our freshman year in college the boys and girls had changed into men and women, yet for years after that little Kay Kay Williams continued to look like she was twelve. The men especially had bulked up, put on ten to fifteen pounds, and not necessarily fat either, just bigger. Their beards were heavier, or their stubble rather, because none of them grew beards back then. And there was some indefinable difference in the women. I suspect it was a loss of innocence that showed in their face and carriage. They weren't virgins any more. (But I was.) By the time of our twentieth reunion I had a hard time recognizing old classmates, especially those that got away. Not so the benighted souls who never had the gumption to get up and hightail it out of Wetside. Them I see all the time, and I swear they've grown old every one of them without maturing or changing; they just withered. They're not like a full-bodied wine that's got richer with age—although most of them are definitely more full-bodied. They're more like dried meat. Yet (name withheld) still looks like she's sniffing something nasty; Buster James's body parts are bigger and more loosely packed, his nose is fatter, his chin smaller and his ears longer, but they're unmistakably Buster's nose and ears and chin; and face lifts and boob jobs have not made (another name withhold) look like she did at thirty, but rather her procedures have made her look like a house of wax replication of herself in her youth.

4

God, life must be exceedingly bleak for those kids who stepped into their parents footsteps—the kid whose father ran the hardware store, who worked for his father throughout high school and college and has now taken over the business, and the same for the dentist working in his father's clinic and the girl with five sisters who is now a mother of six and grandmother of a dozen. And what about the kids who went to City U and majored in math or business management or political science but never worked in their field of study but rather are teaching math and business management and political science to other kids at City U who will someday take their places? I see those kids around town. I recognize them but I don't know them. Gee, those kids are like the little houses built of ticky-tack. The few that got away, on the other hand, I probably wouldn't recognize if I saw them again. Some of them are artists, one I know of is a writer, more than a few are gay, and far too many are dead. Happy, tragic, sweet or mean as all get-out, those that got away are at least interesting. This town is a killer.

On average our old classmates are about forty pounds heavier and ten years older than me. But not my new best friend Jim Bright. Jim could have been plucked out of the 1960-61 yearbook and plopped down on a stool in Barney's Wetside Pub. He looks every bit as dashing as I remembered. Older, sure, gray, a bit of a pouch hanging over his belt, but still with looks to make my pulse quicken.

Comments:

Mary E said: Did it ever dawn on you that women your age who have had facelifts and boob jobs have done it cuz they lived most of their lives in a world where the only bargaining tool a woman had was her looks. So don't belittle them, bee-ach. You're just a jealous, dried up old hag who can't get laid.

Churchlady said: If you think Wetside is such a stifling conservative town why don't you go back to California or Russia or wherever it is you came from?

Jim said: It's nice to know I can still make your pulse quicken.

Chapter 2

Barney's is in the basement of the old Lumberman's Hotel. The hotel shut down in '95 and about five years ago was remodeled into condominiums with retail stores on the ground floor. What had long ago been the lobby of the hotel is now glass-fronted and houses an upscale men's clothing store (an offshoot of Sam Grant's department store), a candy shop, a hair salon, and Bev and Rhonda's Buffet—not the best restaurant in town, but one of the most popular. Alex frequents Bev and Rhonda's because she likes the owners and because it's convenient, only four blocks from her apartment. Bev and Rhonda's is on the Market Street side of the old hotel building. The entrance to Barney's Pub is in the back of the building on the Puget Street side, a short flight down metal stairs to what used to be the delivery entrance to the old hotel's kitchen. Walking down those steps could be treacherous on rainy nights. Slick and dark, a single red light bulb casting a hot glow onto the heavy wooden door with the number 501 punched into a brass plate and no sign whatsoever to indicate there is a pub inside, not unless your idea of a pub is a big city speakeasy from back in the roaring twenties.

Barney's isn't really notorious. The Meat Market is the one that's notorious. It's sleazy and dirty, and aptly named. But Barney's put the gay in gay. It's a local gay icon. Not that it doesn't have its dark side. There was a riot there in 1970. It was like the famous Stonewall riots in New York but never got that kind of publicity anywhere beyond Wetside and Harold Drews' Police Blotter. A cop was killed and a bunch of drag queens were arrested—they called them female impersonators back then. There are framed newspaper clippings from write-ups about the riot on the wall at Barney's. It's a proud heritage.

But a *pub* for Christ's sake. Isn't that a British term? Southwest Washington is no place for a pub. Back when Jim and Alex were first old enough to order drinks in a bar the idea of a pub in Wetside would have been as alien as those pink and orange rubber shoes everybody wears nowadays. Crocs or air shoes or whatever the hell they're called. People in Wetside did their drinking in bars, or maybe even saloons, but never pubs. It even sounds weird. *A pub, a pub; glub glub.* You might expect to find a pub in Boston maybe, but not out here. Most residents of Wetside don't give Barney's a second thought. Except for the super cool of Wetside, the regulars who think of it as *their* pub, the elect, the privileged few who are hip enough to belong; and they always eye newcomers with suspicion. Like who in tarnation do you think you are and how did you happen to stumble upon our little den? Wetside's so called intelligentsia can be pretty damn snobbish.

If a murder mystery were to be set in Wetside the murder would have to take place under the bare red bulb in the well at the entrance to Barney's. On a rainy night. Picture a black body as two-dimensional as a paper doll face down in black black water, the blood like an oil slick as bright as neon.

Inside are plush leather booths and an antique redwood bar salvaged from a nineteenth century saloon in San Francisco and hauled north on a flatbed trailer. Behind the bar hangs a huge, ornately framed mirror, pitted and distorted. A profusion of flower pots hangs from heavy wooden beams above the bar, doubled by the mirror. Music comes from a 1950s-style jukebox loaded with 45-rpm singles from that era—rockabilly from the old Sun studios, Carl Perkins, Elvis, Jerry Lee—plus lots of Broadway show tunes and a smattering of Fats Domino and Little Richard, and the undisputable local favorite, "Louie Louie" by the Kingsmen. Lounging against the back wall are cardboard figures of Marilyn Monroe, James Dean, Elvis in a gold lamé suit, Rock Hudson and Doris Day. There are no beer ads or commercial messages of any kind, but on the night when Jim Bright showed up there was a single political poster featuring a pop art portrait of Barack Obama. It hung over the booth where Alex was seated.

Calling Barney's a gay bar is something of a stretch, even if they do have drag shows once a week. It would be more accurate to call it a bohemian bar, a hangout for artsy types. Alex Martin was not a lesbian and never had been, unless you count a bit of experimenting back in college and that one summer when she and

7

Mary Elizabeth Lucious shared a cabin at Camp Butterfly, which if you asked Mary Elizabeth about, she'd deny on a stack of bibles. Sometimes Alex wished she was a lesbian. Or black, or Native; anything but white. She liked her self: her looks and her mind, but she was not proud of being a member of the privileged and exploitive class. She frequented Barney's because that's where the most interesting people hung out. Wednesday night is drag night. It's the lowest of lowbrow camp and really raunchy. Fridays is cabaret night. Singers, mostly jazz and folk. One of her favorites was a sultry jazz singer named Amanda Bright. Alex realized that the singer's last name being the same as Jim's was pure coincidence, but seeing Jim at the bar was what made her think about her. She hadn't seen her in a while. To Alex it seemed like just a few months ago, but she realized it must have been years.

It was a week before the 2008 presidential election when she first spotted Jim Bright in Barney's. Seeing him just slammed her right back to the dreaded years of high school. She was seventeen again and so, so tongue-tied. She opened her mouth to speak to him, but couldn't force the words out. She desperately wanted to talk to him. But inside her noggin a shouting match was raging between the old id and the old super ego. *How should I act? Throw myself at him? Act all slutty? Or be cool and aloof.* She wasn't even positive it was really him. After all, how much could she trust her deteriorating brain cells to conjure up the memory of a face from so long ago, and didn't this gorgeous man actually look much younger than Jim would be? She would have been mortified if she'd spoken to him and he'd turned out to be someone else. *God! What if this guy turns out to be Jim's son? Could that possibly be?* She figured she'd be embarrassed if it wasn't him and maybe even more embarrassed if it was—mortified for him to see her in such a place. But why be embarrassed to be seen in Barney's? It's the place to be seen, an obviously fashionable drinking establishment. Because he would see through her at first glance, that's why. He would see her as a pathetic old dame destined to be single and lonely until her dying day, finding what comfort she could in the arms of men picked up in bars. Married men for the most part, men who were anxious to get her into bed but then couldn't wait to hop out and head home to their wives as soon as they got their rocks off at three o'clock in the morning, or more commonly men who were too drunk to get their rocks off and just gave it up and mumbled excuses and went home after pathetic attempts at sex. Men who whined and complained about the very wives they ran home to, men who broke her heart almost every time, even though she knew from the first bat of an eye that it was going to be a one-night stand. Or gay men who just wanted to see what it was like with a woman. Ageing queens who came out late in life and wanted to try the old way one last time and invariably chose the one woman in the place, Alex, who reminded them of their exes or even, god forbid, their mothers. (The tragedy of the gay men who used her for their occasional hetero experimentation was that most of them were more satisfying lovers than the straight men she went out with, but it was only the inadequate and much married heteros and never the hot gay guys who came back for a second date.)

She told herself to cut it out. That was the old super ego talking, she assured herself. *I'm really not that bad. I'm a reasonably well adjusted, intelligent and attractive woman. I'm sixty-six years old for Christ's sake, and I've got a college degree and I've been everything from a social worker to a somewhat successful businesswoman to an adjunct college professor. So what if I do hook up in bars now and again? It's not like I get it on with just anyone in pants. I'm not desperate for love; I just happen to be liberated and free from hang-ups.*

He climbed off his barstool and sauntered across the floor to the juke box and dropped in some coins and punched a few numbers, picking the few country and western selections. Heading back to the bar he took her in without appearing to look her way. Tall, statuesque, silver hair. She followed him with her eyes across the floor and back, never noticing that he glanced her way. His posture was effortlessly straight. When he perched on his barstool and pivoted back around to face the mirror the whole top half of his body was reflected in a weird funhouse mirror way and then straightened out, a phenomenon common to the old mirror giving rise to the saying that everybody in Barney's Pub is a little bit bent. Despite the gray hair, he looked no older than, say, forty-five. Fifty tops. Alex thought of herself as looking like early fifty, too. She often swelled with pride when she discovered that someone who looked much older was actually her age or younger. She wondered if that was common among elderly people who cannot see themselves the way others do or if she really was as well preserved as she thought. Alex colored her hair not to hide the gray but to enhance it, getting rid of the dirty yellow tones. She imagined that it looked lustrous in the dim light of Barney's. Likewise, she was confident that the spiderweb lines around her eyes and mouth did not show. Makeup and a push-up bra helped, even though she was naturally firm for her age and could have done without the uplift. But in her less confident moments she was convinced that without the makeup and hair coloring and all she'd probably look like Melody Sauer. She had the impression that Jim had not had to do anything to achieve his youthful look. Some people get all the breaks.

She decided that if, for whatever reason, Mister Everything From Half A Century Back could just waltz into her favorite pub, then there was no reason she couldn't sashay right up to him and say, "Hello, lover. Long time no see." She had certainly never been shy about approaching other men. She watched him nurse his beer. She wasn't watching him directly. She was looking at his reflection in the mirror. The hazy reflection gave evidence that Barney's was empty. Just Alex, Jim (if it really was him) and Randy the barkeep. It was early yet. Within an hour the place would be packed. Jim was wearing loose fitting cargo pants in a dark brown tone and a plain white T-shirt with a sports coat thrown over. His eyes met hers in the mirror, and he kept his gaze on her as he tipped up his glass and took a big swallow of his beer, set it down and topped it off from the bottle. *Did I see a twinkle of recognition in his eyes?* He was drinking a Budweiser, not exactly the choice of brews for a man with class. That didn't bode well. Neither did the political button over his breast pocket: *Ron Paul for President.* "Yikes," she said to herself. Alex was wearing a button of her own. *Obama.* Momentarily set aback by the Ron Paul button, she constructed a hopeful spin: *If*

James Carville and Mary Matalin could make it, why not me and a Libertarian Republican?

There had been a televised debate the night before, and Obama was scheduled to give a speech later that night. Randy would tune it in for sure. Barney's was Obama country all the way, as was most of Wetside.

Wondering if she should have been surprised that he was a Republican she tried to recall what she had known about Jim Bright and realized it was actually very little considering how close they had once been. Other than the general impression of him being a high school hot shot, just about all she could remember was that he had been good at sports and was a good dancer and had dated most of the more popular girls in school. He must have been smart, since he was class president, although she was bright enough to realize that could be a faulty assumption, class elections being more about popularity than qualifications. Beyond that brief outline there was very little she remembered about him, even if they had known each other since they were twelve years old. She realized it would be stupid to try and judge him now based on who he had been then. He had the look of someone who was comfortably wealthy but at ease with the rabble—*meaning me, meaning he was slumming?*—so it made sense that he might be a Republican. But Ron Paul wasn't even in the running any longer, so what was that all about?

She drifted into reverie. She remembered witnessing a big screaming match between Jim and his father and his older sister. It was not the first thing she remembered about the Bright family, but almost the first and definitely the first thing to come to her mind when she tried to dredge up her old memories. Jim's older sister was named Wanda. She was in the ninth grade. She had problems distinguishing between right and wrong when it came to the urges that wanted to govern her body, especially when in the presence of an expatriate Cajun named Jean Herbert. She had been told that if she had sex before marriage she would spend eternity in the fiery lakes of hell, which she didn't quite believe. Yes, she had been warned more than a few times about the perils of sex, but she had never been taught about the mechanics of the act or the possible earthly consequences, meaning pregnancy among other things. Wanda got pregnant. The boy was the lovestruck kid who had followed her all the way from Louisiana. He had dropped out of school and was living in a one-room apartment above a liquor store down on the Eastside. Her father kicked her out and disowned her. He called her a harlot and a Jezebel and said she brought shame down on the family.

Jim and Wanda's old man was a preacher in one of those real redneck churches like footwashing Baptist or Holy Roller or something (actual name: Clearwater Baptist), and he was very strict with his kids. He was dead-set on Jim becoming a preacher too, and had demanded model behavior from him. All four Bright family members and Jim's uncle Brad too, for the short time he lived with them, got up every morning at 5:30 and prayed until 6:30 when Mrs. Bright trudged out to the backyard chicken coop and gathered eggs for their breakfast. Their house was one of very few inside the city limits that had a chicken coop. Some of the neighbors complained, but Mrs. Bright gave them eggs and they quit complaining. She served her family eggs with a side dish of grits or sometimes pancakes. No meat. The Bright family did not believe in eating meat.

Cussing, smoking and drinking alcohol were not allowed in the Bright house. Neither was music allowed other than gospel. Reverend Bright controlled what radio stations they listened to, and there was no TV in the house. Slip up and let a cuss word out and Reverend Bright's hand would whip out faster than a cobra's bite to slap your face. Jim said his sister got slapped lots more than he did. She was the defiant one; Jim learned to play nice at home. Naturally, talk about sex was verboten. Wanda was not allowed to date and not allowed out of the house at night without a chaperone, but on school days between three o'clock and five she was free to go where she pleased, and where she went was Jean Herbert's apartment and his bed. Jean worked nights. Wanda told her parents she was practicing with the school choir. They were very proud, and the old man kept asking her when they were going to get to hear the choir.

Jim, being the boy, was given a little more freedom. He was at least allowed to date after his sixteenth birthday, but double dating only—the theory being that he couldn't have sex if another couple was in the back seat. Alex had no such restrictions to contend with. Her parents were among the most radical of radicals in Wetside. They had grown up in New York and had hung out with bohemian types in Greenwich Village and had been active in the labor movement and had been pacifists during the Second World War and believed in free love. When Alex was thirteen her mother taught her about birth control and told her, "I know you're not ready yet, but it won't be long before you want to have sex with boys, and when you do I want you to be sure and protect yourself," but Alex was in no hurry to lose her virginity. She had a few crushes but did not experience, until much later, the kind of sexual desires other girls talked about. Funny, she thought, other girls are dying to do it but are convinced that it is sinful and dangerous, and I don't think there's anything wrong with it, but I don't see what's the big deal.

When she did date, it was usually very casual and always double dating with another couple—often with Jim and one of his many girl friends. Typically they'd go to a school dance or a film down at the Strand and top it off with a root beer float at the Red's Dairy Bar, and sometimes they'd go to the Beverly Drive-In or park near the West River, in which case Alex would fend off her date's advances while listening to heavy groans and sighs from the other couple, except when one half of the other couple was Jim Bright. She never knew him to make out with anyone when double dating with her. Still, Jim had quite a reputation for being a Casanova and she figured such a reputation couldn't have sprung out of nothing.

Jim behaved like an alter boy at home and a wild child away from his family. That was the way he assured his popularity at school and peace at home. Alex was the only person who was allowed to see both the alter boy and the wild child. Nobody knew him the way she did. She was more than the girl next door; she was the girl who replaced Wanda in his life. He told her things that he'd never tell other people. But she suspected there was a private side to Jim that even she could not reach, and that included a sex life that he tried to keep to himself. She more than suspected it, she knew it, if certain girls could be believed. Jim was never a kiss-and-tell kind of guy. In fact, when other boys at school bragged about their exploits, which they often did, or when they attempted to spread rumors about any of the girls—like the vicious crap they spread about Kay Kay Williams—Jim would blast them in a manner that would have made his hellfire preaching daddy proud. But Alex knew he was not completely innocent. She knew it because Mary Elizabeth, for one, admitted letting him go all the way and Ophelia Sullivan never denied it when she was asked. What Alex never knew was how many of his many other reputed conquests were true.

So Jim was a lover. He was also a cut-up, something of a clown. He impersonated teachers, snuck out of class, drew a hilarious caricature of an unpopular English teacher on the blackboard, and told wonderfully entertaining tall tales. Typical of Jim: one day he wrote on the blackboard in algebra class "draobkcalb eht dniheb deppart m'I pelH," and when he had a rash on his hand and Alex took his hand in hers and asked solicitously, "What is this?" he said, "I forgot what the doctor called it, but he said it was highly contagious" and guffawed at her when she jerked her hand away.

Everybody expected he would end up as a writer or a television personality. He pretended to be wild, but he seldom strayed far from his father's strict rules. He talked to Alex about wrestling with his personal demons, about wanting to be good and wanting to have fun and how frustrating it was that what was fun was sinful and everything that was considered good and desirable was so goddamn boring. It didn't take long for the having fun part to win out.

Alex dated boys who were safe, who were either not interested in her as a sex object or were afraid to try anything. Like Leslie Grant and the youngest of the Barnes brothers. They would spend hours at Red's. Everybody loved Red's Dairy Bar, and everybody loved Red Rogers. Such a nice guy. He often sat in the booths with some of the kids when it wasn't too busy, and they thought it was cool that he seemed to accept them as equals. His favorite kids were Bubba Austin and some of his football buddies. The story was that Red had been a football star in his youth, but somebody said he had been the kid who helped take care of the equipment.

The dairy bar was on Glouster near the park. If you cut through the woods and across Miller Creek it was no more than three blocks from Jim's house, but if you stayed on the streets it was a good twelve blocks getting around the creek.

•

A little smile broke out on his face when he saw her pick up her beer and walk toward him. The same bright smile that had broken hearts in high school, a smile of supreme confidence, just the kind of smile you'd expect from someone who recognizes a long-lost friend for the first time. But she knew that was not the case. He couldn't possibly have recognized her. She had changed too much for that. That confident smile had little to do with Alex as a person but a lot to do with Alex as a woman like any other woman who might approach him in a bar. His mind was saying I'm gonna get laid again. She knew that the clue to him was that it was her coming on to him and not the other way around. Their ideas about pickup protocol had been cemented in an era when men were always the instigators and if women did make the first move it was a clear sign of desperation.

When she got closer to him she noticed that his close-cropped hair was thin on top. So he'd become one of those guys who wears a buzz cut to hide that he's going bald. Was she disappointed? No, she was relieved to see at least that one little sign of aging—something to bring him back down off Olympus and into the cesspool with the rest of the oh-so-fallible mortals.

"Hi," she said. "Mind if I join you?"

Her voice trembled ever so slightly, but he didn't seem to notice. He said, "Not at all. My name's Jim."

"Hi, Jim. I'm Alex."

"I love that name. The first girl I ever loved was named Alex."

Be still my freakin' heart. Did he really say that?

She slithered onto the stool next to him in what she intended to be a rather provocative manner, crossing her long legs so that a lot

15

of thigh showed. She had always been proud of her legs. Muscular calves and thighs, lengthy but not too thin. Definitely her best feature. At five-foot-eleven she was pretty damn tall for a woman. Gargantuan and terribly sensitive about it in her youth, but comfortable with her size now that taller women are more common and are looked up to (figuratively and literally). Look at how tall the hot super models are. And if she was not as thin as she once was she was no fatty either. Solid, that's the word, with ample hips and small breasts that were still fairly firm. Her hair was short. She had high cheek bones and a strong jaw. She wore glasses and tasteful but moderate jewelry. That night she was wearing coral colored lipstick and just a touch of eye liner.

She settled in next to Jim, and Randy the bartender set a fresh coaster down in front of her and asked if she'd like another beer.

"Sure. Thanks." And then to Jim she said, "Randy's a sweetheart."

"I'll get it," Jim said, and he plopped a twenty on the bar and ordered another for himself. "What's that you're drinking?"

"It's a porter."

"Hmmm, never had one."

"Well you should try. Randy, bring him a porter instead of that slop he's drinking."

Still not one hundred percent certain that Jim was, indeed, her Jim, she began to fish with innocuous questions. "Do you live around here?"

He said he did. "Not far from town in a little house down by Rock Creek."

"Country living, huh? Do you like that?"

"Yeah, it's great. Peaceful. What about you?"

"Oh, I live right around the corner. Over on Harvard. I'm kind of a regular here. Neighborhood pub, you know."

Her home was a one bedroom cottage with a small kitchen separated from the combined living room and dining room by one of those doors like they use in restaurants that you can shoulder open from either side with arms loaded. More than the occasional house guest had been banged in the nose by that swinging door, and her cat, Fred the fat calico, darted for cover every time she opened it. Her dining area was barely large enough for the little circular table she had picked years ago in a rummage sale, and the living room was just roomy enough for a single couch, a TV and a floor-to-ceiling and wall-to-wall bookshelf. The apartment was built over a two-car garage and store room with steep steps leading up to the entrance. The garage had been an art gallery before Alex bought the place back in the late eighties (built as a garage, converted into an art gallery and later returned to its original function). The guys who ran the gallery had lived upstairs. Like most of the galleries and bookstores and coffee shops and gift stores that young entrepreneurs just out of college were constantly opening in Wetside, that one promptly went bust, and she got the place for practically nothing.

"Well maybe I'll become a regular here too," Jim said. "There aren't any good watering holes in Rock Creek."

"Is this your first time here?"

"First time in a long time."

He gnawed his lower lip for a second. They looked at each other's campaign buttons but didn't comment. He took a sip of his beer and shivered. "Wow! That's bitter."

"Yeah, well it takes a little getting used to. It'll grow on you."

He said, "I grew up in Wetside, but I've been gone for over thirty years. I retired a few years back, and then my wife died."

It was becoming clear that he didn't know her and hadn't an inkling that she knew him. *How could he not remember me? Could Batman forget Robin?*

She told him she was sorry to hear about his wife.

"Yeah, thank you. After Nancy passed I kind of got homesick. So here I am starting life all over again back where I came from."

"Starting over must be tough."

"Yeah. I guess it's like this beer; it takes some getting used to."

He talked for a while about his wife. He said, "I loved her till the day she died, but I don't think she ever loved me. Oh, she pretended for a while, but I could tell."

She was surprised at how matter-of-factly he revealed that. He said, "She ripped my heart apart, but I'm coping OK now. Besides, I understand. She fell in love with a chimp, and how do you compete with that?"

That had to be a slip of the tongue. "A chimp?" she asked, "Do you mean a like a chump or … or a jerk?"

"No," he said. "I mean a chimp. A chimpanzee, a big, ugly hairy chimpanzee named Manlow. You see…" and he stopped to take a deep breath and for just a second she thought she detected a glint of something mad in his eye. Was he mad? This gorgeous hunk of man? Could it be he was completely bonkers? He let out a big, melodramatic sigh and then said he'd better get another beer, apologizing for not liking the porter, so they waited until Randy brought him another Bud, and after all of that he explained:

"This may be a little shocking, but I might as well just come right out with it. My wife was a sex performer. A stripper, a porn star, a really high class exotic dancer. And when I say high class, I mean it. She didn't dance in sleazy strip joints. Oh no. She danced in places where the cover charge was a week's pay for me and the cheapest drinks were twenty or thirty bucks. She performed her very unique act in very private clubs where the wine started at $500 a bottle and the exclusive clientele were flown in on private jets. And what was her very unique act? You guessed it. Sex with a chimp. And she liked it. I swear she did. Hellfire, she loved it. Manlow had what I didn't have. To be more accurate, he had a lot more of what I had just a little of, if you know what I mean. Oh sure, she said I was out of my mind when I accused her of being in love with the damn animal, but she was."

Alex was flabbergasted. How could she possibly respond? She turned to stone right there on her barstool. Lot's wife in Barney's Pub. She felt as if she couldn't even lift her drink to take a swig or make a move toward getting away from him, which she felt like she ought to do. Fast. Like a trapped animal she stared at him.

She could not have been more astounded if his face had just metamorphosed into that of some kind of monster primate.

And to make the situation even weirder than it was, he seemed to be getting turned on. He was staring at her cleavage, and... she wasn't absolutely sure of this and didn't want to look closer to confirm it, but it looked like there was a bit of a bulge in his pants. Was he getting an erection?

He was. He knew it, and he was pretty sure she knew it. That was too much for Alex. Way, way too much. She said, "I'm sorry. I can't, uh, I can't do this. I got to go," and she quickly stood up, and leaving a full beer stein on the bar she spun around and headed to the door as quickly as those long legs of hers would carry her, and that was when he shouted, "Hey Slugger, come back here. God! You're just as gullible as ever."

That stopped her in her tracks! Slugger! No one had called her that since eighth grade when she outshone most of the boys at baseball. She could hit the ball farther than any boy in the neighborhood except for Bubba Austin and Carney. It was Carney who started calling her Slugger, and the name stuck for a while.

Best Friends – Jim and Alex's blog

A Dream
by Jim Bright

In my dream we had just rented a country home across a dirt road from a farmhouse. I was married, but my wife in the dream wasn't Nancy or anyone else I knew. She was a generic wife. And I think there were children. Yes there were. I remember because they were skipping along with us when we walked across the street, skirted the side of the farmhouse, opened the gate to the pasture and walked to the small cottage there. We went in. It was a sparsely furnished two-room shack. The woman inside was plain, with dull hair. She wore a shapeless tan dress. We told her we'd come to see the art exhibit, even though the only thing that could possibly pass for art in the drab cottage were two or three amateurish landscapes and flower paintings on the walls. Looked like they'd been dug out of a trash heap.

She informed us that she owned our house. If she was our landlady, I can't imagine why we didn't already know, except, you know, it was a dream. Then she asked if we had any beer. My not-Nancy generic wife invited her over to our house for a beer. I cringed at the thought.

This harpy of a landlady kept brushing up against me in unmistakably intentional ways. My not-Nancy generic wife didn't seem to notice. When the landlady stepped through the door into the back room she lifted the back of her skirt to expose her backside. She wasn't wearing underwear. Now I know where the term butt ugly comes from.

Now here's the thing that was disturbing about that dream. I was turned on by her come-on even though both her looks and her personality were repulsive. Given the right opportunity, I would have slept with her. I don't mean in my dream. I mean this is what I realized when I woke up. That's a thing about me that I'm ashamed of—not that I'm highly sexed, I long ago accepted and embraced my lascivious nature; but that when it comes to a roll in the hay taste doesn't come into play. She could be insane and carry weapons and it wouldn't matter so long as she looked halfway presentable.

In the dream I walked into the back room and looked at the single painting on the wall, a particularly ugly picture, and said, "I like this one." I wasn't lying. I truly appreciate great art, but crappy art is OK too. That's just the way I am, and that applies to art, music and sex partners. Like I said, zilch for taste. Not something I'm very proud of. I told Alex about this character flaw, and she said I should write about it as a way of coming to understand it. Alex writes constantly. She's been journaling for years and has this blog where she writes about politics and whatever else comes to mind, and after a lot of talk she wore down my resistance and talked me into collaborating with her on this blog, which is to say that's how we got started on this. We kind of envision it as reminisces about growing up in the old neighborhood in Wetside and about our current life as best friends with opposing views and beliefs (I think of myself as a libertarian, and she's a party-line liberal).

I called her Slugger when we were kids. She was a real tomboy, gangly, strong and plain looking. I thought of her as one of the guys, was hardly even aware of her as a girl. I distinctly remember being surprised by her breasts. It was like she'd had them all along, or at least from about the time we met at age twelve or thirteen, but I never noticed them until one day they were just there. It was like, hey, looka there. She really is a girl.

After noticing her girl parts our friendship became more complicated. She stirred feelings in me that conflicted with the nature of our friendship, and the nature of our friendship as it was, was something I valued too much to risk by bringing something new into it. I was already girl crazy at thirteen or fourteen, but I never pursued her, the girl I liked the most. We parted ways after we grew up and didn't reconnect until many years later, but we quickly became best friends again. Oh, and about the dream. That was all there was to it, or all I can remember.

Chapter 3

He hopped off his barstool and stood with arms wide and welcoming, a delicious grin plastered on his face. Redfaced in the doorway and waiting just a second to regain her composure Alex spun on her heels and marched back to the bar sputtering, "I beat the crap out of the last guy that called me that." And she gushed, "Jim Bright! I knew it was you. I knew it all along. I swear I did. But I wasn't sure, and …and …and then when you didn't… oh man, you really had me going there. You were just playing me, and I fell for it as usual."

Jim lifted his hands in a signal of resignation. His smile was sheepish. She said, "I could jerk your hair out if you had any left."

"Oooh, that's low." He laughed with her as she reclaimed her seat next to him at the bar. He said, "Of course I knew you the moment I saw you. How could I ever forget you? You were probably the one girl I never should have let get away."

"Aw come on," making a mental note that he had twice now indicated that back in the day he had perhaps had feelings for her that he had never expressed.

"I mean it. Really. I liked you better than any of the girls I dated, but I think we were too close to, you know, to see each other as boy and girl."

"Aw, I was just the neighborhood tomboy to you."

Towering over most of the boys and skinny as a sapling, with a bad case of acne to boot (thank God that finally cleared up), she had never been the girl fifteen-year-old boys lusted after.

Jim said, "You were pretty tough for a girl. Geez, I remember one time when we were playing baseball you hit what probably should have been a double at best, but you barreled over Rolly at second, knocking him flat on his ass. Man, I'd never seen a girl play so aggressive."

"I don't remember anything like that. You must have dreamed it." (She remembered it as if it had happened yesterday. If he could lie to her, she figured turnabout was fair play.)

He said, "Oh no, I remember it all right, clear as can be. You beat the pitch to third, and when the next batter came up you stole home. Christamighty, gal, you were the toughest guy on the lot."

She bowed her head as demurely as she could and looked up at him with a shy but flirtatious glint in her eye, thinking, if he doesn't see the signals I'm throwing out now he must have suffered brain damage sometime between then and now. He wasn't blind to the signals but kept his response platonic, somewhat. He said, "Ah yes, you definitely were a tomboy. But by senior year you blossomed into quite an attractive woman."

"Now you tell me. If you'd a told me back then you mighta got laid."

Jim laughed. "Oh woe is me. The opportunities we let slip through our hands."

They sat quietly for a moment and smiled at one another in delight. At last Alex said, "So I guess there wasn't really a wife named Nancy."

"Actually there was. You knew her. Nancy Hendrix, my next door neighbor. And she did die not long ago. Cancer. She fought it for years but finally gave up last summer."

She could see in his eyes that he was telling the truth. She said, "Oh my god, I don't know what to say. But why in the world would you make up that crazy story?"

"I don't know. I just do that. Maybe it's my way of blocking out the pain."

It seemed sick to her, but she decided to give him the benefit of the doubt. Who was she to criticize how other people dealt with grief when she'd never had to herself?

•

It was after ten o'clock, late for old folks. They'd had a few too many and were slowing down. They'd relocated from the bar to a corner booth where it was quieter. Not that Barney's was loud to start with. There was a pretty good crowd by then. The usual: a few gay boys and lesbians, but some straight couples as well. Barney's attracted a mature crowd. A lot of literate types. Not your loudly laughing and shouting bar crowd, but people who talked earnestly about books and politics and movies, but mostly flung sarcasm in the direction of their neighbors and their bosses and their favorite target, City Hall. Portraits of literary figures adorned the walls, primarily Western writers: Raymond Carver, Wallace Stegner, David Guterson and, of course, Tom Robbins, who was still dearly loved in Western Washington from his days as an art critic in Seattle—all the regional heroes plus a few other modern giants such as Joyce and Hemingway and Salinger.

Regulars at Barney's had their own beer mugs hanging on hooks with their names on them. There were fifty named mugs and a waiting list to get one. Conventional wisdom said somebody had to die before anybody new could get a mug. Alex had been on the list for three years with few prospects of ever actually getting a mug. Some people say they'd kill for one, but so far no one actually had.

Alex was forced to push with her hands to get up to go to the ladies room. She felt herself stagger a bit and hoped Jim didn't notice. He did, and he knew if he got up he'd stagger even worse, which was why he waited until she was at the ladies room door before he went to empty his bladder. They had to find new seats when they finished. Hunger pangs started gnawing at Alex, so she was pleased when he said he was hungry and asked if she wanted something to eat. They ordered burgers and fries, a Portobello mushroom burger for Jim. He was still vegetarian. Alex asked if he'd seen the latest Police Blotter by Harry Drews. "The headline said no foul play in a murder. How can that be? And then he called it an accidental murder."

"It's Harry Drews. He's been getting it wrong for as long as I can remember. Him and his old man." For something like thirty years Harold Drews had written the daily police report for the *Daily Journal*, and his son Harry took over when Harold retired. They were both notorious for inaccurate reporting. The *Journal* published two versions of Harry's column, one in print and one on a blog called Rain Drops. The print version had the benefit of copy editing. It was terse and to the point. The online version was longer and had the added attraction of uncensored comments from readers, most of which were entertainingly moronic. The particular edition of Harry's column Alex was referring to bore an oxymoron of a title: *Transvestite murdered, no foul play involved.*

Harry wrote:

What was presumed to be the body of a drowned woman was found by hunters in East River Saturday morning. There were contusions to the head, and the body was tangled in a chain caught on a log.

Police spokesman Snake Collins said investigators initially suspected homicide but later determined the death was probably accidental. "We won't know until they do an autopsy," Lieutenant Collins said. "When they found the body the initial assumption was the victim had been beaten and then chained to the log, presumably to keep the body from floating. But the murder could just as well have been accidental. She might have fallen in the water, got washed into the logjam by the swift current and got tangled up in what was most likely an anchor chain from a shipping vessel."

Her sleeves and pant legs were in tatters. "When the medical examiner removed the victim's clothes he was shocked to discover that the female victim had male genitalia," Lieutenant Collins said. He went on to describe the victim's long hair and torn clothing and the spike heeled boots she was wearing, one on her foot and the other buried in the mud near the body. "I've heard of such things, but I've never witnessed it with my own eyes. Whatever hybrid gender he or she is, the parts were not prosthetic. They were as real and natural as can be," the medical examiner said. He even reported her bra size, 34C.

The victim has not been identified. Police are seeking information on any known transvestites that may have gone missing in the past forty-eight hours.

The report was followed by dozens of inane comments. Alex said, "I wonder if the oxymoron was a misquote by Harry or if he and the cop are equally dumb."

Jim said, "I've learned to accept malapropisms and mangled facts from Harry, but what really gets me is the way he sensationalized the whole transgender issue. Can you imagine what the victim's parents and friends must have felt when they read that crap about the size of her boobs? Jesus."

"I wonder if the parents even knew that their child was transgender."

Jim said, "That crap about *he or she* and the body parts was sensationalism. If she identified as female, which she must have, then by god they should have shown her enough respect to refer to her with a feminine pronoun. And saying she wore a 34C was just salacious."

Alex was surprised by Jim's passion on the subject.

"Wow, I wouldn't have expected a Republican to be up on that stuff, or to care."

"Oh, I'm just full of surprises."

Bringing up politics opened a door she'd wanted to open all night. She said, "Speaking of Republicans, didn't anybody tell you that Ron Paul is no longer in the race?"

"Yeah, I heard that, but I like to tease the Dems and other Socialist sympathizers." He tapped the button "I'll probably vote for McCain, if you really want to know."

"McCain and Palin or Ron Paul and whoever. It's like comparing dog doo doo and bird droppings. They're both catering to right-wing lunatics. The only difference is one of 'em believes it and the other is convictionless."

"Thanks for the bird and dog comparison. Now I understand the difference between Barack and Hillary."

They glared at each other for a full thirty seconds, and then burst into laughter. A change of subject seemed in order, and a return to reminiscing about the past seemed pleasant and safe enough. Jim said, "That was a great neighborhood we lived in, wasn't it? What a bunch of kids!"

•

Alex and her parents had lived in the neighborhood longer than anyone else. From her vantage point in what they called the butt end of 18th Street, she had watched them build the newer part of the neighborhood where Jim lived. She watched them rip out an acre or so of forest and flatten the ground with bulldozers and put up his house and then the houses on either side, and she had been one of the first to welcome him to Wetside. Most everybody in the neighborhood was friendly, with a few very notable exceptions, such as Old Man Singleterry, who owned the land and built all the houses on Woodlawn Street. Everybody knew everybody else. Not like today when you can go for years without even getting to know the guy across the street. Jim was twelve years old when his folks moved into the house on Woodlawn. Theirs was the first of the new houses on the street. The old man lived across the street. "What a strange and grumpy old asshole he was," Jim recalled. "During the ten years we lived across the street from him I don't think he ever spoke to me, not once."

Mister Singleterry's house was a monstrosity compared to all the others. It was in need of paint when the Brights moved into their new home, and it had still not been painted when Alex graduated from college ten years later. During that time Jim and his father painted their house twice. Alex's folks never painted theirs during that time. They just weren't that into keeping up appearances, and besides, their house wasn't as faded as old man Singleterry's or half again such a noxious color as Jim's. The first time the Brights painted their house it took four coats of white to hide the horrible Pepto-Bismol pink the original contractors had painted it. The second time they painted it yellow. There were no trees in their yard and no grass when they first moved in, but they quickly planted a mimosa by the car port and four pecan trees in the back yard, and a little magnolia that for some reason never grew (never died either, just remained six feet tall forever), and flower beds along the front of the house and low shrubs on two sides. Jim's mother could be seen tinkering in her flower beds every day during that summer. She

27

weeded in a flowery housedress. All the other neighborhood women wore shorts for gardening.

Jim's house was one vacant lot west of 18th, close enough that he and Alex could pitch baseball from their respective front yards. Unlike Woodlawn, 18th Street had been developed long ago and was fully populated with young families. Most of the adults were in their thirties or forties with children ranging in age from six to twenty. All of the houses on the block faced west toward Jim's house. In Barney's Pub Jim and Alex made a game of seeing if they could recall all the kids on that stretch of 18th by name and match each to his or her house color.

Best Friends – Jim and Alex's blog

The Neighborhood
by Jim Bright and Alex Martin

This is where we grew up, going house-to-house starting on the corner at 18th and Park. First house, baby blue shingles and twin mimosas in the front yard. The redheaded kid lived there. His dad was a shoe salesman and his mom ran a beauty shop in their converted garage. She was a looker, his mom, thin and vivacious and full of energy. - *Alex*

Flaming red hair and green eyes and a knockout figure. She flirted outrageously with all the boys, but just in fun. I mean I can't imagine that she ever actually did anything more than flirt (not like Jimi Sue, for instance—oh boy!) but man oh man did we ever imagine it back then. - *Jim*

Her name was Margaret—Margaret something-or-other. Her kid was an only child. He was wiry and full of energy. We just called him Red. I don't know if anybody knew his name. He was a real daredevil and accident prone to boot. I remember him swinging out on the rope swing over the creek and dropping into the water below. It was a good thirty feet. He landed smack on a broken Coke bottle and slashed open his foot. Took fifteen stitches to fix him up. He walked around with his foot bandaged for about a month. - *Alex*

He was showing off for Lara Cockburn and the Darling Debs. He wasn't the only kid in town trying to score with them. - *Jim*

Next to the daredevil in the baby blue house was Leslie Grant in the mint green house. Leslie was one of the few boys I dated when I was growing up. Everybody called him a sissy, but so what. I thought he was nice. We held hands in the movies. He had the softest hands, and a voice like a stage whisper when speaking normally and impossible to hear when actually whispering. I suspected he used that whispery voice as an excuse to get closer. "What did you say?" I'd ask him and he'd say it again with his lips brushing my ear. "What's that?" I asked him once in the Strand while we were watching some beach party movie, and he whispered, "I said you smell like honeysuckle," and I turned my face and I kissed the softest lips I'd ever touched. Leslie ended up marrying Susan Smith from down in Centralia. She was a good bit older. They had four children and about a dozen grand kids. - *Alex*

As it turned out he really was gay after all, just like everybody suspected. He didn't come out until he was in his fifties, but Susan said she knew it all along. It's all right if I say it here. Their story is no secret. They became very active in gay rights and actually went around to churches and civic organizations and told their stories and eventually created a website where they told the whole world how they had stood by each other as he discovered that he was gay. By then they had a bunch of kids and grand kids, and their marriage had become pretty much sexless anyway (again, they were completely open and honest about that), so they stayed together and loved each other as they always had. I don't know if he had boyfriends on the side or not. Doesn't really matter, I guess.

Leslie's father was kind of old for having a kid our age. I think he was already retired when Leslie was twelve or thirteen. I thought he owned Grant's store but I found out that was a different Grant. Mr. Grant had a runabout with a big Mercury outboard, and he used to take a bunch of us kids water skiing. He was a skinny guy, smoked a pipe. And I sure as shooting remember his mom. She was a toucher and a gusher. We used to dread seeing her coming. Lord have mercy, she was always hugging and kissing and calling you sweetie and honey bumpkin, and she looked like she was old enough to be somebody's great grandmother. They were both kind of ancient for parents. Come to think of it, maybe they weren't his parents. Maybe Leslie was raised by grandparents.

Next to the Grants in another pink house were the Delks. The old man was a drunk. He was a cop. Useless bastard. They had three kids. The oldest was about ten in fifty-four—that's when I first met them—and the youngest was six. He was a real hellion, that little one. Then there were the Sullivans. The two girls, Ophelia and Trisha. Their house was white, and somehow it looked older than all the rest even though they were all built at the same time. Ophelia was a couple of years older than us. I don't think anybody used the term slutty back then, but she was as slutty as slutty can be. - *Jim*

You should have seen Jim's response when I mentioned Ophelia Sullivan. He rolled his eyes heavenward and looked at me like he wanted to stuff that name back down my throat. If it was true that he'd done with her what the other kids said he had, it probably wasn't anything he wanted to be reminded of. Ophelia was a big girl, standing about five-foot eight, not fat but big boned with muscular arms and legs and a well-endowed chest. She had a hard look about her even at fourteen, like some babe you'd expect to see in a honky tonk. She probably grew up to be a roller derby dame.

Pretty much everything I knew about sex in junior high—and that wasn't very much—I learned from Ophelia. Don't get me wrong, I'm talking theory not practice. She taught me stuff my mother never told me, and mom was pretty open minded.

Quite the opposite of Ophelia, her little sister was quiet and shy and never flirted with the boys. Pug, they called her. Sometimes Pugly Wugly. She was much shorter than her sister and what we diplomatically called pleasingly plump. But she was sweet. The boys in the neighborhood liked her a lot better than her sister, despite big sister's undeniable sexual allure. Fact was Ophelia scared the crap out of most of them. Pug was safe. - *Alex*

The Barnes brothers were like male counterparts to the Sullivan girls. They moved in to the new house on the south corner of 18th and Woodlawn in about fifty-nine or sixty. Yellow house. Bill Barnes was tall, handsome and gregarious, and his little brother Rodney was pudgy and shy. Not surprisingly, they started dating the Sullivan girls, Bill with Ophelia and Rodney with Trisha. That was also about the time the Hendrix family moved in next door and some of the neighborhood boys (I won't print their names) started messing around with their housekeeper. There was stuff going on in that block that Grace Metalious couldn't have dreamed up.

Next to the Sullivans in another mint green house lived Bubba Austin and his half brother, Reggie Sheffield. Bubba played fullback on the Jefferson High School football team, and he had a

31

reputation for being a tough cookie. He liked to pick fights. But only with guys he knew he could beat. He wasn't as dumb as he looked.

Bubba might have been tough, but he met his match when he decided to pick on Dudley Strong. Dudley was a big kid and sweet and shy, and very clumsy. He walked on his toes and always looked like he was about to topple over forward, like one of those blow-up punching bag characters, like he had to keep moving to keep from falling. Why Bubba decided to pick on Dudley, nobody knew. But he egged him on and teased him and did things like slapping him on the back of the head and shooting him with spitballs until finally Dudley couldn't take it any more, and he fought back with deadly earnestness and a machinelike barrage of left jabs and right crosses that had Bubba backpedaling until he finally dropped to his knees and begged for mercy. Unbeknownst to Bubba, Dudley had been training for Golden Gloves, and much to the surprise of everyone he soon went on to win the state championship in his weight class. Dudley is now a county judge. - *Jim*

In the sand colored house next to the Austins was an older boy named Snake. Snake grew up to be a police officer. As a kid he was a bully. As a policeman he probably still was but managed to hide it. Once he held my head underwater in the creek until I thought I would drown. Old Snake snarled, "If you gonna act like one of the boys then you can damn well get treated like one of the boys." He hated it that I dressed like a boy and could beat the boys at most of their games.

Despite being about five years older than me, Snake wasn't much bigger, and it took all the strength he could muster to hold my head underwater. I was kicking and flailing my arms, and I was truly horrified. Thank God Carney Jones saw what was going on. Carney lived in one of the newer houses Old Man Singleterry built on Woodlawn. He was even older than Snake and a lot bigger, a linebacker for the City U football team. He was six feet tall and weighed two-fifty. Nowadays that's not particularly big for a lineman. There are running backs bigger than that, even in high school. But in the late '50s that was huge. He had a big belly, but it wasn't soft. He let guys hit him in the gut just to prove how tough he was, and if they ever hurt him at all he never let it show. He was perpetually jovial in a way that's common for a certain type of big man. In his old age he grew a fluffy white beard and now he plays Santa Claus in the mall every year. He's a used car salesman. Carney was one of three college boys on the block. They all lived together in a rental house that belonged to Carney's parents. One of the other boys was named Jerod something or other. He moved out after a short time. The other one was Buster James. Buster was cool. He was short, about five-foot-six, and not exactly what you'd call handsome, but the girls loved him. He had a big nose and his lower lip and chin kind of folded into his neck. That makes it sound like he was pretty dumb looking, but he wasn't. He was cute. His clothes were always the latest fashion, and he drove a hot sports car and could really cut a rug on the dance floor. High school girls swooned over him. Kimzy Williams called him a dreamboat, and (name withheld) once snitched one of his shirts off the line and kept it under her pillow. "She hugs the shirt and cries herself to sleep," Kimzy said.

Carney and Buster didn't play along the creek bank like we did. I guess they were too old for that. But they sometimes took a shortcut to Glouster that cut across the creek. That's what Carney was doing when he saw Snake holding my head under water. He grabbed him and snatched him up and slapped him a good one, and Snake turned and ran away, and Carney kicked him in the butt as he was leaving. I jerked my face out of the water sputtering and cursing and crying all at once 'cause I was mad and scared and embarrassed, and I swear to god if I could have got my hands on a baseball bat I'd a taken after Snake and cracked his skull. - *Alex*

Notice to Snake and Bubba: It was Alex that dropped your name here. I never would have said those things. No sir, I love you both. I think you're the greatest guys in the world. So if you want to come after us for saying that stuff, come after Alex. It's never too late to drown her - Jim

•

Randy brought them another beer each, with fresh glasses. It was their fourth or fifth, and neither of them was used to drinking

33

that much. They quietly sipped their beers for a few minutes, enjoying the atmosphere of Barney's. As warm and welcoming as a fireplace in winter, Barney's is sparsely and tastefully decorated. The interior walls are old brick, and there are heavy wood beams. Added to the portraits of writers and the personalized beer mugs on the wall are exhibitions of paintings by local artists displayed in lighted recesses. At the moment "Some Enchanted Evening" was playing on the jukebox, and one old couple was dancing. If you could call what they were doing dancing. Propping one another up while swaying to the rhythm would be a more accurate description. Two men were playing chess at another table, and every barstool was occupied. The warmth, the low lighting and the pleasant buzz put Alex in mind of sitting around a campfire at night, something she hadn't done in many years, not since her first marriage. Among the few pleasant memories of that marriage was camping with Donny and the girls. She pictured Jim by the campfire instead of Donny.

Jim stretched and put his hands together and cracked his knuckles. "Those were the good old days," he said.

"Yeah, I guess. If you were white and middle class and male."

"Oh crap," he said. "I don't think I want to hear this."

"But it's true, you know." Everybody talked about how wonderful life was in the '50s. The Internet was replete with paeans on the subject lauding the games people played and the ads in magazines for long-gone products, and longing for a time when mothers stayed at home to take care of the kids while the dads worked and nobody ever had to lock their doors and everything was ridiculously cheap. Yes, George Baily, it was a wonderful life, at least for the privileged class in small towns and suburbs; but life was not so peachy for minorities and people in the inner cities and even, as Alex tried to tell Jim, for women no matter where they lived or how much money their husbands made. But she backed away from pursuing that argument with Jim Bright.

"Fill me in on the last thirty years," he said.

"Well, let's see. I was married twice and divorced twice, and I worked at more stupid, dead-end jobs than you could shake a stick at, and that's about it."

"You're not married now?"

"Nope. Nobody'd have me."

Is he fishing to discover if I'm available? Things are looking up.

Alex married Donny Brooks in 1974. Yes, that really was his name. She was thirty-one and he was forty. She was living in Seattle at the time. He was suave and exciting. A lady killer. In retrospect she could see that he might have been a substitute for Jim, but if that had been her motive it was deeply buried. Donny had two daughters from a previous marriage. They were ten and twelve. It was for them that they got into camping. Neither Donny nor Alex was so keen on outdoors stuff. Alex actually detested it, was horrified of bears and cougars and snakes, not to mention crazy mass murders who would surely sneak into their tent and kill them in their sleep. But she pretended to enjoy it for the girls' sake. Donny was an actor and the heartthrob of Southwest Washington. Women threw themselves at him. Girls really, and the younger the better, as Alex eventually found out. Donny was the leading man in a number of community theater productions in the area. He played all of the roles you'd expect of a dashing glamour boy with a halfway decent singing voice: Tony in *West Side Story*, Cabel in *South Pacific*, Sky in *Guys and Dolls*. Alex got to know him through her job. At the time she was working for a public relations firm, and he had recently founded a theater company and hired the firm to do some promo work. He gave her a comp ticket to *Hello Dolly*. He was not in the play, he was the producer. When she showed up opening night she discovered that he had given her a seat next to him. At intermission he told her he was going out to dinner with the director and some of the cast members after the show and asked if she'd like to go with them. Alex was soon swept up in the world of theater. It all seemed so glamorous. From one show and a casual dinner Donny and Alex slipped seamlessly into steady dating.

It bothered her at first to see the way young women fawned over him. But she soon came to accept that people in his world exchanged kisses as casually as other people shared handshakes. It wasn't until after they were married that she discovered there was a lot more than kissing going on. She overheard two cast members at a rehearsal for *Romeo and Juliet* whispering that Donny was sleeping with Juliet. He denied it, but once it had been brought to her attention she couldn't help but pick up on the looks they shared. Next it was one of the dancers in *South Pacific*, and then a stagehand. Donny was diddling everyone in the theater. It wasn't really so much his sleeping around that pissed her off as it was the looks of pity cast her way by everyone from the lighting director to the girl who fed the actors their lines in rehearsal. She was the outsider in his world, the one everybody whispered about, wondering *What's he doing with her*? She couldn't take knowing what they all must have thought about her. *Poor little innocent, can't imagine what her husband's up to.*

"Speaking of two-timing spouses," Jim said. "Did you ever know the poor jerk that married Mary Elizabeth Lucious?"

"No, but I always thought whoever got her would be pretty lucky. The way I remember it half the guys in our class had the hots for her."

"Yeah. But she wasn't such a great catch as you might expect." He said, "She married some guy from Eastern Washington and cuckolded the crap out of him. At our twentieth class reunion she made out with Bill Barnes in the parking lot while her husband was inside trying to strike up some kind of business deal with Johnny Delgado. And Johnny, well Johnny was hitting on *him*, Mary Elizabeth's husband, but the guy was too dense to see what was going on."

"Well that doesn't surprise me. I knew Johnny was gay."

"You did? I never would have suspected."

"Oh yeah, definitely. He's been out for years. Even in high school he let a few of his trusted friends know it."

"Including you, I presume."

"Uh huh. And now he heads up the local Pride parade."

"Anyway, that must have been some reunion. Too bad I missed it. I can't even remember why." There had been a lot of hanky panky at the twentieth reunion. Half the class was hitting on the other half, not to mention how many of them had married classmates and then divorced them and married other classmates. It was wildly incestuous.

"But anyway, back to me. After putting up with that creep as long as I could stand it I married Larry Billings. That was romance on the rebound, a huge mistake."

Larry was at least closer to her age than Donny had been. He was thirty-five when they married. He was a bank teller. Before they married he lived with his mother. That should have been a tip-off that something was wrong with him. Did an inner voice scream Mama's Boy!? If it didn't, it sure should have. Larry doted on his mother. She did his laundry. She brought him lunches at the bank. Larry and Alex had dinner at his mother's house every Sunday. Larry expected Alex—demanded of her—that she do things just the way his mother did, from cooking to alphabetizing books on their shelves to rubbing his shoulders when he came home from work and squeezing his damn pimples. She couldn't take it after six months. Two marriages, and never an anniversary.

Their talk flowed through the night and through the years without chronology, jumping from subject to subject. They talked about how they had thought Mary Elizabeth Lucious was a joke and how they had despised Bubba Austin and loved Kimzey Williams. Alex talked about her various jobs—waitress, secretary, office manager, bookstore clerk, and adjunct college professor (she had majored in math but used her degree only for that one part-time teaching gig). They discovered, or rather re-discovered that they both loved art and literature (Jim had majored in art and worked in advertising, giving them something else in common—advertising/marketing, same thing). They talked about who had been killed in Vietnam (three of their classmates that they knew of and many more of the younger brothers of classmates since most of the men from their class were a little too old for service in Nam unless they were career military). And, since they were in a gay bar, they naturally talked about who else they had grown up with who had turned out to be gay (two more that they knew about and some who were highly suspicious, plus, most significantly, Jim's uncle Bradley).

Uncle Brad, of course, Alex thought. That explained so much. Like why a super stud heterosexual who was conservative to boot would hang out in gay bars. Jim loved his Uncle Brad. "Uncle Brad brought me here about the time you were discovering your Johnnys and Donny's."

Mostly they talked about the good times. Jim said, "Hide and seek football, what a wild game that was. Remember hide-and-seek football?"

"Oh yeah, how could I forget?" They played an especially rambunctious brand of hide and seek in the neighborhood. "Remember when I knocked you on your ass when you were licking an ice cream cone?"

She attempted to demonstrate by making a blocking motion with her forearm. It was kind of a reflex action, and she overdid it a bit. She bumped his arm and sloshed beer on his shirt. "There you go again," he said while she hurriedly dabbed his shirt front with her napkin.

He laughed and said, "That's just the way you dabbed at the ice cream." He asked her why she stayed in Western Washington all this time.

"Mostly inertia, I guess. I did get away for a while, but at some point in between jobs I had nowhere else to go so I came back home and kinda got stuck. What about you? You're the last person I ever expected to see back here."

"I never left."

"Oh." She was surprised. "I thought you said you'd been gone for—what was it? Twenty, thirty years? What was that about?"

"Did I say that? I don't know what I was thinking."

Jim had been so obviously destined for success that she assumed he would have lived in some major metropolis in an upscale neighborhood with a goddess for a wife and three perfect children, but he had been right here all along living in the country

38

home he inherited from Uncle Brad. He had majored in art at City University, which she had known at the time but had forgotten, and had worked in advertising all these years with, he admitted dolefully, unexciting clients the likes of Grant's department store and Smith's Sporting Goods.

She asked if he had children or grandchildren, if he'd had any exciting adventures in all the years since she'd last seen him.

"Nope. No children, no grandchildren. No adventures. I've had a pretty dull life, if you must know. Not counting the years when I led a secret life as the most famous female impersonator on the West Coast." He added this last with a sly wink, and she said, "Yes, of course. You must have been on the same bill with your ex wife and the monkey."

She thought it was sad that someone with so much promise as a youth would have had such a dull life as an adult. It just wasn't right. There must have been a whole passel of adventures he didn't care to talk about. The romantic in her yearned to discover he really had lived another secret life. Maybe he'd been a spy, or he'd made a fortune on Wall Street and lost it all. *Silly me.* She changed the subject. She asked, "What about Rolly? Whatever happened to him?" Rolly Simpson had been one of their closest friends.

Jim said, "He married Molly Robbins."

"Rolly and Molly. Good name for a Vaudeville act."

"Or a pair of rabbits."

"I wish you hadn't said that. Now I'll never get it out of my head."

He told her that Rolly was a disc jockey.

"In Wetside?"

"Uh huh. KLOW Soft Rock. He's been there since the late '60s. I still run into him every once in a while. I've done some work with them, so our paths cross now and then."

She noted the present tense. "You said you were retired."

"Basically I am, but I still take on a few odd jobs now and then. I work at home. In my pajamas. You can't beat that."

She said she never would have imagined Rolly and Molly together. "At least he didn't marry Kay Kay. That would have been a disaster."

"Yeah, and he knows that. But I think he's always been a little bit in love with her."

Kimzy Williams, or Kay Kay as her parents and her few friends called her, was as sad as an abandoned puppy, as sweet as banana cream pie, and as crazy as a kitten with a snoot full of catnip. Kay Kay stood less than five feet tall when she reached her full growth at thirteen (she kept hoping to grow more, but it never happened). Her stringy, rust colored hair fanned out from the sides of her face as if constantly shocked by static electricity. Pug-nosed and wide-eyed, her face was surprisingly round and cherubic in contrast to a body that was all knobs and angles—a face like Trisha Sullivan's and a body like a stick puppet. When she graduated from Jefferson High at sixteen after skipping two grades, she still looked pre-pubescent.

People said she was crazy and predicted she would wind up in the loony bin, which she did. They said she was a nymphomaniac, among other diagnoses (clinical and otherwise), which she wasn't. Who knows why people spread damaging rumors about other people? But they sure do. Especially kids. It must be the same in every school in the U.S. There is some girl rumored to be the town whore, and nine times out of ten there's not a smidgen of truth to it. How they pick who they're going to smear is beyond understanding. More often than not it's wishful thinking on the part of the boys. Some poor girl through no fault of her own is graced with a certain look and a figure that drives boys wild, and somebody's fantasy becomes somebody's exaggeration and then an outright lie that spreads like influenza. Or maybe it starts with anger over being rejected. In Kay Kay's case there seemed to be no reason at all. She was no sexpot, and if she ever spurned anyone's advances it was not in a mean way, although there was one little incident everyone heard about that might have been what sparked the rumors and nasty remarks and outright lies about her—hurtful lies that flew through the halls and were scribbled on bathroom walls at Nisqually Middle

40

School and later at Jefferson High School. Graffiti about Kimzey was the stuff of adolescent legend, and hardly any of it was based on anything real. Yeah, she did have some emotional problems, she did spend time in a mental hospital, and she might have been a little bit on the wild side—*might*. But even if she did let some of the boys go a little farther than she should have, which probably only Rolly Simpson would know for sure, that didn't make her any wilder than half the other girls in Wetside's schools. Being so little and scrawny, and with that look of fear about her, you'd think people would want to protect her and not say all those nasty things about her.

From what Rolly said, it started with her first "real" date, meaning the first time she went out with a boy without a chaperone. It was one of the Ross brothers. They were notorious liars.

She was just a child. Thirteen? Fourteen? Something like that. The middle Ross boy claimed she went all the way with him.

Jim said, "He said she gave him a hand job."

"Somehow that seems worse. Don't ask me why. It just does. I don't understand how people were so quick to believe him."

"I don't know. They were quick to believe the most outlandish things about her. Is it human nature? Is it as simple as that? Do people need drama and excitement so badly they'll believe anything that's a little bit juicy?"

Was Kimzey aware of the things kids were saying about her? Surely she must have been. Probably not all of it, but she must have gotten wind of some of it. She certainly saw the nasty messages that were scrawled in the girls' bathroom. She might have told her mother about it. She might have told Mary Elizabeth. For a year or so at least Mary Elizabeth was her only friend. They lived across the street from each other. Alex said she often wondered why Kay Kay never stood up for herself. Why didn't she just say it was all a pack of lies? Maybe she was afraid that would make it worse. Sometimes people hope that if you ignore something it will go away.

Jim said, "They wouldn't let her in the Debs. Remember that?"

The Darling Debs, a junior high school sorority. All the most popular girls were members. Kay Kay really wanted in, but they

41

didn't want her, and her mother raised hell about that. She was just trying to take up for her daughter, but she went about it all wrong. Kay Kay's folks were pretty screwed up. There was something very strange about their home life. She was an only child. Everybody said she was spoiled rotten. Her parents were pretty wealthy, but they didn't live like rich people. They lived in a fairly modest house in a regular neighborhood just a few blocks from Jim and Alex, closer to the high school and the park. Throughout elementary school and junior high her daddy drove her to school every morning, long after most kids her age were old enough to get there on their own. If it was raining or snowing he'd even take her when she was in high school, and Jefferson High was a mere two blocks from her house. In many other ways she seemed to depend on her parents more than other kids did. Once, for instance, when she was in grammar school she started crying and wouldn't stop, and it took the teacher a long time to coax out of her what she was crying about. Her daddy forgot to kiss her goodbye. Finally the principal had to call her father and he came to the school and kissed her, and then she was all right.

Jim said, "With parents like hers, I don't guess she ever had a chance. I think Kay Kay started out all right. It wasn't until the town went all *Town Without Pity* on her that she went nuts herself."

"Didn't her mother get a bunch of money in a court case against Lara Cockburn's mom?"

"Yeah, I think so. You're talking about the pie thing, right? I don't think it ever went to court. I think they settled out of court. The newspaper said it was an undisclosed amount. That's what they always say. I heard it was more than a hundred thousand dollars."

•

Bartender Randy turned on the television over the bar. It was a rarely used TV. Tailoring the programming to the crowd at Barney's, Randy tightly controlled what shows were allowed. No sports, no quiz shows and no reality TV. They watched special events only, and only those Randy wanted to watch. Randy said, "Listen up, everybody. Obama's speech is coming on."

There was a scuffle of chairs as bar patrons jockeyed for a good view of the twenty-one inch screen. Randy turned up the volume.

The speech was all about the economy. Obama said, "They said they wanted to let the market run free but they let it run wild," and Barney's went wild with applause. There were shouts of "Right on!" and "Ain't that the truth!"

In a matter-of-fact tone Obama said, "We talked about the economy for forty minutes (referring to a recent debate) and not once did Senator McCain talk about the struggles that middle class families are facing every day."

The Barney's Pub crowd commented that McCain was out of touch with regular people and recalled that Obama had worked on housing issues in the inner city. Somebody said, "I want to know what he's going to do about Don't Ask Don't Tell," which was when someone else said, "Shut up and listen. We can talk about it after he's done."

The only other interruption was when Obama said, "I believe that our free market has been the engine of America's great progress."

Someone muttered "Screw the market. See? He's a sellout just like the rest."

"Whaddaya expect?" someone else said, "There are no good politicians."

After the speech Barney's erupted in chatter about the campaign. The consensus was that Obama had a clear understanding of the issues and McCain was an idiot, although no one was willing to quibble with his standing as a war hero. Jim didn't say anything.

"I guess you feel kind of like an outsider," Alex said.

"More like a maverick, if you know what I mean," he replied with a conspiratorial wink as if he thought she'd approve of his clever use of the term maverick.

Her response was, "Mavericky. Palin's new term."

"She never said that. That was what's her name who said that. The comedian that does impersonations of Palin."

Jim said that he was gratified that at least some of the liberals in Barney's were skeptical about the free market. "It doesn't matter whether it's Republicans or Democrats, the Clintons and Bushes and everyone else in Washington thinks the market is the answer to everything, but it's the market that got us into the mess we're in now. And the fat cat bankers."

"At least we can agree on that," Alex said, "but look, I'm not one hundred percent against McCain either. Well, yes I am. But I can kind of see why you might like him. I even admired some things about him. Like the McCain-Feingold bill. I was all for that. But you've got to admit that picking Sarah Palin for a running mate was a dumb move. She's an idiot. The thought of her becoming president scares the shit out of me."

Jim conceded that she might be right. He said, "I don't know yet. I don't think anybody really knows enough about her, but I think she might be brighter than people give her credit for."

"Yeah, right. And Charlie Brown's actually going to kick that ball and the Brooklyn Bridge is still for sale. But here's what I predict: Obama's going to trounce McCain, and then after the election McCain will swing hard to one side or the other just to survive in politics. Left or right doesn't matter since he's got no principles at all. And Palin will get her own late-night talk show and become the darling of the right wing."

Arguing the presidential campaign morphed into a more general argument over political ideology. Jim said he was more libertarian than conservative, in theory at least, but thought libertarian theory didn't always work out so well in practice. He said he considered himself a social liberal but a fiscal conservative. Alex thought that was promising because that stance had been a stopping-off point in her journey from right of center to the far left. He said he liked Obama and would love to see the U.S. elect its first black president but was afraid Obama would be too soft on terrorists. "Any other time in history I would vote for him, but with radical Muslims out to destroy America we need a strong military man like McCain in the White House."

"That's exactly what we don't need," she countered. "We had that with Bush, and look where it got us: loss of freedom, the Bill of Rights flushed down the toilet and a president acting like a goddamn schoolyard bully challenging other countries to a fight. *Bring it on*, for godssake."

"Coddling criminals, inviting the enemy in. That's what we'll have with Obama. That's just what the enemy wants. I know all you bleeding hearts want to give everyone a fair hearing, but there are terrorists in the world who want to kill us, and they'll never listen to reason. McCain understands that. Your boy doesn't."

"Boy! You call him boy?"

"I didn't mean it that way."

They came close to blows. If they were two men instead of a man and a woman it might have come to that, but they talked it out and found areas where they could agree. They agreed, for instance, that McCain was catering to the extreme right wing in the campaign for purely political reasons. "He's got to do that to get elected," Jim said. "But once in the White House he'll tone it down a bit. He's much more moderate than his campaign rhetoric implies. Every president does it. Look at Bush. Remember how he talked about compassionate conservatism but dropped the compassionate part once he was elected? And he talked about tightening the boarders during the campaign but then wanted to give amnesty to illegals."

"No he didn't."

"And Clinton. Look at him. He talked a liberal game but turned out to be much more centrist than anyone imagined, and was owned by big business just as much as any Republican."

She said, "I hope you're right about McCain floating to the middle. Not that it matters. He doesn't have a chance."

They'd had similar arguments way back in college. Their senior year. It was the first time either of them had been politically active. He was working with the campus Republicans on the Goldwater campaign, and she was supporting Johnson. She reminded him of that. "Remember Goldwater and Johnson? That almost destroyed our friendship. Now that we've reconnected, I'd hate to see a repeat of that."

"We were young and passionate, and let's face it, we had started to drift apart anyway. Hopefully we're more sensible now."

Around about midnight they finally ran out of things to talk about. They were both pretty slammed, too. Jim offered to walk her home. The night was cool and an almost invisible drizzle slanted down in the glow of streetlights. Jim had an umbrella. He walked her to her door a short four blocks away. He sheltered her with the umbrella and they staggered into each other and giggled like kids. Faced with ascending the stairs to her front door she said, "Oh my, I don't know if I can handle this." She felt woozy.

He said, "You can make it, Slugger. I got faith in you."

She grabbed the rail and started climbing. The steps were steep. It felt like her feet could not lift high enough to get from one to the other. He put hands on her butt and gave a push, and kept his hands cupped on her cheeks longer than necessary to push her up, removing his hands only when she turned to face him at her door. He stood by while she fitted her key in the lock. What now, she wondered. Do we kiss goodnight? Hug? A handshake? Was he feeling me up or just giving me a push up the stairs? The script should have been easy enough to follow. She'd seen it acted out in countless movies. According to the script he was supposed to say, "Aren't you going to ask me in?" and she would make up some weak excuse, and then they'd have to drag the tension out over a series of silly scenes until they finally wound up—a month later in real time but only two minutes in movie time—in a compromising position but fully clothed or discretely hidden from full view, mind you, because she was thinking about the way the script would have run in one of the movies they saw together at The Strand in 1960. In a more contemporary movie they'd shake hands and then grab each other in a fierce embrace and clothes would fly; hot pulsing music and quick cuts for a million camera angles, and she'd leap on him and wrap her legs around him and he'd carry her fast and stumbling to bed, and in ten seconds flat they'd be fucking each other's brains out—with just enough left to the imagination to avoid the dreaded NC-17 rating.

I could go for us acting out that script, oh yes I could.

But he did not kiss her or grab her in a fierce embrace. No he did not. He offered her his hand. She could have been a blind date he wasn't overly impressed with. He said, "This has been fun. We should get together again."

"Yes, let's do."

Halfway in she paused while propping the door with her foot. "Wait," she said. "Call me. Here. I'll give you my number," digging in her bag for pen and paper.

•

A week later they found themselves together in an old familiar place, the basketball court in Chief Leschi Park on Nisqually Drive by the old school, Jim dribbling the ball side to side and Alex trying her best to guard him, warily waiting for him to make his move to the basket. She often shot baskets on that court. Hardly anyone else ever used it. It was mid morning and she had been there by herself trying to get in a little exercise before going to work. She was surprised when a Hyundai Santa Fe pulled up to park by the curb. On the curbside door was a Bright Marketing logo. The driver stepped out and waved at her. It was Jim Bright. "You still play, I see," he said as he approached the court.

"I shoot a few baskets now and then. That's about all I'm up to these days. Trying to run the court would probably kill me."

She was taken aback to see him there. Dropping by without calling first was a bit presumptuous, a little bit like stalking. But hadn't she dropped in on him a thousand times in their youth? But she knew that was different. They weren't kids any more; they were virtually strangers if you came right down to it, and she was irritated that he would be so presumptuous. But happy to see him. You're such a pushover, she said to herself.

Chief Leschi was a typical inner city basketball court, a concrete slab about half the size of a regular court with goals on either end. Both baskets had long since lost their nets.

"You up for a little one-on-one?" he challenged.

No, she wasn't. It had been decades since she had actually played against another competitor. She figured a dozen trips running up and down the court, even as small as it was, would do her in. But

47

she wasn't about to let him scare her off. He brought out the old competitiveness in her, so against her better judgment she said, "Sure, hot shot. I can take you on." Even if she couldn't run, she figured she could beat him on set shots alone. That was what she practiced the few times she shot baskets, fifteen and twenty-foot set shots. She sunk nine out of ten on average. Not bad for an old lady. In high school she had played forward and had led the girls' team in points and rebounds. She'd been a terror on both offense and defense. And in pickup games she held her own with the boys as well. As outstanding as Jim had been at most sports, basketball had never been his strongest. His performance against other boys had never been quite as good as her performance against other girls, but against each other they had always been fairly equal. They enjoyed playing one-on-one with each other when they were sixteen. The prospect of taking him on at sixty-six was fraught with fears of muscle strains and broken bones or collapsing from exhaustion. She pictured them both having heart attacks and being rushed to the hospital together.

She tossed him the ball. Slowly, deliberately, he dribbled hand-to-hand, chatting with her. Trash talking like Gary Payton in his prime. She planted her feet and feinted left to right as he moved his upper body, keeping her eyes on his hands but also on his eyes. The feet and the hands can fool you, but the eyes never lie. She knew that he would always look in the direction he was going to move.

"Ah yes," he said, the ball going *pa-pa-pa* against the concrete, "this is going to be like old times. Gonna give you a drubbing like I did before." He started singing, "Gonna twist again like we did last summer," *pa-pa-pa.*

"You never gave me a drubbing."

"Oh yes I did. And yes I can."

"We'll see about..."

He suddenly darted to the left, catching her off guard, zipped to the basket in a half dozen steps and deftly scored an easy lay-in.

"Two to zip!" he exulted.

"No fair. I wasn't ready."

"That's the breaks, honey buns."

"You were traveling. You took at least five steps without putting the ball on the court."

"How would you know? You never even turned around enough to see me before I took my shot. I coulda dunked it too, but I didn't want to show off."

He bounced the ball to her. She circled slowly, dribbling, feinting as if to go around him and rise up for a jump shot, but he held his ground with feet planted and slapped the ball out of her hands just as she started to make her move. Damn. He was quick. And better than she expected. Before she could position herself in front of him he raised up for a jumper of his own. It caught rim and bounced off. She ran after it, circled around him and pulled up for a ten-foot set shot. Sunk it. Two to two.

"Pure luck," he said. "That's the last one you're gonna sink."

He backed her down, methodically pushing against her with his back. It was like Charles Barkley backing down Sue Bird. She didn't have the strength to guard him. From five feet out he hit a nifty hook shot. Four to two. She knew he could do that all day. The only way she could beat him was with speed, if she could muster any. But it seemed like he had more speed than her, as well as superior strength. A short burst to the goal was all she could manage, followed by gasping for breath. It wasn't very long before they were both huffing.

While she tried her best to just stay on her feet he repeatedly forced his way to the basket with his superior weight and strength, tossing up lay-ins and short hooks. But he missed as many as he hit. She used head feints and crossover dribbles and what bursts of speed she could manage to get to the hoop, where she connected more often than she missed. He had the best moves, but she was a better shot. Both of them kept up a stream of trash talk, even if their insults did increasingly sound like last gasps. They were both beginning to sweat. It was a cloudy day and might start raining at any moment.

Alex felt a rip in her right calf, a painful knot. She tried to not let him see her limp. He tried to not let her notice how hard he was breathing. They were both praying the other would call it quits. She was the one who finally gave in. Clutching the ball to her chest she walked off the court and plopped down on a bench, her long legs stretched out in front, head reared back. She set the ball on the ground. "I've had it," she said.

He said, "Thank God. I don't think I could have gone another minute."

"But you were too proud to quit."

"Can't help it. It's a guy thing."

She chalked it up as a minor victory that he had not noticed she had been pretending just as much as he had.

Half an hour later they were drinking coffee at her kitchen table. Her cat, never afraid of strangers, had climbed onto his lap. She had set her computer to play a random selection of girl singers: the Indigo Girls, KD Lang, Sheryl Crow and others. Talk of healthcare had come up, a topic of contention in the current political campaign. "I'm concerned about the millions of people that don't have health insurance at all," she said, "I also worry about the ones who have insurance but not enough to cover their expenses and about the people whose premiums keep going up and up."

"I know. I agree. And I'm all for making affordable health insurance available for everybody. But the way Obama wants to go about it is all wrong. It's socialized medicine."

"What would be so bad about that? It seems to work pretty well in Europe."

"Yeah, right. You can't pick your own doctors and it takes months to get approved for hospital care. I don't want Nancy Pelosi telling me what doctor I can see, and if I have a heart attack I don't want to have to wait for some government bureaucrat to decide when it's OK to let me in the hospital."

She didn't want to call him stupid, but that was her immediate reaction. She said, "Where do you get ideas like that?"

"People who have done studies of socialized medicine in Canada and Europe have found that it always comes to that. Not at first. They have to ease it in. But sooner or later when you put the government in charge of healthcare that's what it comes down to. Let's face it, when has the federal government ever done anything right?"

"Oh? What about Social Security? What about the WPA and the first man on the moon? Those were things the government did that private enterprise could not. And what people are you talking about, anyway? What studies?"

"I don't know. I can't remember the details, but I've read about it."

That was when she did call him stupid, more or less. She said, "I thought you had better sense than that. Do you believe any old crap you read on some right wing blog without even checking to see if it's true? Nobody's asking for government control of healthcare. They're just asking for the government to finance it, and for sensible regulation of the insurance companies. And it's a myth that they have long waits for medical care in Europe. It's free and quick and just as good as it is here. Did you see Michael Moore's *Sicko*?"

"Now there's your bullshit, that right there. They call his movies documentaries, but they're just his warped opinions. I wouldn't believe anything he says."

"Why not? He backs stuff up with hard facts. He doesn't just make up facts like some people I know." In the back of her mind was the nagging realization that she was accepting the supposed facts on her side of the argument just as unquestioning as he was. But she was pretty sure some of the Republicans and some of the commentators on Fox news made up stuff willy-nilly, and she was confident that the left wingers, being boring policy wonks for the most part, backed their stuff up with facts and figures. (She spent a lot of time watching MSNBC.) She was getting frustrated. She was also beginning to wish he wasn't so handsome. It's hard to argue politics while your heart's going pitter patter.

Assuming he'd want more coffee (after all, she downed one cup after another and didn't everyone?) she picked up his half empty cup and her empty and carried them to the counter and refilled them. He said, "We gotta have some system of determining who's deserving and who isn't."

That pissed her off. "Deserving!" She shouted, "Jesus Christ Almighty. Are you saying you gotta earn the right to healthcare? No, no. It can't be that way. If you need it you should get it. That's all there is to it."

"Maybe," he said. "Maybe for the truly unfortunate. Maybe for people who are disabled or mentally ill or something where they can't get a good job and can't afford insurance. But most employers provide insurance, and most poor people could get jobs if they wanted to."

"Man, what world have you been living in?" She snatched a paper towel off the roll and dabbed at the coffee ring her cup had left as if it were his mouth she was wiping away. She said, "Look at me. I'm a prime example. I'm a decent, educated, hard working person. Like they say, I play by the rules. But I've been poor all my life. Through no fault of my own. You know, it's… it's partly my upbringing. When we were young they didn't prepare girls for careers because we were expected to find husbands who could support us. When I went to college girls were expected to major in how to find a husband. Those of us who actually wanted to learn something were herded into social work and English lit and other majors that kind of guaranteed low wage jobs. Well, I found a husband all right, two of them. They were pretty good providers but lousy husbands, so I divorced them. Was I supposed to stay in shitty marriages just because they were good providers? And then I wasted the rest of my life with one lousy job after another. Despite a good education and willingness to work I couldn't get decent jobs. Some of them had benefits, but most didn't. There were times when if I had come down with some really serious disease I woulda been shit out of luck. I coulda died. And now…"

She paused dramatically, having a sudden inspiration of how to make her point and drive it home, no longer thinking about how her little heart went all aflutter when looking into his deep brown eyes but wanting desperately to win an argument. She reached into her mouth and pulled out first her lower and then her upper dentures and placed them on the table in front of him. "I got no fucking teeth. I loft 'em little by little over a lifetime becawf what little insurance I had didn't cover dental. I had to save up for a year to get these false teeth, and during that year I practically stayed in hiding the whole time becawf I was ashamed of the way I looked. I always looked down at the gwond or covered my mouf when I talked. And dammit, I had toothaches, lots and lots of toothaches, and when I did I would put off going to the dentist as long as I could becawf I couldn't afford it, and when I should have had root canals or implants all I could do was let 'em pull the teeth. I got to where I couldn't eat much of anything but soft foods."

"I'm sorry, honey. I guess I didn't realize how bad it could be for some people."

She thought she'd made her point, but then he said, "But there are charity programs for the truly needy. Besides, I'm pretty sure you must be the exception. Most people who don't have insurance could get something if they really tried."

She said, "What's that? I couldn't hear you. I forgot to tell you that I'm also half deaf, and Medicare won't pay for hearing aides." This last little dig was a slight exaggeration. She did have some slight hearing loss, but whether or not she needed hearing aides was borderline.

Raindrops, the blog of the Daily Journal, Wetside, Washington, October 30, 1954

POLICE BLOTTER
By Harold Juniper Drews

Indecency on the Range

Aubrey Smithfield, 16, was caught in an indecent act with a horse in a pasture on the Smithfield family farm Thursday afternoon. Sheriff's Office spokesperson Gene Whitney said, "It's bad enough that the kid committed an illegal and indecent act, but he had to go and do it in full view of innocent passers-by. Shouldn't nobody have to see something like that," Whitney said. The pasture in question fronts a major highway, and motorists had called in to the Sheriff's Office to report the incident. "My six-year-old daughter was in the car, and she asked why the boy was riding the horse without any pants on," reported one witness who asked that her name be withheld. "Now how was I supposed to explain that to a six-year-old?" the witness said.

In defense of his actions Smithfield said, "I thought I was too far from the road for anybody to see. 'Sides, it didn't hurt the horse none." He was remanded to juvenile authorities.

Best Friends – Jim and Alex's blog

Little Houses
by Jim Bright

The neighborhood where we grew up was something special. Maybe the place you grew up was special too. Maybe that's true for everyone, but I doubt it. I don't think kids of the '80s, for instance, think there was anything special about where they first tried to moonwalk along with Michael Jackson. Their friends weren't their neighbors but kids they met on the soccer field. Nowadays I drive through residential neighborhoods and I don't see the kind of camaraderie we enjoyed. I don't see neighbors chatting with each other. Suburban houses don't have front porches to gather on; they have garages, huge double car garages. Sometimes they have basketball goals in the driveway where you see a solitary kid shooting hoops. You never see gangs of kids playing chase. The only place you see gangs of kids nowadays is hanging out on street corners downtown, and they're scary.

The houses in our old neighborhood were small and not very interesting. We didn't know it at the time, but when they put up all the little houses on Woodlawn and along the butt end of 18th it was part of a nationwide phenomenon in which young post-war families were moving in a kind of monstrous migration to little houses on little streets where all the homes looked alike and all the families lived identical lives. It was mostly a suburban thing, but there were also pockets of similar development in most towns. We were smack dab in the middle of town in an area where buzzsaws and bulldozers had leveled pine forests to put up cheap houses, and as for our neighbors being clones of one another, they'd never admit it. Alex's parents would claim they were liberal and the Grants middle-of-the-road and the Austins ultra conservative, and they'd be right, but in the ways they lived and dressed and entertained and gathered around the TV they were just alike.

All the houses were on concrete slabs, had three bedrooms, one bathroom, a small storage-slash-laundry room, a single-car carport and hollow-core doors that you could punch through with fist or shoe (I know, I saw Rolly Simpson do it). And we didn't have porches either. That thing about porches I mentioned earlier was me being nostalgic for something I never actually had. The only thing special about my house was the beige shag carpet, wall-to-wall throughout the whole house, except for the bathroom (God, it was hideous) and the sporty den with pine paneling and pop's stuffed fish on the wall—a 110-pound tarpon he caught on a fishing trip to Florida and a 12-pound smallmouth bass he caught in Serenity Lake. Pop closed in the carport to build the den, and we parked our cars in the drive.

Across 18th Street behind Alex's house was what remained of the pine forest, and about a hundred yards or so south of us was Miller Creek, which ran through the woods to the high school and past the swimming pool and on downtown. Across Woodlawn lived the Barnes brothers, and next to them was Old Man Singleterry's house, which was set back from the street by a long driveway canopied by ancient oaks. It *did* have a big front porch. His house was almost completely hidden from view. From the back side, which neighborhood kids could glimpse when playing along the creek bank, was a hodge-podge of sheds and a vegetable garden and a succession of brokedown cars and the notorious cottage where the mysterious Abilene lived. Old Man Singleterry owned the whole street from 18th to Rebel and built all of the houses from carbon-copy blueprints, individualizing them with token differences such as moving a carport from the left side to the right or putting up different style shutters and painting each house a different pastel color, from pink to yellow and blue to a milky pea green.

Chapter 4

Jim's house was right across the street from the old man. It was a sickly pink house with white trim, the usual carport, which they later enclosed, and a concrete patio in back. Jim used his bedroom window on the patio side for sneaking in and out after bedtime. Most of the boys in the neighborhood did that. When they moved in the street wasn't even paved. Damn muddy piece of a road that started on 18th right at Bubba Austin's front yard and came to a dead stop at Mr. Singelterry's driveway where they hadn't yet built the rest of the houses on Woodlawn. From there to the next corner was a dirt path with posts and flags marking off where the street was going to be if they ever got around to finishing it, and delineating quarter-acre lots for eight more houses.

Old Man Singleterry's house had been his father's farmhouse back when the whole neighborhood was the Singleterry Dairy— bought out by some big farming conglomerate during the Korean War and moved to a ranch ten miles east of town with offices downtown still under the Singleterry brand name. Over the years the old house had been added to in haphazard ways, and what had once been servant quarters in back had been remodeled and became Abilene's apartment. Abilene was as ghostlike as Boo Radley, but nowhere near as scary. She was Old Man Singleterry's first wife. Local legend had it that she had been committed to the state insane asylum years ago and that a clerical error resulted in the old man being notified that she had died. They must have sent a notice intended for somebody else. He never questioned it. He had never visited her when she was in the hospital, not once, and he never bothered to go fetch the body when he was notified she had died. If he had, maybe he would have found out she wasn't dead. What he did do was to immediately marry the younger woman he'd been having an affair with for years. Later he got another letter explaining the mistake, which he tore up and pretended he'd never got, because by then he was already married to his hot young mistress and wanted any evidence of Abilene's existence out of his life. For the next two years he got rid of all the letters from Abilene that landed in his mail box. When she was finally released and came home to find her husband living with another woman she threw a hissy fit. A fit wasn't all she threw. She threw frying pans and a rolling pin and a kitchen chair at the old man and at his new wife, who crouched behind the kitchen table. When Abilene ran out of ammunition and came at them with a butcher knife they scooted out the kitchen door and ran through the woods for safety, splashing through the creek and emerging way out on Glouster by the zoo, where they sat on a bench by the monkey cages and plotted how they could safely return home. By the time they finally crept back into the house Abilene had calmed down.

After coming back home Abilene lived in the cottage out back and the old man continued to live in the big house with his new wife, Jessica, who was half his age. The old man proved himself adroit at pleading in getting both women to accept the situation. Why either one of them put up with it defies reason. Jessica could have found a better man and one closer to her own age. Abilene, on the other hand, could plausibly have been coaxed or bullied into it. She was nothing but a shell of her former self. Repeated shock treatments had robbed her of any strength of will she may have once had. She was willing to go along with whatever her husband wanted, and what he wanted was his sexy new wife. Rolly Simpson said the old man took turns sleeping with first one and then the other. Jim believed it, but Alex didn't. She said she didn't believe the old man ever even knocked on Abilene's door. "She could have died in that little cottage and nobody would have known it until she started stinking," she said.

After a few years Abilene was once again sent to the insane asylum and that time she never got out.

If Old Man Singleterry wasn't shtupping two wives, there were a lot of other people in Wetside engaging in other kinds of hanky panky. People tend to think that before the so-called sexual revolution in the '60s everybody was uptight and circumspect. But there was a lot more going on than you might imagine. There was even a notorious incident when a local sex club was discovered. Wife swapping and group sex, some of it even involving children and adults. It was some kind of religious thing, some weirdo preacher telling people God wanted them to all share their bodies and a bunch of horny folks eager to buy into it. And what all went on right there in the neighborhood was enough to make your hair stand on end. Like Ophelia Sullivan doing a strip tease for the entertainment of the neighborhood boys. That one happened shortly after the Brights moved to Wetside.

Down by Miller Creek there was a maze of winding paths through the trees and brush that the kids called the jungle. Jim was wandering around down there one day, and he had to pee. He stepped behind a tree to do his business. He thought he was well hidden. He was in mid stream when he heard a girl's voice tease, "I seeeee you."

Quickly he stuffed his penis back in his pants and swung around, and there she was. He hadn't met her yet but knew immediately who she was because Alex had told him all about her and described what she looked like: hair as red as fire and huge boobs. Somebody said they were 40-Ds. They weren't quite that big, but big enough. Her hair was not only flaming red, it was such a wild tangle that it looked like a burning bush. To Jim, caught off-guard, she looked like a grown woman, even if she was only a year older.

Jim said, "You didn't see anything."

"Did too."

"I had my back to you so you couldn't a seen much."

"I seen enough," she said.

"Naw you didn't."

"Did too. I seen your little pee pee."

He blushed, and she said, "You wanna see mine?"

He didn't know what to say. She said, "For five bucks you can see me all the way buck naked. Would you like that?"

"I don't know," he stammered. "I guess so, but I don't have any money with me."

"Gimme the money later, then tonight after all the lights go out come over to my house, but don't let anyone see you. Watch my bedroom window. It's on the back. There's a dog house back there. You can hide behind it if you're scared somebody'll see you. Don't worry, there ain't no dog. He got run over. Be there at exactly ten-thirty or you'll miss the show."

Jim snitched the money from the cash jar his mother kept hidden in a kitchen cabinet. As soon as his folks turned to the ten o'clock news that night he excused himself and went to his room. He locked his bedroom door and turned out the light and opened the window and climbed out, and then he ran across to Ophelia's yard and slid like a base runner behind the dog house. Wham! Right into Rolly Simpson, who was also there so see the show. So was the oldest Delk boy. They were both crouched behind her dog house. "Shhh," Rolly said.

They watched her window. After a long wait and just about time they were ready to give it up and slink home, her bedroom light came on. They saw her shadow moving about behind her blinds. Her wavering shadow walked up to the window and then back across the room and out of sight. Maybe she had to go to the bathroom or something. "Is that all?" Rolly asked. "Shit. That weren't worth five dollars."

"She made me pay ten," the Delk boy said. Rolly snickered. Actually he hadn't even paid the five bucks. Why should he? Once he heard she was going to do her show, there was nothing to keep him from showing up. Payment was on the honor system and Rolly didn't honor it.

And then she came back into the room and back to the window, and she raised the blinds and stood in the window just as she had promised, completely naked. At least it looked like she was. The yellowish light from a three-bulb overhead fixture was behind her, so her body was partially a silhouette. And then she moved into the light and the boys could see a little bit more than the dark shape of her body. For a second Jim thought she was wearing a two-piece swim suit because she was tanned such a deep bronze all over except for the stark white imprint of her swim suit, and there were also large shadows cast across her body, so there was probably more imagining than nakedness seen that night.

Ophelia put her hands on her hips and did a little dance and stuck her tongue out at them, or at the spot where she imagined they were crouching in rapt attention. She couldn't see them peeking around the edge of the dog house, but she knew they were there. In her mind she could see Jim's wide eyes and the big round opening of Rolly's mouth. She moved toward them until her silhouetted shape filled the window, and then she reached up and closed the blinds. The whole show lasted no more than a minute. "She does it all the time," Rolly Simpson told Jim. But you can't ever see very much."

"I did. I seen it all," the Delk boy said.

Rolly said, "She puts out, too. If you don't believe it, ask Bubba Austin."

•

Alex was born in Wetside and had never been more than thirty miles away. The Reverend Bright and his wife and children moved to Western Washington from some little town in Louisiana when Jim was thirteen. Reverend Bright hitched a trailer behind his 1950 Ford pickup and his brother, Jim's Uncle Bradley, hitched another trailer behind his car, and together they caravanned cross country, sleeping in tents at night.

Jim and his sister loved the new house. After years of sleeping on twin beds in a shared bedroom in a two-bedroom shack with peeling wallpaper and cracked linoleum the new house was luxurious. "It's like a mansion," Jim said. It seemed much larger than it really was because they didn't have enough furniture for so much space. The combined living and dining room was as big as their whole house in Louisiana. They moved in on a Friday in early June, the summer between elementary and junior high. They had barely started to unpack boxes before Alex showed up in their front yard saying to Jim, "Hi there. My name's Alex. Are you guys moving in?"

He was all snarky right from the start. He said, "Ain't that obvious? What are you, brain damaged or something?"

His mother said, "Now you be nice to the young lady, honey."

Alex didn't let his attitude bother her. She was used to it. She thought that was the way all boys talked. She said, "Nah, I'm not brain damaged, and there's no call for you to be such a wisecracker."

"I was just fooling with you," Jim said.

His mother introduced herself and said, "This here's our son, Jim, and in yonder (pointing to the kitchen) is our girl, Wanda. And that sourpuss over there is my husband, The Right Reverend Bright."

"Hi there. Nice to meet you."

She jumped right in and started helping them unpack. She picked up a box marked *dishes* and carried it in to the kitchen. She helped them unload everything and put stuff away, and then she took Jim on a tour of the neighborhood. They walked three blocks down Park Avenue and past City Park to the old baseball park, and then they wandered through the construction sites where they were building the new high school, the construction crews gone home for the weekend, and next door to that the swimming pool, which was also under construction. He jumped down into the deep end, a ten-foot drop, and ran the length of the pool to climb out in the shallow end. Watching him make that leap was exhilarating to Alex. He hit bottom and started running, and she took off in a dash around the edge of the pool to meet him at the other end and said, "That was pretty neat, but you coulda broke your leg."

"Naah," he said. Then they explored the jungle and walked along about half a mile of Miller Creek to where the pipe goes across. It was a water pipe that fed water to a station in the nearby zoo. It was about two feet in diameter and five feet above the surface of the water. It was quite a challenge to walk the pipe. Some of the kids would sit astraddle and scoot across on their butts, but Alex and some of the more athletic boys could walk it pretty easily. Jim and Alex sat in the middle with their feet dangling. She told him that Rolly and some of the other kids had stick fights on the pipe, acting out that scene with Robin Hood and Little John. She said, "Rolly always wins, and the other kids always wind up in the creek."

Jim said, "I bet I could beat him." For all he knew Rolly could have been seven feet tall and strong as a bull. Such confidence.

Miller Creek meanders all over town. It ran from the Little League park, past the Singleterry house and through yet another park, under the bridge by the high school and the old baseball park. Yes, there were three baseball parks in Wetside, and all in the same neighborhood within easy walking distance. The largest of the parks had been a professional baseball stadium back in the days of the old Negro Baseball League and was later used for high school games and for professional wrestling with a ring set up between the pitcher's mound and home plate. The neighborhood kids loved sneaking in when the stadium wasn't in use. The gates were locked but there was a gap they could squeeze through. Sometimes they'd chase each other around the bases and maybe hit a few, but mostly they liked to climb up in the stadium seats and just sit up there. The thrill of it was being where they weren't supposed to be. That was where the kid from the corner house broke his arm. It was also where Bubba saw Lara Cockburn kissing Bobby Johnson and told Lara's mother (Lara was grounded for a week).

Miller Creek skirted the outfield wall and ran on throughout the town until it finally spilled into the river. Normally it was no more than two feet deep and five feet across—a few inches of fast moving water over rocks as smooth as marbles, but it had high banks and when there was a big rain it turned into a raging river. Kids would dive in and swim with the current, and sometimes float on makeshift rafts imagining they were rafting wild rapids such as never actually existed in the little meandering creek.

Just below Alex's house there was a wide spot in the creek where the water stood about five feet deep or more, even in the driest part of summer. It was the swimming hole. The water was icy year round. Jim and Alex, who were the same height, could stand up in the middle and the water would come to their chins, except right after a solid rain when it was over their heads. It was there above that swimming hole that Rolly Simpson hung the swing rope from the branch of a magnolia tree. Rolly and Jim liked to swing out and drop far into the water below. But most of the boys would just swing out and back, never managing to work up the nerve to let go and plunge into the water. Alex did it, too. One time only, just to prove she could.

Across the creek from the swing was the jungle. Mottled light streamed through a dense canopy of foliage. The paths that wound through fir and ash and cottonwood trees and thick ferns and around tangles of blackberry bushes were of the kid's making, beaten down by tramping through. Alex led Jim on an excursion through the jungle that day, and they told one another everything about their lives so far. She told him that she had an aunt who was a nurse and that probably that's what she'd be when I grew up, and she told him that her hero was Helen Keller. His hero, he said, was Jim Brown. She didn't know who that was, but he told her he was the greatest running back who ever lived. She found it fascinating that Jim (Bright, not Brown) was from Louisiana, a place as exotic to her as real jungles in Africa or South America. She wanted to know all about what it was like down there. Seeing her reaction he laid it thick. He said in the summertime it got to be 130 degrees. He said the humidity was so high you could hang a wash rag on the line for an hour and squeeze water out of it. He told her about alligators that could swallow a dog whole and about a kind of vine called kudzu that smothered houses and cars, and about swamps filled with snapping turtles and water moccasins, and that the cockroaches were as big as a half grown cat and a swarm of them surprised on their kitchen cabinets when the light was flipped on at night looked like a black rug that squirmed and pulsed and quickly scattered into cracks and crevices.

She said, "I think we're going to be the best friends ever."

After thoroughly exploring the neighborhood Jim said, "I better get my rear end back home and help the folks unload."

She said she'd help. It was getting on toward lunch time when they got back. Mrs. Bright asked if she'd like to have lunch with them.

"Yes ma'am, that would be nice," she said.

Mrs. Bright prepared sandwiches and chips and brought them out to the patio with iced tea. Wanda helped. And they ate off plates balanced on their laps. After lunch some of the other neighbors started dropping by to welcome the Brights. The first to come were the Delks, Sergeant Delk in his police uniform but without his sidearm and cap, and with his shirttail hanging out; his wife and kids trailing dutifully after. He brought a six-pack of Falstaff "to christen the new abode." Nobody used words like abode. He was so pretentious, but really nothing but a redneck.

The Reverend Bright said, "We thank you, sir, but we're not drinking people."

"Well, ya'll mind if I imbibe?" the sergeant asked. Another out-of-his-league word, *imbibe*. Everybody was gathered on the patio. Sergeant Delk had already grabbed one of the folding chairs that was stacked against the wall, and flipped it open one-handed and plopped his fat ass down like meat on a platter without so much as a may I and without offering his wife a seat or bothering to introduce her. She was a skinny thing and totally under his thumb. He popped open a Falstaff using a can opener in a belt holster, saying, "I always carry a church key just in case. You never know when the Lord might be calling you home. Haw Lord."

Slow on the uptake, Mrs. Bright said, "No, you go right ahead" in response to his earlier "Ya'll mind if I imbibe?" and when he didn't respond to that she mumbled under her breath, "That's quite all right. You're welcome." Only Alex noticed the sarcasm. She was starting to really like Mrs. Bright.

The kids sat off to the side and chatted among themselves while halfway listening to the adults. One of the Delk boys had brought a softball, and they tossed the ball around in the back yard. Wanda asked if Alex would like to look at her pictures. "Sure," Alex said. Jim was torn between playing with the Delk boys and looking through Wanda's pictures with Alex. He decided to stay with the girls.

Wanda went into the house and brought back a scrapbook. They sat close together on patio chairs with Wanda in the middle and the scrapbook spread out on her lap and Alex and Jim on either side of her. The scrapbook held photographs and drawings and notes signed by someone named Jean with lots of hearts and Xs and Os. "That's my boyfriend," Wanda said. "He's going to come all the way up here from South Louisiana to be with me. Mama and daddy don't know he's coming. He wants to marry me as soon as he can get a job."

Alex asked if Jean was going to live with them. "Oh gosh no," she said. "Daddy would never allow that."

They looked at baby pictures of Jim and Wanda, including the inevitable embarrassing naked kid photo (Jim about four years old) that made Wanda and Alex laugh. There were a number of drawings of fashion designs that looked like they were copied out of catalogs. They were not bad. There was one that looked more stylish and competently drawn than the others. "This one's really good," Alex said.

"That's Jim's," Wanda said. "He did that one."

"Oh, wow. You're quite an artist."

All the time they were looking at Wanda's scrapbook they were partially listening in on the neighborhood policeman. It quickly became evident that Sergeant Delk was already drunk. He spilled the beans on all the neighbors who had had run-ins with the law or done anything scandalous. He told about Old Man Singleterry's two wives and how his first wife had been caught shoplifting on numerous occasions and had once been put in jail for drunk and disorderly after she baited a couple of drunks at the American Legion Hall into fighting over her. "She hinted that she would let whichever one of them won the fight take her to bed. But the thing was, see, she'd already decided which of 'em she wanted to... well, you know, fornicate—'scuse my French, ma'am—and she figgered she knew which one would win the fight. But she had it wrong. So when the man she didn't want to mess with got the other'un down on the floor she jumped on his back and started slapping him in the back of the head. Lord, you shoulda seen it. It took three men to pull her off him."

He also told a tale on himself. He said, "I got to admit that I sometimes drink a little more'n I oughta, and little Billy, that's the youngest one out there, he kinda set me straight one day. He weren't but about six at the time. It was a Sunday afternoon, and the preacher come calling. I reckon you can relate to that, Brother Bright. So we was talking with the preacher and little Billy climbed up on my lap and he asked me to give him my car keys, and then he asked for my wallet and all my money. I played along. I thought he was being really cute. And after I gave him my keys and my wallet and all my change he jumped off my lap and scooted away, and then he said, 'Now you sonofabitch, let's see you go get drunk.'"

Mrs. Delk laughed sheepishly, but nobody else did.

Later that day Leslie Grant and his mother came over. Mrs. Grant helped Mrs. Bright put away stuff in the kitchen, and Wanda went to her bedroom to organize her belongings while Leslie and Alex helped Jim unpack the boxes they'd already stacked in his bedroom and while Reverend Bright turned on the television to watch a baseball game. In Jim's room they unpacked books and shelved them. Leslie was thrilled to see that they had read a lot of the same mysteries. They both loved Sherlock Holmes. Alex got miffed. She sat on the edge of Jim's bed and sulked, feeling ignored and jealous. Neither one of them wanted to talk about the book she was reading, Irving Stones *Love is Eternal*. When she mentioned it Leslie said, "Yuck."

Leslie pointed to the Sears and Roebuck catalog that was opened face down on Jim's bed and asked, "You been shopping for something?"

"Nah. I just like to look at stuff."

Leslie picked the catalog up and saw it was open to a page of women's lingerie. "Ah ha! Now I see. You've been looking at the ladies."

Jim jerked the catalog away and shut it. "I wasn't looking at that. That's just where it fell open." His face turned red, and Leslie and Alex both laughed at him.

There was a tap on the door, and Mrs. Bright poked her head in to say, "We're going to have some homemade ice cream. Would you boys and young Miss Martin like some?"

"Yes'um, that'd be nice," Leslie said.

"Well let's take it out to the patio, then," Mrs. Bright said.

The patio was getting a lot of use. It was gorgeous out, not a cloud in the sky. Leslie's mother was holding a glass of ice water that she pressed to her forehead. "That feels good," she said. "It's awfully hot."

Mrs. Bright said, "Hot? If this here's what ya'll call hot then we've done moved to heaven on earth."

"Somebody's here," Jim said. He had spotted a white station wagon pull up out front. Two women got out holding what appeared to be shopping bags.

"Run around and see what they want," his mother said. "Tell them we're back here."

It was the local Welcome Wagon with coupons for discounts at local stores. "I declare," Mrs. Bright said after they left, "This must be the friendliest town in the whole state of Washington. Just about ever'body's come to make us welcome."

"Don't let them fool you," Mrs. Grant said. "Those Welcome Wagon ladies are married to businessmen, and they just want your business. The tall one, she's crazy as a loon. Last year at Christmas she showed up at the A&P drunk as a coot wearing a fur coat with bare legs and bare feet sticking out and filled her cart with ice cream. Can you picture that? Her feet must have been cold as ice, and I can't imagine what she was going to do with all that ice cream. And the other one, well her husband's a car salesman. Give her the slightest bit of encouragement and next thing you know she'll be pestering you to buy a car from him."

Alex hung around all afternoon. Around about five, just as Mrs. Bright was rummaging through the pantry to see what she could fix for supper, Mrs. Simpson and her son, Rolly, came over and brought a steaming hot dinner of meatloaf, potatoes, sweet peas and carrots. The Simpsons lived kitty corner to them. The farthest corners of their back yards touched right at their gate, which Rolly never opened; he climbed over. Within two years, after Jim and Rolly had each grown a good four to six inches, they were able to vault over the fence by grasping the top with one hand, and not long after that Jim mastered the art of leaping the fence without touching it with his hands. It was a good six inches higher than the high hurdles at the school track. None of the other boys in the neighborhood were ever able to make that leap. The redhead tried it once and almost broke his leg.

•

Almost every night throughout the summer before seventh grade, the summer when Jim moved to Wetside, groups of ten to twenty neighborhood kids played what they called hide-and-seek football. Definitely not a girls' game, it was a rough and tumble brand of hide-and-seek where the person who was IT had to not only find the other players but tackle one of them, who would then become IT for the next round. Not that there were rules; that's just the way it was generally played. As usual with the rougher boys' games, Ophelia and Alex were the only girls playing. Ophelia played with the boys because it gave her a chance to flirt with them. There was a lot of touching going on, and she played right into it. Alex played the boys games because that's who was there to play with. The only other girls in the neighborhood were Ophelia's little sister and Mary Elizabeth and Kimzey, who lived three or four blocks away and never joined in. Mary Elizabeth said hide-and-seek was a kid's game no matter how you played it, and she wasn't a kid any more. Alex liked the rough and tumble. She liked to show the boys she could run and tackle just as well as them. Ophelia was just the opposite. Big and bawdy and kind of rough around the edges as she was, she acted all girly. When she ran she fluttered her hands, and she squealed when the boys caught up with her. It was all an act. She made sure she got caught. And you better believe there was a lot of groping and rubbing going on when the boys tackled her. As far as she was concerned the game could have been called hide-and-fondle.

The game ranged throughout front and back yards from Park to Woodlawn and west to Rebel, including about an acre of forest land that had yet to be developed. Kids scurrying like an army of squirrels all over the neighborhood. The first time Jim got in the game it was by accident. It was just at dusk. He was walking home from the Dairy Bar, licking an ice cream cone. He had taken the dirt path from the other end of 18th and walked the pipe across the creek. Alex had just run around the corner of her house and was heading down to where the path comes out of the woods—excellent hiding places down there—just about the time Jim stepped out onto the road, and she ran smack into him, and they both went down in a heap. He landed on his back with Alex on top of him, and they would have been mouth-to-mouth (an accidental kiss) if there hadn't been a squashed scoop of chocolate ice cream between their mouths.

It took them a moment to shake their heads clear and untangle. They both apologized and helped one another to their feet, and wiped their faces with their shirttails. She offered to buy him another ice cream cone, insisting on it when he tried to say it wasn't necessary. So they walked through the woods and across the creek in the dark to Red's Dairy Bar and ate their ice cream there instead of carrying it back. They took the long way home because it had gotten too dark for cutting through the woods. By the time they got back all the kids had quit playing and gone home. They lingered for a while in front of his house until he finally said goodnight. She came close to kissing him goodnight but chickened out at the last minute.

Before hide-and-seek football the big craze had been chasing the mosquito spray trucks, running in the fog behind the truck. They had no idea that it was highly toxic, but no more toxic than smoking cigarettes, which most of the boys were beginning to take up. Most of the boys and Ophelia. Even Alex sometimes snuck a Chesterfield out of her mom's pack. After a few weeks they grew tired of first chasing the mosquito truck and then playing hide-and-seek, and Jim and Alex started taking long walks around the neighborhood in the early evenings when many of the neighbors were out in their yards watering the grass or grilling burgers on their patios or, like Jim and Alex, strolling around the block. They would stop and chat with everyone, most frequently that summer with Kimzey Williams, who lived a few blocks away.

•

Kimzey Williams. Crazy little Kay Kay. She was unfairly targeted in a smear campaign. It started when she made the mistake of going out with Jimmy Ross, her first ever date. She was thirteen and he was sixteen. They went to see *The King and I* at the Strand. She loved it; he made fun of it throughout, whispering snide remarks. Afterwards they parked by the damn at Serenity Lake. Serenity was the place where all the kids went to park. He reached over and pulled her into the circle of his arms and planted a kiss on her lips. She didn't resist because she understood that was what was expected of girls on dates. Besides, she wanted to kiss him. Jimmy was a good looking boy. But she didn't want what came next. Jimmy shoved his hands up inside her blouse and under her bra, and grabbed her tiny breasts with his big hands and squeezed them, and she felt as if she were being smothered and mangled and pinched, and it hurt, and she didn't know what to do. Somehow she'd got the notion in her head that it was a woman's duty as a member of the weaker sex to endure that sort of thing.

That was the pattern for the few dates she had in her middle school years. She wanted to be liked. She let the boys go further than she wanted to go, and the boys talked. Boy, did they ever talk. And the boys embellished to beat the band. And then there was the incident with Doctor Collins' son, Snake. He tried to force himself on her in the front seat of his car. She had been willing to put up with boys mangling her breasts, but nobody had ever reached up her dress and slipped a hand inside her panties and touched her in that very private place. She reacted instinctively. She slapped him. It wasn't a vicious slap, but it was hard enough that his head snapped around and his mouth slammed into the review mirror of his car and broke a tooth. "You crazy little bitch! Look what you did. I'm bleeding. God. Oh shit." he reached into his mouth and pulled out a shard of the broken tooth.

When his father asked him the next day what had happened to his tooth Snake said that Kay Kay had attacked him. "We were at the drive in, and she started trying to kiss me. I didn't want to kiss her. I tried to push her off and she got mad and slapped me, and my mouth struck the rearview mirror."

He told the boys at school that she bit his lip. The next day someone said, "Is it true that she grabbed your dick" Snake said, "Yeah, she did." And the story grew.

Doctor Collins told some friends at the country club about it. He said, "She's obsessed with sex. The girl can't help herself. She's a nymphomaniac. Can you believe it? That little whore practically tried to rape my son, and he's a leader of his youth group at church. Never even kissed a girl. He was shaking when he told me." Since

Doctor Collins was a doctor, the rumor mongers had it from a medical authority that Kay Kay was a nymphomaniac.

Poor Kay Kay. She never did anything to invite the rumors that escalated from tales told by kids to tales known by the whole damn town. She didn't dress provocatively, and she didn't flirt with the boys. She never cursed or told dirty jokse. She was Catholic, and she went to mass not just every Sunday but week days too, and she had grown up being pampered by parents who were over protective—the kind of parents who would come down to the school house and raise hell with the kids and teachers alike if they heard about their child being mistreated, which they did on more than one occasion. *Oh Lord, here comes Kay Kay's crazy mama again. She's probably going to make them shut down the cafeteria just 'cause nobody would sit with her precious little girl.*

Pre puberty and pre rumors Kay Kay had been popular enough with the kids in school and at church, but then the other kids started shunning her. From about the ninth grade on the boys continued to ask her out on dates, but never publicly. They'd sometimes take her to the drive-in movies and try to neck in the car, or they'd go for rides and end up parked at Serenity or at the East River overlook out on Highway 99, and then there was the kissing that usually started out pleasantly enough but always ended with grabbing hands and the boys either pleading so pathetically for what she was not willing to give them or trying to force her or saying things like, "I know you did it with (so and so). What's wrong with me? Ain't I good enough?" And she would have to say, "I never did it with anybody," but they never believed her. And the worst would be the next day at school when the boy she'd been out with the night before would pretend he didn't even know her.

She wanted so very, very much to be liked, but she was sickened by what seemed to be the only way to win affection, which was to let them maul her. And making friends with the other girls wasn't much easier. Her only girl friend for a while was Mary Elizabeth Lucious, and Mary Elizabeth's friendship did not last long. In later years when she saw what was becoming of Kay Kay, Alex wished that she had reached out to her more, but she never did. At least she was nice to her in a casual way even if she didn't make any real effort to be her friend.

Fifties kids were readers. They didn't watch TV very much, but they read a lot, Kay Kay more than most. She'd walk to and from school with her nose buried in a book, hardly even looking when she crossed streets. She daydreamed. Her test scores put her right up there in the genius range, but in high school her grades started plummeting because she didn't study and she got to where she couldn't concentrate. She'd let her mind wander out the window and around the world during class. On top of rumors of promiscuity, rumors of mental illness began to fly.

It was almost by chance that Rolly started dating her. He was a nice kid—everybody's best bud. He was not particularly bright but no idiot either. He was the kind of kid who goes along with whatever the crowd is up to.

Like winter swimming in the East River, a typical kind of Rolly Simpson misadventure.

"Ya'll wanna go swimming out to the river?"

"Are you crazy? It's forty degrees out there."

"That's just it," Stew Ross said. "Not many people know this, but it's a fact. When the outside air is cold the underwater temperature warms up. It'll feel cold when you first get in, but when you get all the way in it's like a sauna. Man, you'll love it."

Poor Rolly believed that. He said, "OK. Sure. Might's well, can't dance."

They pulled up in Stew's chopped-top Ford under the overpass on River Avenue, and piled out—six of them in the car, Stew and his brothers and Rolly and two other kids. They ran across the vacant lot behind the parts store to the river bank, where they stood in an excited clump. "Are we really gonna do it?"

"I don't know. Reckon there are snakes?" the youngest Ross brother said.

"I'll do it if everybody else will," Rolly said.

Stew said, "I bet you five bucks you won't go first."

"Five bucks. Wow, man, you're on." Rolly took the dare. He changed into his bathing suit in the back seat of Stew's car and ran down a sloping bank to plunge into the filthy river water.

"Oh God! Oh God! Oh God!" he spluttered as he pushed himself up spitting mud and water and shivering. He scampered out on the bank and rushed to dive in the car and hug himself for warmth using his own clothes to dry off because there was nothing else to use, and by the time Stew dropped him off at home half an hour later his body temperature was just beginning to approach normal.

Or like shoplifting.

"Let's see what we can shoplift from Woolworth's," one of the boys said.

All but Rolly said OK. He said, "I don't know. It don't seem right."

"You're chicken."

"No I ain't. All right. I'll do it." He couldn't stand being called chicken.

So they went to Woolworth's and, according to Bubba Austin's plan, split off to troll different sections of the store so that the clerks couldn't watch them all at once. It drove store clerks crazy to see a bunch of teenagers come in and split up to roam the aisles. They knew what they were up to, but all they could do was try and keep an eye on everybody. On that day there seemed to be only one clerk on duty. Bubba sidled up to Rolly near a rack of T-shirts. "When I get in front of you grab one of them shirts," Bubba said. "They won't be able to see you with me in front."

Bubba got in position, and Rolly grabbed a shirt and stuffed it under his jacket.

They continued wandering the aisles of Woolworth's. Rolly and Jimmy approached a display case featuring cheap costume jewelry and even cheaper decorative knick-knacks where there was, after all, another sales clerk, this one posted behind the counter. She was talking to a customer. The sales girl from the clothing department sidled over nearer the jewelry section. Jimmy nodded in her direction and whispered to Rolly, "See if you can distract her while the rest of us load up."

"How am I supposed to distract her?"

"Talk to her."

"What am I supposed to say to her?"

"I don't know. Make something up. Ask her about her mama and them."

So Rolly approached her and said, "Excuse me, ma'am. But, uh, how's your mama and them?"

"What? What do you want, kid?"

"I uh, oh nothing. I'uz just trying to be friendly like."

"Well that's nice, I suppose. But I really ain't got no time for chit-chattin'. So maybe if you ain't going to buy nothing maybe you better go on out, you hear?"

"Yessum. OK, uh, thank you."

As he turned to walk away the pilfered T-shirt fell out from underneath his jacket.

The sales girl grabbed his arm and called for the manager. Panicked, he spun away from the hand grasping his upper arm and darted out the door. The other boys casually walked out one by one. None of them got caught. Rolly got away, but he had been spotted as a thief so he could never go back into that store.

Average size and average in the looks department, Rolly wore a flattop starting in the seventh grade and on up through college when flattops were long since out of style.

In the tenth grade he started hanging out with a bunch of Eastenders like the Ross brothers and Marvin Tuttle and some others. Guys who had bad reputations. As in many towns, Wetside's social structure was based on geography (east equals squalor, west equals wealth). The town sits in the crotch of a river that splits just north of the city limits and flows in two branches commonly called East River and West River. Today a landscaped boulevard runs alongside West River. On the town side of the boulevard are residential homes, some refurbished houses from the late nineteenth and early twentieth centuries, and in some areas new town houses and condos. Between the boulevard and the river are stretches of manicured lawns with walking and biking paths along which, any time of year, you can see young people in sweats or shorts or the latest running gear walking or jogging or biking. The new town swimming pool is there, the one they built in 1970, and tennis courts and a putting green and covered picnic areas. None of that was there when Jim and Alex were growing up. Most of the land surrounding West River Drive was undeveloped forest land except for a stretch of colonial homes on the north end.

Miller Creek started near the top of West River Drive and meandered south and east through most of the town, finally flowing into East River on the southeastern edge of town. There was an elevated highway that ran along East River, and underneath the highway was River Avenue, a street that was commercial toward the north end with a stretch of cheap bars and food joints, hardware and mercantile stores, garages and used car lots and small factories giving over to cheap housing toward the southern end. People in that part of town were called Eastenders.

Wetside's few blacks and its growing population of Asians lived in the poorest and southernmost part of the East End. For the most part, Wetside's predominantly white population was blind to even the existence of blacks, who made up less than one percent of the population. De facto segregation and housing covenants in the wealthier parts of town, plus social habits brought with them from the South kept most blacks segregated. In the '50s there was one black-owned restaurant in town, Nelly's BBQ Shack. And even though blacks could legally eat anywhere they wanted to, they didn't feel comfortable anywhere but Nelly's. Similarly, people of African descent, most of whom had migrated from Mississippi and Alabama and Louisiana, always sat together in the balcony in the town's movie houses. Asians, who were much more plentiful and mostly lived in their own little section of South East End, were segregated by all of the same forces plus language barriers. Once in the tenth grade one of the Japanese-American kids read his essay about the interment camps. That was the first many of the kids had ever heard of them. They had been babies at the time of the camps, and they were never taught about them in school. The kid who gave the report was born in one of the camps, but he had no memory of being there. He got his information from his folks and his older brother. To the white kids in class his report was interesting. They agreed that it was a terrible thing his family had to go through, but it seemed like something from another world and another time, and when he went home at the end of the day he might as well have gone back to Japan. That's how foreign his little section the East End was. Whites called it Chinatown, but it was mostly Japanese with a few Chinese and Koreans mixed in. Alex's mama took her down there once to buy some stuff in a Japanese grocery store. She wanted to give it a try. She always encouraged trying new things. They didn't like it very much.

Of course there were class differences between Eastenders and Westenders, but it was the parents who were more acutely aware of it. The midtown kids hardly noticed. They knew that kids from different parts of town tended to hang together, but they didn't think of the Eastenders as being lower than them. Or not much lower. That was because the poor in Wetside were not extremely poor and the rich in Wetside were not extremely rich—the point being that while it may have been unexpected that Rolly Simpson would start running around with a bunch of Eastenders, it was certainly not beyond belief, and yet when Rolly got in trouble his mother naturally blamed it on the evil influence of those East End boys. She said, "Hang out with trash and you become trash."

The youngest Ross brother, Jimmy, was Rolly's age, and the middle one, Roy, was a senior in high school. The oldest of the Rosses, Stew, had dropped out of school a few years back and was working as a mechanic at a shop over on River Avenue. He had a customized 1950 Ford with a chopped top and dual carbs and a glass-pack muffler. It was just about the coolest hotrod in town.

Rolly and Jimmy Ross took to sneaking out of school during third period. Rolly was in Mrs. Evans' math class. She was half blind, and the kids thought she was senile. They pulled crazy stunts on her like putting cigarettes in the chalk tray, knowing she'd mistake a cigarette for a piece of chalk. She'd pick it up and try to write with it, and the cigarette would crush in her hand. The kids would laugh at her and she'd fume and spew about how whoever did it was going to get caught one of these days. The way Rolly would sneak out of her class would be he'd go to the pencil sharpener, which was right by the door, and pretend to sharpen his pencil while keeping an eye on Mrs. Evans, and as soon as she would turn to the board to write something he'd dart out the door and down the hall and out the back door between the cafeteria and the shop. The Ross boy was in shop third period. Sneaking out of shop was even easier than sneaking out of Mrs. Evans' class because the shop teacher was hardly ever there. He'd call the roll, get the kids started on some project, and then head to the teachers' lounge to smoke. Whenever Rolly and Jimmy got caught playing hooky, which happened about three times that year, their punishment was a one-day suspension. To them that was just like getting to play hooky again, only without having to worry about getting caught.

They never did anything special when they played hooky. Once, in the late spring, they went swimming in Serenity Lake and once they broke into Old Man Singleterry's storage shed and stole a bottle of his homemade wine and got stinking drunk. Most times they just rode around in Stew's hot rod.

What got Rolly in trouble was when Stew and the boys gang banged Melody Sauer. What was called gang banging back then was not what's called gang banging now. Melody was a young hooker. She'd been working the street down by the railroad station and in the lobby of the Lumberman's Hotel since she was fifteen years old, and a whole generation of Wetside boys had been initiated into sex by Melody. It was like a sacred tradition.

Every boy in town knew this little ditty:

> We all love Melody Sauer
> She's a lovely spring flower
> Her lips are sweet
> Her tits are neat
> And she charges by the hour.

She was thirty-two years old. Everybody knew her age because when the newspaper wrote something about somebody they told how old they were. Like "Melody Sauer, 32, was arrested for prostitution."

In the garage where Stew worked there was an old Cadillac hearse that belonged to a banker named Judson. He had outfitted it as a camper with a fold-down table and bench in back that converted into a single bed. There were no side windows, and the single back window sported a black curtain, so there was complete privacy inside. "It's a rolling bordello," Stew said. He "borrowed" Judson's hearse, meaning he simply drove it out of the garage without permission, and he picked up Rolly and Jimmy and Marvin, and they picked up Melody and drove out to the old drag strip east of town where they took turns with her in the back of the hearse. Twenty dollars each. They passed around a bottle of Jack Daniels and puffed on filter-tip Marlboros while waiting their turn. It was a bright Sunday afternoon in early April. Rolly was just about to take his turn when a cop car careened around the end of the stadium with lights flashing and slammed to a stop next to the hearse. The cops leapt out and one of them corralled Rolly and Stew and Jimmy while his partner jerked open the back door of the hearse to reveal Marvin Tuttle with his pants and underwear around his ankles humping Melody, who was still dressed but had her skirt hiked up and had tossed her panties on the floor.

"Get your ass out here!" the cop shouted. Marvin and Melody hurriedly dressed and climbed out. The cops herded them all into the squad cars. One of the cops poked Stew in the chest with his billy club and said, "We're gonna charge you with auto theft and illegal possession of alcohol and indecent exposure, and since we know damn good and well these here other boys are under eighteen we're going to tack on contributing to the delinquency of a minor. You're looking at a couple years in the state pen."

They held the boys at the station for an hour or so, an hour in which they horrified them with tales of prison. But they didn't book them. They did book Melody, but she got out on bail within an hour. They hit Stew with a fine and let him go. They called the owner of the hearse to tell him what happened, and where he could pick up his vehicle. And finally they personally escorted Jimmy and Marvin and Rolly home to their parents. The reason they treated Stew differently was because he was older and a lost cause. They thought the other boys' parents would straighten them out.

"Mrs. Simpson," one of the cops said, "We caught your son consorting with a prostitute in the back of a hearse. And oh yeah, he played hooky from school, too."

She said, "I appreciate you bringing him home, officer. I'll see to it that he's suitably punished."

"Yessum, you better do that. Elsewise he's gonna end up in jail the next time."

"Yes sir. Thank you, officer."

The other parents shrugged the whole incident off with mild reprimands to their sons, but Rolly's mother hit the roof. She took him out of school and packed him off to a military academy, where he stayed for two years. "Maybe they'll teach you some manners," she said.

So Rolly wasn't seen around town very much after that, other than summer vacation and Christmas and spring breaks. Every time he came home he managed to get in trouble. He was a trouble magnet, even though he never did anything really bad. One time, it was on spring break, his mom was out of town and he invited a bunch of boys over to spend the night. They got pretty drunk. Rolly and Bobby Johnson had an argument about something or other, surely something trivial. Rolly lost the argument. The rest of them took Bobby's side. That pissed Rolly off. Around about two o'clock in the morning they all piled onto makeshift bedrolls on Rolly's living room rug. Most of the boys had kicked off their shoes and stripped down to their underwear. Out for vengeance, Rolly grabbed Bobby's shoes and pants and ran outside with them and started trying to toss them on top of the Hendrix house next door. He couldn't hit his mark, and the clothing ended up in some bushes.

When Bobby saw what Rolly was up to he slammed and locked the front door. Then ran for the back door and locked it. Rolly started banging on the front door demanding to be let in. "It's my house, dammit! You can't lock me out of my own house."

The front door sported a trio of little decorative windows, each about six inches square. Glaring through the middle window,

Rolly and Bobby squared off like pugilists, nose-to-nose, Rolly hissing, "Let me in" and Bobby sticking his tongue out at Rolly. Already fuming, Rolly flew off the handle when Bobby stuck his tongue out at him, and he hauled off and tried to punch Bobby in the nose right through the window. He broke the window and cut his hand but didn't touch Bobby, who instinctively stepped back when he saw the punch coming. Probably the dumbest thing Bobby could have done then was unlock the door, which was exactly what he did. It was a reflex reaction to Rolly smashing the window. It never dawned on him that Rolly—who was out for blood (his)—would then push his way in and grab him around the waist and tackle him and pound the hell out of him. Which he did. They punched each other and wrestled on the floor for a while until finally Bobby said, "I'm sorry, man. OK, you win. Let me go."

Rolly said, "You made me break my window. My mama's going kill me when she finds out."

Bobby said, "I'm sorry. If you want to, you can come over to my house and break one of my windows."

Speaking of windows, the really crazy thing was when Rolly dove through Alex's bedroom window. She was sound asleep. It was around midnight. Her window was wide open. People think it never gets hot in the Pacific Northwest, but it does. For about three days every summer there is oppressive heat that hangs on late into the night. It was one of those nights. Her little oscillating fan was huffing in a feeble attempt to cool her icky sweaty body. She was wearing frilly pajamas that were more or less see-through, not the kind of thing she would have been wearing if she'd known Rolly was going to come calling in the middle of the night. He startled her awake by banging on her window sill. He whisper-shouted "Let me in! Let me in!" Desperation in his voice.

She unlatched the screen. Rolly lifted it out and dove head first through the window and burrowed under the sheets. She caught a fleeting glimpse of his bare butt shining white under the light from the corner light pole, noticing he wasn't wearing a stitch of clothing. After however long it took her to gather her wits she asked what was going on, whispering for fear that her parents would hear them and come in and find them. They'd have had a hard time convincing them it was all innocent, him in his birthday suit and her in her shorty see-throughs. Her folks were pretty open minded, but not that open minded.

He whispered, "The cops are after me."

"Geez, what'd you do, rob a bank?"

"Went swimming."

He'd been swimming in the municipal pool just a few blocks away. Long after closing time for the pool. A bunch of boys had been doing it pretty much all summer. They'd been making late night visits to the pool, climbing the fence and going skinny dipping. This time somebody saw them and called the police. The cops sent a squad car with lights flashing. The same cops who had caught Rolly and the boys with Melody Sauer.

The redheaded kid, the one whose name nobody ever seemed to remember, was standing on the diving board when he saw the cops coming. "Police!" he shouted, and everybody scrambled, some diving into the pool and others running for the locker rooms and out the front door, dressing on the run or buck naked and carrying their clothes. Rolly was standing on the side of the pool near the diving board. He dove. The redheaded kid dove at the same time. Caa-rack! Their heads collided, a glancing blow knocking them both temporarily blind and discombobulated. They floundered like flopping fish in a net, Rolly shaking his head and blinking his eyes and the redhead swimming in circles for a few moments. His head was bleeding. "Are you all right?" Rolly asked.

"Yeah, I think so. Kind of dizzy."

"Shhh, not so loud. We better get the hell out of here. Can you make it?"

"Yeah, I think so. Kind of dizzy," he repeated. "What day is it?"

"What difference does that make? Are you all right?"

"Yeah, I think so. Kind of dizzy. What day is it?"

He'd obviously been knocked silly. They climbed out of the pool and scrambled into the dressing room while the police were getting out of their car. The cops rushed to the fence where they shone their flashlights across the surface of the water, but by then all the boys had made their getaway. All but Rolly and the redhead, who were crouched in the shower. "Let's make a run for it," Rolly said. The cops were on the north side of the pool. The front door faced Rainier Street to the west, and directly across Rainier was the stretch of woods that ended right at Alex's back yard.

They ran out the front door and across the street to the cover of woods just ahead of the cops' flashlight beams, which were sweeping the area. They ran through the woods, both bare-ass naked, brambles and branches slashing their bodies. They emerged from the woods and split in different directions. The red headed kid aimed for · the safety of home and Rolly ran for closest place he could flee for sanctuary—Alex's house.

So they huddled under a sheet in her bed and watched through the window as the cops pulled up to his house. (As everyone would find out from Harold Drews' column in the next day's paper, Rolly had left a clue behind that sent them to his house.) The policemen spent a long time standing at Rolly's door talking to his mother. All the while their red lights were flashing, and porchlight after porchlight snapped on up and down the block as neighbors stepped out on their front stoops to watch. Meanwhile under the sheets things were happening that neither of them expected. Pumped on adrenaline, Rolly could not hold still, and Alex became intensely aware of flesh touching flesh, which was kind of nice and kind of scary. They touched and drew apart and touched again, and finally settled into comfortably snuggling. Body-to-body felt good to Alex even though she knew they were the wrong bodies, and she thought that someday it would be nice to find someone she could do this with every night, and Rolly found himself wishing he could settle so comfortably in Kay Kay's arms. With Kay Kay it was always either desperately clutching or not touching at all, and he never knew which is was going to be.

It was a long time before they noticed that the cop's lights were no longer flashing. They lay still for a while longer and then she asked if she should get him some clothes.

"Uh huh, yeah, maybe you better," he whispered.

She tip-toed to her closet and rummaged in the dark to get him something to put on. Fortunately for Rolly a lot of her clothes were boys' clothes and they were close to the same size. He dressed under the sheet. They stayed together in her bed for another half hour, talking a bit in careful whispers, but mostly in silence. There was a minute or two when she thought maybe they could be boyfriend and girlfriend, but he was in love with Kay Kay; and she might not have ever said it out loud but if you looked at the name scrawled all over her notebooks you'd have thought she was in love with Jim Bright.

•

Kay Kay was in the eighth grade. Her heart's desire was to join the junior high school sorority Darling Debs, a kind of junior auxiliary to the so-called real sorority Debs of Jefferson High. But the Debs blackballed her. Repeatedly.

The Debs were a snotty bunch. All the most popular girls belonged. Not just the rich girls from the West End but also a lot of middle class girls from the neighborhood. Alex was a Darling Deb too, although she gradually lost interest and quit going to meetings, and never joined the Debs of Jefferson. The DDs met once a month in the homes of various members, usually Westenders whose mothers didn't work and who had large enough houses to entertain between twenty and thirty girls and had house keepers to serve snacks to the girls and clean up after them, meaning hosting duties alternated between the same three mothers: Heather Cross's mother, Lara Cockburn's and Betty Black's. Heather and Betty lived in mansions on West River Drive that could have been used as sets for *Gone With the Wind*, and Lara lived in one of the newer homes on Serenity Lake about five miles west of town—a low slung, blend-into-the-woods ranch house with a wraparound deck overlooking the lake.

Whenever a new girl was put up for membership they'd vote by passing around a bucket and each girl would cast her ballot by dropping in a black ball or a white ball. White you're in, black you're out. And none need ever divulge which color ball they dropped in the bucket. (They didn't use actual balls. They used checkers pieces.)

It was Mary Elizabeth who kept putting Kay Kay's name up for membership, so it fell to Mary Elizabeth to give her the bad news. She did it by phone.

"Isn't there anything you can do?" Kay Kay asked.

"I can bring your name up again, but whoever blackballed you—and I really, really don't have any idea who it was—can just do it again, and you'll be hurt all over again."

Kay Kay put the phone down, and she cried. She used up half a box of tissues. When her mother heard her sobbing a good ten minutes after Kay Kay had hung up the phone and tentatively tapped on her door, Kay Kay didn't answer. Mrs. Williams slowly eased the door open and stepped in to wrap her daughter in her arms and coo, "What is it, baby? What's the matter with my sweetheart?"

Seated on her bed in a skirt and socks with her ankles crossed and knees raised, her skirt shoved down between her legs like a collapsed tent, Kay Kay was surrounded by crumpled Kleenex, her cheeks glowing with tears.

"Nobody likes me," she sobbed.

"That's not true, honey. Your daddy and I like you very much."

"But you're my parents. I mean real people."

It took a lot of soothing talk and hand patting and cheek kissing for Mrs. Williams to coax from Kay Kay the story that the Darling Debs had rejected her.

The next meeting of the Debs was at Lara Cockburn's house on Serenity Lake. It was the second meeting of the school year. There were fifteen girls and three of their mothers in attendance. Most of the girls were seated on couches and chairs and sprawled on cushions on the floor of the Cockburn family room overlooking the lake. Mrs. Cockburn had left the sliding glass door to the deck open to let smoke out, since all of the mothers were puffing away inside. Some of the girls complained about the cold, so Mrs. Cockburn shut the door. "If it starts to getting too warm in here, you girls just let me know," she said. The thermostat was set for seventy degrees.

Anna Shemper and Beverly Ryan were at the table cutting autumn leaves out of red and orange construction paper to make decorations for an upcoming Halloween party. Three seventh graders stood with their backs against the wall. On strings around their necks they wore pink baby bottles and dangling signs that read: *I am a Darling Debs pledge. I am the lowest creature on earth.* The pledges were not allowed to sit down.

Reba, the Cockburn's Negro maid, shuffled in and out with trays of cookies, cheese and crackers, potato chips, Fritos, onion and shrimp dips. All of the girls dug into icy water in a big tin washtub to pull out Cokes and Pepsis or Nehi grape or orange drinks. Also on the table were cream pies on plates: banana, Boston cream and chocolate. Nobody was allowed to touch the pies until after all business was completed, at which time the pledges would serve the members before serving themselves.

The house was filled with the hum of chatter when Kimzey Williams' mother slung open the front door without bothering to knock. The girls, the maid, the mothers all froze in mid-movement when Mrs. Williams stormed in and demanded to know, "Which one of you little pretentious witches blackballed my daughter?"

Her face was red and her hands were shaking. Anna and Beverly grabbed onto each other for mutual protection and ducked as if they thought Mrs. Williams was going to hit them with her purse. It took a few stunned seconds for anyone else to react, and then Mrs. Cockburn said, "And just who do you think you are and who said you could come barging into my house?"

"Brenda Cockburn, you know damn good and well who I am. And just who on God's green earth do you suppose you are, these girls' den mother?"

"This is not a Girl Scout troop."

"It's certainly not," Mrs. Williams said. "The Girl Scouts would never allow one of their members to humiliate an innocent girl with a secret ballot. That is the cruelest thing I have ever heard of. It's cruel when they do it in college and it's extra double cruel when they do it in junior high school, and I will not stand for it."

"*You* will not stand for it," Brenda Cockburn shouted. "Again I ask, just who in tarnation you think you are, Jesus Christ Almighty?"

As if watching a tennis match, the girls heads turned from mother to mother with mouths agape as Mrs. Cockburn said, "What these girls do is none of your business, and just what do you plan to do about it anyway?"

"I plan to sue the club and you personally, and don't bother reminding me that your husband is a lawyer because mine is too and he beat your husband the last time they faced off in a courtroom and you know it."

Mrs. Cockburn marched across the family room to face Mrs. Williams across the table. They were like Bobby Johnson and Rolly Simpson on either side of Rolly's door, only bigger and with more vicious glares. Mrs. Cockburn took a step to the right, Mrs. Williams to the left, then back the other way. Stop. Move. Jostle for position like wrestlers ready to pounce. It looked like Kay Kay's mother was going to cold-cock Mrs. Cockburn. But it was Mrs. Cockburn who moved the confrontation to violence. She picked up the banana cream pie. She drew back her hand with the pie like a baseball pitcher winding up.

"Don't you dare!" Mrs. Williams shouted.

"Oh, I dare all right." And she let fly and smashed Mrs. Williams in the face with it. Mrs. Williams screamed, "I'm blind!" and whirled around and careened across the floor stumbling into chairs and bumping into girls seated on the floor while trying desperately to wipe the cream out of her eyes. She bumped into an end table and knocked it into the sliding glass doors onto the deck, which shattered outward in a crystal shower, and Mrs. Williams sprawled forward and landed face first on the broken glass, resulting in minor cuts to her knees and arms and a rash of bloody red slashes in her very expensive white blouse. Half of the girls were stunned into silent statues, while the other half broke into loud laughter and somebody screamed. The only person to spring into action was Reba the maid. She grabbed a towel off the kitchen counter and rushed to where Mrs. Williams lay and dropped to her knees and started simultaneously wiping cream pie out of her eyes and trying to help her to her feet while saying, "Oh dear, Miz Williams, are you all right?"

And Mrs. Williams pushed her away and shouted at Mrs. Cockburn, "Get your monkey off of me!"

"Now, now, Mrs. Williams. There's no sense in taking it out on the maid. She's just trying to help you," Mrs. Shemper said. She stepped over to where Mrs. Williams was still on her hands and knees and leaned down to offer her a hand. Kay Kay's mother was a bloody mess. She took the helpful hand, and together they hobbled into the bathroom. When she came out she had a couple of Band Aids on her cheek and one on her arm. She had removed her blouse and had wrapped one of Mrs. Cockburn's towels around her torso and was clutching it tightly at her throat, her bloody blouse hanging limp across one arm like a carcass. Her cuts were all superficial.

"You make sure to return that towel now, you hear?" Mrs. Cockburn said to her retreating back.

For a week or two after that Kay Kay avoided everybody, ashamed of her mother and ashamed that she'd been rejected so publicly by her classmates. But she poured everything out in letters to Rolly.

The letters had started very soon after Rolly left Wetside. He had hungered for her for quite some time, but had never told her how he felt. He had fantasized about kissing her and about dancing with her and holding her tight in his arms, but had never asked her out on a date. Like flowers yearning toward the sun's warmth they had eyed each other from across the dance floor at the Friday night sock hops at the community center, where she often sat alone on the bench against the far wall, but he had never asked her to dance. Thinking of her while on the long bus ride to the academy, he pulled a notebook and pencil out of his bag and started putting his thoughts into words. He filled pages of lined notebook paper with professions of his love, finding that he could say in writing what he could never say in person—six pages worth by the time he got to his destination. From the Greyhound station there was a shuttle to Exeter Academy. Across the street from the station sat a post office as if squatted there just for him. Quickly, before he lost his nerve, Rolly darted across the street, bought an envelope and a stamp, and mailed his missive to Kimzey.

Oh my dear sweet Rolly, she wrote back in a flowery hand, *if only you had told me how you felt. I feel the same as you. I really, really do. I dream of you at night. I keep your picture from the yearbook on my mirror. I want to kiss you a million jillion kisses.* She signed with a line of X's and red lipstick kisses.

Week after week in letters sprinkled with kisses, she told him everything that happened in school, and he wrote back with letters filled with plans for the future, dreams that changed week by week but always involving her as his partner in whatever the current week's vision of the future happened to be—not grand or exotic dreams but the simple things he thought he might do when he grew up: *If we saved up we could buy that little restaurant on the bank of East River with the windows overlooking the water, and you could do the cooking and we could have a band and put in a dance floor* or *we could live in a little house in the valley south of Rock Creek and it could have a little fishing pond right in the back yard and twin hammocks for you and me*, or *maybe we could take a rafting trip down the Colorado River, just you and me, or go camping on Mount Rainier*.

She told him about her mother storming in to the Darling Debs meeting and getting smashed in the face with a cream pie and stumbling through the plate glass. Nisqually Middle School was abuzz with talk about that, and Kay Kay was mortified. "You made it worse, mother," she wailed when she got home from school that next day. "How could you? Now everybody hates me."

"How could I what? Stand up for you? You ought to be thanking me, darling."

She wrote to Rolly:

The cuts mother got were nothing, but she wore great big bandages for weeks and weeks just to show how badly she'd been hurt, which really wasn't very bad at all. But she's going to sue Lara's mom, so she's wearing the bandages to convince the judge how terribly hurt she was. She talked about renting a wheelchair for her court appearance. Can you believe it? But daddy talked her out of it.

It was bad enough that somebody went and blackballed me. I bet it was Lara, the snotty creep, I just know it was, but then mother had to go and interfere and—Ha!—get smashed in the face with a pie for her troubles, and now she's trying to sue Lara's mom. Jesus Christ Almighty, I wish I could get a million miles away from here. I told mother everybody's making fun of us and she's making it worse. I hate her, hate her, hate her.

The worst of all was Mary Elizabeth. I thought she was my friend. But did she stand up for me? Not on your life she didn't. She acted like I didn't exist. In the cafeteria the next day Lara was sitting right next to Mary Elizabeth. In my seat. Everybody knows it's my seat. Lara told me to get lost, and Mary Elizabeth, she should have stood up for me, but no, she turned her head away and wouldn't even look at me. I know she still wants to be my friend, but she can't because then Lara and all the Debs would turn against her.

Raindrops, the blog of the Daily Journal, Wetside, Washington, August 23, 1957

POLICE BLOTTER
By Harold Juniper Drews

Swimming pool break-in

At 1:30 a.m. this morning a bunch of teenage boys were spotted swimming illegally and, according to police reports, most likely in the nude, in the municipal swimming pool on Rainier Street. Police investigated when an unidentified citizen called to report he had seen what "must have been twenty or thirty of them scallywags" climbing over the fence to the pool, according to police spokesman Adam Spitzer. The boys (police spotted no more than five) scampered away when the police got to the scene and turned on their spotlights. Spitzer said, "They was buck naked and carrying their clothes and they ran into the woods off Rainier Street like a bunch of deer."

"It looks like there was a fight. There was blood in the water. A pair of boys' bluejeans was left at the scene with a wallet in the pocket containing identification for one Rolly Simpson, a delinquent who has previously been in trouble with the law. He had ten cents in his pants pocket. We went to Rolly's house and talked to his mother, but he was not at home. Anyone knowing the whereabouts of Rolly Simpson is urged to contact the police."

Best Friends – Jim and Alex's blog

Rock and Roll, Ya'll
by Jim Bright

I remember the birth of rock and roll. I was there. I was in the seventh grade. Some people claimed it started much earlier. Not so. Rhythm and blues started earlier, but rock and roll was born in 1953 in the South, as I was fond of telling my new friends in Washington. Memphis, Sun Records. First the white boys playing black and then the black boys cutting loose on their own. Elvis, Carl Perkins, Jerry Lee Lewis, Bill Haley and the Comets, Ray Charles, Little Richard, Fats Domino. (They claimed Ray Charles was from Seattle, but I corrected them. He *moved* to Seattle from Georgia, bringing with him a heavy dose of pure Southern rhythm and blues.) And let's not forget the fabulous rockabilly girl singers, Patsy Cline and Brenda Lee—as Southern as grits. We snatched up all the latest hit records on those little big-hole 45rpm records and had impromptu dance parties in friends' houses.

I know everybody's got their own favorite memories of the music of their youth, but unless you were there for the birth of rock and roll you don't know music.

Comments:
Alex Martin said: Well aren't you smug! Rock and roll may have been born out of a synthesis of hillbilly music and rhythm and blues, but it didn't become the force it is today until the Beatles and the Stones. The British rockers took the raw material they'd discovered—and yes, granted, it did come out of the South—and made real music out of it.
Deadhead222 said: Don't forget psychedelia.
Seattle Sam said: Long live Jimi!
Jim Bright said: Long live The King!

Chapter 5

Practically the whole school went to the Strand to see *Rock Around the Clock*, with music by Bill Haley and the Comets and The Platters and a couple of other more forgettable rock and roll groups. All over the country kids were getting up and dancing in the aisles during the movie, and riots were reported in a number of places. Jim went on a Saturday afternoon with Rolly. (It was right before Rolly got shipped off to military school.) Just like kids in New Jersey and California and everywhere else, they danced in the aisles. On the TV they said it was a spontaneous eruption in theaters all across the country. Somewhere that might have been true, but in Wetside it wasn't as spontaneous as claimed at the time. The kids started dancing in the aisles because they'd heard about it happening in other places and they liked the idea. They went to the theater knowing that was what they were going to do. The old ushers and ticket takers and the policeman who lounged against a back wall— there was one on duty during every movie, and he usually dozed through the show—had never seen anything like it.

The white kids were all downstairs. Up in the balcony there was a United Nations of Asians and Mexicans and Indians from the Nisqually and Puyallup tribes, and a handful of black kids. That seemed natural to Jim because where he came from movie houses were segregated, blacks *had* to sit in the balcony. Wetside was not segregated, but the blacks sat in the balcony anyway. They tended to hang out with each other, as did the Asians and Indians and a few Mexicans, none of whom felt very comfortable with or welcomed by the dominant white culture. Defacto segregation was the unspoken law of the land, and even though Wetsiders bragged about being untainted by racial prejudice when, a few years later, civil rights became the hot news of the day in other parts of the country, more than a few of them were just as bigoted as rednecks in Arkansas.

The Strand was a huge art deco theater built in the twenties, with velvet ropes and red carpeting and ashtrays built into the arms of the seats even though smoking was not allowed (a universally ignored law). Most of the boys smoked, cupping their cigarettes to hide them when the ushers came by.

Kay Kay came to the theater alone. It was early autumn. Morning drizzle had slicked the streets and sidewalks and wet leaves glistened like Jello when the sun broke through. Kay Kay's hair shone orange in the sun. She wore a plaid skirt and a light blue cardigan tossed over a white blouse. Noticing her in line for tickets Jim said to Rolly, "She looks younger than the rest of us, like a little girl all decked out for Easter Sunday."

Rolly mumbled, "Oh, I don't know. But I guess she does look kind of cute."

Kay Kay smiled at classmates standing behind her and nodded her head in greeting. Rolly acknowledged her greeting with a slight grin but then quickly looked away, like he didn't want anybody to know he liked her. Jim raised his hand in greeting and smiled at her. The rest of her classmates ignored her. In line at the concession stand once everyone got their tickets and crowded into the lobby, larger kids bumped into her without noticing. After she finally got her popcorn and made her way to a seat down front, she was told, "This seat's saved. You'll have to sit somewhere else." Like an emptied container no one wanted to dispose of, she was passed from seat to seat, every one of which seemed to have been saved for someone. She found a seat in the very last row under the overhang of the balcony. The whole row, traditionally claimed by a bunch of Eastenders, was empty. But not for long. Immediately after she settled in, Marvin Tuttle, the Ross brothers and a few of their buddies grabbed seats on either side of her. "Do you want me to move over so you can all sit together?" she asked.

"Hey, thanks Babe," Marvin said.

She moved over one seat and scrunched down, trying to make herself invisible.

The Eastenders plopped down and propped their feet on the backs of seats in front. One of the Ross boys pulled a whiskey flask from an inside jacket pocket, and they passed it back and forth. The previews hadn't started yet. The auditorium was a hornet's nest of loud chatter. Kids were throwing popcorn at each other. The boy sitting next to Kay Kay leaned close. His hand slid across her leg. He kept it there for a minute. She pushed his hand and jerked away from him and stood up and left. "Come back, baby, come back," he said with mock supplication. They all laughed at her, but she ignored their taunts and scooted into the aisle and out to the lobby where she stood alone by the stairs to the balcony. Nearby the uniformed policeman guarded the doorway to the main auditorium. "Those boys were getting fresh with me," she told him, pointing to where the Eastenders were seated.

"Well just stay away from them, honey," the cop said. "They just boys. That's what boys do. Can't blame 'em none."

She backed away, turned and darted into the ladies' room, and ran water and splashed her face with shaky hands. She heard rock and roll music strike up, and she pushed out of the ladies' room and made her way once again to the doorway into the auditorium and stood in the dark to watch the previews and the beginning of the movie from there. After a few minutes she went upstairs to stand by a rail at the front of the balcony. When kids started hopping out of their seats to dance in the aisle Kay Kay squeezed ever closer to the rail and the wall as if under her daddy's protective arm. But soon the infectious music seeped into her soul and she began to get a little wiggle in her shoulders and then her hips. Other kids were crowding the aisle. Girls' wide skirts and flaring petticoats flying. Nearest to Kay Kay were Smiley Russell and Christine Rocker, an unlikely looking couple who would never have dated each other had they not been the only African-American students at Nisqually Middle School. Smiley stood all of five-foot-five and was chubby. When he danced, his arms and legs and cheeks and belly jiggled in time with the music. Christine was tall and boxy in build, with square hips and wide shoulders. She danced stiffly, mechanically—she a plodding machine, he a whirling dervish.

Smiley swung Christine in a wide turn, and she bumped against Kay Kay, knocking her violently to the side where she bumped against the hip-high rail. Christine started to speak in apology and reach out with a steadying hand just as Smiley twirled around and crashed into both of them. Already off balance, Kay Kay was knocked head over heels across the rail. Her scream brought all movement in the crowded theater to a sudden stop, all but the movement on the screen, because Bill Haley never herd Kay Kay scream. Every head swiveled toward the sound. Kay Kay tumbled down twenty feet to where Jim Bright was dancing with Mary Elizabeth Lucious. It happened faster than Superman changing in a phone booth. Jim looked up just in time to reach out to catch her, but not soon enough to set his feet to brace her fall. Wham! All ninety-nine pounds of her right in his arms. The force of her fall knocked him off his feet, but since the whole auditorium was a mass of dancing kids the bodies of other kids cushioned their fall. With Kay Kay still sprawled in his arms, Jim landed unhurt on his backside in a tangle of sweaty bodies.

Mary Elizabeth stood speechless and helpless for a few seconds while other kids reached down to help Jim and Kay Kay to their feet. Rolly and Alex steadied her on either side and helped walk her out to the lobby. Jim smiled sheepishly and stood motionless for a few seconds and then followed them into the lobby. Mary Elizabeth shook herself out of her stupor and rushed into the girls' restroom and back out with a damp cloth with which she patted Kay Kay's brow. It was probably the first and last time Kay Kay ever received that kind of loving attention from her classmates. Mary Elizabeth tried to relieve the seriousness of the situation by quipping, "Really now. Was that any way to cut in?"

Kay Kay smiled weakly in acknowledgment.

While they tended to Kay Kay, the cop on duty ran hell bent for leather after the supposed perpetrator, whoever he might be. He had no idea who knocked her out of the balcony or whether or not it was an accident, and apparently didn't give a damn if she was hurt. He was on a mission from God to collar someone, anyone, any of those dark skinned heathens in the balcony. He blew his whistle and took the stairs three at a time to the balcony where he grabbed the most likely looking suspect and hustled him downstairs and out the front door and pushed him into his squad car and hauled him off to jail and into an interrogation room. The likely suspect he had grabbed was Smiley Russell, the first boy he saw in the balcony and coincidentally the boy who actually had knocked Kimzey over the rail.

"What did you do to that white girl, boy?" the cop asked the startled thirteen-year-old kid.

"I didn't touch her." His hands were trembling and sweat soaked his starched white shirt.

"You shoved her over the rail."

"Nawsir. I didn't touch her. I didn't even see her there."

"She said you grabbed her titty and she tried to jerk away and went tumbling over the balcony rail." *From what deep well of racist claptrap did he dredge that one up when she never said anyone up in the balcony had grabbed her but said only that someone she didn't see bumped into her?*

"What? N-n-no sir, I didn't. I swear to God I didn't e'em touch her."

"Don't you lie to me, boy. I know what happened. You got to listening to that jungle music and it got you all excited like it does. I know how you people get all excited when you hear that African music. When that poor little white gal come up there you just couldn't keep your dirty mitts off her. We seen it all. You tell the truth now and we'll let you go this time."

"It was a accident. I musta bumped into her. I didn't e'em see her. I swear to God."

In screaming fonts of descending sizes the headlines in the daily newspaper the next morning read:

ROCK AND ROLL MUSIC CAUSES RIOT IN LOCAL THEATER

NEGRO ACCUSED OF MOLESTING WHITE TEENAGER

LOCAL TEEN SAVES GIRL'S LIFE WHEN SHE FALLS FROM BALCONY

When the police questioned Kay Kay she told them that an unintentional collision of dancers caused her to fall off the balcony, that nobody pushed her.

"Did that colored boy touch you inappropriately?" the policeman asked her, and she said "The only boys who touched me inappropriately were white boys downstairs."

"That must have been accidental when they caught you after you fell."

"No sir, that was Jim Bright that caught me, and he didn't touch me in any wrong way. The boys that tried to put their hands on me were in the back row up under the balcony, and it happened before I went upstairs. I reported it to the policeman that was in the theater, but he didn't do anything about it."

Since the police couldn't find a single witness to say Smiley had pushed her they had to let him go, but they warned him they'd be keeping a close eye on him.

•

Wanda got knocked up. Jean Herbert (pronounced the Cajun way, Zhen A-bare) was the father. Wanda's family didn't even know Jean had followed them to Wetside when they moved from Louisiana. They hadn't told a soul. He camped out in the back of his car until he finally got a job on a construction crew and rented a room down by the East River. Wanda was sixteen when she got pregnant. The old man hit the roof. She probably wouldn't have told him if she could have kept it a secret, but how do you keep a thing like that secret when you're starting to look like you're holding a basketball under your shirt? Reverend Bright told his daughter he would not allow an unwed teenage mother in his house. "Can you imagine what people at church will say? They'll gloat 'cause the preacher can't even control his own daughter. I'll be a laughing stock. The Lord will rain down retribution."

Mrs. Bright said, "Can you think about someone besides yourself for once? Can you think about Wanda?"

"I am thinking about her. I'm thinking she's the whore of Babylon right here under my roof and she brought shame and degradation to this family."

The old man told Wanda she could no longer live in his house. He also told her he would not give his permission for her to get married. Since she couldn't legally get married without parental permission she moved out of the house and in with Jean, thereby living in sin and piling further shame on the Bright family. She dropped out of school.

Raindrops, the blog of the Daily Journal, Wetside, Washington, Nov. 1, 2008

POLICE BLOTTER
By Harry Drews

Transsexual found murdered

A transsexual woman was found murdered in Seattle's Gasworks Park Saturday morning. The body was discovered by early morning joggers who called police around seven a.m. The cause of death was listed as a single gunshot wound to the head. The coroner's office said the time of death was sometime between midnight and two a.m. Not until the body was brought to the medical examiner's office and stripped of clothing was it discovered that the victim was a transsexual. He or she had both male and female sexual characteristics. The coroner speculated that the victim was in the process of transitioning from male to female, a process that begins with hormone treatments and is followed up with one or more surgeries, often over a period of time, according to Miriam Heart from the Gender Identity Center in Seattle in an email. Transitioning may take up to a year or longer, Heart said.

This murder is the second in Washington in the past month. In both cases the victim was of ambiguous gender.

There have been two other deaths within the past twelve months that may be in some way related. They were investigated as possible homicides but ruled accidental. The two cases were similar to the recent murders in that the victims, while not transsexual, were men who dressed as women. In one case a driver plunged off a mountain road going to the Mt. Saint Helens visitor center. In the other case a hiker fell into a deep ravine on the Pacific Crest trail.

Even two murders in one year is unusual for this area. Two in two months is almost unheard of. Wetside police spokesman Snake Collins said they may take a closer look at the two supposed accidental deaths. If it turns out that they were staged accidents; i.e.,

100

murder, they may be victims of the same killer. "The similarities can't be dismissed," Collins said.

A personal note: I am a crime reporter, not a police investigator, but I can't help but see an obvious connection.

Seattle Police spokesperson Adele Long said the similarities are troubling but do not necessarily indicate a pattern. Long said the homicides may or may not be hate crimes. She said, "There is no reason to suspect any connection between the two murders other than a generalized hatred of persons who are seen as being different from the norm. Transgendered persons are among the more commonly targeted victims of hate crimes, so there is that in common but nothing else. There are no suspects at this time."

As for the earlier deaths, which were ruled accidental, Long said, "The apparent connections are most likely coincidental, although we will continue to investigate if further evidence surfaces."

I suspect a single perpetrator, and I suspect that the murderer is a person with an unreasonable hatred for gay, lesbian, or transgendered people who does not distinguish between them but sees them all as being the same.

Unrelated but of interest to crime buffs: The last recorded murder in Wetside took place more than 50 years ago in 1954 when two men engaged in a poker game in the lounge of the old Lumberman's Hotel shot each other. The men, Albert Frost and J.D. "Lefty" Smith, were both independent loggers who competed in business. Witnesses said Smith accused Frost of cheating, and they drew guns and shot each other. Neither had a license to carry a concealed weapon. Since both victims and perpetrators were killed, no one was charged with the crime.

Chapter 6

Celebrating an election victory had been such a rare event for Alex that she was totally psyched going into Election Day 2008. Surges in the polls over the past month or two had boosted her hopes sky high. She remembered briefly feeling the elation of victory in the '90s when Bill Clinton won. How well she remembered singing "Don't Stop, thinking about tomorrow…" But man oh man did Slick Willie ever turn out to be a disappointment! He was such a wimp that he fired his Surgeon General because she dared to talk about masturbation. On the heels of the Clinton letdown Alex had to endure eight years of George Bush, cementing her distrust of politics from a lifetime of watching right wingers and middle-of-the-roaders win almost every single local and state election. She knew in her gut that finally there was going to be reason to celebrate, and she wanted to be glued to the TV screen election night. But she had to work that night.

She was keeping her post behind the cash wrap at Stellar Light, where she had been working part-time for the past year and a half. Grumbling, anxious, curt with customers, she thought it was a sin and a shame to be stuck at work instead of home watching the returns come in. She had begged people to swap shifts, but nothing doing.

Stellar Light was an independent bookstore in the same old building that housed Barney's Pub. Alex didn't really need the job for the income since Social Security was sufficient for her modest way of living, but she did need something to keep herself busy. She had tried retirement for a while, but it hadn't set right with her. She found herself hanging around the house far too much with nothing to do. She started putting on weight, and felt listless most of the time, so in an effort to pull herself out of the doldrums and restore her once firm body she took on the bookstore job and starting walking on the paths in West River Park every morning. She enjoyed the walks, but she felt like an urchin in a fancy restaurant because all the other walkers and joggers and bikers wore fancy warm-ups and running shoes while she typically wore shorts or jeans and cheap tennis shoes from the half price shoe outlet.

The walking was actually a compromise after she had tried running and got excruciating cramps in her calf muscles. The constant standing in the bookstore didn't help with the cramps either, but at least it got her out of the house for something other than booze at Barney's. The job and the walking did her a world of good. She was very slowly but definitely beginning to feel stronger and more energetic until she went and overdid it playing basketball with Jim Bright. You'd think by the time she reached her mid sixties she would have learned not to let herself get goaded into foolishness like that. Three days later she was still sore.

From her post in the bookstore she kept not-so-surreptitiously glancing at her watch, anxious to get home and watch the election returns. She also kept glancing at Jim, who was stealthily returning her gaze from his spot in front of the magazine rack. He was thumbing through *Architectural Digest* but looking at her. Weird, she thought. Should I be flattered or frightened by his attention?

The polls were scheduled to close at eight o'clock. So was the store. Her watch showed a quarter till. On the East Coast and in the Midwest most of the election results were already in, and although certain critical states were still too close to call it was already as clear as the ringing of a bell that Obama was going to pull off a huge victory. Throughout the night clerks from adjacent stores had been popping into the bookstore to announce updates on the election. Somebody said, "They showed it on TV, already there's half a million people crowding into the park in Chicago where Obama's going to make his acceptance speech, and they ain't even called North Carolina or Ohio yet. Won't call the West Coast for hours."

Alex didn't want to have to deal with Jim Bright. Was he going to expect her to go out with him after they closed? He had shown up about an hour earlier dressed all nattily with a dark charcoal overcoat and a matching fedora, a multi-colored scarf wrapped loosely around his neck even though it was not very cold out. *God, he was good looking.* She mouthed the words, "What are you doing here?"

Setting the magazine back on the rack and approaching her, he said, "I wanted to see where you worked. Is that all right?"

"Well yeah, I guess. But it kinda seems like you're stalking me." There, she said it. She chuckled to cover up the sudden fear that maybe he was.

"Do you want me to leave?" he asked.

"No."

She didn't want to hurt his feelings. She did want him to leave. No she didn't. She couldn't make up her mind.

Comments on the election returns from bookstore browsers left little question about which candidate was the favorite among their shoppers. Among all the people who had voiced their opinions—many shouting "We're winning!" or confidently stating, "It's going to be a new day!"—there had been only one McCain backer, and he was totally whacko. He came in and started ranting about how Obama was secretly a Muslim and that his whole campaign had been masterminded by Osama Bin Laden and paid for by Hamas. Other than that one guy, Jim seemed to be the only person in town who was not for Obama, which was another reason Alex was in no mood to spend time with him.

The store had cleared out. Other than Jim, there had not been a single customer in the store since seven-twenty. The clock on the face of her cell phone showed five minutes to closing time, and she knew in her gut there would be something of a rush at closing time. There always was. She had become convinced that there was a whole tribe of bookstore customers who purposefully waited until right before closing to browse. Sure enough, a minute later three customers came in—enough to constitute a rush to her way of thinking. Two of them headed for the sci-fi section. The third, a lady wearing a floppy hat and lugging a big shopping bag, came up to the counter and said, "I'm looking for a book."

How many times have people said that? Of course you're looking for a book; you're in a bookstore. This time Alex didn't even wait for the inevitably inaccurate description of the book—

"It's an autobiography by..." (someone other than the subject) or "It's a mystery" (actually a true crime story) or "It's nonfiction" (how's that for specificity?). She said, "No you're not, lady. If you were looking for a book you'd be out there perusing the shelves."

"Well I never!" the woman said. She spun around and stormed out of the store. Good thing the manager wasn't there.

The two guys with their sci-fi books were still checking out at closing time when the polls closed on the East Coast. Immediately, the pundits declared Obama the winner. But Alex missed the announcement.

"All right, guys, it's closing time, time to go home."

Twenty minutes later, after closing the register and counting the money and sweeping the floor, she left work with a smiling Jim Bright by her side. She was anxious to get home and watch the rest of the election returns on television, and she wondered whether she should invite him to join her or find some excuse for ditching him.

It was colder out than she had expected, with gusty wind, the hanging sign outside Stellar Light swinging and bits of paper blowing across the street. The only protection from the elements she had was a thin cotton jacket, which she pulled tight at the neck. Jim pulled his scarf off and draped it around her neck and shoulders. "This'll help," he said.

"Thanks. But what about you? Aren't you cold?"

"I'm fine. Are you on foot?"

"Yeah. It's just a few blocks. Remember?"

They stepped around the corner to Market Street where— suddenly deciding she had to confront him and find out where this thing, whatever it was, was going—she grabbed his arm and pulled him to a stop in front of Bev and Rhonda's Buffet. Jim turned to face her. He opened his mouth to speak. So did she. She was going to put it to him point blank: "What's going on here? What are your intentions?" But before she could say anything he asked, "Are you hungry?"

She hesitated. She said, "Look, this seems too much like a date, you know what I mean? I can't date you."

"Why not? Come on, I'll buy you dinner. We don't have to call it a date. Just old friends having dinner together."

She decided she was being silly. Compared to some of the guys she'd left Barney's Pub with Jim was harmless. He was her oldest friend, even if she hadn't seen him since Johnson was in the White House.

"Is this place any good?" he asked.

"It's not bad. Most of their entrees are pretty bland, but they make great pocket sandwiches and a chocolate mousse to die for."

"So come on, let's get a bite."

She said, "All right, if you promise no political arguments."

Inside it was noisy and crowded, the party atmosphere jacked up a notch. Jim took her arm and steered her past the bar.

"I appreciate your chivalry," she shouted above the den.

"Comes from growing up Southern," he replied, but she couldn't hear him.

While making their way through the mesh of bodies Alex noticed a large man at the bar who seemed to be watching them. He was wearing a black trench coat and a wool cap. When he caught her eye he touched fingers to his brow in a kind of salute. There was something creepy about him.

They found a spot in the back dining area not far from a long party table against a wall. It was almost as noisy as it had been in the bar. They still had to almost shout to hear each other. Alex said, "Did you notice that big guy at the bar that was looking at us?"

"Yeah. I think I might have seen him before."

They waited for someone to take their order. After a while Alex said, "You have to tackle wait staff to get any service in here. Our best bet might be to go to the buffet first and then grab a drink from the bar. Leave our coats here and nobody will grab our table."

As they passed the bar again on their way to the buffet the man in the wool cap greeted Jim. He said, "Hidy."

Jim said, "Hey," and walked on.

It took them longer to get their food and drinks than to eat. TVs were placed throughout the joint, and all of them were carrying election commentary. A huge cheer went up. Alex patted Jim's hand as if placating a child. "Don't worry," she said, admittedly gloating a bit, "It won't be as bad as you think. You'll see."

"I hope you're right," he said. They were practically nose to nose, which was the only way they could hear each other over the restaurant noise. "It's not that I don't like Obama..."

Here he goes, she thought, right after promising no arguments. He said, "I do like him. He's charming, he's smart. To tell the truth, I almost switched to his side when McCain picked Palin. But the international situation scares me to death, and Obama doesn't have the right kind of experience to handle international affairs. He won't stand up to the terrorists, and I'm afraid that's going to make us vulnerable to another attack on America."

"You're wrong, you know. If Bush and company hadn't been such imperialist assholes the attacks on the twin towers never would have happened."

"That's such bullshit."

"At least Obama said he'd go after the people who actually attacked us instead of waging war on Iraq. Not that I want them making war on anyone."

He backed off. He said," Can we drop it for now? I like you too much to let politics come between us."

She liked that. She mentally scolded herself because he was being nicer than she. "OK," she said. "No more politics. For now." But she was still mad at him for interrupting her plans for the evening. She wanted to be home where she could actually hear what was being said. On the other hand, the celebratory atmosphere in Bev and Rhonda's was intoxicating. Wetside is a hotbed of liberalism, and it was their time to howl. Too bad Jim couldn't comfortably join in. She almost felt sorry for him.

During a momentary lull in the constant clatter and chatter, someone at the big party table quietly said, "Yes we can," the mantra Obama had repeated so effectively during so many campaign speeches. Someone else repeated it. "Yes we can." It went around the table like a chant, everyone whispering. It was lovely, almost other worldly. Suddenly Jim could take it no more. He'd been conciliatory and polite, but something about the chant pushed his buttons and suddenly he started ranting like a mad man. He pushed himself up from the table and shouted, "You're going to regret this. You'll see. Obama's not who you think he is. This is the start of a slide down the slippery slope to Socialism. Our defenses will be weakened to the point where we'll be vulnerable to terrorist attacks, and next time it will be even worse than before. You'll see. You'll see what tragedy this election will bring."

Alex jumped to her feet and hissed, "I don't even know you!" Mortified, holding her bag up to hide her face like some criminal being led to jail, she ran out of the restaurant.

"Wait!" Jim shouted, but she was already out the door, and she wasn't about to stop. She trudged down Harvard toward home but veered onto West Pike and went into the park and plopped down on one of the swings and cursed Jim Bright. Still with his scarf wrapped around her neck. Well I'll just keep the damn scarf, she thought. I certainly don't want him coming around to pick it up.

After she left he pulled out his wallet and threw two twenties on the table, plenty enough to cover their bill plus a generous tip. Jim had always been generous. He rushed out after her, but she was long gone. On the sidewalk out front he looked in both directions to see if he could spot her, and he stood for a while in front of Bev and Rhonda's trying to figure out what to do. The street was not as crowded as when they had first arrived. Two women stood at the bus stop on the corner, and a few feet away from Jim stood two young couples. One of the men pointed down the street and said, "Look, here comes that crazy old whore again."

Jim looked in the direction the young man had pointed and saw a woman carrying a lighted sparkler, skipping down the street in joyful abandon. He recognized her. She was kind of a local celebrity, an eccentric character he'd known of since he was a teenager. Melody Sauer, the old whore who had introduced three-fourths of the boys in Jefferson High School to the joys of sex, now in her seventies or eighties and well known as one of Wetside's more colorful characters. She constantly showed up in Harry Drews' Police Blotter. She rode on floats in the Pride Parade and the River Fair Parade, often as an invited "celebrity," knowing she was being made fun of but enjoying it nevertheless. She skipped past Jim. He watched her skip on down the street until the fire of her sparkler went out.

The door to Bev and Rhonda's opened and out came trench coat man. He took a few steps and stopped five feet away from Jim and looked in both directions. He was slightly taller than Jim and heavier. His face was shadowed with stubble of salt and pepper. His eyes met Jim's, and he nodded in greeting. Jim nodded back. The big man moved closer and said, "Hidy."

"Hey yourself."

"I think I know you."

"Really? I don't think so."

"Oh yeah, I do. I met you in the Meat Market."

"You must be mistaken. I've haven't been in a meat market in over ten years. I'm vegetarian," pretending he didn't know The Meat Market was Wetside's other gay bar.

The guy laughed at that. Jim said, "You must have me confused with somebody else."

"Maybe it wasn't The Meat Market after all. Maybe it was that other one, Barney's Pub. Yeah, that's where it was. You don't remember seeing me in Barney's?"

"No. Sorry. I don't think I've ever seen you before," Jim said, which was a lie. He had seen him before, he just couldn't remember where and he didn't want to remember where because the guy looked scary.

"All right," he said, "but I know I know you. Maybe it was the Barracuda." (Another gay bar, this one in Portland. It seemed like the man was going to mention every gay bar in the Northwest in hopes Jim would admit to frequenting at least one of them.)

Jim was getting nervous. He was afraid that if the guy kept it up one or both of them would remember from where they knew each other, and he didn't want to know. Jim didn't frequent any of the bars he had mentioned, but he had been an active ally in gay politics ever since his gay uncle died many years ago and had likely met this man before. The guy had probably tried to pick him up, and judging from the way he was acting now, had probably been very persistent about it.

Jim said, "Sorry man, but I never heard of any of those places, and I'm pretty sure I've never seen you before."

"I'm sorry. I guess you just look like someone I know. What's your name anyway?"

"Jim. Jim Bright."

"Oh. Well, that name doesn't ring a bell. I guess you're right. Sorry." He paused a moment and then said, "But hey, what the heck. You look like you could use a drink. What say? I'm buying."

"Thanks, but no. I've got to get going."

"You sure?"

"Yeah."

"All right then. Hey, what happened to your lady friend? "

"That's none of your business," Jim said.

"I'm sorry. You're right. Well, have a nice night." ...and one last stab at conversation: "Nice about Obama, right?" He turned and walked away. Jim walked in the opposite direction. He headed to the little park at the intersection of Pike and Pine just around the corner from Alex's house, the park where she was... waiting? A block away a black SUV passed him and the driver waved. It was trench coat man.

She should have known he would come there looking for her, meaning she knew it in her heart, meaning she was hoping he would, meaning she was beating herself up for hoping he would. It was a dinky little park no larger than your average suburban home site, but there was a swing set for kids, and a slide and a fountain and benches facing the sidewalks along West Pike and Pine. Triangle Park had been one of their special places, even when she lived much farther away. When they were kids and not dating as such, but often going to movies at the Strand together or taking long walks downtown and back, they loved to stop at the park—empty of kids at night—and swing side by side. She was swinging when he got there. He took a seat on the adjacent swing and matched her rhythm. "I'm sorry if I embarrassed you," he said. "I shouldn't have done that."

"No, you shouldn't." She heard the sound of her own voice and knew she sounded like a petulant child, but that couldn't be helped.

For a long time they were pendulums swinging silently in counterpoise, and then they settled at the lowest point, twisting their seats and shuffling their feet in the dirt, and their eyes met.

"I'm sorry," he said.

"You said that already."

"What else can we talk about?"

"I don't know. Oh, yes I do. Your sister. What was her name?"

"Wanda."

"Yes, Wanda."

Since the dramatic episode of her father kicking her out when she got pregnant, Alex had not heard anything about her. Jim said, "She's a grandmother now, living in Port Arthur, Texas. Still married to Jean Hebert. He's working for some oil company down there. Despite all the odds against them they built a good life together."

"And your folks? What about them? Is your old man still preaching?"

"They passed away a few years back. Yours?"

"Yep, they passed too."

They talked of this and that. Everything but politics. Mostly reminiscing again about old times. There were still a lot of memories they had not fully explored. It was still cool out, but the wind had died down and it wasn't too bad. Their talk went back to Kimzey Williams. "You know what I think?" she said, "I think the kids who treated her badly in seventh and eight grade, by the time we were all in high school they really regretted it and wanted to make it up to her, but they just didn't know how."

"Yeah," Jim said. "It's hard to admit you were wrong, and peer pressure is a powerful thing when you're a kid. Besides, by then Kay Kay was beginning to show definite signs of mental illness, and nobody knew how to deal with that."

"Did Rolly ever talk to you about that?"

"Very little. All he said was that he had to be really patient with her. He said when she went off the deep end he'd just wait her out and after a while she'd come back to her normal self. But he wasn't around that much either. Remember? It wasn't until after we graduated that he started dating her steady. But I remember how freaked out he was the first time he witnessed her having some kind of psychotic episode. A bunch of us had gone swimming out at the gravel pit. I think it was the summer before our senior year. They had been writing each other while he was away, but they hadn't dated very much. They snuck off over that little hill on the south side to find some privacy where they could make out, and they were smooching pretty hot and heavy when all of a sudden she started talking about midgets chasing after her. Get that, a whole tribe of nasty little people out to get her. She jumped up from the ground and ran back over the hill and dove in the water and swam across to the other side and took off running toward the dump like the devil himself and all his minions were after her. That dump was a dangerous place to run through, especially barefooted. There were all kinds of old cans and boards and stuff. Rolly had to run around the gravel pit and chase after her. When he finally caught up with her, fortunately before she got into the dump site, he held her while she hyperventilated and kept talking about the midgets that were going to hurt her. He said she kept it up about ten minutes, and then she snapped out of it and she was herself again and didn't seem to remember anything about it later."

Alex mentioned remembering that there had also been something very strange about her family. "Her dad was some kind of big muckety-muck in local government, wasn't he? Local or state. District attorney or something like that. A lawyer anyway. And he got arrested for something or other. I think it was that big sex scandal thing. That satanic cult thing."

"It wasn't a satanic cult." It's just the freakin' Christians, anything that's weird or evil they figure it has to be satanic. It was a cult all right, but it was a Christian cult. The leader claimed to be King David reincarnated, and like King David, he was allowed lots of wives."

"Whatever it was, there was a big scandal that was quickly hushed up because Mr. Williams had all the right connections or greased all the right palms or something."

"Yeah. But that weird sex club scandal, that was all over the news."

"Uh huh. Yeah, I know. It was run by a preacher, some bizarre pseudo-Baptist church. My daddy knew him. They were friends until all that stuff came out, but then daddy disavowed him, called him the antichrist."

"Oh, I remember a lot about the sex cult thing. My parents talked about it a lot, but I don't think Kay Kay's father was involved. What I remember is that what he got in trouble for was some kind of illegal business deal or investment scheme or something like that."

Neither of them had known what was going on. They were just kids. They might have skimmed an article or two in the newspaper or maybe caught something on the evening newscast— Alex more than Jim. She was more interested in that sort of thing. But mostly they just caught snatches of conversations here and there. Alex remembered that her folks talked about it a lot. But she probably forgot more about it than she ever knew. Jim's memory was even sketchier. They tried to put together their piecemeal bits of memory. They both remembered that Kay Kay's father got arrested. Jim thought it was both parents, but Alex thought it was just the father. It was a big scene. A whole bunch of cop cars pulled up to his house and he was hauled away in handcuffs with half the neighborhood watching. It was a Sunday morning near Easter. Maybe even Easter Sunday. Beautiful weather. Neighbors in their Sunday best out on the sidewalks on their way to church. There were two churches nearby, one Baptist and one Episcopalian. People were parking and getting out of their cars, walking in family groups. They all stopped to watch lawyer Williams get hauled away. Did they arrest Mrs. Williams too? They couldn't remember. Alex couldn't remember why she was there either. She certainly wasn't walking to church. Her family never went to church. The thing she remembered most clearly was that the sun was in her eyes and the cop cars and the cops hauling Mr. Williams in handcuffs were a blur like a desert mirage. In her memory bank she pictured it as surreal and played out in slow-motion.

Jim thought Mrs. Williams had been arrested too. Memory can be strange. Somehow he conflated the arrest of Mr. (and Mrs.?) Williams with the ruckus at Mrs. Cockburn's house and wanted to think that's what the cops hauled them off for, even though he knew within reason that couldn't be right. If anybody had been hauled off for the pie fight it would have been Mrs. Cockburn. Jim said he actually dreamed about it, not just once, but repeatedly. But in his dream Mrs. Williams and Kay Kay were one person. The image was Kay Kay, but somehow Jim knew it was really her mother, and she was defending herself in court and her husband was there—Mr. Williams on a leash with a collar like a dog.

Harold Drews wrote that the price Mr. Williams paid for keeping out of jail and hushing up the scandal was that he could no longer practice law in Wetside. They left Wetside, but Kay Kay stayed behind. She went to live with her grandmother who lived over in the East End. Rumors flew around town for a week or so, but nothing else ever showed up in the paper or on the six o'clock news. Even Harold Drews was mum on the subject. It was like it officially never happened, except Kay Kay's parents were gone and she was living with her grandmother.

Alex said, "Maybe there wasn't anything in the news about Mr. and Mrs. Williams, but there was plenty about the sex scandal. And not just from Harold Drews. It was all over the news. They even had somebody from one of the networks come out here to do a report on it. Harold said they were devil worshippers…"

"But they weren't," Jim reiterated, and Alex said, "I'm just telling you what he wrote. He said they performed satanic sex rituals in the basement of the church. He interviewed the preacher and some others who were arrested. He said there were children involved. It was really ugly. The preacher and some of the others were sent to prison. I think there were, like, some really prominent people involved, but I can't remember who. "

Jim said, "I think Harold Drews exaggerated and sensationalized the whole thing."

"Maybe, but they confessed to some kind of group sex thing. That really happened. And there really were kids involved. They were having sex with kids.

They agreed that if Kay Kay's father really had been involved it was certainly believable that he could have got the whole thing hushed up. Or any mention of his part in it. He had those kinds of connections. If he had taken part in the sex stuff, then probably his wife was involved too, and if Kay Kay had been forced to take part—well, one or both of them might have been molesting her all along, and that could certainly have been the cause of her mental illness.

They let it go, knowing they'd never know. It was close to midnight. A police car drove slowly past the park, circled the block and stopped, and watched them long enough to decide they were harmless. That was their clue that it was time to call it a night. Jim walked her the rest of the way home, and just like the first time he had walked her home, they paused in front of her door and she wondered if he expected her to invite him in. Was their friendship heading in the direction of romance or were they just a couple of old farts connected only by nostalgia? Jim took her hand ever so gently and said, "Could I..."

She thought he was going to say kiss you goodnight and she was thinking yes, yes, yes.

He said, "Have a hug."

Relieved but a little disappointed, she said, "Sure. You can have a hug."

His hug felt really nice, strong but not crushing. She told him she was glad he stopped by the book store.

She climbed the stairs, got ready for bed, fixed herself a hot chocolate. Wearing her winter robe she plugged in the space heater and sat close to it and picked up her copy of Barbara Kingsolver's *Poisonwood Bible,* but didn't start reading right off. MSNBC was still running election commentary, so she watched until they started repeating everything. She was drifting off to sleep with the book open on her chest half an hour later when the phone rang. It was Jim. He said he thought someone had followed him home. "There was hardly any traffic on the streets when I climbed into my car to drive home, so the headlights behind me were real obvious. They turned every time I turned. I told myself it was just a coincidence. Anyone on the road downtown at that time of night would more than likely be headed for the freeway. Once I got on I-5 the traffic was a little bit heavier, but when I got off in Rock Creek the car behind me got off too. Maybe I was just being paranoid, but I kept an eye on him all the way. He didn't slow down when I turned into my drive, so I figured I was worrying about nothing, but it was spooky."

She agreed that it was kind of spooky but probably nothing and asked why he called to tell her about it. He said, "I just wanted to hear your voice again."

Chapter 7

Meeting at Barney's became a routine. Alex introduced Jim to Randy the bartender and to a gay couple whose names he could never remember, both of whom were professors at City U, and to other regulars. "It seems like you know everyone here," he said.

"That's not a good sign, is it?" she countered. "It just shows I spend way too much time hanging out in bars."

"Yeah, you're a regular sot. I can tell," he kidded.

She reintroduced him to an old high school friend. "Jim, this is Johnny Delgado. I'm sure you remember each other."

"Of course. Good to see you, Johnny."

With a third person to reminisce about what Jim called the good old days and Alex called the dark ages they began tossing names around. Remember so-and-so? What about what's his name? Somebody mentioned Bubba Austin.

"That bastard," Johnny said. "If ever I wanted to kill somebody it was Bubba Austin."

"Why?" Jim asked.

"He was a bully. He picked on me constantly."

"I guess you're right. He might have been a bully, but I have to confess that I admired the hell out of him. I guess it was the old macho thing, his athletic ability. I took to copying his swagger. Remember how he used to kind of roll his shoulders and pull his head into his neck like a turtle? I started doing that too. And for a while in junior high I wore my hair flat on top and brushed back in a ducktail just like Bubba."

As a role model Bubba was the worst choice possible. Jim said, "I have no excuse except that I was young and impressionable."

Bubba was the toughest boy in school. The next toughest was his half brother, Reggie. But it was Bubba who struck fear in the hearts of boys like Leslie and Johnny Delgado.

Jim said, "I'm kind of embarrassed about my childhood infatuation with the bastard, but it didn't last long, and you got to admit he was clever in a nasty sort of way. Like I remember him saying, 'The meek are gonna inherit the earth, but not before I rub their faces in the mud.' See I mean? That was clever."

"It was just mean, if you ask me," Johnny said.

Bubba enjoyed seeing the small and the timid quake in his presence. He bragged about kicking ass. He was disdainful of teachers, cops and parents. Bubba and Reggie were both on the football team. Reggie played defensive back. He was fast, and he was vicious. He'd rather tackle the pass receiver than intercept a pass. You could give him a clear shot at an interception and nothing but grass between him and the goal line, hand him a touchdown on a silver platter, and he'd rather let the receiver on the other team catch the pass and then cream him than go for the easy interception and touchdown. Scoring points meant nothing to him; he just liked to smash into opposing players with all his might. Bubba too. They were not team players. Bubba was the fullback. Just a straight-ahead, hit-the-line kind of runner, always good for needed short yardage. He wasn't very big, but he was solid muscle. He had lost his front teeth after being head-butted with a helmet. He wore dentures off the field but liked to show his big gap during games. His toothless leer intimidated opposing linemen.

Jim's worship of Bubba Austin didn't last long. It was on the practice field that he first began to lose respect for Bubba. He played dirty. He blocked from behind, which was not only illegal but very dangerous. On defense—back then everybody played both offense and defense—he hit people out of bounds or after the play was over. He tried to hurt people unnecessarily. His own teammates, not just players from rival schools.

Bubba and Reggie seemed to be obsessed with queers, especially Bubba. They talked about them constantly, told queer jokes, called anyone they didn't like a fag or a fairy. There was a Spanish teacher at Jefferson High. His name was Jesus Gomez. He was thin and wore his coal black hair slicked back in a big pompadour and slid his feet as he walked down the hall, almost as if he were ice skating. Mr. Gomez taught at Jefferson for only half a year. One day Bubba Austin painted the word *FAG* on the side of Mr. Gomez's car. When he drove to school the next day you could

118

see the faint ghost of the word where he had painted over it with a blue that almost matched the color of his car. That day someone threw rocks through his windshield, and a few days later someone taped a threatening note to his chalkboard saying *we don't tolerate fags in this school.* The day after that he didn't show up at school. There was a substitute teacher in Spanish class. "What happened to Gomez?" the class asked. The substitute said all he knew was that he had been asked to fill in until a permanent replacement could be found.

"He quit?"

"Let's just say he'll not be teaching here any more. That's all I was told."

"He got fired?"

"I don't know the circumstances."

None of the kids were willing to ask the principal about it.

"I don't think he got fired," Bubba said. "Old man Sutter ain't got the guts to fire anybody. I think the little fairy just took off because we scared the shit out of him."

Mr. Silver, sixth period history and football coach, said, "We do not talk about people behind their backs." But in the locker room after school he said, "Whoever ran that pansy off did this school a favor." Coach Silver felt camaraderie with the football players that allowed him to let his true feelings out in their presence.

Up until that moment Jim had never been the kind of boy who would stand up for something he believed in, especially not against someone he looked up to. He had always been a go-along-to-get-along kind of guy. He wanted everyone to like him. So calling out Bubba Austin *and* the football coach was a big deal. And it was over something he didn't even understand, the bullying of someone suspected of being gay. But more specifically it was a matter of simple decency. True, he had a gay uncle that he loved, and after his uncle came out and Jim realized he was still the same lovable Uncle Brad he grew to despise gay bashing, but in his junior year in high school he hadn't yet come to understand that about Uncle Brad. He just knew that what Bubba and the coach were doing didn't seem right. Mr. Gomez had never done anything to hurt them. So in the

119

locker room after football practice, still dripping from the shower when Bubba made some smartass remark about Mr. Gomez and the coach joined in and laughed right along with him and the other boys, Jim shouted, "You shut your mouth!"

It just came out.

"Screw you, Bright. What are you, some kind of fag lover?" Bubba rushed him like a maddened bull and slammed into him and drove him up against the wall of lockers. They fell to the floor and wrestled. Bubba got the upper hand. He rolled Jim onto his back and straddled him and choked him. Jim broke his hold on his throat and pushed him off. He said, "I don't want to fight you, dammit," and he stood up and tried to step away, but Bubba came after him again. All the other boys gathered round to watch, and the coach stood by, leaning casually against the lockers.

They just wrestled. No blows were exchanged. When talking about it later Jim said, "I think the truth of the matter was neither one of us wanted to fight. We were teammates. I think Bubba regretted it the moment he attacked me, but his pride wouldn't let him quit. Finally I guess the coach decided it had gone on long enough, and he stepped in and pried us apart and told us to get dressed and go home."

Not long after that Bubba and Reggie started hanging out a lot with Red Rogers, the guy who ran the dairy bar. A lot of kids did, but not like Bubba and Reggie. Red was the one grown-up the kids knew who could talk to them on their own level. He was like a big brother. The kids needed someone older they could talk to about the things they couldn't talk to their own parents about. Teachers and even the school guidance counselor couldn't fill that role because they were authority figures, but Red Rogers fit the bill perfectly. He was kind of an unofficial street counselor. Red was in his mid-thirties. He was single and lived alone in a small house near the college campus. There were rumors about wild parties at his house with lots of booze and some of the wilder fraternity boys and their dates, but the high school kids were not invited. He knew better than to invite underage kids to a party where there was lots of booze—the exception apparently being Bubba and Reggie, if you could believe them. Bubba bragged that they were invited to Red's parties. He bragged about some of the hot shot football players from the college that were there and about the stripper Red hired to entertain at one party and how one time they played spin the bottle and ended up with everyone making out in a big heap of writhing bodies.

Senior year Bubba got drunk at one of Red Rogers' parties, and on the way home he drove his car off a bridge and busted himself up pretty badly. Broke both legs and had big cuts on his face and arms, and lost one eye to a flying shard of glass. He spent a long time in the hospital, and when he came back he was never able to play football again. The rest of that year he kind of kept to himself. It was almost like he wasn't there. There was some question about whether or not Red was liable for serving alcohol to an under age kid, but Bubba had recently turned eighteen.

Raindrops, the blog of the Daily Journal, Wetside, Washington, Dec. 19, 2008

POLICE BLOTTER
By Harry Drews

Quick thinking clerk and Jesus catch robber

In one of the strangest cops-and-robber stories this reporter has ever had the privilege of reporting, a quick-thinking 7-11 clerk invoked the name of Jesus and used sympathy and understanding to catch a crook. You can catch more bees with honey than with vinegar.

Saturday evening a young man with long hair and a fake beard entered the 7-11 on Highway 101 North, approached the counter, pulled out a gun and instructed cashier Christine Rocker to empty the cash drawer. Miss Rocker said, "Jesus will get you for this."

Afterwards she reported to the police that the robber said, "(expletive) Jesus."

"Well it just made me mad to hear him talk about the Lord that way," Rocker said. "I was so mad I was right on the verge of slapping him, but thank you sweet Jesus I had good sense enough to remember he was holding a gun on me, and then I calmed down a little bit and thought 'What Would Jesus Do?' and I told him he must be awfully desperate to hold up a store and that I was going to pray for him. Then, miracle of miracles, he broke down and started crying and said he was hungry and he had a little baby girl at home that needed food and diapers, and he just needed enough money to hold him over until the welfare check come. Well now, I been there before and I knew what he was feeling."

The would-be robber was a singer in a rock and roll band that goes by the name Austin City Limit. He said his band hadn't been able to play for pay in over a month and he got laid off from his job at the Ace Hardware. Miss Rocker told him if he would give up his life of crime she would help him get a job at the 7-11, and she gave him an application, and he filled it out on the spot while still holding a gun on her. And then he went ahead and robbed the store anyway, getting $187.53 from the cash drawer, an undisclosed amount of milk and baby food, a six-pack of Pabst Blue Ribbon and a carton of Camel Lights. She said he was still crying and apologized as he walked out with the loot.

Miss Rocker called the police after the robber left. His name and address were on the job application, real name George Ash. Police went to his home and arrested him. The gun he had used in the robbery turned out to be a cap pistol.

There will be a court hearing next week, at which time bail will be set. Ash is being held in the county jail. His wife is asking for help to raise bail money and money to help feed her nine-month-old daughter. Miss Rocker said she has placed a donation jar on the counter at the 7-11 to help raise money for the family. As for the job application, she said her manager agreed to give it "due consideration" and will "discount the attempted robbery."

Best Friends – Jim and Alex's blog

Love and Politics

The way we slipped into couplehood was gradual but natural once we got past the political thing. But oh the political thing. That was a tough one. For me, anyway. Jim sloughed it off, but politics means a lot to me. Everything else in my life is just entertainment and relaxation, or just getting through the day—books, movies, the half hour a day I devote to keeping my tiny house in order, my joke of a social life. But who gets elected and what they do in office matters a lot. I spend a lot of time reading political blogs and watching Olbermann and Rachel Maddow, and sometimes even the right wingers just to see where they're coming from. Jim calls me an armchair liberal. He said if my political views really meant anything I should be out on the picket lines, I should have been with the kids that got arrested trying to stop the shipment of military goods to Iraq. - *Alex*

It's all talk with armchair liberals. They get all weepy and touchy-feeling, but not many of them are willing to put their asses on the line. Alex accuses me of being a hypocrite about that because I'm not out campaigning for my side either, but it doesn't matter to me the way it does to her. We've had good and bad politicians in office and they've passed wise and wonderful laws and perfectly horrible laws, and somehow the country has survived. Besides, we're going to destroy the planet anyway, and you and I won't live long enough to see it happen. - *Jim*

Damn you, Jim Bright. I hate to think you might be right, and you're not.

It's not just theoretical with me. It's visceral. I hate right wing nutjobs. Hate them with a vengeance. They make my skin crawl. I want to rip their eyeballs out.

And goddamnittohell I found myself falling in love with a Republican. Or a Libertarian or whatever he's claiming to be this week. Mostly he calls himself an independent. Whatever. His politics are horrible. He quotes Rush Limbaugh for chrissake. And he laughs about the tea baggers or whatever they're calling themselves protesting against Obama's supposed determination to get rid of the second amendment (which he's never said a word about) by showing up at rallies toting guns. And to think, we'd called George W. Bush a cowboy. – *Alex*

But you do love me, and love heals all wounds. – *Jim*

Chapter 8

There was a time during the summer when they almost came to blows... again!—over the hot political topic of the day, healthcare. Variations on the argument they'd had at her kitchen table back in the fall were being acted out all over the country as legislators back in their home states were holding town meetings on the topic and the meetings were being packed by protestors who often got so belligerent that violence lurked along the edges. "It's the fringe groups sending troops in to disrupt meetings. They make it impossible to discuss anything rationally," Alex complained.

"Yeah, fancy that," Jim countered, "Conservatives acting just like liberals from back in the day. Remember when they accused protestors of being outside agitators?"

"Yeah, but this is... well shit, I don't know what to think. The Democrats have already wimped out on single payer and the public option. We've given away the store trying to placate the Republicans, and the damn Republicans aren't going to vote with the Dems no matter what."

Sara Palin, still pissed about losing the election, was talking about what she called death panels, claiming *they* (whoever they were) were going to euthanize everybody's grandparents rather than provide them with medical care, and most of the right wing picked up on that and used it as a rallying cry. Mobs showed up at the town hall meetings and shouted down the speakers. They came with signs calling Obama a Socialist, with pictures of Obama with a Hitler mustache, of Obama with face paint and a bone in his nose.

It was ugly. Jim didn't go to any of the town hall meetings, but he argued on their side. Often just to goad Alex. When film clips of the rallies were shown on TV he'd point out the most outlandish signs and laugh at them. "That's horrible," she'd say, and he'd come back with, "Sure it is, but you got to admit it's clever," and she'd say, "Yeah, just like you thought Bubba Austin picking on people like Johnny Delgato was clever." Alex had no sense of humor about those matters.

At one point in August she got so mad at him that she refused to talk to him for a while. He just laughed it off like it was no big deal, and that made her even madder. Finally he told her he was just teasing, and he apologized, but she didn't know whether he meant it or not. That was the other thing that infuriated her. Half the time she couldn't tell when Jim was serious.

Alex liked to be able to put things in their proper boxes, and it drove her crazy when Jim jumped from box to box. She got flustered when they argued because half the time she didn't know what to say, couldn't anticipate whether he was in agreement or opposition. That tickled him pink. He loved to argue. The things that aggravated her stimulated him. His final word in most political arguments was that people who follow a party line, meaning Alex, don't think for themselves.

"Are you saying I let other people think for me?"

"If the foo shits." (She vaguely remembered that being the punchline to some old joke but couldn't remember the lead-up.)

Joke or not, he had her on that one, and he knew it. It wasn't that she didn't know what was right and what wasn't, but she couldn't keep details in her head and it seemed like he could quote facts and figures about any argument. She marveled at his memory but suspected he made half of it up, and it irritated her that she couldn't prove it.

Full of contradictions, he was all for small government but believed in spending whatever it took to have a strong defense, even though he said the war in Iraq was immoral and illegal. Not that he was against war; he was just against that particular war. On the other hand, he was all for sending more troops to Afghanistan, which put him in the Obama camp, and he thought we ought to bomb North Korea and Iran.

Cutting taxes? Naturally. He was for that. In fact, he wanted to completely do away with income tax. "We don't need the IRS," he said. "Let the marketplace govern itself."

He was a most charitable person. He gave freely to causes he believed in, but he thought charity should be a function of individuals, not government, in theory at least if not always in

127

practice. He tended to lump together members of ethnic groups and minorities and buy into myths about them in the abstract while showing real concern for individuals within those groups who may have been trampled or ignored by the system. He was not a simple man. He insisted that poor people as a whole were a bunch of lazy bums feeding off the system and she could not convince him otherwise; yet when they passed beggars on the street he'd not only give them a five or a ten but then he'd pull over to the side of the road and get out of his car and engage them in conversation. Alex, for all her empathy for the downtrodden, would not do that. She suspected beggars of being just the kind of bums Jim accused them of being, plus she was repulsed if they looked dirty or unkempt. "I can't help it. I'm just afraid they might have something communicable."

Jim was no bigot. That was the one thing she couldn't have put up with. He hated bigotry as much as she did. She loved it that at least they had that in common. He complained that a lot of his side's opposition to President Obama was pure and simple racism thinly disguised. Those folks were threatened by a black man in the White House. "They give conservatives a bad name," he griped. He was also a champion for gay rights, he identified so much with gays, in fact, that if she didn't know better she'd assume he was gay himself. *Wouldn't that be a fine kettle of fish if he turned out to be gay?* "Blame it on Uncle Bradley," he said. "He was queer as a three dollar bill, and I loved the heck out of him. He was the only male role model I had growing up."

When, during his years in college, Jim got so fed up with his old man's self-righteousness that he left home, he stayed not in a dorm on campus but with Uncle Bradley in his country home in Rock Creek, the property he inherited when Brad died in 1990.

Alex said, "I'll be goddamn if you're not the most liberal conservative and the gayest straight man I've ever known."

"That's why you love me," he quipped. But love between them had never been mentioned accepted in such a toss-away manner.

128

Once, after about the fifth time they went out together, when he gave her his usual goodbye hug at the door, she turned her head and planted a big smacker right on his lips. He didn't exactly respond. He *let her* kiss him, and she felt the slightest return pressure, but there was no clinging of bodies, no ramming of his tongue down her throat. He at least smiled appreciatively. The smiled said something like "that was nice of you," but she had the impression he would have been more grateful if she'd baked a sheet of brownies for him.

The next time they kissed he initiated it. That gave her a ray of hope—*is there perhaps some spark of romance in him after all?* —but the kiss he initiated was no more passionate than his response to that first kiss. Despite a paucity of evidence she began to suspect sometime near Thanksgiving of the second year of their renewed friendship that they had made not the leap but the tentative step from being friends to being in love. If you'd asked her why she felt that way she would have been at a loss for an answer. He certainly didn't act like he wanted to grow old with her. He didn't even act like he wanted to get her in bed, and he'd been about the beddingest guy she'd ever known. *What's with him anyway? Has he forgotten what boys and girls do together? Has the stud horse of Jefferson High School totally forgotten how to make a move? And why, for God's sake, am I waiting for him to make the first move. Am I not a liberated woman?*

She told herself that maybe he was simply not attracted to her in that way, but in all honesty she really had a hard time accepting that and, frankly, it would be pretty damn insulting seeing as how she saw herself as a very attractive and desirable woman. Hadn't many a man made that clear, and not just men of their age, but many younger men as well? But apparently not Mister Most Handsome and Most Likely to Succeed from half a century ago. Maybe he hesitated because they had too much shared history. Once a certain type of relationship is established it is hard to change it. Could that be it? Could it be the platonic nature of their friendship had been so well established that he either didn't want to or didn't know how to change it?

And then it hit her. He was sexually dysfunctional. God knows it happens to most men his age. Isn't there a huge pharmaceutical industry making a fortune on just that? Couldn't he just take a pill? She psyched herself into dealing with it. *Performance Anxiety. Erectile Dysfunction.* Pop a pill and everything's all right. It just takes someone to let him know there's nothing to be embarrassed about. She would be Little Miss Patience. She would coax him back to life. She would raise his flag of desire.

And then it happened in early December—not a flag waving but a simple question. With no preliminaries and nothing leading up to it, coming in fact as the tail end of a conversation about changes in the advertising business in the age of the Internet, he said, "Are we going to ever sleep together or what?"

Caught off guard she voiced the first silly thought that popped into her head, which was "Abstinence makes the heart grow fonder."

"And the gonads ache," was his quick-draw comeback.

They fell into eye-watering laughter at that. Finally, collecting himself, Jim said, "Really, are we going in that direction or not? If that's not what this is, then let's get that out in the open; and if it is, then what are we waiting on?"

It was about time. He was ready, willing and apparently able. She said, "I thought you'd never ask."

"Well, it's 'cause, you know..." in that crazy, rambling never-quite-lost-the-Southern-accent way of his when he was trying to be funny (usually inappropriately), "Sex is so goddamn nasty and disgusting."

"Nasty and disgusting? You've got to be kidding me."

"Oh no, no, not at all. Tell the truth, I can hardly stand to even think about it, much less actually *do* it. And yet I must. I'm programmed that way."

That was when she knew he was kidding. He continued, "God in his infinite wisdom and probably in a fit of truly sick humor created us in such a perverse way that the very places where we kiss and fondle and make love are the same places where we chew our food and spit and vomit and shit and piss. Lordee, it makes me want

130

to puke, yet here we are compelled to rut like barnyard animals, driven by undeniable urges built into us by that self-same all-loving and all-knowing jokester, Godalmighty." He beamed at her and topped it off with, "I know about that shit because I'm a preacher's son."

A huge, huge grin from Jim, eyes watering, and then, "Well, are we going to do it or not?"

"I don't think so," she said. "Not after all that. Somehow I seem to have lost the desire."

He had destroyed the mood with his childish grossout humor. *Did you have a good laugh? Was it worth ruining your chance to get laid?* He wasn't concerned about killing the moment. He knew that once the subject had been broached they would eventually come back around to making love, which they did after a couple of drinks and an evening of watching a delightful romantic movie called *Amélie.*

They undressed with backs turned, sitting on opposite sides of the bed to take their shoes off and standing with backs still turned to slip out of pants, shirts, underwear. Each of them was afraid the other would be turned off by the sight of their aging bodies. She quickly slipped under the sheet. She pulled the sheet to her chin and then, embarrassed about being so modest, she folded it back down to expose her breasts. She barely got a glimpse of his naked body when he scooted in beside her. She tented the sheet to take a long gander at what she remembered as a Greek god body. Not bad. Slightly more flaccid than she remembered, perhaps, except for in one critical area, but otherwise pretty much the same as in his youth. He lifted his side and joined her in their mutual inspection of old bodies. The unspoken conclusion was "not bad."

Their approach to lovemaking was slow. They touched tentatively, not much foreplay. It didn't exactly rock their world, but it was all right.

The next night he stayed all night, and the lovemaking was more fulfilling. And again the night after that. She knew she had him hooked when he brought his favorite coffee cup from home and put it on her shelf. It was a cup with a picture of Alfred E. Neuman, the What Me Worry kid from *Mad* magazine.

"Do you mind if we don't do anything tonight?" she asked after spending eight nights in a row together. "I'm not used to making love as a nightly ritual. You're wearing me out."

"Thank God," he said. "It's been a strain trying to keep up with you. You're quite the dynamo."

"Me? You're the one..."

"You mean we've been faking it?"

•

He suggested they should celebrate Christmas at his home in the country. In all the time they'd been seeing each other she'd never yet seen his house. She said, "I'd love to see it. But you don't mean stay over, do you?" She was terrified of country living. Her only experience with it had been a week spent with her aunt and uncle on a farm near Shelton when she was ten years old. Aunt Belinda and Uncle Art. They were ancient, or so it seemed to her at the time. Actually they were much younger then than Alex now. Uncle Art was a logger. He kept his truck parked by the barn, and little Alex loved climbing on it. The old truck was dirty and smelled of pine and gasoline. The cab was green and the bed was an indistinguishable color, ninety percent rust. The spotty lawn between the barn and the house looked like a plowed field from the deep ruts gouged out when Uncle Art maneuvered his truck to turn it around. Discarded near the truck was a big tire that she used as a trampoline. When the ground was wet, which was practically all the time, she could take a running start and slide on her butt from the muddy road across to the patch of grass by the tool shed. Once she was thoroughly muddied Aunt Belinda would help her shuck out of her clothes and wash under the hand pump by the back porch (the first few pumps always bringing forth rusty water) and wait impatiently while wrapped in a towel for her to launder her clothes in the washer and drier that rattled the back porch. It wasn't that they didn't have indoor plumbing. They did. But not an indoor toilet. They had to use an outhouse. It stank to high heavens. Alex told Aunt Belinda she couldn't go out there at night. Aunt Belinda told Alex she could use a slop jar. That was disgusting, but it was better than trekking out to the outhouse in the dark.

Jim said, "Of course I meant stay over. Why not?"

"Because I get scared out in the country."

"You? You've never been scared of anything. Don't be silly. You'll love it. There's nothing like a country Christmas. It'll be perfect."

Neither of them had family to go to for the holidays, and despite her country living trauma, the thought of an old fashioned rural Christmas was enticing. "You do have an indoor toilet, right?"

"Are you kidding? Naw, it's primitive living, back to nature."

"Oh god, not an outhouse."

"Nope, not even an outhouse, but I do keep an old Sears and Roebuck catalog tied to a fir tree down by the creek. For wiping, ya know."

She said, "Crap!" and he said, "Of course. What else would you be wiping?"

As usual, there was a time delay before the joke dawned on her.

Jim's house sits a quarter of a mile back from the main road. The driveway is canopied with oak trees that stand like giant umbrellas on either side with, at the end of the drive, two purple madrones, the kind with the weirdly peeling trunks. It had snowed the night before. Beads of ice hung from overhead branches. The tires of Jim's car made a crackling sound on a bed of crisply frozen leaves on the drive. It was lovely, but she could picture it at night as a haunted roadway leading up to a dark castle. The house was no castle. It was a ramshackle ranch style with whitewashed wood slats and a large, screened front porch. A couple of dilapidated vinyl-covered kitchen chairs sat on the porch alongside a stack of firewood. Inside the expansive front room there was a large fireplace. Much to her relief there was indoor plumbing complete with a very modern flush toilet and a walk-in shower big enough for them to shower together without feeling cramped, which they did that first night lingering long until the hot water turned tepid.

They got there about four o'clock Thursday afternoon, Christmas Eve. Large, multi-colored Christmas lights were strung across the front of the house in a line of pine boughs stapled to the fascia. A Christmas tree stood in a bay window. She was holding a wrapped present for Jim that she placed under the tree. The area surrounding the tree was already loaded with stacks of wrapped gifts. Jim took her bags into the master bedroom, and while he was out of sight she snuck a quick peek at tags. All of the presents had her name on them.

"I only got you the one," she said when he came back out into the living room.

That's OK. The ones for you are all cheap. How about something hot to drink?"

"Sure. Sounds good. It's cold in here."

"Maybe I should get the fire started first."

Soon they settled in on chairs in front of the roaring fireplace with hands clasped around mugs of hot mulled cider. The crackling logs sent sparks flying that she was sure would set the house on fire.

"It's going to be a wonderful Christmas," he said.

"Just being able to share it with someone is special. I can't remember the last time I had anyone to share the holiday with, and I haven't bothered with decorations in I don't know when."

Dinner was take-and-bake pizza picked up on the way and heated up in the oven. Later, they had popcorn cooked in a long handled popper over the open fire.

He said, "I was scared to death the first time we made love."

"You're kidding. Why?"

"Because maybe I'm not the lover I once was" (a rueful chuckle). "After all, I've got a reputation to uphold"

She steeled herself for more banter about how repugnant sex was, but he had milked that bit of humor for all it was worth. Teasingly she said, "Oh, you're aware of your reputation, huh?" The boys in school called him a cocksman. First time she heard that she thought they meant coxswain and didn't understand why they would say such a thing.

He said, "I was not only aware of it, I cultivated it with craft and guile."

"No you didn't." Jim had never been one of those boys who bragged about who he slept with. He might make up whoppers, but they were never malicious.

"You can tell me now," she said. "Who all did you sleep with?"

"That's none of your business."

"Aw come on. You can't sully anyone's reputation fifty years after. Besides, if you don't tell me I'll just assume you banged everyone the rumor mills said you did, and that pretty much included the class of '61."

She noted a glimmer of a suppressed smile, indication that he was, after all, a little bit proud of his reputation. She said, "I know about Mary Elizabeth Lucious and…"

"How do you know about her?"

"I just do. Who else?"

"Umm."

"Lara Cockburn. I know about her too 'cause she told us."

"Told who?"

"Just about everybody. In the girls' gym. She was apparently very proud of herself."

"Did it ever occur to you that she might have been lying?"

"No. Boys lied about who they slept with, girls didn't. If anything, they pretended to be virgins when they weren't."

"Is that what you did?"

"No. We're not talking about me. We were talking about you and… and let's see, who was it? Lara. Did she lie about it? No way. She might have lied about everything else, but not that. What about Anna Shemper?"

"That's for me to know and you to find out."

That meant yes. She was on a roll. She wasn't about to drop it. For once she had him back pedaling and blushing. It was usually the other way around. She said, "All right, let's talk about Mary Elizabeth some more. Was she as good in bed as everybody thought she'd be?"

"No, but I was." He snickered.

It was as if some malicious spirit had inhabited her. She'd never been one to get off on hearing all the steamy details of his or anybody else's sex life. She'd always figured who did what to whom was none of her business. But because it was Jim and because his sexual partners would have been the kids she grew up with (many of whom, she knew, had pretended to be purer than they really were) she was dying to know. Their generation had not been as super casual about sex as today's youth. Not in the 1950s. Not even in the early '60s. It was all secretive and titillating, and often very shameful. So it was great fun now to hear that Miss Hotty Pants Mary Elizabeth was no great shakes in bed, and she'd love to hear that Jim had slept with, say, someone like Anna Shemper, who acted all prim and proper and pretended to be offended by dirty jokes. But he flat out refused to talk about it any more, and she realized that the more she pressed the subject the more gleeful he became.

Their chatter dribbled into languorous silence. The fire had settled to a single blackened log with pockets of red and a pile of glowing coals. She stretched and yawned.

"Ready for bed?" he asked.

She was sleepy but she didn't want to leave the comfort of the hearth, and memories of nights with Aunt Belinda and Uncle Art had her dreading going to sleep so far from civilization—as far as she was concerned a country home a mere ten miles south of the city and a quarter of a mile off a busy freeway might as well be an isolated cabin on a mountain top. He said there were night clothes in his closet that she could wear. She said, "I brought pajamas and a robe."

"I know, but take a look anyway. You might find something fun."

That sounded very much like he had a surprise for her. Was he implying there was something special stashed away in his closet? *Nasty boy, he must have bought sexy lingerie, wanting to play out some kind of kinky fantasy.*

He walked with her to the bedroom, opened the door and turned on the overhead light. "It's like a woman's bedroom," Alex said. It was roomy and homey. There were lace curtains on the single window and an old four-poster bed with a flower pattern bedspread. Against the wall stood a dressing table with a large mirror. Framed family portraits were hung on the wall along with a few show posters that must have belonged to Uncle Brad and a copy of the infamous photograph of the drag queens at Barney's from 1970. Without responding to her remark he pointed out a closet with sliding doors that took up most of one wall, and he suggested she see what she could find to sleep in. He got undressed and slipped under the covers.

A few minutes later she stepped out of the closet dangling a black lace teddy from her fingers. "What's this?"

"It's a teddy."

"Yes, I can see that, but it's... There's a whole damn wardrobe of women's clothes in there. Is that what you wanted me to see? Are you trying to tell me there's another woman in your life? Or a whole damn chorus line? Or... oh my god, did you go out and buy all of that for me?"

"No and no and no," he said, "It's my way of broaching a rather delicate subject." He paused. He looked around as if suspecting there was someone else lurking in the house. He said, "They're mine, all mine. The women's clothes. I wear them."

"Yeah, right, and your ex-wife made love to a chimpanzee, and you think Barack Obama is an illegal alien."

"No, really, I'm serious," he said. "I'm a cross dresser. I have been nearly all of my life. For a short time right after college I was a drag performer. Quite famous in certain circles if you want to know the gospel truth. I told you before but you thought I was kidding. I started cross dressing back when we were in high school."

"I don't believe you. I'd a known. We were like brother and sister. We told each other everything."

"Not everything. Didn't you just now ask me who I slept with? If we'd told each other everything you would have known."

Touché. He had her there.

He told her that he performed in drag under the name Amanda Darling and later reappeared as a jazz singer using the name

Amanda Bright. "Now I know you're making it up. I've seen Amanda Bright perform. At Barney's no less. She's one of my favorites. She's a lot younger than you and doesn't look a thing like you."

She did have the same last name, and it was not a very common name. Alex noted that that was an unlikely coincidence. She tried to picture Amanda Bright. She couldn't call anything more than a vague, generalized image to mind. Could he be telling the truth after all? No, not a chance.

"*Was* one of your favorites," he said. "She hasn't sung in more than six years. And yeah, maybe she did look a little younger then. Believe it or not, I really was Amanda Bright and long, long before that I performed as Amanda Darling, the darling of Barney's Pub."

"Yeah, and I guess you were Minnie Mouse too. Jesus! You're such a liar."

"No, I'm not."

"But you're straight," she said. And after a pause added, "Aren't you?"

"So what? Lots of cross dressers are straight, a lot more than you'd imagine. I'm talking about the ones that are serious about it, not your everyday campy queen. The drag queens at Barney's aren't serious cross dressers. With them it's all theater. They're just gay boys having fun. But the men like me who are… how do I say it? — compulsive. We're different. There's something in us that drives us to dress in women's clothes. When I'm dressed like a woman—I don't think of it as being in drag—I feel like I'm really me."

"Well that makes it sound like you're a transsexual."

"I know, but I'm not. I can't explain it, but I know what I am. I'm not trans, I'm not gay. I just have this compulsion to wear dresses and lipstick. It somehow completes me. Always has. And I know it's maybe weird and it may repulse you…"

"No, it doesn't repulse me. But I'm afraid I don't get it," she said. "Do you promise you're not putting me on?"

"I promise."

"Then tell me everything. Tell me how you discovered this thing about yourself and what it feels like and how often you do it. Is it sexual or just dress-up? I want to know everything. And I still want to know who all you were screwing in high school. You're not getting out of that one so easily."

"Don't forget junior high," he said.

"My god! You started in junior high? OK, junior high. Grammar school, kindergarten. Whatever. Start with Mary Elizabeth and Lara. And all the others. God, did you do it with Ophelia Sullivan? What about... wait, maybe we'd better have a drink first. I'm suddenly wide awake."

He glanced at his watch. It was almost midnight. He added a log to the fire and stirred the embers, and went into the kitchen to fix them each a Scotch and soda, and he told her about his exploits with Ophelia and Lara and Mary Elizabeth and Anna, and he said, "That was all. Four girls in six years. Not exactly what you'd call a harem, but I guess that was a lot for the times and for my age at the time, and life did get even more interesting in college and after."

"Meaning you screwed everything on two legs?"

He smiled and shrugged his shoulders. He told her that he had rejected his father's puritanical religion and adopted a hedonistic or libertine philosophy steeped in embracing all things sensual, and said, "There's a term, polyamorous. I think that kind of says it. There's not much of anything I haven't done over the years, but don't worry, I've kind of settled down in my old age."

And then he told her how he became, as he put it, a world famous female impersonator. He said, "I did perform at Barney's and for quite a long time. But I was quite different from the regular drag queens."

"So when you said you were there the night of the riot, you weren't there as a customer. You were there as a performer?"

"Uh huh."

"So you were lying to me when you said you left?"

"Oh no, I was telling the truth. I left all right. I was scared to death. I snuck out the back." He still wasn't ready to tell her the complete truth.

139

Still dangling the teddy in her hand she asked, "So what do I do with this? Should I wear it or should you?"

"I don't know. What would you think if I wore it?"

"I don't know either. I think maybe I'm not quite ready for that."

"Then let's not."

She draped it across the top of a chair and stepped out of her clothes and scooted under the sheets. She nestled into his arms and for a few minutes they lay in silence, and then she said, "Do you want to do anything?"

"Maybe. Sort of. But…"

"It's too late and you're too tired?"

"Uh huh. The mind is willing but the body isn't."

"That's OK. I kinda feel the same."

•

The wind kicked up outside. The howling of it was unnerving to Alex. She heard a screeching sound like chalk on a blackboard.

"What's that?"

"It's a limb on the fir tree scraping across the roof. I've been meaning to cut it off, but this winter's been cold and wet, and I haven't been able to muster up the gumption to climb up on the roof with a chain saw and I'm hardly ever out here anyway."

She was sure the limb was going to crack and fall through the roof. Maybe the whole freaking tree.

His bed sagged. It hurt her back. What with the uncomfortable bed and the frightening wind against the windows and the crackling of tree branches and thoughts of Jim Bright cavorting on stage as Amanda Darling, not to mention plowing through a string of polyamorous bedroom affairs like a glutton in a chocolate factory, it took her a long time to fall asleep. At three o'clock in the morning she was startled awake by what she was sure must have been a bear scratching at the door that opened out from his bedroom to the screened-in back porch. She heard the chalkboard screech of the screen door being nosed open and the rasp of claws against the door. She clutched Jim's arm and shook him awake. "There's an animal trying to get in."

140

"It's raccoons," Jim said, "They come up here all the time. Nothing to worry about. Go back to sleep."

He was crazy to think she could simply go back to sleep, and she resented his ability to do just that. He was sleeping again in seconds, and she couldn't even will herself to close her eyes. Shadows danced along one wall and across the ceiling. She listened to the chu-chu-chu of the clock. Later she heard the mournful hoot of an owl, and then the clamoring of dogs off in the distance—or could they have been wolves or coyotes? The explosions of ice-weighted limbs cracking in the wind went on all night long. "I'll never spend another night in this house," she told him the next morning. He thought she was kidding, but she meant it. Her little one bedroom cottage in the heart of downtown was perfectly fine for both of them in her estimation. Jim kept a robe and a couple of changes of clothing in her closet. No dresses. He stayed over two or three nights a week. For the foreseeable future that seemed like a nice enough arrangement.

Christmas morning he made instant oatmeal and coffee, and they opened gifts. Her gift to him was Al Franken's book *Rush Limbaugh is a Big Fat Idiot*—given in a joking spirit but in hopes it might open his eyes. His gifts to her were many, mostly silly little trinkets that he said he had picked up at the Goodwill store. There were cups and glasses and little statuettes of turtles and a couple of children's books, and—not from the Goodwill but with a tag from a high-end specialty shop—a lovely blue alpaca scarf.

Raindrops, the blog of the Daily Journal, Wetside, Washington, Dec 23, 2008

POLICE BLOTTER
By Harry Drews

Brewster Crockett cleared of robbery charges, buys Grab-N-Go

Evelyn Spitzer Ramsey, owner of the Grab-N-Go espresso stand on Rainier Street, recanted allegations that local businessman Brewster Crockett was behind a recent string of robberies. Crockett had been lobbying Ramsey for months to sell the establishment to him, and when her business was repeatedly robbed she accused Crockett of hiring crooks to commit the robberies as a way of driving her to bankruptcy and thus forcing her to sell out. Last week she gave up and sold him the business.

The espresso stand, which was not insured and which Ramsey said was operating at a loss, was robbed four times in the past two months at a cumulative loss of $4,750.00 according to statements by Ramsey.

Ramsey had been Wetside's first police woman. She retired from the force in 1998 and opened the Grab-N-Go in 2005. Ramsey reported to Wetside police that Crockett, also a retired policeman, "hired thugs" to rob her business in order to bankrupt her. She spoke of a long-standing family feud stemming from when Crockett and her father, Adam Spitzer, served together on the force.

Crockett's career on the police force was marked with allegations of excessive force and corruption, although none of the charges against him were ever proven. In 1970 he was one of the policemen involved in the May Day Riot at Barney's Pub. Crockett's partner, Fred Felts, was shot and killed in the riot. His death was ruled accidental.

In 1976 confiscated drugs valued at $20-$30,000 were stolen from the police evidence lockup and Crockett was implicated in the robbery. Ramsey's father was one of Crockett's fellow policemen who went on record as accusing Crockett of stealing the drugs. Ramsey said her father was "essentially hounded off the police force" for "turning on a fellow officer." An internal investigation found no evidence implicating Crockett in the drug heist.

"Brewster is a man who holds grudges," Ramsey said. "He never forgave my father, and he took his spite out on me."

Police said there was no evidence connecting Crockett to the robberies of Grab-N-Go. Crockett owns several rental properties in Wetside and interest in Grant's department store. He purchased the Grab-N-Go for an undisclosed amount. "I had no choice," Ramsey said. "It was either sell it to him or declare bankruptcy."

Crockett said it was an ideal business in an ideal location and with proper management should be profitable.

Chapter 9

His birthday was in February. She gave him a Victoria's Secret catalog. He loved it. She couldn't tell if he was excited about the sexy pictures or the clothes. She asked him when she was going to get to see him in drag, and he said, "One of these days, if you're lucky."

Invitations to their fiftieth high school reunion arrived in Alex's mailbox. The reunion was to be held on May Day, but she got the invitation months in advance. Jim said he couldn't think of anybody in their class he wanted to see again, and she kind of agreed with him, but at the same time she was curious about some of their old classmates. "I may not like many of them, except maybe Kay Kay and Rolly, but it might be interesting to see what some of them look like now and find out what they've been up to." Quite a few lived in and around Wetside, yet they'd completely lost touch with nearly everyone, and it was only recently that either of them had become curious about seeing some of them again. Alex said, "We had great fun reminiscing about the old days when we first got together."

"And that's the way I want to remember them and the way I want to be remembered," he said.

He was not particularly proud of the life he'd made for himself over the years, aware that he hadn't fulfilled even a little of the grandiose hopes that had been invested in him. He didn't particularly want to be recognized as no longer the most handsome and talented boy in the class but rather as a small town man running an unimposing marketing business that he knew was still operating on a 1960s model because he hadn't had the gumption or the smarts to update methods and technology. And he was ashamed for even giving a damn what they might think of him. Alex was just the opposite. She thought of herself as more sophisticated and more intelligent than her peers. She could see herself strutting into the reunion on the arm of the most handsome and talented boy in their class and she could easily picture every eye turning her way in envy.

He said the date was a problem because it was the fortieth anniversary of the riot at Barney's. "What? Are they having a reunion too?"

"Not a reunion. I don't think there's anybody left who was there except for Barney and Randy. But it's an annual celebration."

"I knew that, but I've never been." Next to the Pride parade in June the anniversary of the riot was the biggest annual event for the gay community. It was Wetside's version of Stonewall.

"I've never been either, but I was hoping we could go this year."

The riot was not something you talked about. For people who frequented Barney's and for many more people in Wetside it was a constant but seldom thought-about historical event, a harmless ghost that unobtrusively hovered over the town and was hauled out and shined up once a year and then promptly relegated once again to a single photograph on the wall at Barney's. Until Jim's big confession about cross dressing Alex never suspected he might have any interest whatsoever in the riot.

Jim said, "Maybe we can stop by and hoist a glass after the reunion."

"Maybe. We'll think about it. It's not like it's next week. No reason to make a decision now."

The planned reunion was three months away. There would be a dinner at seven followed by a dance starting at eight at the Country Club. For the time being they decided maybe they could go for the dinner and then cut out early and go to Barney's.

•

Wednesday nights were drag nights at Barney's. Jim and Alex had started taking in the show even before he told her about his past. Now they never missed drag night, even though it seemed like the only reason Jim went was to criticize. He said the performers weren't nearly as good as the ones from his day. Naturally none of the old performers were still there, not even in the audience. Jim knew half of them were dead and he assumed the rest would have long since moved to some other town. Maybe they're all in an old folks home for aging queens, he thought. Alex thought the current

145

crop of performers were fabulous. "I love 'em," she gushed, and he said for about the umpteenth time, "I've seen better."

"Yes, I know. You tell me that every time."

They were driving home from Barney's via a quick run out to his house to pick up a change of clothes. They'd left the pub a little before midnight and driven all the way down to Rock Creek and back. She waited in the car while he ran in for his stuff. She refused to go back inside that house. The rain had started on the way there, a typical Northwest drizzle—such a fine mist that after about the third swipe the windshield was too dry to use the wiper and too wet not to. The rubber started squeaking on the glass. Jim turned the wipers on and off, put the intermittent setting on slow, then medium then fast. "If it's going to rain, I just wish the hell it would go on and do it," he said. And it did. The mist changed into a steady rain and then built to a gully washer. They got sandwiched between two eighteen-wheelers and couldn't see anything but swirls of gray, dim taillights in front and a haze of headlights in the rearview mirror. The truck on their tail looked to be no more than a car length behind, and Jim was driving just that close to the truck ahead.

"Slow down," Alex shouted.

"I can't. That asshole's so close behind I'm afraid if he'll crawl up our rear end."

He held steady at sixty miles per hour, hands squeezing the steering wheel. "There's the exit," she said. It was barely visible in the spray. He let off the accelerator and guided his car onto the off ramp while dropping gradually to fifty and then forty, and then he braked hard but steady as they approached the stop sign at old Highway 99. Alex eased off the death grip she had on the arm rests.

The old highway ran through an industrial section where there was little traffic at night. With streetlights on every corner and none of the spray from big trucks they were able to clip along at a comfortable forty-five. "This is better," Jim said, then, "Where were we? Oh yes, the drag queens at Barney's. Those guys are just about the most pathetic drag queens I've ever seen. Their makeup was atrocious."

146

"Yeah, I know. You've told me that a jillion times, and I keep telling you they aren't trying to look like real women. They're supposed to look ludicrous. It's camp. Surely you've heard of that."

"Heard of it? We had the queens of camp in my day."

A monster Humvee sped past them and threw up a sheet of water. "Slow down," Alex said.

He said, "What they do at Barney's is not even good camp. To make camp work right you need a foil, a contrast. You know what I mean? In the really classy clubs they always have at least one knockout beauty that plays it straight, no pun intended. A counterpoint to all the silly babes with their big hair and balloons for boobs. The way to do it right is to bring on the seven-foot babes in bad makeup first, and then follow up by bringing on a gorgeous woman you'd never suspect was really a man, a real singer who doesn't lip sync but sings like an angel."

She knew and he knew what was coming next: some variation of *that was me in Barney's in my heyday*. He gloated, "You should have seen me..." followed by the feigned modesty of "I might not have been the greatest singer in the world, but I had a nice enough voice."

Yes he did. She remembered from high school musicals.

"The acts that came on before me would be real bawdy and would have the crowd all riled up, and then I would calm them down with a sweet song like 'Georgia on My Mind.' And then... and then came the act that made me famous. A striptease."

"You're lying." He'd bragged about the singing and his feminine beauty, but this was the first she'd ever heard of stripping.

"No, I'm not kidding. I did a striptease, and not just any old strip, but a class act. No raucous music, no tassel twirling, no G-string and pasties, no bump and grind, none of that. I would slowly walk on stage to the strains of lush orchestral music, recorded of course, wearing a long gown and a mink stole and elbow-length gloves. I didn't dance, I walked, gliding to the music while slowly disrobing all the way down to brassiere and panties. I had them mesmerized. I was the Gypsy Rose Lee of drag. It was sophisticated and tasteful, and of course I always ended it by pulling off my wig and taking a bow."

Another car pulled up behind them really fast and then passed, cutting in way too close. Instinctively Jim swerved and their car went into a skid. They hit the curb and skidded to a stop. The driver of the other car slowed as if he was going to stop and then hit the gas and made a wide turn onto Highway 101. It was a large black SUV. "I recognize that guy," Jim said.

"How could you?" All she had seen was a blur of motion.

"I got a look as he was passing us. He's the guy that tried to hit on me that night in front of Bev and Rhonda's. Remember? I told you about that."

"Uh yeah, sorta. Are you OK?"

He felt shaky but all right. He was talking in gasps. He said, "I'm fine. You sure you don't remember me telling you about that? It was election night."

All she remembered about that night was what a huge surge of hope and good cheer there had been right after the election results were announced, and then how he had ruined it with his asinine crap about John McCain and how mad she had been and how sweet he had been later when he apologized. She remembered being dizzy with contradictory emotions.

Jim got out in the rain to check for damage to the Hyundai. Got back in after circling the car and said, "Looks like everything's all right."

They were quiet for a while and then she said, "You didn't really get a good look at the driver. You couldn't have. It was dark. He was…"

"I know, but I did. It was just for a second, but I'm pretty sure I recognized him. I think that guy has been trailing me. I don't know why."

In bed that night she questioned him some more about transsexuals, drag queens, transvestites. She couldn't get the terms straight in her head. Which ones actually had the operation to change their gender and which ones just pretended, and why, why, why?

"The variety is endless," he said. "People tend to lump us all together, but we're as different as can be. Transsexuals have physical bodies that don't match their psychological makeup. Some of them take female hormones. Or testosterone if they're female-to-male, but I'm talking about male-to-female. They grow breasts. It's the hormones. They lose body hair, but usually not enough so they undergo painful electrolysis. Transitioning takes guts. Some have operations to turn their penises into clitorises."

She shuddered. "So then are they gay or straight, and are they able to have sex?"

"They become fully female. Or male, depending. And yeah, their sex organs work. Some of them are attracted to the same sex and some to the opposite sex, and I've heard that some of them may start out as, like men who deep inside feel like they are really women but they are attracted to other women, meaning if they transitioned they would become lesbians, but then when the start taking hormones they begin to be attracted to men. It can be really confusing, and I'm no expert. I only know about it from hearsay. Cross dressing is different. There's a million reasons men dress in women's clothing."

"But they're not necessarily gay or transgender?"

"No. Most of them are straight. Drag queens are different. Like I said, drag queens are usually gay, not trans. Most of them are in it for the theater. "

She had to ask. "Are you sure you're completely heterosexual? You're not maybe just a little bit bisexual?"

"Nope."

"But maybe you are and don't know it."

"Oh, I think I would know."

He said in the old days a lot of the queens at Barney's led double lives. Outside of the club they were closeted as much as it was possible, meaning some of them couldn't hide it to save their souls.

"Living in the closet meant constantly watching what they said. It meant being on the lookout for tell-tale gestures and inflections. In other words, it was hard work. They lived in constant fear of slipping up. Being openly gay was much more dangerous back then. They might have been accepted in certain circles, but there weren't many places where they could be themselves. The only time they could express themselves openly was on drag night at the club, so it was a great relief for them to be able to be themselves or play out their fantasies that one night a week. But Jesus, even Barney's Pub wasn't safe all the time. The cops raided the joint regularly, and queers got beat up all the time. And a lot of the boys could no more hide their gayness than a fat man could hide his fat. On the other hand, some of them, you'd never suspect. Some were even married."

"Did their wives know?"

"Most didn't."

She asked him if pretending to be a woman was a sexual turn-on.

"For me? Yes, it definitely was. I don't know if that's typical or not. I suspect it might be a turn-on for a lot of men if they gave it a try. At first it scared me. Scared me that I liked it. I tried to suppress my feelings. I was tortured with guilt. I thought there must be some kind of deep psychological sickness inside of me. But, you know, it was the '60s when I started. We just kind of accepted that everyone had his own turn-on. What was the saying? Different strokes for different folks. I got over the guilt trip. Besides, it was show business. I did theater in high school and college. I even sang with a rock and roll band for a while. Performing can be addictive. You ought to be able to understand that. You were married to a theater guy."

"What about now? Do you still dress up in women's clothes? Or do you still want to?"

"I think about it," he said, "but it's been a long time since I've worn a dress."

"But you still keep dresses in your closet."

"Uh huh."

•

By some kind of cosmically weird coincidence, Harry Drews' Police Blotter the next morning was about the murder of yet another cross dresser. Alex read the column out loud. Harry wrote that a man's body was discovered in the woods by teenage hikers. Two bullets were lodged in his head and another in his heart. Any one of the three shots could have killed him. Because there were three potentially fatal wounds, police spokesman Snake Collins was quoted as saying it was probably a crime of passion.

Harry reported that the victim was identified as Raymond Craig, 70, a Seattle resident. He was identified by the driver's license in his pocket, and the body was subsequently identified by a neighbor. The neighbor said the victim lived alone and kept to himself. "He wasn't married and it didn't look like he had any kids or grand kids. Nobody ever visited him," the neighbor was quoted.

Harry Drews stated that items found in the victim's house gave evidence that he had been a performing female impersonator in his younger days.

"Another one from Barney's," Jim said.

"You're right. Listen. Harry wrote, 'Among other items found in the victim's home was a copy of now famous photograph of the drag queens from Barney's Wetside Pub in 1970. There were also posters and playbills advertising drag shows in Seattle, some of which identified the victim's stage name as Honey Jewel.'"

Jim said, "Honey Jewel. What a great dame he was."

Jim was sipping his first cup of coffee while Alex cooked breakfast. He sat his coffee cup down, pushed up from the table to grab plates and silverware, and then he sat back down, took another sip of coffee and then shook his head as if in disbelief. He said, "Somebody's killing off the queens. I suspected it earlier, but now I'm pretty sure. Somebody's killing them off one by one, all the queens that were there in the seventies. It's methodical. All of 'em, all of 'em. All the queens that were in the riot. They didn't identify the earlier victims. But if they did, I bet you'd see. It was Anita and Bonnie and Liza Jane. Was that all? They all performed at Barney's. They were the ones that started the riot, the ones that are in that picture. All victims. God! Maybe even Miss Tammy who they ran off long before the riot. That means I'm probably on the list too, except maybe not because few people knew me. I kept my male and female identities strictly separate."

Repeating himself as if muttering some kind of chant, he said, "One by one they're killing them off. All the queens. They got a list, or it's someone who was somehow involved."

Breakfast was ready. She scooped fried eggs and link sausage out of the pan and put them on plates and brought them to the table. Buttered two slices of toast and got out the orange marmalade, his favorite. Jim's theory—that's all it was, just a theory, it had to be—didn't make sense to her. If what Harry had written was true, two transsexual women and one cross dresser had been killed. Plus, he speculated there was a possible link to a couple of earlier accidental deaths. She said, "I know Harry Drews seldom gets anything right, but it seems like he may be right that there's no pattern to these murders and no connection between them and those earlier deaths."

"Oh there's a pattern all right. But nobody's seen it yet."

She argued, "The methods were not the same, and why would he wait so long between killings? Didn't the first ones come close together? And then there were none for a while, and then this one."

"There could be any number of reasons. Maybe the killer got sick. Maybe he was out of the state for a while and then moved back. Maybe he got arrested for something else and spent time in jail."

Alex said, "I'm not sure if I have this right or not, but the two back in the fall were transgender and then this one was a cross dresser. From what you told me about the difference between drag queens and transsexuals it doesn't make sense that a killer would target both. You said the performers at Barney's in 1970 were all gay men, not transsexuals, so the early victims were probably not performers at Barney's."

"Not unless they were trannies but just didn't know it yet."

Jim then rattled off details so exact that Alex was really surprised—flabbergasted to realize he had paid such close attention. The first murder victim, he reminded her, was reported on Halloween day '08. She was a pre-operative male-to-female with both male and female sexual characteristics. She was found in the river, either beaten or drowned. She had been taking hormones, had well developed female breasts and very little body hair, but still had a penis. The next one, also a pre-op male to female, was shot in the head. So, a different method of killing. She was found just a couple of weeks after the first one. Then there was Raymond three months later, a former drag queen but not transsexual. As for the two so-called accident victims; one drove off the road near Mt. St. Helens and the other fell into a ravine in the Olympics—no apparent connection except that they were both cross dressers.

"Doesn't that prove my point?" Alex said. "They weren't all transgender. Plus, some of them were shot and one was beaten to death. If they were all killed by the same guy, wouldn't the methods be the same?"

"Maybe, but..."

"And the others probably weren't murdered at all. Where's the pattern?"

"The connection that the police haven't figured out yet is that they all performed at the same club thirty years ago," Jim insisted. But he admitted that was just a gut feeling. He didn't have any proof of that. Only one of them had been identified.

With a mouth full of scrambled eggs she mumbled, "All right, Mister Know-it-all, maybe you ought to go to the police and tell them what you know."

He said, "I can't go to the cops."

"Why not?"

"Because it would be like reporting a UFO sighting. Nobody would believe me. They wouldn't investigate. Plus, that nut Harry Drews might get ahold of it and write something about it and use my name, and then the killer would come after me."

Best Friends – Jim and Alex's blog

How I became a polyamorous libertine
by Jim Bright

They called me a pussy hound, a cocksman, a lady killer. Blame it on my old man, the uptight, repressive, holier-than-thou son of a bitch. The more he preached about the sins of the flesh, the more enticing those sins became. He told me that if I had sex before marriage I would go to hell. But that wasn't the half of it. He said all I had to do was think about it. "Anyone who looks on a woman with lust has in his heart already committed adultery. It says that right there in the Bible."

Ah yes, the Jimmy Carter sin. I figured I was doomed anyway, so what the hell. I made chasing tail my *numero uno* passion. And half a century later Alex started pestering me to tell her all about it. "Why?" I asked (teasing, of course), "are you jealous cuz you didn't get any of that action way back when? You got me now, and you're the only one."

Yes sir, I'm a one-woman man now.

I didn't so much chase after girls as they chased after me. I couldn't help it that I was good looking. From an attractive mother and a rather plain looking old man I inherited looks that drove girls wild. It was a blessing and a curse. And here's the thing. I discovered that I liked it, and it didn't matter if the girl was fat or skinny or young or old. I became a totally indiscriminate lover. I loved them all, and I have to confess that it was the infirmities of age and that alone that made me settle down to a single partner, and believe you me, my eyes still wander even if my body can't.

Comments:
Alex said: I didn't start this blog so you could brag about your sexual exploits. And guess what, folks. He ain't that good.
Aubrey Smithfield said: If you were truly poly you wouldn't be a one woman man, you wouldn't even be a woman only man or a human only man. Let's strike out for true sexual freedom.

Churchlady said: What is Aubrey Smithfield talking about?
Sexylady said: The so-called infirmities of age shouldn't lay you low, not if you have any imagination. Give me your phone number if you want to find out what I'm talking about.

Chapter 10

Ophelia Sullivan was his first. It was 1954. He was twelve years old, awfully young to get started down the path of sin and debauchery. She was fourteen. They did it down by Miller Creek in that stretch of woods they called the jungle, a wonderland of trees so tall they almost obliterated the sky. They did it on an old quilt tossed over a bed of moss. He wondered who had put that quilt there and why, and had decided it must have been Ophelia and for exactly the purpose they had put it to. Ophelia was all about sex. She lived for it. It was all she ever thought about, or so it seemed to Jim and Buster and the other boys. You could tell it from the things she said, the looks she flashed at the guys, the sultry expressions, the way she tossed her hair, the surreptitious ways her hand would graze a thigh, a chest, an ass. She did it with Buster and Carney and the Barnes brothers and who knows who else. She just oozed sex. Jim never knew girls could be like that. At least not real girls. The women in the Bible were all Jezebels and wanton whores, from Eve right on down the line—with the one exception of the Virgin Mary, of course. But in the real world wives acquiesced to their husbands' lust as was their duty and without pleasure, and any woman who engaged in sex outside the bonds of marriage was a horrible sinner doomed to eternal hell. That was the whole of love, sex and marriage according to the preaching of Jim's father.

So he was scared shitless of Ophelia Sullivan and, at the same time, helplessly drawn to her. She wasn't bad looking, but she was pretty coarse. Rough skin, stained teeth and sometimes bad breath. She was stocky built with big breasts and wide hips, thick wrists and biceps more muscular than some of the boys. They did it in a hurry, sweating and panting, completely dressed with britches pulled down, and without kissing or foreplay. She was the aggressor; Jim let it happen, not that he was exactly what you'd call reluctant, but he didn't pursue her either, and truth be told his father's exhortations against anything sexual must have been clanging like a fire bell in his mind. He was terrified. He had only the vaguest idea of how to go about it. Couldn't even get it in at first until she reached down and guided it. And then the feeling that first time. It was like when the spirit took hold in a tent meeting. How could anything that felt so good possibly be sinful? They did it two or three times that summer, but never again. He never knew why they quit.

He didn't get laid again for four years, although he came awfully close many, many times. Mary Elizabeth was the next one. They were sweet sixteen. She seduced him. A pattern was beginning to emerge, not so much playing hard to get as being a babe in the woods grateful to be guided in the art of love. If he had planned a strategy for getting laid, he couldn't have found a better one. Mary Elizabeth asked him to help her with a history assignment. She invited him to her house when her parents were out. His mother had warned him about that. She said that even if it was completely innocent, it could ruin the girl's reputation. So he tried to beg off, but Mary Elizabeth insisted.

"Would you like to kiss me?" she asked. They were seated together on her couch with their books spread out on their laps. He kissed her cheek. "Not like that," she said, "On the lips."

It escalated from there, not all at once but step by step over a period of time, every Wednesday and Friday afternoon until they finally ended up in her bed after about six weeks. They were both disappointed, and they didn't do it again. She made an A in history, by the way, and he took that as a real tribute to his tutoring ability because, as he later told Alex, she was dumb as a fence post.

It was the year after that when Lara Cockburn made love to Jim under a tree behind Temple Beth Israel during Anna Shemper's seventeenth birthday party. Anna came next, and then Betty Black, and it almost happened with Kimzey Williams and Cheryl Rogers, but they both got a sudden case of good sense. He never told Alex about Betty or Kimzey or Cheryl.

All of his adolescent sexual adventures were rushed, blind groping with clothes on, afraid to say anything or make the slightest noise, only once in an actual bed, and only once completely naked (not the time in bed with Mary Elizabeth) and never particularly romantic except the one time when Lara seduced him in the water while skinny dipping in Serene Lake after dark on a summer night standing chest deep in water near the end of the Cockburn's boat dock. That was the one and only completely naked time. Lara's parents were supposedly keeping an eye on them while grilling hamburgers on the patio about fifty yards away, but they knew her parents could barely see them. Lara slipped her bathing suit off and dared him to do the same. They draped their suits over pilings on the dock within easy reach. All her folks would have been able to see if they looked their way would be two heads bobbing on the surface like a pair of otters.

When Mrs. Cockburn shouted, "Come on, kids. The burgers are ready" Lara shouted back, "We're coming," and they were.

There was one girl he petted with a lot but didn't have sex with until many years later. She was the girl he ended up marrying, Nancy Hendrix. She lived next door on the corner of Woodlawn and 18th, where there had been a vacant lot for about four years after the Brights moved into the neighborhood. All that time Woodlawn had remained unpaved and unfinished, and then all of a sudden the developers got to work, and within a few months the road was extended from 18th to Rebel Road and paved, and new houses were built, and they said they were going to put in sidewalks but they never did. Carney and Buster and the Barnes brothers and Nancy moved into the new houses. A rock and roll cacophony permeated the area because of all the kids, all the open windows in the summertime, radios blasting KNEW-AM and record players blaring all the latest hits. Everybody got a laugh out of the time a neighbor a block away on 18th called Buster and asked him if he was the one playing "Chantilly Lace." When Buster confessed and said he'd turn the volume down the caller said, "No, no. I just want to know if you got any other Big Bopper records."

The Sullivan girls had dances on their patio on summer evenings, and dozens of neighbors and school mates showed up. While everyone else was dancing, Ophelia would sneak off down by Miller Creek with Buster or Carney or the older Barnes boy, but they grew tired of Ophelia when Jimi Sue moved into the new green house on the corner next door to Jim. Jimi Sue was a grown woman, a sexy, slatternly, semi sophisticated woman, more tempting even than the legendary Melody Sauer. And who doesn't remember her? *We all love Melody Sauer, she's a lovely spring flower...*

Jimi Sue was the Hendrix's live-in housekeeper, one more thing about the Hendrix family that made them seem exotic. Nobody else had a live-in housekeeper, not in their neighborhood, especially not one that looked like Jimi Sue. She was like a big sister to Nancy, who was an only child, and she was a real temptress—Jimi Sue, not Nancy. The neighborhood boys were absolute putty in her hands. She was a lot younger than Nancy's father and not a whole heck of a lot older than Nancy. Naturally everyone assumed she was sleeping with Nancy's father. He was about forty-five. She was probably in her early thirties. The father was hardly ever at home and was never very friendly when he was. He went by the nickname Greasy. He was a mechanic. He was in the National Guard, too. That's one of the reasons he was gone a lot. The housekeeper was a substitute mother to Nancy, whose real mother lived with her new husband in Portland, something else the neighborhood kids thought was an exotic arrangement because, one, they didn't know many families with separated parents—it was the 1950s after all—and, two, when normal families did break up, which was rare, the mothers got custody of the kids. Can you believe it? Right there in the heart of Wetside, Washington, teenage sluts and grownup sluts and people running around naked and climbing in and out of bedroom windows and not one but two men who kept concubines.

Nancy was fifteen when Jim was seventeen, and right off the bat he pegged her as a royal pain in the ass. She was smitten with him at first sight. She slipped love notes under the screen of his bedroom window where they would fall onto his pillow. Imagine finding mushy love notes on your pillow. She slipped notes into his locker at school or in the books left on the side table on the patio. At first the notes were gushy and simple and horribly pretentious with some of the worst metaphors ever penned by man or woman. *My heart beats for you. I swim in the pool of desire for you.* She read a lot of steamy romance novels. She signed the notes *Your Secret Admirer* or *Your Secret Love.* She copied entire love scenes out of books in florid handwriting on scented and pastel-colored paper, substituting their names for the lover's, and then she left the pages where he would be sure to see them. She was not very subtle.

Concrete slab patios in their back yards were separated by two feet of flower beds. On Jim's side were lush flowering plants that his mother tended religiously; on the Hendrix side mostly bare dirt and scraggly plants with few flowers. During the summer Jim often lounged on a plastic chair on his patio with a book and his favorite soft drink and music blasting on the little portable record player that he plugged in with an extension cord snaked through the bedroom window.

The record player was one of those that looked like a suitcase when it was closed, the chair was one of those with the plastic webbing that stuck to your thighs, and his favorite drink was an RC Cola.

Nancy liked to sunbathe on a blow-up air mattress on her patio, her ample flesh on display in a succession of bathing suits, a yellow one and a pink one and a blue one with white flowers and another with swirling patterns of what looked to be seaweeds in green and blue. Her thighs and belly were soft and brown, her shoulders round and unevenly tanned. She would strike provocative poses and furtively glance his way to see if he noticed. She didn't seem to realize, or care, that she was fat. Sometimes she would lie on her stomach and reach behind her back to unsnap her top and slip it off and then every once in a while kind of wriggle around and rise up on her elbows, resting her chin on her crossed arms so that her balloon breasts were almost but never completely exposed. She must have practiced that pose. She would slather her front and arms and legs with suntan lotion while watching Jim watch her. She smiled wickedly his way and called over, "I can't reach my back. Won't you please come over and rub it in for me?"

Reading *Peyton Place* and already aroused by thoughts of Selena Cross, he put the book down and unwound himself from his chair and slowly sauntered over to where Nancy lay on her belly with the top part of her suit cast aside like a semaphore. Her skin was warm and slick to the touch. The lotion smelled sweet and felt slippery. He rubbed up and down across her shoulders and down below the small of her back to where her muscles dimpled at the waist band, and around in a circular motion, and as his hands moved to her sides she lifted up slightly, and he was suddenly cupping her weighty breasts. It was almost like they just jumped into his hands. *Whoopsy daisy, what's this?* He just held them for a long time as if shocked to find them in his grip and not knowing what to do with them. At long last he began to move his fingers a little to explore the rubbery firmness of her nipples. She sighed deeply but did not move. He wasn't sure if he wanted it to go any further or not, but that was never his decision anyway. He always let the girls take the lead. That was his way. He figured some kissing would come next, but he was hesitant to kiss her. Her lips looked kind of wet and floppy. He was afraid it might be too slobbery. But holding her boobs was nice. He wished she would turn over so he could get a good look at them, but she never did. Her rule seemed to be touch but don't look.

For a good ten minutes he held her breasts, and then she said, "That's enough," and reached for her top and squirmed into it, still without turning over, still managing—with skills worthy of a magician—to prevent complete exposure. She asked him to please not tell anyone she had let him touch her. When he promised she said, rather indifferently, "Thank you. Now snap me up, please."

It became a routine they repeated as a silent ritual once or twice a week throughout the summer. He grew to love the smell of Copper Tone lotion. While rubbing her back and shoulders and breasts he thought of Jimi Sue. She was the one he really wanted, and he suspected Nancy knew it. Just like Nancy, Jimi Sue gave every imaginable hint that she yearned for him. She would sometimes invite him in for cookies and a soda, and she would often touch his hand or put a hand on his shoulder—a motherly touch, he thought, but he wasn't sure. Sometimes her touch seemed much more provocative. He thought of her as a more experienced and much subtler version of Ophelia Sullivan.

Sometimes she joined Nancy sunbathing on the patio, and sometimes she would wash her car in her driveway while wearing a two-piece swimsuit and cast big eyes Jim's way. Like Nancy, she sent out signals and then held back. Pseudo-mother and pseudo-daughter playing him like a fish on a line.

•

Nancy was in summer school and Greasy was off at National Guard camp. It was the summer before Jim's senior year. Jimi Sue said, "Dance with me." They had been seated on her living room couch, a plate of cookies on the coffee table and an iced soda in a sweating glass. She stood up and kicked off her yellow sandals and began to dance alone, holding out her arms in invitation.

He said, "I'm not too good at dancing."

"Just let yourself sway with the music."

Hesitantly he pushed himself up and went to her, following the signal of her fingers and her undulating hips, which were beckoning to him like a hula dancer as she backed away in rhythm. She took one of his hands and placed it on her waist and guided his other hand to the middle of her back. She wrapped her arms around him and pulled his body tightly against hers, and pressed her cheek to his chest. Slow dancing, barely moving, bodies grinding together.

He had a boner and a half, and there was no way she could have not felt it. She pressed her groin even harder against him. It was sex through their clothes to the beat of the music. It was hot, scary, intoxicating and infuriating. He was angry at her for playing with him as if he were a kitten and she was the person dangling a play-pretty on a string, and like that kitty he could not stop leaping for the dangling toy.

They did it again a few days later, and then a week after that. As with Nancy, the sex play became a routine. Through July and August and then tapering off but not stopping altogether after school started in September. It was as if he had been captured and put in a cage by Nancy and Jimi Sue and every once in a while let out to play. But by their rules only. Why couldn't he be a man and tell them either they take it all the way or they quit? Were they teasing him? Did they get together and giggle about it when he wasn't there? They kept giving him a walk to first base but never any farther. He thought maybe first base for him was a home run for them. He thought Nancy wanted to go all the way home but was afraid. After

162

all, she was still young and a virgin. As for Jimi Sue, he figured he was an appetizer for her before whichever main course was to come later.

Keeping it up wasn't easy. He was kind of glad when football season started with the daily practice that took him away from them. After football season there was the school play (he was Peter in *Peter Pan*), followed by another summer vacation and right back into his fur-lined cage.

Jimi Sue had read all the dirty novels with the burning sex scenes that he had only heard about. Like *Tropic of Cancer* and *Lady Chatterley's Lover*. She sometimes read passages to him (another way of teasing) and sometimes loaned him books. If his daddy had found them he would have destroyed them and prayed over Jim and used his transgression as a basis for his next sermon, calling Jim his prodigal son or some such.

Jim was also fascinated with Jimi Sue's clothes and her jewelry. He loved women's things, the feel of fabric, the smell, the sparkle of jewelry. At that point in his life he had no premonition of what direction that might take him. He had sort of thought about working in the fashion industry in some manner, maybe as a designer or as the guy that took pictures at fashion shows. How hard could that be? He inherited his fascination with fashion from his mother. It was a life she dreamed of but knew she could never have. More than once she said, "I could have been a model if I hadn't married your father," and Jim thought but didn't say, "You can always divorce him." She was right. She could have been a model. She had the looks for it, tall with high cheekbones, a swan's neck and the svelte body, although not so svelte as it appeared in pictures from before Jim was born. She talked about what it might be like walking down the runway. She brought home fashion magazines, and she'd point out dresses and hats and ask, "What about this one? What about that? Can you picture me in one of these? Wouldn't I look marvelous?"

Jim mentioned to his mother that he might want to study fashion design. She said, "Oh, I think you'd make a great designer. You're already quite the artist."

163

That was only partially true. He liked to draw, but he was only moderately good at it. His mother said he could get better with practice. She said the world of fashion was not only glamorous, but there was lots of money to be made. "Gobs of money," she said, "and making money is not necessarily evil, despite what your father says."

Her fascination with fashion was of the window-shopping variety. Her personal wardrobe was meager and consisted of "sensible" clothes the old man would approve of. Nothing flashy, no bright colors, and nothing that accentuated her figure. Jimi Sue, on the other hand, had sexual parts to spare and knew how to accentuate them. She was a walking Sears and Roebuck catalog. She was mad for clothing, and her taste in fashion was bolder but not so discerning as Mrs. Bright's (That was Jim's assessment; truthfully, Jimi Sue's taste was trashy.) Jimi Sue did much more than window shop through catalogues. She wheedled Greasy Hendrix into buying her dresses and blouses and coats that hung in perfect order by color and style in her giant walk-in closet, and shoes that she carefully arranged with heels next to heels, flats next to flats, boots and slippers all grouped by style. And she had wigs, half a dozen wigs lined up on Styrofoam heads sans features along the length of a shelf like fashionista soldiers standing for inspection—red, two shades of auburn and three blondes.

She had a dress with a big bow over the breast and a swing style skirt, pink with a delicate flower pattern; a luncheon dress, also with swing skirt, blue with a broad white lace band around a deep cut square collar; a pleated red poodle skirt that she wore with a whole bunch of stiff petticoats that fanned outward when she sat down; and for everyday wear she had a dozen or so pedal pushers with mix-or-match blouses, and she wore faux pearl necklaces, rhinestone brooches, jeweled bracelets, and wild rose and pansy earrings. Looking back, it's a wonder that anyone could make that stuff look sexy. She would have really been something if today's fashions had been around then.

•

"What's that called?" Jim asked her, pointing to a necklace.

164

"It's just costume jewelry. Why do you ask?"

"I don't know. What about the skirt, is that a Dior? "

"What do you know from Dior? It's just a skirt. Why are you so interested?"

"No reason," he demurred.

"There's a reason for everything. What is it? Do you like to wear women's clothing? Are you maybe a little girly guy?"

"Gosh, no," he said. "That's crazy." As if unconscious of what his hands were doing, he reached for a silk blouse and rubbed the material between his fingers as he told her how he talked with his mother about fashion all the time and how he thought he might want to be a fashion designer when he grew up. "But don't tell anyone I said that. The boys around here would think that was some kind of sissy thing to do."

She gently took the silk blouse away from him and laid it on her bedspread. She said, "The boys around here are about as sophisticated as farm animals. Don't pay them no never mind. I think it would be wonderful if you became a fashion designer. Designers make oodles of money and women love them."

"That's what Mama said, but Bubba Austin said they're all queers."

"You didn't tell Bubba, did you, about wanting to be a designer?"

"Heck no. It just came up. Mama was watching TV and we were in the room and something about fashion was on."

"Well don't you ever listen to that idiot."

From her closet she took a long black skirt that matched the silk blouse and spread it on the bed next to the blouse. "Would you like to see what these look like on?"

"Oh yes, I'd love to."

Without another word she wriggled out of her pink pedal pushers, completely blasé about stepping out of her pants in front of him. He watched her bend forward and thrust her hips side to side as she pushed the pants down below her calves and stepped out of them. Then she pulled off her blouse. Standing in front of him in her pink silk panties and matching lace bra, she asked, "Do you like my little pink undies?"

Speechless, breathless, he silently nodded his head. He didn't know if it was her panties and bra or what they barely concealed that had him in a sweat. Was it the clothing or the sexual provocation? It was both, but he couldn't comprehend that at the time. She stepped into the skirt and pulled the silk blouse over her head, and then took a turn in her bedroom as if on a runway, and then after asking if he'd like to see more—to which he answered with more speechless head nods—she slipped into a succession of skirts and blouses and showed off her various wigs. You could have wiped him off the floor with a sponge.

"I always wear this one with the poodle skirt," she said as she pulled her short hair up in back and put on one of the blonde wigs. He watched wide-eyed sitting on the edge of her bed, his hands clasped together between his legs.

She sat down on the bench in front of her dresser and pulled a Marlboro out of a pack and lit it with an ornate lighter. She inhaled deeply and blew a perfect smoke ring. "I wonder what you'd look like in one of these," she asked. "Want to try something on?"

For a long time he didn't answer. He looked down at the floor. She took his chin in her hand and lifted, forcing him to look at her face. "Don't look away from me. I know you want to try it."

"N-no I d-don't. I told you I didn't want to do that."

How could she possibly know? It was like she had sneaked inside his brain.

"I bet you'd make a really cute girl."

"Aw, don't be silly."

He held out one hand to see if it shook as much as he was afraid it would and was relieved to observe that it was fairly steady. She had uncannily zeroed in on the thing he had never even allowed himself to admit: that he didn't really want to design women's clothing so much as he wanted to *wear* women's clothing. He didn't know why, but he had thought about it often, even while denying to himself that such thoughts ever crossed his mind. How many times had he imagined the feel of lace and silk and quickly pushed the

166

thought away? How many times had self-images in women's clothes come to mind unbidden, looking in his mind's eye at his reflection in his mother's big mirror and seeing a woman's face stare back, with a dress and wig and makeup. Did his obsession with women's clothing mean he was queer or aberrant in some way? He'd heard about some man in Sweden who had an operation to turn himself into a woman. He'd heard about transvestites and female impersonators. Were those two words for the same thing or something different? Was it just a game some men played, or was it some kind of horrible sickness? How does a boy find out about things like that? There were no books on the subject in the Wetside library. Nobody talked about such things, and he didn't dare ask. He knew there were womanly men in the world and they were objects of the worst kind of scorn. He didn't think he was one of them. He knew a couple of boys who were most likely gay, but they didn't wear dresses or prance around in wigs and lipstick. He was pretty sure he wasn't gay either, although he didn't think, even way back then, that he would have been ashamed of it if he was.

He stammered, "I… I'm not going to dress up like a girl."

"Aw come on. It'll be fun. And no one need ever know."

She pulled from her closet a soft white dress that was designed to cling to the hips and fall straight to mid calf. "Here," she said, "Just slip into this one. Come on, do it for me. No one's going to know."

He demurred, but she was insistent. Finally he said, "OK, but I have to take my pants off."

"Of course, sweetie."

"But you're…"

"I'll turn around."

Hastily he stepped out of his pants and jerked his shirt off. He couldn't decide whether to take his briefs off or not but chose to play it cautious and leave them on. He ever so carefully stepped into the dress and pulled it up. It buttoned up the front. It wouldn't close over his stomach. "It's too small," he said.

She turned around and looked. She said, "You're adorable."

"No I'm not. I must look ridiculous." He quickly wriggled out of the dress, this time not caring if she saw him in his underwear, and got back into his own clothes and concocted a lame excuse to go home.

That was his first step down the road to fame if not fortune as the seductive Amanda Darling. It was a long and winding road. First he had to try on women's clothes many more times, starting with some things of his mother's when she was out of the house. Her stuff fit much better than Jimi Sue's. Her panties—nylon he supposed they were—felt so much more sensual than his old cotton Jockeys. He snitched a pair and then later bought some and kept them in his dresser drawer underneath the *Playboy* and *Nugget*, and wore them almost every day, but never at school because of gym. And then Jimi Sue went out and spent money (Greasy's money, naturally) on clothes in his size that she kept in her closet for him, and she taught him how to apply lipstick and mascara and eye liner; and then one day she stuck her head out her bedroom window holding her curtain closed under her chin, which made him think (hope) she was naked behind the curtain, and she called him to come over saying she had a special surprise for him. *She is! She's absolutely all the way naked and she's going to be lying in bed waiting for me.*

He rushed over and entered the door to her kitchen without knocking and started down the hall, and she called from the living room, "No, in here."

He turned around. He saw that she was standing in the living room decked out in black pants and a white shirt, her already short hair brushed back behind her ears and topped with a man's black hat. "I thought we could swap," she said. "I could be the man and you could be the woman. You can call me Jim, and I can call you... what? What name would you like?"

Amanda was the first name to come to mind. Amanda had been his first girl friend back in Louisiana in third grade. He got dressed in a skirt and blouse, and she said, "Amanda, darling. Let's dance."

•

It was bound to happen. Greasy Hendrix came home unexpected one day and caught Jimi Sue in bed with another man. It was Carney. They were going at it so hot and heavy they didn't hear Greasy slam the kitchen door and stomp down the hall to the bedroom. The way Carney told it, he was on his back and she was astraddle shouting, "Ride 'em cowboy!" He made that part up.

Greasy slammed open the bedroom door so hard that the doorknob smashed through the wallboard. He didn't make that part up. Jimi Sue jerked her head around at the sound, and Carney pushed her off and rolled off the bed, scrambling across her to grab his clothes while Jimi Sue clutched the sheets to her naked body. Greasy lowered one shoulder and blocked Carney to the side, which he never could have done if Carney hadn't been off balance, because Carney was a lot bigger and stronger, and he rushed past him and jerked open the closet door and grabbed the unloaded double barrel shotgun he kept in there, all with agility and strength you'd never suspect from such a scrawny man. He spun around, lifted the gun and placed the butt to his shoulder and pointed the two big barrels at Carney, but Carney's reaction was lightning fast. Instead of trying to duck for cover he stepped forward, grabbed the shotgun by the barrel, jerked it out of Greasy's hands, slammed Greasy in the belly with the stock and tossed the gun to the floor. The gun went skidding across the floor and right back into the open closet, and Greasy crumpled where he stood, doubled up and clutching his belly. Carney jumped over him and ran out the door and out of the house, still naked as the day he was born.

It was three o'clock on a Saturday afternoon in August. Jim and Alex were next door playing badminton in Jim's back yard. They saw Carney streak past with his big bare body shining in the sunlight, and they quickly threw their racquets to the ground and ran around the house to see where he was going. Alex had never before seen a completely naked man, especially not one so huge, with a big white belly and something like a little worm flopping between his legs. It was the briefest of glances because when Carney saw her he

169

covered his privates with the clothing he'd been clutching in his hands.

Leslie Grant and his younger girl cousins were jumping rope in the middle of Woodlawn, with the girls on either end of the rope and Leslie jumping. Carney almost ran into Leslie, tripped on the rope, fell to the pavement, rolled over, scampered to his feet, and kept running home. Leslie shouted some kind of expletive. Carney ran right by Jim's mother, who had been digging in the flowerbed in the front yard and had stopped to chat with the new city councilman who had recently moved in next door in the house that separated them from Carney. They stood speechless as their eyes followed the two-hundred and forty-pound man streaking past while clutching a bundle of clothes to his crotch. Jim and Alex almost ran into Jim's mother and the neighbor when they streaked around the corner of the house. The councilman said, "Holy shit!" Mrs. Bright just laughed.

•

Greasy Hendrix fired Jimi Sue and kicked her out of his house. Nobody in the neighborhood knew where she went. Nancy went to live with her mother, and in the fall Greasy sold the house to Greg and Nellie Jones, who had nine children ranging in age from three to seventeen. Quite a crowd for a three bedroom 1,700-square-foot house. Within a year or two all of the kids in the neighborhood went off to college or moved away. Jim went to City U. So did Alex and a few of their friends, but not many. Alex lived at home with her folks, but Jim moved in with Uncle Brad. Reggie Sheffield went to Portland State on a football scholarship. Bubba went to work in the mattress factory down in Rock Creek. Jim never saw him again until many years later, even though he was living in Rock Creek then and has been there ever since. Rolly came back home after graduating the military academy and got a job at Red's Dairy Bar and then later at the radio station.

Alex and Jim remained friends during their first year in collage, but drifted apart soon after. Jim studied marketing, but his true love was theater. He'd been in a couple of musicals in high school and was in three more in college. He also took a class in fashion design but barely passed it. Drawing was not his strong suit, although he did eventually develop enough drawing skill to create halfway decent ads. Alex got involved in theater, too, behind the curtain. She was mostly a gopher.

Halloween night of their sophomore year at City U, Kimzey Williams flipped out once again. This time in the Jones's back yard. In the two months the Jones family had lived in Nancy's old house on the corner their kids had done significant damage. They had drawn on the walls with indelible markers, broken windows and ripped out screens. Their yard was a minefield of scattered and broken toys. After trick or treating Kyle and Doyle, the Jones twins, were in bed but not asleep in the room that had once been Nancy's. Buzzing excitedly about what they'd seen on their adventures around the neighborhood knocking on doors, how the guy named Carney came to the door in a Frankenstein costume and scared them half to death and how Mrs. Martin gave them candied apples like you get at the fair. It was a warm night, and their bedroom window was open despite the missing screen. "Looka yonder," Doyle said, "It's a lady ghost and she's jaybird naked." —As we're beginning to discover, nakedness ran rampant in the neighborhood and most of the excitement seemed to involved bedroom windows.

Kyle pulled his head out from underneath the covers, and both boys propped elbows on the window sill and looked out at the ghostly pale figure of a woman standing by Rolly Simpson's bedroom window. It was Kay Kay, her pale hair and skin casting off a dull milky sheen under a harvest moon. She was clawing at Rolly's window. "Let me in," she pleaded in a scratchy whisper, "I've got to talk to you."

"I can't," Rolly hissed through his screen. "You've got to go home. If you get caught out like this you'll be thrown in jail."

"Well if you let me in I won't get caught." A thread of good sense beneath her insanity.

"I can't," Rolly's voice a strained whisper. "You know that. My mama would kill me and you both if she found you up in here without any clothes on."

"If you don't let me in I'll do something crazy."

171

"Crazier than running around naked in the middle of the night? You've got to go home, honey. Please."

They had been at Red Rogers' Halloween party. It was the first time they had ever been to one of his parties. Most of the people were in costume. Kay Kay was dressed as a vampire; Rolly was not in costume. Bubba Austin was there, and Buster James. Otherwise no one Rolly and Kimzey knew. The rest looked to be college students or adults closer to Red's age. There were two young women wearing Cat Woman outfits who stayed in the kitchen the whole time talking to each other. The rest were men who chatted in small groups. It seemed to Rolly and Kimzey that each little two- or three-person satellite was absolutely isolated as if no one knew anyone outside their clique, and none of them made any effort to welcome Rolly and Kay Kay.

Rolly was unusually withdrawn. They felt out of place and left early. Rolly drove her home, parked in front of her house and said, "We've got to talk, honey."

"I don't like the sound of this. What is it?"

"It's you, honey. I'm worried about you. I think you need to see a doctor."

"A doctor?"

"A psychiatrist."

"You think I'm crazy?"

"I think you need help."

She flung open the car door and stepped out on the sidewalk. Standing with the door open she said, "Well I ain't gonna. There's nothing wrong with me."

"But there is, honey, and you know it. We've talked about it before. You have spells when you don't know who you are. You hear voices. You've told me that. Maybe you can live with it, but I can't. I can't take it any more."

"No, no, no. I didn't mean it when I said I hear voices. I was kidding you."

"No you weren't. And sometimes you act like you're a different person altogether. You don't even recognize your own name. Sometimes you say you love me and sometimes you say you hate me, and sometimes you don't even know who I am."

"That was before. I'm better now."

"No you're not. You're getting worse, not better. If you don't get help, I can't keep seeing you."

Rolly was desperate. He loved her, but he couldn't take her craziness.

Incredulous, she said, "You're breaking up with me?"

"If you refuse to see a doctor, yes. I have to. I can't put up with your moods any more."

They argued. She pleaded. She said, "Please, please, don't break up with me. I can't live without you." She said, "I'll kill myself. I'll cut my wrist. I'll climb up to the top of the Highway 99 bridge and jump off." (The highway 99 bridge was notorious for suicide jumps, but nobody had actually succeeded in killing themselves by leaping off because it was not a high bridge, and the water below, while dangerously frigid, was not swift running, and it was possible for a halfway competent swimmer to reach shore before hypothermia could set in.) Kimzey cried, she screamed, she beat frantically on the roof of his car, she collapsed into a blob of tears, and he helped her out of the car and walked her up to her porch and pushed on the door, but it was locked, so he rang the bell and stood there holding her until her grandmother came and opened the door, and together they walked Kimzey into the house and sat her on the couch. She was shivering even though it was not a cold night. Her grandmother wrapped a blanket around her.

"Thank you for bringing her home."

"I... I hope she'll be..."

"She'll be all right. You go on home now."

Rolly walked to his car and drove home. An hour and a half later crazy naked Kay Kay was scratching at his window begging to be let in, her Halloween makeup smeared across her cheeks. Rolly refused to let her in and begged her to go home. Finally giving up, she turned and walked across his yard and through the gate to the Jones house.

Kyle and Doyle thought she was some kind of ghostly apparition. But they were brave boys, brave and foolhardy. Screaming for their parents to come quick, they hopped out of bed and rushed outside to do battle with the monster. They were eight years old. They rushed at her like a two-person lynch mob with loud yells and wielding badminton racquets as weapons. Their mother, seeing the naked girl in the yard, ran back into her bedroom to grab something to wrap her in. Kay Kay started screaming about killer midgets, Kyle and Doyle apparently triggering a flashback to the vision she had at the gravel pit. She ran around the house with the boys in hot pursuit. Finally their mother caught up and slung a sheet around her and held her while she violently shook. Meanwhile, Mr. Jones called 911 and they sent a police car. When the police arrived they started to haul Kimzey off to jail, but Rolly and his mother came out and talked them into calling her grandmother, who came to take her home. The next day Kay Kay was admitted to the state insane asylum in Steilacoom.

Jim was still living with his parents at the time, so he was there to witness the excitement Halloween night. He had also been to a Halloween party earlier. He had just come home and crawled in the bed when he heard the commotion. He looked out but couldn't see anything but the lights flashing on the cop car. It was Rolly who told him about it later. It was shortly after that when he moved in with Uncle Brad. By then his dad and Brad were no longer on speaking terms. Coming out as gay had destroyed what little brotherly love remained between them. Mr. Bright hit the roof. He said, "I knew it. I knew it all along. I prayed it wasn't so, but I knew it."

He told the whole damn congregation in church the next Sunday and asked them to pray him straight. Uncle Brad was there, sitting right in the middle of the second pew. He was Episcopalian by then, had long since left his brother's holy roller church, but he sometimes went for the sake of the family. He went that day specifically because he knew deep down inside that his crazed preacher brother was going to pull something like that, and he didn't want to hear about it from someone else. Maybe there was some kind of internalized self-loathing going on. Maybe he was heading full-throttle down the railroad tracks on a handcart and a train was coming and he was mesmerized by its headlight. In church he sat like a statue while his brother the preacher told everyone that he was homosexual and doomed to the fiery lake of hell. He never went back to that church again and never again spoke to his brother. Jim quit going to church too, and after he moved in with Uncle Brad his father was convinced the gay was going to rub off on him. It wasn't pretty. Jim went home to see his mother only when he knew his daddy was not at home.

Uncle Brad was terrific. He was funny and kind hearted. Jim remember that he had pet sayings that he thought were hilarious at the time but that in retrospect didn't make much sense. Things like "take it easy, Greasy, you've got a long way to slide" and "nervous as a cat with his tail in the washing machine," or his favorite threat, "You wanna eat soup through a straw?"

Friends came over and they would watch TV together or drink and tell jokes and sometimes dance with one another. His friends were mostly closeted gay men. Some of them you'd think anyone could tell, but others you'd never suspect. Among themselves they were outlandishly gay, and they laughed at gay references that would have been painful to hear if uttered by outsiders. Their favorite entertainers on television were Liberace and Paul Lind.

Jim learned to recognize the code words, the inside jokes. He was curious about gay sex, and in his naiveté asked Uncle Brad what men did together and what it felt like and if they kissed, didn't the beards scratch. "Why do you want to know," he asked. "Do you think you might be gay?"

"Oh no, I'm just curious."

"Well forget it, Bud. I'm not going to tell you about my sex life, and you can't use my K-Y either."

So he decided to find out for himself. He asked Leslie Grant about it. He wasn't very graceful or sensitive. He caught up with Leslie in the library and sat down by him and whispered, "Hi Leslie."

175

"Hi," he whispered back, tossing Jim a suspicious look that he didn't notice.

"I need to ask you something."

"All right. Go ahead." He bookmarked and closed the book he was reading.

Jim said, "Are you gay?"

"What? Are you kidding? No, of course not. Why would you ask such a question?"

He told him his uncle was gay and said he was cool with it and wanted to know what it was like. Leslie said, "Are you trying to say you want to try it?"

"Yeah, I guess so."

That changed a lot in Leslie's mind. He decided to take the chance. He confessed that he was gay but not exactly experienced, and he made Jim swear on an actual bible he'd never tell another living soul, and then he said. "If you want to experiment I'd like that. I'd like it a whole lot."

They did it in Leslie's car parked on an isolated road near East River. It was fun. Not as much fun as with a woman, but enjoyable. At leas it was not as repulsive as he feared it might be, as almost everything he'd ever heard about it indicated it should be. So, did that mean he was a latent homosexual? That there were deeply hidden urges he had been repressing? Actually, no, he decided. No soul searching, no tormented guilt and no self-loathing. He didn't know why he was so casual about it. He just was. Maybe he'd inured to guilt after discovering over the years that most of his old man's speechifying about sin was pure bull.

That, at any rate, was the nonchalance he pretended to. In truth, between dressing in women's clothes and enjoying his little experiment with Leslie, he had to wonder about it some, so he told Uncle Brad about his experiences and asked him if that meant he might be gay. He also told him about his cross dressing. "That kind of sews it up, don't ya think?" Brad said. "I'd say it's a pretty good bet you're one of us. I never knew a drag queen that wasn't gay, and if you got off on making it with another boy, that oughta tell you something."

"But I don't *feel* gay," he said. "I was just curious. I've never felt sexual attraction towards a boy."

"If you ask me, that sounds a heck of a lot like denial, especially so soon after having Leslie Grant's dick in your mouth."

"But it's not," Jim insisted. "If I was really attracted to boys I wouldn't be ashamed of it."

"Well now you're confusing the shit out of me, but I reckon it takes all kinds. Sexual orientation by definition is who you're attracted to. If you're not attracted to the same sex, then you're not gay. Lots of straight boys experiment with it. If some gorgeous woman wanted to have sex with me I just might do it and I'm sure I would enjoy it, but that wouldn't change me being who I am, a gay man."

He made it sound so simple.

He told Jim about the drag shows at Barney's and said he'd take him to see them if he wanted. Jim was barely old enough to be allowed in. The show was hilarious. The queens camped it up to high heaven, and everything was sexual. Double entendres, puns, and outlandish dirty moves. And then the star of the show came on, Miss Tammy Tucker. Jim had never seen anyone like her, except maybe Kimzey Williams when she was at her loveliest. Miss Tammy was beautiful and sweet, and she sang—not lip synching but really singing—tender country ballads.

"I could do that," he told Uncle Brad.

Brad said, "Look before you leap, Buddy. Coming out in public as a cross dresser could be dangerous. These queens, they do their show and leave the club, and before they get half a block away some big bully jumps their asses and beats the crap out of them. I'll bet you there's not a one of them that hasn't been beaten up. Some of them have also been fired from their jobs, all because they like to wear lipstick and falsies."

They went back to Barney's a few more times. After about the third or fourth time Jim said, "What if I made myself into such a perfect woman nobody would ever suspect I was a man?"

"What would be the point in that?" Brad asked. "If they wanted to see a woman perform they'd go to a club where women perform. They want to see men pretending to be women."

He couldn't argue that, but the beginning of a crazy scheme was taking root in his mind. If they wanted to see a man pretending to be women wouldn't it be even more exciting if they had no idea until just at the climax of the act?

Brad and Jim began to observe women as they had never done before. They watched how they walked, how they took a seat and how they stood up, how they tossed their hair, how they held their hands. Everything about them. They bought clothes and shoes and worked together on perfecting his makeup.

When Jim finally worked up the nerve to audition at the club he went there already in drag, and when he got the gig he always got ready at home. If anyone saw a woman leaving Brad's house and driving his car, they would just assume he had a new girlfriend. Besides, they lived way out in the country where no one would see him leave the house. The only dangerous part was that the big finale of his act was revealing that he was a man. A quick bow and quickly scoot off stage, run into the dressing room and change into boy clothes. From the back hallway there was a door into the kitchen. He'd hang out in the kitchen for a long time, and finally come out trusting that people would assume he was the cook or the dishwasher. None of Barney's customers knew the identity of the man under Amanda Darling's makeup.

•

After college he got a job doing marketing for Grant's department store. Buster James got him the job. Buster was manager of the men's department and had more or less been adopted by the owner, Sam Grant, who was grooming Buster to some day take over the business. Jim's job was putting together newspaper ads and in-store posters, dressing the mannequins and setting up window displays. Both Sam and Buster assumed that a marketing degree qualified him for the job. And as the saying goes, he faked it until he could do it. Grant's was an upscale store. Their biggest customer base was from young businessmen in town and from the fraternities and sororities on campus. Buster had started working there part-time during his sophomore year in college. He was a charmer, a snappy dresser, a brand-conscious connoisseur of all the best, from his choice of a watch or a fine leather wallet to the brand of rum he used to mix a daiquiri. He never had a lot of money, but he spent what he had judiciously. So when he told his fraternity brothers Grant's had the best men's clothing in town they bought their suits and shirts and shoes from Grant's, and since their frat was considered a trend setter on campus—frat boys being lemming-like—most of the other fraternities followed their lead, and their girlfriends in Chi Omega and Delta Gamma and Tri-Sig started shopping the women's departments at Grant's. As far as Sam Grant was concerned, that sealed the deal. Buster was his man.

They had not been friends in college. Jim was a few years younger and had not been interested in the fraternity life. They invited him to pledge Buster's frat and a couple of others, but he turned them down. It wasn't until after college that he started hanging with Buster, and then only because so many of their friends from high school and the old neighborhood had moved out of town, and they were left with nobody else. Buster introduced Jim to golf. Golf turned out to be the one sport other than basketball Jim was not very good at it. He didn't like the game enough to buy his own clubs, but always used Buster's. They also played handball at the YMCA. That was a game he could get into. He was much better at it than at golf, easily beating Buster, who was smaller and not particularly athletic. He even trounced him on the basketball court. Weekends they often ate together at Bev and Rhonda's, which was called something else back then, and after dinner they hung out at the bar where they would pick up salesgirls or sorority chicks from City U and take them back to Buster's apartment for drinks, and sometimes a joint or two.

Buster was a big fan of the blues, a carryover from his fraternity days when slumming at Nelly's BBQ had been fashionable. Nelly's featured big name blues bands the likes of Son House and John Lee Hooker and Big Joe Williams, plus some of the hottest rock and roll bands in the area, including The Kingsmen of

"Louie Louie" fame, who hailed from just up the road in Tacoma. And yes, if you're wondering, Hendrix played at Nelly's. The music and Nelly's famous barbeque sauce drew people from as far away as Seattle and Portland. Students from U-Dub and even carloads of blues aficionados from Vancouver, B.C., were known to drive down to Nelly's. It was the only club in the area that turned people away at the door.

Buster could always get a table because he had an in with the owner—not Nelly Turner, who founded the club during World War II and passed away in the '60s, but Nelly's son Ned. Buster's special connection with Ned was this: Ned was a clothes horse, but at five-foot three, he had a hard time finding clothes in his size. At Grant's they used the smallest sizes in men's clothes for the window displays, and always discounted them when the displays came down. So Buster would call Ned and let him know when something in his size was going on sale. It wasn't exactly quid pro quo, but nevertheless, there was always a table for Buster at Nelly's.

On one of the hottest nights in August the summer after Jim graduated he and Buster went to Nelly's to hear a band called Little Bill's. The place was dark and hot. No air conditioning. Ceiling fans stirred the stale and smoke-filled air. They bought bottled Budweisers at the bar and carried them to a small table near the dance floor. It was a round table on uneven legs. When Jim propped his elbows on the table it wobbled a bit and sloshed beer out. He grabbed a handful of napkins from a dispenser and wiped the spill up. The band was playing some growling blues song with fuzztone guitar and a heavy bass beat. There was only one couple on the dance floor, an interracial couple, a rare sight at the time. He was short, slightly chubby and sporting an afro. His partner was the hottest hippie chick ever to peer through a pair of granny glasses. She was slightly taller than him with a luscious figure and a river of hair that flowed down to the small of her back. She wore a deep-cut blouse adorned with turquoise necklaces and one of those peasant skirts with the tiered layers that swished like so many tropical fans when she moved. Under the red lights near the bandstand both of their faces glistened with sweat. They danced as if to different

180

music, he jiggling and bouncing and she swaying in sultry rhythm. Jim recognized the guy at once. He was Smiley Russell, the kid who had bumped into Kimzey and knocked her over the balcony rail at *Rock Around the Clock*. He was not so quick to recognize the girl, but when he did... well bless my soul, this vision of sensuality was none other than Nancy Hendrix looking hotter than he'd ever imagined. She had lost about thirty pounds. With her slimmer figure and the hippie clothing and long hair it was no wonder he didn't immediately recognize her.

She caught his eye and sent him a joyful glance of welcome while still dancing. When the song ended and they started back to their table she waved, reached out a hand to stop Smiley, and they came over to where Buster and Jim were seated. "Hi," she said. "Far out seeing you here, man. This here's my man Smiley. Remember him?"

"Oh yes, I remember Smiley," Jim said. "How's it hanging, man?" He shook hands with Smiley, whose grip was surprisingly strong for the chubby kid he remembered as being pretty shy.

"Pull up a couple of chairs and join us," Buster said. He stood up and grabbed a chair from another table, and Smiley grabbed another one, and they all squeezed in close together around a table meant for two.

The band played their raunchy blues version of Ray Charles' "Georgia on my Mind," and Jim asked Nancy to dance, wondering if Smiley would be jealous. Was he the kind of guy who'd fight over a girl? He didn't think so. Smiley had been quiet and well mannered in high school. "It's cool, man," Smiley said, and Nancy said, "Are you sure you want to dance with me? I'm not Jimi Sue, you know." She winked.

She knew he remembered her as a chubby girl with a bad complexion, and she knew that even if they had played around a bit it had always been Jimi Sue he danced with, not her. He could read her thoughts. She was thinking, *You want me now, uh huh, uh huh. Well watch out, bub, you might get more than you asked for.*

On the dance floor she wrapped both arms around him and swayed like a tree in the breeze. Smiley and Buster watched them.

As it turned out—revealed through snatches of conversation throughout the evening—Nancy and Smiley were not a couple after all. They lived in the same apartment building on Harvard, the old Luzon Building, run-down apartments built at the turn of the century that should have been condemned. It's now a parking lot that Jim and Alex can see when they look out Alex's kitchen window. Smiley and Nancy were in the same night class at City U. Smiley had married his old girlfriend Christine Rocker, and they had a six-month-old baby. He had Nancy had come out to Nelly's after class. No hanky-panky, just friends.

After the club shut down they passed around a joint in the parking lot. Nancy handed Jim a scrap of paper with her phone number. She said, "Give me a call."

He called a few days later and asked if she'd like to go out "for a movie or maybe for dinner. Whatever you'd like."

Her response floored him. She said, "You chauvinist pig."

And then she paused as if waiting to see how that set with him, and then she laughed. She said, "How come you never asked me out when we were neighbors, huh? I wasn't good enough for you then, was I?"

"Oh god, I'm sorry. I..."

"I threw myself all over you. Made a damn fool of myself. You were happy enough to play with my boobs, weren't you? Uh huh. And all the time you were laughing behind my back. But you snubbed me at school, pretended like you didn't like me. But now that I'm a fox you're more than happy to take me out."

He felt like swallowing the phone. Had she given him her number just so she could berate him? *Call me sometime, handsome, and I'll grind my feet in your face.* After ranting a bit she started laughing again, and then she said, "I'm kidding you, man. Hell, you can't help being a man. Men think with their wieners. I can dig it. But you've got to admit, I was nothing but a pair of boobs to you when I was a fatty. You were ashamed to be seen with me. You were willing to mess around all right, as much as I'd let you, but you never asked me for a date back then. In public you hardly ever even acknowledged I existed."

She was absolutely right, and he was absolutely mortified. But he could tell that despite it all she really did want to go out with him. She just had to give him a bit of come-uppance first. He shrugged.

"What can I say?"

"You could say you're sorry."

"I am. I'm really sorry. You didn't deserve that. But we were kids and I was all concerned about my reputation. Mister cool, you know? But we're not kids any more. We're grown up now. We've both changed."

He took her to dinner at Fisherman's Cove that night. They sat on the deck overlooking the river. After dinner they went to the mall just to wander around, window shop, watch all the people. First they smoked a joint in his car. The weed kicked in nicely about the time they decided to sit down by the fountain in the food court, and it was like all of a sudden everybody there was some kind of Fellini character. Snatches of conversation were like weird poems or atonal music. They fell into giggling fits. They got the munchies and practically bought out the cookie store and munched on cookies for half an hour. Brushing crumbs off his lap looked like a starry explosion. Later, when he took her home she invited him in, and she kissed him—their first kiss ever, which was really bizarre considering their almost endless foreplay over two seasons of high school.

About that kiss. It was a kiss to remember, and not in a good way. It was not the kind of first kiss a romantic soul wants to treasure for a lifetime. He shuddered involuntarily and jerked away from her. It was a shudder of sheer panic. Never had he experienced such a kiss. He had assumed that she would have been experienced in the arts of love. She certainly presented herself as a girl who had been around. But nobody who had ever kissed another person more than once or twice would have kissed the way she did. It was sheer torture. She rammed her tongue down his throat and whipped it side to side so rapidly that it felt like a hummingbird in his mouth. He said, "Jesus! Who taught you to kiss like that?"

Momentarily confusing the horror in his voice for excitement and sounding very pleased with herself, she said, "You like it like that, huh?"

He said, "No. No I don't. It was... God, it was horrible. I'm sorry. I shouldn't have said that. But it... it was not good. Oh my lord, I shouldn'ta..."

She was crestfallen, and he wanted to take it back. The phrase *bite my tongue* came to mind, but that was too close to the horror he had just experienced. He said, "I am sorry, honey. I didn't mean to hurt your feelings, but I'm afraid that wasn't pleasant at all."

"Well my last boyfriend taught me to kiss like that. He liked it that way. At least he said he did. He said men always like a little tongue."

"A little, yes, but geez, honey. You need to take it easy. It was like a bumblebee in my mouth or like a fire hose going full blast with nobody holding it."

They had been in each other's arms on her couch, but after he jerked away and shouted at her she bolted upright and paced the floor in a jerky walk for a nervous moment and then sat back down birdlike on the edge of the couch with her knees together and her head bowed. "I'm sorry," she whimpered, "I guess I don't know how to do it. I'm so embarrassed. I know you think I'm all liberated and experienced and all, but that's an act. I've never ever been kissed except by Billy Joe, and that's the way he did it."

"I don't want to hear about Billy Joe, whoever he is. Did you go all the way with him?"

"Just once, and that was the worst mistake I ever made." She pushed him away, and she tried to push the tragedy of Billy Joe out of her mind. One time only, and she got knocked up. Billy Joe refused to acknowledge that he was the father, and Nancy had an abortion that almost killed her. She wished she could banish that whole year from memory.

Jim reached for her hands. She jerked them away, jammed them under her backside. He said, "Maybe we can try it again, huh? But maybe just move your tongue around very slowly."

"I don't know," she said. "I'd like to, but I'm kind of out of the mood."

Years later, long after they were married, she told him that at that moment a picture had come to mind of bits of unmasticated food all mixed up in saliva and flowing like some kind of sewage in and out of their mouths. While she was picturing a flood of food particles, he was still reeling from the memory of her tongue—could it be the longest tongue in human history?—buzzsawing inside his mouth. She said maybe they could have a Coke first and then maybe give it another try.

"Yeah. That would be good." Their high had worn off. He said, "Hey, you got a joint around here? I could use another hit about now."

"We're sitting on it." She laughed.

She dug her stash out from beneath her couch cushion and handed it to him. "Roll us one while I get the Cokes."

•

She called him her old man and he called her his old lady, which in the vernacular of the day meant they were a committed couple. After dating only two weeks she moved in with him and helped him decorate his little room in Uncle Brad's house to fit the hippie mold: stacks of colorful throw pillows and ragged bedspreads, book shelves made of planks on concrete blocks, a portable stereo on a worn Indian rug on the hardwood floor. They made tie-dyed curtains out of cheap sheets bought off the sales rack at J.C. Penney, painted the walls yellow and scavenged junk stores for more shelves and an easy chair and bric-a-brac for decoration. They piled more throw pillows against the wall.

Brad's only complaint was that they played their music too loud, but it thrilled him to have someone else to cook for. After they had been together a month or two Nancy asked Jim if he still liked to wear women's clothes. It was a Sunday morning. They were having their morning coffee in bed. Postum, actually. Weird pseudo coffee that they suffered for a while because it was supposed to be healthy. Brad was gone for the weekend, so they'd not bothered to get dressed. Jim was wearing nothing but Jockey briefs and Nancy was wearing white panties and a T-shirt. The little black and white TV she had brought from her old apartment was tuned to "The Today Show." Barbara Walters and Hugh Downs were talking about nothing of importance. Jim and Nancy weren't paying much attention. Without any preliminary or warning Nancy popped that question. "Do you still like to wear women's clothes?"

She said *still*, he thought. But of course. Jimi Sue would have told her. He stammered, "What? Are you... where did you..."

"Don't pretend you don't know what I'm talking about. Jimi Sue said it got you all hot and bothered." Her penetrating look and gotcha smile dared him to deny it. She said, "If you fess up, who knows? It might get me all hot and bothered too."

He said "Far out."

She hopped off the bed, took him by the hand and coaxed him over to the dresser. He watched in the mirror as she picked up a tube of lipstick. He smiled shyly as she applied it to his lips. Not since Jimi Sue's pampering touch had he felt so giddy, and cared for and sexually charged. The smell and feel of rouge dusted on his cheeks, the eye liner that made him blink, the delightfully shared laughter when she smeared it and had to wipe it off and start over. After she finished painting his face she said, "OK, where do you keep your falsies and your panties?"

"My what!"

Denial was futile. She said, "Aw, quit playing all innocent. I know you got 'em hid somewhere."

"In a box on the shelf in the closet," he whispered, barely able to breathe. She scrambled to the closet and reached the box down off the shelf and fished out the fully stuffed bra and helped him slip into it and snapped it in back for him and helped him wiggle into the panties, and then she pushed him back down on the bed.

Sweating and exhausted and gasping for breath between peals of laughter half an hour later, with lipstick and rouge and eyeliner smeared liberally over both their faces, she asked, "Would you marry me?"

"You bet," he said.

•

The first few years of their life together were determined by the nature of the times. The now familiar litany of drugs, sex and rock and roll. They stayed high most of the time, danced to the Grateful Dead on the hardwood floor, saw a lot of movies, and played around with a lot of kinky stuff together and with friends who were as much into the make-love-not-war culture as they were. He didn't discover the essential Nancy until long after they got married. She was remarkable. Nancy gave herself over to causes wholeheartedly. She volunteered for the Red Cross. She served soup to poor people at the mission. She was the most Christian person he'd ever known, and she didn't even believe in God. He had always thought that charity and morality had to have a religious basis. How would people know about the golden rule if they didn't go to church? What incentive could they possibly have to be good if they were not bucking for a reward in heaven? Nancy disavowed him of that notion. She had never regularly attended any church, although she did visit a few out of curiosity. She had read the Bible and said she thought Jesus was a wonderful man but not the son of an all-powerful and all-knowing god. Yet she was more charitable and self-sacrificing then anyone else he'd ever known.

At first his attraction to her had been purely physical, seeing how knockout gorgeous she had become in the few years since she moved away from the corner of Woodlawn and 18th, but it was her generous soul that he learned to love. Even when she put all the weight back on plus some. She got fat, and he loved her even more.

The single room in Uncle Brad's place was too cramped and, for Nancy, too far from town. Smiley Russell had moved out of the Luzon Building and into a duplex on Pine Street across the street from the cemetery. He told them the other half of the duplex was vacant. They took a look, the price was right, so they moved in. From the outside it looked like the houses they grew up in if you shrunk them a bit and glued the sides of their houses together. They spent a lot of time with Smiley and Christine and their baby. On weekends they often carried their lunch picnic style into the cemetery. They enjoyed reading the tombstones and speculating about the dead.

Nancy and Jim decided not to have children. "Look at the world we live in," Nancy said. "Wars, pollution, overcrowding, our food chain poisoned. It would be cruel to bring a child into this world." It was not until sometime in the '70s that she confessed, tearfully, that she'd been kidding herself about not wanting children and would really love to but couldn't. She told him for the first time about the self-induced abortion that had destroyed something inside of her. He said they could adopt, but she said if they couldn't make a baby themself she didn't want one.

In her fifties she developed diabetes. Neuropathy almost destroyed her legs. She couldn't walk a city block without the help of a walking stick. Despite bad health, when hurricane Katrina hit the Gulf Coast she went down to New Orleans and spent two months helping out with whatever she could. Somewhere along in there Jim had started performing at Barney's again, this time in the guise of Amanda Bright, jazz singer. Nancy was often in the audience. Then she got breast cancer. Chemo, hair loss, and remission, and then it came back again. She tried to hide how much pain she was in. She never stopped smiling till the end.

Raindrops, the blog of the Daily Journal, Wetside, Washington, March 3, 2010

POLICE BLOTTER
By Harry Drews

Protests over bikini clad servers

Police say five baristas are in trouble for offering more than just coffee at a Wetside espresso stand.

Police spokesman Snake Collins said police concluded a two month investigation where they found "terribly inappropriate and lewd behavior" on the part of bikini clad baristas at Grab-N-Go Espresso. The baristas have been charged with violating the city's Adult Entertainment ordinance.

Police started their investigation after tips came in from customers. Collins said, "For extra money these women would expose their bodies. While wearing skimpy bikinis, regardless of the weather outside, they would lower their tops to flash their breasts, and in some instances in was reported they would turn their backs and 'moon' customers. There were also complaints from citizens that they were performing 'whip cream shows.' There were also unsubstantiated reports that they were prostituting."

The owner of the business, Brewster Crockett, says the women who work at the Grab-N-Go are required to sign a policy prohibiting the kind of behavior alleged by the police investigation. Crockett says the policy will be strictly enforced and any violation will result in immediate termination.

"Any girl caught doing anything illegal will be fired on the spot," says Crockett. "Every girl that works for us knows that our policy clearly states what is and is not acceptable attire for work. They must cover their bottoms and their tops. Pasties are not allowed."

Crockett says no whip cream on bodies or sexual gestures are allowed.

He says he can't control every moment of every girl that works for him. "What they do after work is none of my business," Crockett said.

If convicted the women could face 90 days in jail and a $1,000 fine.

Protesters lined the sidewalk across the street from Grab-N-Go Saturday morning. "These young girls serving coffee are practically naked," said protest leader Lara Cockburn Grant, who pointed out that the stand is situated near a school and swimming pool and caters primarily to "impressionable" area youth.

Baristas in bikinis have become a fad recently, and there have been complaints at other espresso stands in the area of baristas exposing more flesh than is allowed by law. Some communities have tried to outlaw such espresso stands or to limit where such coffee servers can work, wanting to relegate them to adult-only areas as some towns limit adult movie houses and strip clubs.

Mrs. Grant said the protesters would not object to coffee servers wearing bikinis if "their salacious behavior never went any further. After all," Mrs. Grant stated, "We all know that sex sells. We've come to expect and accept a certain amount of salacious pandering and we're willing to allow it in its place, even though we don't like it. But such blatant displays of sexuality should not be forced on our youth. This particular coffee stand is located close to areas where young people congregate. If they are still in operation this summer when the swimming pool opens, greater numbers of innocent youth will be exposed."

Crockett pointed out that girls routinely wear skimpy bikinis in the swimming pool located within fifty yards of Grab-N-Go. "If we were located in the lobby of the opera our servers would wear tuxedos," Crockett stated.

Chapter 11

Jim and Alex moved in together in March. He still had the old home down in Rock Creek, but he moved the essentials into Alex's place—most of his clothes, his laptop, the books he hadn't yet read or thought he might want to read again, and his favorite coffee mug, the one with the picture of Alfred E. Neuman from *Mad* magazine. His home had always been Spartan; he couldn't imagine needing much more than that, but he was wrong. It seemed like at least once a week he had to tool down to the old place to get something or other. When he did, he would sometimes linger for hours looking at the trees, listening to the sounds of the surrounding forest, smelling the clean air. And then he would go home to Alex and cook dinner. (She could scramble eggs and cook hamburgers, and that was pretty much the extent of her culinary prowess; fortunately for both of them Jim enjoyed cooking.)

For dinner he prepared one of his favorite dishes, a tortilla casserole dish. After dinner he helped himself to a beer from the refrigerator and turned on the television. Alex said, "Aren't you going to get dressed? It's Wednesday night."

"Oh, I forgot. Hey, what if for once we skipped drag night?"

"Why? Are you not feeling well?"

"No, I feel fine. It's just that I'm a little tired of going every week. It's the same thing every time."

"That's true. So what do you want to do instead?"

"Let's just stay home and watch TV for a change."

She said, "Does this mean the honeymoon is over? Now we're going to settle into being every other middle class, mid-America couple. Eat on the couch, watch TV all night and go to bed too tired to have sex? Oh, and I forgot the requisite after dinner beer for the man."

He lifted his glass as if in a toast and laughed. He said, "Is that really so bad?"

"Not unless it becomes the whole of our life. It would be nice if we could go out once in a while."

Very quickly after that their life eased into exactly the kind of routine she had forecast, but it wasn't as bad as she feared. They both grew comfortable with it. They still argued politics, with the added point of contention of whether to watch Rachel Maddow and Keith Olbermann or Glenn Beck and Bill O'Reilly. And they argued over other TV shows. He liked crime shows and courtroom dramas and she liked documentaries and sit-coms. They both detested reality TV on principal. "I prefer stories with characters and plots," Jim said, "Not assholes being assholes."

She agreed.

They routinely turned the set off at ten o'clock and went to bed and read to each other, taking turns reading. Shared reading plus morning walks in West River Park and an occasional evening out for a movie or a play at the Little Theatre kept them from slipping into absolute torpor and mindlessness.

And they continued to post on their shared blog, although less frequently. Her posts were mostly political rants, to which he responded with sarcasm, and his took the form of short stories but reality-based with names withheld. "Your posts are reality TV in print," she teased.

Raindrops, the blog of the Daily Journal, Wetside, Washington, April 10, 2010

POLICE BLOTTER
By Harry Drews

The drag queen murders

An anonymous tip to police resulted in an investigation which uncovered evidence that a body found in the woods off the Pacific Coast Trail in the fall of 2008 and ruled as an accidental death at the time may be that of a murder victim and possibly a serial killing. The victim was identified as Larry Butler, a gay man who performed as a female impersonator at Barney's Pub in Wetside in the late 1960s and early 1970s under the name Liza Jane.

The anonymous caller claimed the victims were the performers at Barney's who had been involved in the May Day Riot of 1970, and evidence seems to point in that direction.

Earlier, on Feb. 8 another murder victim, Raymond Craig, whose body was found in a secluded area north of Seattle, was also identified as a former female impersonator at Barney's Pub. Both Craig, whose drag name was Honey Jewel, and Butler were participants in the infamous riot. Police now suspect that an unidentified body found near Mount St. Helens and two murder victims from the fall of 2008, both of whom were transgendered individuals, may be victims of the same mass murderer. One other noted connection is that all of the victims, including those that have not been identified but whose ages were determined by forensic examination, were elderly. The youngest was 65 and the oldest 80, making them the same ages as the drag queens who were arrested in the 1970 riot.

Unofficially, the police are calling the case the drag queen murders.

There may or may not be further connections. Murders of transsexual and cross dressing individuals constitute a large portion of hate crime victims in this country, a type of crime that is on the rise. One recent estimate reported on the Internet indicates that there is a murder of a transsexual person every month in the United States, and those are just the reported cases.

Best Friends – Jim and Alex's blog

Life after Nancy
by Jim Bright

Life after Nancy died was a blur. There were months I can't even remember. I must have functioned somehow. I must have taken care of business. I remember people telling my I had to get on with my life and I'd say, "Yeah, I know," or I'd ask how I was supposed to do that and they'd say, "You just do it" like life was a goddamn Nike commercial. I started drinking a lot. I started hanging out at Barney's again. One funny thing happened. I saw an old high school teammate in Barney's one night. He left with another guy, and it was pretty obvious what they were up to. The guy had been the queer hater of all queer haters back in high school. How typical. I wished for a moment I could go back in time and blab it to everyone at Jefferson High School. (The reunion's coming up; I'll be tempted, as much as I despise outing people. But no, I can't do that. Sorry folks, name withheld.)

Nobody can tell you how to handle your own grief. It never goes away. You have what's called grief attacks. You see someone who has the same kind of walk as your lost loved one or you drive past one of your old haunts or you hear a certain song, and you're flooded with memories and unimaginable grief. Maybe it lasts no more than a few seconds. With time it becomes less frequent, but it never vanishes.

When I met Alex that Halloween eve two years ago I didn't want to talk about Nancy. When she asked if I was married I made up some stupid story, and for reasons I couldn't explain I pretended like I'd never before been in Barney's.

When I finally told Alex the whole truth she expressed admiration for Nancy and empathy for me. "It's always the care taker who suffers the most," she said. And then to lighten the mood after I recited every good deed Nancy had ever done Alex went all smartass on me and said, "All right, I get it. She was a saint. Now let's get back to the kinky stuff"—the kinky stuff being all the sordid details of my sex life (you already read all about it right here on this blog). She couldn't get enough.

Chapter 12

When Alex read Jim's latest smart-aleck remarks about his youthful sexual exploits she said, "That's the easy stuff to brag about. What I'm waiting for is the day you come out in your blog as a cross dresser."

Their old friend Rolly Simpson was also waiting for the big revelation. Rolly emailed Jim. He said:

> Hey, old buddy. I've been reading your blog. Fun stuff. We ought to get together sometime, maybe for coffee or a beer. Guess what? Every time you write "name withheld" I know exactly who you're talking about, including all the chicks you nailed and the homophobe you spotted in Barney's. They probably recognize themselves too, if they read your stuff. So if you're planning on coming to the reunion, watch out. They're liable to gang up on your ass, and some of those chicks can do serious damage. BTW, the queer hater was Bubba A. I had it figured out about him and Red Rogers way back. But what I want to know is why you don't come out about your career as a drag queen. Yeah, I saw you as Amanda Darling. You were hot, buddy. But I knew it was you.

Alex no longer doubted he had been a drag performer. He had called the police with his suspicion that someone was killing off all the old queens from Barney's, and his call had spurred their subsequent investigation proving that at least two of the victims were who he claimed they were. She was proud of him for going to the authorities, but now that Harry Drews had made it public information she hoped it would quietly die. Jim, however, became obsessed with the case to the point where she got sick of hearing about it. And he had still not let her see him in drag. She couldn't figure out if he was teasing her, dragging it out to build up the anticipation, or if maybe he was afraid that now that he was much older he wouldn't look as good.

She said, "What I want to know is when you wore women's stuff did you and Nancy pretended to be lesbian lovers?"

"No," he said. "We didn't pretend to be anything."

"Yeah you did. You pretended to be a woman. That's what you told me."

"But it wasn't like that. I never tried to *become* a woman. In the club it was just acting, and at home it was something else. I don't know how to explain it. But the thing is, the reason I married Nancy was because she understood it or at least accepted me for what I was, complete with my fetish or obsession or whatever it was and without being judgmental. That was huge. That was like… well, I can't explain what that meant to me. The fact that it was a turn-on for her also was sweet dessert."

She wondered if he would expect or want it to be a turn-on for her as well if he ever did let her see him as a woman, and would it be? She didn't think so, but she knew you never could anticipate what might trigger arousal. She asked, "Did you always dress as a woman before you had sex?"

"No, but when I *did* dress as a woman it always seemed to lead to it. But hell, we were young and newly in love. Everything led to sex. Watching Johnny Carson led to sex, eating ice cream, shoveling snow."

Alex said, "I'm jealous." And Jim said, "No you're not. You just miss being young and in love."

"I can't miss it," she said, "Because I never had it."

"Never had sex all night long?"

"Maybe. I can't remember. But I don't think I ever felt it the way you're talking about. I was never in love."

"Really? Never?"

"I had crushes when I was a girl. Some pretty big ones, including a major crush on you if you must know. But I never fell in love with someone who loved me back."

"That's so sad. It really is. But you've got it now."

She was thankful to hear him say that, but she also noted that he didn't say the actual three words she wanted to hear from him.

She asked if Nancy went to Barney's with him when he performed.

"She came, but not as my wife. That would have screwed up the illusion I tried to create in my act. A good actor never breaks the spell. She came with Uncle Brad. She was his beard. Except they didn't use that term back then. They called 'em fag hags. How's that for politically incorrect?"

The guys at Barney's bonded like soldiers in battle, performers and customers alike. They watched out for each other. When they were absolutely sure there were no undercover cops or gay bashers in the club—and you better believe there were homophobes who came to Barney's just to harass the gay boys or to get their jollies laughing at them—they'd flirt with each other and generally gay it up to high heaven. But they were good at spotting the enemy.

Alex wanted to know if the fag hags were lesbians. "You keep asking about lesbians," Jim teased. "Is there something I ought to know?"

She chuckled, licked her bottom lip, lifted eyebrows.

He told her that back then lesbians and gays didn't get along very well. He never understood why; they just didn't. The popular notion was that dykes were man haters. Gosh. You reckon they had reason? It wasn't until the AIDS epidemic that lesbians and gays began to understand that they were on the same side. Gay men were dying in droves and not getting support or comfort from anyone. It was lesbians who were the first to wake up and say, hey, we got to help them.

Jim kept his true identity hidden. Barney and Randy the bouncer and the other performers knew his real name, but nobody else. After his act he'd change out of costume and come back in as himself and join Uncle Brad and Nancy if they were there. He introduced them to his friends as Uncle Brad and his lady friend. Usually, if Nancy wasn't there, Jim would just go home after his act. He didn't always feel safe alone in Barney's. Once or twice he tried to sit at the bar while still in drag, but that usually didn't work out too well because customers of both genders would try and hit on him. "What can I say? I was gorgeous."

The beat cops that patrolled Barney's were a pair of big, ugly, macho dudes that the queens nicknamed Walrus and Warthog because that's what they looked like. Both had big mustaches. Walrus's curled up and Warthog's drooped down. Sometimes they would arrest guys if they caught them dancing or holding hands. Any outward show of affection between two men was grounds for being hauled off to jail. But jail was more often a threat than a reality. They didn't usually get that far. They'd take them out on the street, threaten them and sometimes rough them up a bit. Walrus and Warthog would threaten to out them to their bosses or their families. Imagine the horror. Two beastly cops sneeringly ask a closeted gay man, "Does your wife know you're queer? How 'bout your children? Wonder what little Janey's gonna think when she finds out her father sucks dick." And then they demand a payoff (or payment in kind, like a blow job—it happened) and threaten, "We gonna slap your faggy ass in jail. Next morning your wife is gonna see something in the paper saying you been arrested for an immoral and perverted sexual act with another man. Your kid's gonna hear about it at school."

They lived in constant fear of Walrus and Warthog, who in addition to harassing everyone were on the take from Barney. He paid them off not to bust the joint. It was the price of staying open. Barney was a sweet guy, but not without dirt on his hands. There were shenanigans going on in his pub that could have gotten him shut down and maybe worse. Hustling. Some minor drug dealing and other stuff. Walrus and Warthog were definitely getting some of that action, but the payoffs were not enough stop the cops from occasionally getting their jollies from the boys.

It was not at all unusual for a cop to slap somebody upside the head or poke them in the belly with a nightstick. That was the milder stuff. Sometimes they'd wait in ambush outside and hustle the gay boys down the ally and really beat the shit out of them. Viciously. There were some serious injuries. Naturally they were never reported. They also raped a couple of the boys. More than once. Despite what some may believe, the perpetrators of rape of homosexual men are more often than not heterosexual. The one everyone knew about was Tom Rogers, who performed under the name Miss Tammy Tucker. Tom was in his forties. When not in drag he looked like a bookkeeper. He usually arrived wearing a dark suit and tie. He was terribly skinny. Miss Tammy performed in a blonde wig and a cowgirl skirt and sang country and western ballads. Jim was Miss Tammy's protégé when he first started. He often sat next to her at the bar waiting their turns on stage, and the two of them were so convincing as women that straight men who wandered into Barney's sometimes tried to pick them up.

Walrus and Warthog raped Tom in the alley at gunpoint. The big sons of bitches took turns molesting him. The first one had his way with him from behind, and then the other one held his service revolver to Tommy's head and told him to turn around and get down on his knees and go down on him. That was not a smart thing to do. No matter how weak or how scared a person might be, anybody can reach a breaking point and react violently and suddenly without thinking of the possible consequences. Tommy fought back. They never expected that. They never thought Tommy would do anything but meekly follow orders. Desperate, insane with fear and anger, Tommy bit his attacker's penis. He clamped down on him like a snapping turtle. Inside the club they heard his scream, and Randy the bouncer—the same Randy that's now the bartender, only he was twenty-five, tough as leather and toting a pistol back then—rushed out to the alley just in time to see one of the cops bent double and clutching his crotch, black blood under the lurid light in the alley seeping between his fingers, with his partner on one knee in front of him like he was praying. Tom was crumpled and bleeding on the ground. One or both of the cops had beaten him with their night sticks. Walrus and Warthog claimed they caught Tom in the alley performing oral sex on another man. The one that had been bit turned his back to Randy to zip up. The other one said, "When we tried to arrest them, they fought back. We had to subdue them with force. This one fought like a tiger. He might be little, but he's tough. The other one ran away before we could grab him."

201

Tommy didn't say a word.

Everyone knew the cops were lying, But what difference did it make? It was the word of a bouncer in a gay bar against that of two police officers. They practically killed Miss Tammy. Tom. He was not in drag when they attacked him. They called for an ambulance and took him to Mercy Hospital.

The incident was never discussed openly, but some of the drag queens talked about it among themselves. They said Tom was terribly traumatized but managed to laugh a little about biting the cop's dick. Sadly, that ended Miss Tammy Tucker's singing career. She never came back to Barney's. Anita Mann, the other queen those cops raped, said Miss Tammy moved to San Francisco. The one that got bit, Warthog (real name Fred Felts), needed some time to heal. For the next week or so Walrus showed up on his rounds with a different partner. There was a hush in the club when they were there. When Warthog finally did show up in the club again he was surlier than ever.

The other rape victim's real name was George. Jim said, "George was pretty much the roughest, macho drag queen I ever met. Even in the club when not in drag he had a tough guy swagger, and outside of the club he was proud to tell people he was homosexual. I guess he was the only one who was so open. He practically dared the bigots to say anything about it."

George was six feet tall and didn't take any shit from anybody. But he was no match for pistols and nightsticks. Besides which he knew that if he fought back the whole might of the police force would come crashing down on him. So when they told him to drop his pants and bend over he took it silently, and then he went directly to the police station—marching into the viper's den—and reported the rape. He thought he knew how to get them to investigate. There was a newly appointed citizen's review panel made up of police and civilians. Its function was to investigate cases of alleged corruption within the department. Harold Drews had recently written about it in the Wetside *Daily Journal*. George reported the rape to the officer in charge of the review panel on the slim chance they could find at least one or two cops on the force who wouldn't cover for the rotten apples. They said they would investigate, but they never did.

George moved to Portland, where he became famous as an outlandishly comical drag performer and frequent MC at Pride celebrations. When the AIDS epidemic hit he became an outspoken member of the activist group Act Up. He lived with the same partner for thirty-something years. In 1989 they adopted a child who grew up heterosexual, got married and gave them two beautiful granddaughters. When Multnomah County legalized same-sex marriage they were among the thousands who got married in Portland. They came from everywhere. There must have been forty gay couples from Southwest Washington who went down to Portland to get married. Jim went down there to witness for a friend and bumped into George and got to see him take vows. That was before an amendment to the state constitution almost immediately nullified those marriages and made same sex marriage illegal again. So much for progress. Married or not, George and his partner were happy together for the short time they had left. His partner died of AIDS-related pneumonia in 2007. George died about a year later in what was first reported as an automobile accident. He was found in his car near Mt. St. Helens. He was never identified, but Jim had no doubts. It was George. He was murdered and his car was pushed over that embankment.

Raindrops, the blog of the Daily Journal, Wetside, Washington, January 1, 1969

POLICE BLOTTER
By Harold Juniper Drews

Preacher calls Wetside 'New Sodom,' threatens lawsuit against Journal

Rev. Samuel Bright, minister of the Clear Water Baptist Church, threatened the Wetside *Daily Journal* with a lawsuit for refusing to run an editorial as a paid advertisement. In the editorial, Rev. Bright called the city of Wetside "The New Sodom," referring to the biblical story of Sodom and Gomorrah.

It began when the Rev. Bright asked if he could write something for the editorial page and was turned down. "This newspaper is not a public forum," managing editor Ralph Johnson explained. "We publish articles by staff writers and editors and freelance writers, all of whom are professional writers and whose articles are subject to editorial revision. Our editorial board determines what to publish based on numerous criteria."

Bright then submitted his editorial as a letter to the editor, but was told it exceeded the 250-word limit. Failing that, he tried to get it published in the form of a display ad, but was again refused. Johnson said the newspaper could turn down ads if the content was considered slanderous, libelous, obscene or not in the public interest. He said Rev. Bright's ad was "all of that."

In the article originally submitted for publication Rev. Bright called Wetside "The New Sodom," and "a hotbed of licentiousness." He offered "proof" of the city's "sinful nature" by way of articles from this column going back to 1954 in which I wrote about one Aubrey Smithfield, a 16-year-old farm boy at the time, who was cited for having sexual congress with a horse. In 1960 and again in 1964 Smithfield was arrested on the same charges.

Culled from Police Blotter columns over a period of years, Rev. Bright cited the case of a prostitute named Melody Sauer who has been arrested 23 times since the early 1950s on various morals charges and misdemeanors and who is still prostituting herself on the streets of downtown Wetside, "with complete impunity," according to Rev. Bright. He said that in numerous mentions of Sauer I wrote about her with a "sly wink of approval."

He also referred to the authorities "winking" at bars that cater to homosexual clients, one of which features entertainment by men who pretend to be women. "Homosexuality is the worst sin of all," Rev. Bright said. "That's what brought about the destruction of Sodom."

He referenced every mention of licentious behavior reported in this column except for the most notorious, the "sex ring" discovered in 1960 which involved a Baptist preacher and local business and professional men.

The Rev. Bright is calling on Wetside citizens to rally in front of the *Journal* offices Friday at noon.

On a personal note, I am flattered that the Rev. Bright has been such a loyal reader of this column.

Chapter 13

Jim finally gave Alex what she'd been asking for since Christmas—Alex as Amanda. As in his performing days, he decided to dress at home alone, his country home not the home he shared with Alex, and then present himself fully transformed. He bought lip gloss, eye shadow, foundation and a nice but subtle perfume from Nordstrom. "It's all for my girlfriend. Hair and skin tones pretty much like mine," he told the saleslady. The rest he already had, including some sleek cocktail dresses from his days as a jazz singer. The one he slithered into was a little tight but not so much so as to threaten to burst wide open. It looked a lot like the one he had been wearing when they took the group photo in 1970.

When he looked in the mirror he liked what he saw. He made a bet with himself that Alex would not recognize him. He drove to her place and parked around the corner where she would not see his car, and walked to her house and rang the bell. Wary of salesmen and missionaries, she called through the closed door to ask who was there. He told her he was conducting a survey for the city council.

She opened the door and said, "What kind of survey?"

He said, "We want to know why you aren't dressed better."

"What? What right do you..."

Giggling and dropping his voice an octave, meaning reverting to normal, Jim said, "Come on, Slugger. You have a date with Amanda Bright."

"Oh my god," she said. "It's you. You totally fooled me."

"So how do I look?"

She said. "You're beautiful. If I was a man I'd probably be hitting on you right about now."

He said, "You can hit on me anytime, honey. But the million-dollar question is, are you willing to be seen in public with me in this outfit."

"Certainly. Anytime, anywhere."

"All right then. If you change into something with equal class and beauty—I don't want to out shine you—I'll take you out to dinner."

"Great. Where are you going to take me?"

"I don't know. What are you in the mood for?"

"Hmmm, uh, how about Italian?" she said.

"All right. How about Carmines?"

"Wow! You certainly know how to pick them."

He followed her to the bedroom and sat on the edge of the bed and pulled his cell phone out of his pocket and called for reservations while she got dressed. It didn't take her nearly as long as it had taken him.

Carmines is on the West Side overlooking the river. They got a window table. Jim noticed a couple of men eyeing them as they walked to their table. Alex ordered the wine. Jim had long since learned to let her order the drinks, whether mixed drinks, wine or beer. No more Buds or PBRs for Jim Bright. Alex had trained him to appreciate better. She ordered a Merlot. The waiter brought bread and oil, and the wine steward brought out the wine. She did the tasting. "Excellent," she said.

Then she said, "Let's go to Barney's after. See if any old Amanda Bright fans recognize you."

He said, "I could do that. I guess. But I think you might be the only Amanda Bright fan left in Wetside, if there ever were any."

"False modesty does not fit you well."

"Neither does this dress." He tugged at the bodice as if to stretch it. It was a little snug, nicely accentuating curves that Alex could easily envy.

Through the window they watched lights of a fishing boat float by on the black river. Street lights on the farther shore formed a sparkling necklace against a line of trees.

She said, "You told me and I couldn't believe it, but it's really true that nobody would ever suspect you were a man."

"I know. I guess I have girlish features."

"I just thought about your father. I bet he'd a had a hissy fit if he ever saw you like this. He didn't know you were a cross dresser did he?"

"God no. It would have killed him. And I wasn't that into pissing off the old man."

He told her about the time his father called Wetside the new Sodom and about how he tried to organize a protest in front of the *Daily Journal* office. When nobody else showed up he picketed the building by himself, and then that night he went to Barney's and marched up and down in front with a sign that said *Barney's Pub is the Devil's Den*. That was also reported in Harold Drews' column. Rev. Bright hated Barney's. After the riot he was convinced the drag queens murdered the policeman, and he said all of them should be put in prison for life. Jim said, "I can't imagine what he would have said or done if he had known I had been there. In a dress no less."

Jim said, "If he made it to heaven he must have been mystified at who was there and who wasn't. It woulda turned everything he ever believed topsy turvy."

"That would be fitting, but I don't believe there is any such thing as heaven or hell."

"Probably not, but I wish there was just so the self-righteous could get their comeuppance."

While eating dessert he spotted the stalker at the bar. The stalker spotted Jim at the same time. Jim said, "Don't look now, but that big ugly man at the bar is the guy I told you about that tried to pick me up outside Bev and Rhonda's, the one I thought was stalking me. Uh oh, I think he's going to come over here."

"Why would he. You're in drag, remember. He can't possibly know who you are."

She was right. He'd momentarily forgotten. In the old days he could never have let himself forget for fear of slipping out of character and exposing himself. But in Carmines it didn't matter. For a second he even entertained the thought that it might be fun if the guy did come over and try to hit on him again. *I could tease him a bit and then whip off my wig and say, You sure you want to go out with me, honey buns?* But he rejected that thought as stupid and reckless. He didn't want the Boris Karloff lookalike coming over, and he didn't think he would. Whoever he was, the creep was not interested in any old lady or anyone else of the female gender. *He has no idea I'm a man.* He also thought it was really weird that the guy was in Carmines. He did not look like a Carmines kind of guy.

But he was watching them and he did stand up and purposefully walk over to their table. "Excuse me," he said, "But aren't you Amanda Bright the singer?"

Jim was flabbergasted and flattered to discover he had at least one fan after all, even if he was the ugliest man he'd seen in quite a while. For a few seconds he was at a loss. Should he deny being Amanda? But why should he? The guy was an Amanda Bright fan. Nothing threatening in that. But he was still creepy looking, and Jim couldn't shake his conviction that he'd been stalking him. Finally, in character, he said, "Yes, I am. But I haven't been a singer for a long time."

"I thought so," he said. "I used to love listening to you."

"Thank you."

They made polite conversation for a few minutes and then he excused himself and left. "That wasn't so bad," Alex said.

Topping the evening off at Barney's later that night one other person introduced himself as an Amanda Bright fan, but nobody recognized Amanda as Jim Bright. People who knew Jim and Alex as a couple asked where Jim was. Alex said he was at home working on a new ad for Grant's. She said Amanda was Jim's cousin.

•

Flash back to Barney's Pub on the night it made its bid for infamy, the first of May, 1970. Amanda Darling was on stage wearing a white ankle-length gown with a plunging neckline that went all the way to her navel. The piano player went through the opening bars of "Georgia on my Mind." Amanda stepped up to the microphone and looked out over the house. She spotted the cops Walrus and Warthog seated at the bar and looking back and forth from the stage to the front door, which had been propped open to let air in and smoke out. Despite the open door and a couple of ceiling fans it was warm inside, especially under the stage lights. Jim knew not to do his striptease act with the cops there. He always played it by ear, depending on who was in the audience. Sometimes he did a modified striptease, down to panties and bra but still wearing stockings and garter and heels. Other times he'd strip to nothing but panties and end with a dramatic flourish. He'd turn his back to the audience, and the lights would dim. All but a single spotlight on Amanda. With his back turned he would whip off his bra and sling it out across the audience to where the bartender could catch it, and then in one big gesture he would yank off his wig and turn around to reveal his flat chest and short hair.

When there were cops in the house, including undercover cops who were surprisingly easy to spot, he didn't do the strip. He sang his song, bowed, and left the stage. One more reason to despise Walrus and Warthog. Because of them he had to deprive his audience of the big ending, but that was the price he had to pay. He stubbornly refused to let them know his male identity.

That night he sang "Georgia on my Mind" and "Danny Boy." He took his bow and stepped off the stage. Making his way to the bar he gracefully accepted a few pats on the back and a cheek kiss from someone in the audience. He looked away as he walked past Walrus and Warthog. Usually he went straight to the dressing room, but he was feeling nervous that night and flushed from the unseasonable heat. He thought a beer might be just the thing the doctor ordered, so he took a seat at the far end of the bar and ordered a Bud. He swiveled toward the stage to watch Bonnie Parker make her entrance in her Bonnie Parker outfit with the Fay Dunaway hairdo and beret and a string of machinegun clips crossing her breast.

A phalanx of cops stormed the club during Bonnie's act. There were at least a half dozen of them, plus the two already there who hopped off their barstools and advanced on the stage. Whistles blowing, gruff orders shouted out, nightsticks swinging threateningly over the heads of bar patrons. As soon as it started Jim slipped off his barstool and headed for the door to the kitchen. He glanced back for a second as he pushed through the door and saw the cops starting to herd customers out the front door. He couldn't see the paddy wagon, but he knew from previous experience that it would be parked by the entrance to the alley, and he knew the cops would be wielding their batons like cattle prods to force the queens in the paddy wagon and take them to the station. Once in the kitchen there was no place for him to go. The little room didn't offer much of a hiding place, and he knew slipping out the back door into the alley would be useless because the paddy wagon would be blocking the alley entrance. That's the way they always did it. He looked anyway, and sure enough, the alley was blocked. There was no escape. He fully expected to get arrested. Twice before he had narrowly escaped being swept up in a police raid, but both times he had been in drag and they looked at him thinking he was a woman and passed him by.

To Alex he said, "I think it was because I was so beautiful."

"I admire your modesty."

"Yeah, well you can't deny the beauty before your eyes, and excuse me if that sounds conceited, but being gorgeous saved my ass. If they'd suspected I was another of the drag queens they would have jerked my wig off and hauled me in, but they never did. Weird as it might seem, I think they were intimidated by me. I was out of their class. Giving me a hard time would have been like going to the country club and harassing some society dame who probably had pull with the chief or the mayor."

One of the cops pushed open the kitchen door and looked in. He looked Jim right in the face and then turned and headed back into the bar. Jim pushed the door open a crack and watched as they hustled the queens out.

For as long as anyone at Barney's could remember the queens had meekly taken whatever abuse was handed out, but no longer. Something snapped. For once in their lives, just like their sisters in the famous Stonewall riots in New York a year earlier (and inspired by their example), the drag queens refused to cower under the onslaught. They fought back with fists and fingernails and bottles and swinging barstools. They screamed, they scratched, they hit and bit and kicked. The cops were severely outnumbered and overpowered, and the queens were out for blood—ecstatic and vicious in their newfound power.

Some drag queen—Jim thought it was Liza Jane, but he couldn't say for sure—hauled off and threw a beer bottle that hit one of the cops in the back of the head. It was Warthog that got beaned. He crumpled to the floor, and a mob started hitting and kicking him. George was the first to hit him. He clobbered him one with his fist.

George had every reason to want to kill the son of a bitch, but he hit him only once and then was pulled away. The place was pandemonium, and from Jim's vantage point peeking through a crack in the door it was just a blur of movement and sound. There was another gun, the plastic machine gun Bonnie Parker waved around during her act. It went skidding across the floor and someone picked it up and pumped it in the air like a banner and shouted "Hit 'em one for Tammy Tucker!"

One of the cops rushed Little Liza Jane (Larry Butler) with his billy club swinging. Liza used her purse to shield the blows, and two other queens rushed to her rescue and started beating the cop with their purses and clawing him with their fingernails. Suddenly the number of queens had doubled. The word had spread to The Meat Market, another gay club that usually drew a rougher and more outlandish crowd. Barney's and The Meat Market had competing drag shows. The Meat Market shows were not very good compared to Barney's, but they were raunchier. Their clientele was tougher, and a bunch of them spilled out and rushed to Barney's like sharks attracted to the smell of blood.

It was queens and queers with purses and fingernails against cops with nightsticks and guns, and the queens and queers were winning. They backed the cops all the way to the paddy wagon, and the cops crawled in and locked the door to protect themselves from the mob. The mob surrounded the paddy wagon and rocked it. The cops called for backups. The queers had to know that even if they were able to overpower the police their victory would be momentary. They had to have known that sooner or later the cops would call in reinforcements, that sooner or later they would retaliate, that someone was going to be badly hurt or even killed— Bonnie or Miss Tammy or Anita Mann or Honey Jewel with the giant boobs or the flaming redhead Liza Jane. They didn't care. If they were going to be killed, they were going to go down fighting.

Six more police cars arrived on the scene. The cops stormed back in the club. More reinforcements from The Meat Market showed up. Now it was leather boys with whips and chains, but their weapons were decorative, as much for show as the big tits and hair of the drag queens. If any of them pulled out their whips and chains no witnesses could verify it. They hit, they kicked, they clawed. There was blood, there were shouts. The heat was unbearable. Jim, still dressed as Amanda Darling and shaking with fear, cringed behind the kitchen door peeking out.

It was back and forth for half an hour until the cops finally got the upper hand and the queens who hadn't been herded into the wagon split and ran. And in the middle of the melee a single gunshot ring out.

Six drag queens ended up in the hospital with severe bruises and lacerations. Likewise six cops. When the fighting stopped, the cop called Warthog was found unconscious on the floor near the front door where he had taken a bunch of kicks to the ribs and the face while trying to crawl out the door. He was such a bloody mess it wasn't until they had him in the ambulance and were rushing him to Saint Martin's Hospital that they discovered he had been shot in the head. He died in the ambulance.

Policemen investigating the crime scene found the service revolver on the floor under a bar stool. It had been fired once. The weapon belonged to Brewster Crockett, the cop nicknamed Walrus, the dead cop's partner.

The headline in the *Journal* the next morning screamed, TRANSVESTITES KILL COP.

The *Seattle PI* headline was WETSIDE POLICEMAN KILLED IN GAY RIOT.

A Portland paper said TRANSVESTITES GO WILD!

The lead article in the *Journal* included a posed photograph of the drag performers in front of the bar, not a picture taken the night of the riot but a standard group portrait a reporter borrowed from Barney. They were all in the picture. It had been taken New Year's Eve.

A police spokesman said they suspected one of the rioting transvestites must have wrested the gun away from Felts and shot Crockett. The prime suspect was George, drag name Anita Mann. He's the one Walrus and Warthog had raped. They wanted to pin the killing on him in retaliation because he had reported the rape.

213

Speculation in Barney's was split. Half the boys in the club thought Crockett did it, but accidentally. They said he just got careless. He probably meant to shoot into the mirror over the bar or into the ceiling, probably figuring a gunshot ringing out would stop the fighting. But maybe he got jostled just as he fired. Maybe he had his gun out and it went off accidentally. Others swore he did it on purpose. They said the two cops had some longstanding feud going, some said over a woman, others said over money. Harold Drews said in his column that the only fingerprints on the gun belonged to Crockett, which meant nothing, because it was his gun. If George had got his hands on Crockett's gun he wouldn't have left fingerprints because he would have been wearing gloves. He wore gloves in his act, and he was still in drag when the rioting started and when he was arrested.

According to Harold Drews' Police Blotter none of the witnesses saw who fired the shot, or if anybody did they weren't saying. Nobody questioned Jim. Even though Walrus and Warthog had watched his performance and knew he was there, and even though at least one other policeman had seen him in the kitchen, no one thought to question him. Harold wrote: "All but two of the female impersonators seen in the photograph were present the night of the riot, one of the missing performers, Tom Rogers, who performed under the name Miss Tammy Tucker, was not present. The other one, who performed under the name Amanda Darling, had been in the club that night, but according to witnesses had left before the rioting started. Miss Darling is known only by her stage name. Others pictured are, from left: George Newman, aka Anita Mann; Billy Martin, aka Bonnie Parker; Raymond Craig, aka Honey Jewel; and Larry Butler, aka Liza Jane."

All but Tommy were arrested and tried on various charges and served slightly more than a year in the state penitentiary. Jim lost touch with all of them after that, but did see Raymond that one last time when he got married in Portland.

Nobody was charged with shooting Officer Felts. The official conclusion, as reported by Harold Drews, was that Crockett either dropped his gun or it was knocked out of his hand, and in the scuffle someone kicked it and it went off accidentally. The police put a spin on the whole incident that made Crockett out to be a hero. They said he was the one who spotted the ring leaders in the riot and arrested them and then took the lead in putting a stop to the fighting. There were articles about him in area papers and on TV. Only Harold Drews came close to reporting the truth of what happened. He said the police and the rioters were equally to blame and that in order to prevent similar incidents from happening in the future law enforcement needed to "take a long hard look at how homosexuals are treated." The paper was flooded with letters condemning Harold and demanding that he be fired, but the editors stuck by him.

Crockett made detective and was assigned to work on drug enforcement. Sometime in the mid '70s he played a lead role in a big drug bust. They confiscated something like twenty thousand bucks worth of illegal drugs, and then the drugs were stolen from the police. It looked like an inside job since no one other than a small group of cops had access. But nothing ever came of it. Nobody was arrested, and the missing drugs were never recovered. A few years later Crockett bought some rental properties in Wetside—speculation being that the money came from the drug heist—and eventually acquired more and more property. He's still in Wetside. Has an office on the sixth floor of the Securities Building downtown on Market. He owns a bunch of rental properties on the East Side and has an interest in Grant's department store and owns the infamous Grab-N-Go espresso stand where the girls serve lattes in bikinis and have been charged with prostitution. Harry Drews wrote all about it in his column.

Chapter 14

Jim and Alex decided to go back Barney's for drag night one more time. It was early. The show had not started. They were seated at a table by the back wall. Alex was fascinated with a sprightly old man who was making the rounds of the tables. He walked with the aid of a walking stick, but moved quickly. He seemed to know everyone in the joint. He was laughing and hugging and kissing people. To her the scene playing out was like she would imagine if some big movie star from the old days, say like James Cagney or Jimmy Stewart, was making the rounds in his old hometown stomping grounds.

Jim said, "That's Barney Pressman, surveying his kingdom. He's almost 90 years old now."

He said Barney had turned over most of the operation of the pub to Randy but still dropped in from time to time to see how things were going. "He even manages to flirt with the drag queens and some of the young hunks, something he never did in his youth when he and most of his customers were closeted."

"Does he know you?" she asked.

"Of course."

"I mean when you're not in drag."

"Yes, he does. You'll see. He'll work his way to us and then ask to sit down for a while."

"So he knows you were Amanda Darling?"

"Yes, of course. I told you already. Barney and Randy. They're the only ones. Why can't you remember this stuff?"

"Well you don't have to be so snarky."

Sure enough, after schmoozing with all the other customers, Barney made his way to their table. "Hey, Jim," he said, and asked, "Who's this lovely young lady?"

Jim introduced Alex. Barney kissed her hand.

"Wow! Such old fashioned gallantry. I love it," she practically gushed.

Barney asked to join them, just as Jim had predicted he would, and he said, "Jim, my dear, you are the only one left from the old days, and I'd like to honor you on the fortieth anniversary of the riot."

"Well thank you, sir. I'm honored." He asked what he had in mind. Alex beamed. She was delighted with the way they spoke to each other with old world courtesy. She was seeing a side to Jim she'd never seen.

The old man said, "We want to do an anniversary show starring Amanda Darling."

Alex spurted beer out her nose at that. Literally. And Jim almost choked on his beer. He said, "Are you kidding? You expect me to get up on that stage and do my old act? No way. Miss Amanda Darling has grown a little too old for singing and definitely too old for making like Gypsy Rose Lee."

"Oh, don't flatter yourself, darling," Barney said. "I don't want *you* to be Amanda again. I've had enough of you on my stage." (He actually stuck out his tongue.) "I want to hire a beautiful young stud to impersonate Amanda. I'll find the best goddamn singer in Western Washington, and you'll have to teach him all of Amanda's moves. You think you can do that?"

"Including the strip moves?"

"Especially the strip moves."

"No, I don't think I can. Sorry, man, but I can't see myself spending my time coaching some young stud. You just tell him to take it off slowly and without the old bump and grind. Heck, Randy could coach him as well as I could."

"Well all right then, be that way."

It sounded like his petulance was good natured pretense, but Alex couldn't tell for sure. She decided that if he was mad he was not too mad because he stood them beers on the house. He lingered at their table for another ten minutes. After he left she asked Jim to show her who was who in the famous picture of the drag queens. He identified the performers in the photo: Anita Mann and Bonnie Parker, unmistakable in her gangster outfit and ammo straps; Honey Jewel with her gigantic boobs; Liza Jane; Miss Tammy looking sweet in a white cowgirl skirt and blouse with big roses printed over her breasts; and, of course, Jim as Amanda. His dress was tight fitting and cut deep in front. "It looks white, but it was really yellow, and if you could see the back you'd see that it was cut even deeper, I mean almost all the way down to my waist, so the audience could clearly see I wasn't wearing a bra. That was tantalizing even though they all knew I wasn't really a woman. But don't you think for a moment that gay men can't get excited over a woman's body. Anyway, they salivated over Amanda Darling in this low cut gown."

In the photo the performers were posed on the little stage with Anita, Bonnie and Honey seated in front and Liza Jane and Miss Tammy and Jim as Amanda Darling standing behind them. It was a black and white, eight-by-ten photo. Their faces were about the size of a thumbnail, but looking very closely Alex could almost recognize Jim. As Jim talked about the queens she could tell from his tone of voice that he missed them. He teared up for a moment when mentioning Tom Rogers, aka Miss Tammy. While he was talking the stalker made another appearance. He spotted Jim (not in drag this time) and slipped into a seat at a table adjacent to them with his back to them almost as if he wanted to listen in without being seen. Neither of them noticed him until he turned to face them and spoke up. He said, "Excuse me. I couldn't help over hearing. Were you Amanda Darling?"

Jim responded as if he was going to have a seizure. His whole body jerked and became stiff. They were both shocked and confused wondering why he had approached them at Carmines and now here again at Barney's—especially odd because there Jim had been in drag and here he wasn't. The guy was frightening. Had he recognized Jim in drag? How could he? Nobody ever had. He was a big man with wild hair and massive shoulders and practically no neck at all, and even in the semi dark of the club they could see that his face had never recovered from a bad bout of acne as a youth. On the other hand, despite his shocking appearance he had a gentle smile and there was sweetness in his eyes as he stood almost like a supplicant by their table. Not surprisingly Jim was not enraptured by the guy's gentle voice and manner. All he knew was that the monster kept crashing their party. His initial reaction was rage. He blurted, "Who the fuck are you? Why do you keep following me?"

"I'm sorry. I didn't mean to upset you. I'm Harry Drews."

"You're who?" He couldn't believe what he was hearing.

He repeated: "Harry Drews."

"The Police Blotter guy?"

"Yes, I'm afraid so."

"I can't believe it."

"I know. I get that all the time. People picture me in their heads, and this ugly mug doesn't quite fit."

"But you've been stalking me. Actually, I thought you were this other guy... this old policeman. Never mind."

"Oh gosh, no. I'm definitely not a policeman, and if I gave you the impression I was stalking you I'm really sorry. What makes you think that?"

"Well, for starters, you hit on me once. The night of the presidential election. Remember that? Right outside Bev and Rhonda's."

Harry said, "Yes, I guess I kinda did. I thought I'd seen you before, and—forgive me for making assumptions—but I was pretty sure I'd seen you cruising gay bars."

"But I was with a woman," Jim said.

"I'm the woman," Alex put in. She introduced herself.

"Yes, I remember. We met at Carmines. It's nice to see you again."

They talked some more about that night at Bev and Rhonda's. Harry admitted he'd made a bad assumption. "True, you were with a woman, but that doesn't always mean a guy is straight." He said he was pretty sure he had seen him at Barney's, and thought he'd also seen him in the Meat Market, which he hadn't, and he had (stupidly, he confessed) thought he might be ripe for being picked up because he'd seen them having a big fight and seen Alex storm out of the restaurant. That confession did not endear him to either of them.

"I'm kind of awkward socially," he said. "I don't go out much and don't know how to... you know, flirt. When I try I usually screw it up."

He talked at some length about his awkwardness in social situations (which did endear him to Alex a little, but not enough for a complete change of heart). Jim stared at his face as if trying to memorize his every feature (actually, he told Alex later, trying to look into his eyes for some sign of truthfulness). Jim said, "Somebody followed me home that night. I thought it was you."

"Oh no. No way."

Jim admitted he hadn't been able to see the vehicle that was following him, just the headlights. "But the position of the lights was like on a big SUV, and I knew that's what you were driving because I saw you drive away earlier."

Harry said, "Uh huh. I waved at you. And then I went home."

Jim felt silly. Once the thought crossed his mind that he could have been mistaken about the car everything else he had thought seemed like a paranoid delusion. He'd believed Harry Drews was Brewster Crockett just because they were both big and rough looking, ignoring a big difference in their age and forgetting that he had no clear picture in mind of what Crockett had looked like forty years earlier. Ever since he had made the connection between the riot of 1970 and the recent deaths of cross dressers and transsexuals he had been both paranoid and fearful. He was sure that someone connected with the riot was out there picking off the survivors one by one. He had no reason to think it was Crockett, but somehow Crockett had come to be the symbol of evil. He or someone like him was killing off the queens. He or someone like him was stalking him, was out to get him, was waiting until all the rest had been put to death before coming after him.

He admitted he could have let his imagination run wild and apologized for his rude behavior.

Harry said, "That's all right. I tend to spark that kind of reaction. I'm used to it." A minute of sheepish silence ticked by and then Harry said, "I'd really like to talk to you some more if I could. Could we maybe move to a larger table?"

Alex answered for both of them before Jim had a chance to say yay or nay. "Thank you. We'd be glad to join you."

About the time they got settled at their table the evening show began. Outlandish drag queens lip-syncing hit tunes while prancing and jiggling and walking table to table for tips. It was loud. They talked a little between performers, but mostly nursed their drinks and enjoyed the show. After the last performer did her thing Jim asked Harry what he wanted to talk about. "Old times," Harry said. "What it was like doing drag way back when. It must have been a whole different world, and I want to know what that world was like."

"Well, for starters, a lot of the queens were more serious about it. It was fun, too. In one sense it was a lark, and it was liberating. But we constantly watched over our shoulders. And the audiences were different. Look around. Half of these people are straight. Now straights come and laugh with the drag queens. Back then they came to laugh at them. It was a freak show."

Jim saw that Harry listened with his whole body at attention. It soon became clear that he was sincere in his interest and didn't have it in him to stalk anyone. He didn't think in ways a stalker might. No guile, no craftiness. He looked right into their eyes when he spoke to them. There was, as he had said, a kind of social awkwardness in his manner of talking, with a kind of gee-whiz wonder at everything and an unaffected way of asking questions that Jim realized probably worked to his advantage as a reporter. At first Jim was hesitant to tell him anything. He threw out tidbits as if to test Harry's response. As it became clear that Harry didn't think he was weird or perverted, and as Harry assured him that he would not write anything without his permission, Jim began to tell all. Alex was surprised at how easily he opened up after his initial hesitance. Coming out to her had not been that easy for him, and she had to assure herself that he didn't trust this virtual stranger more than he trusted her; it was simply a matter of coming out getting easier with practice.

He told Harry how he had first tested the waters of cross dressing with Jimi Sue and about seeing the performers at Barney's for the first time with his Uncle Bradley and about how long it took him to work up the nerve to ask about being in the show. He said,

"When I auditioned for the gig, it was just me and Barney and one of the drag queens, Tom, better known as Miss Tammy Tucker. It was early afternoon, an hour or so before the pub opened."

"Did you just walk up to Barney and ask if you could do it?" Harry asked.

"No, I was very formal. I sent him a letter, including an eight-by-ten glossy of me as Amanda Darling, and he wrote back and said to call him to schedule an audition. I came to the bar at the scheduled time already in drag. I sang "I Could Have Danced All Night" from *My Fair Lady*. In high school I had played the part of Freddy, but I secretly yearned to play Eliza."

"See?" Harry put in triumphantly. "That right there, that's why I thought you were gay."

"Because of something I'm saying now you decided two years ago that I was gay. That's some power of observation you got there."

"No, you might not have said anything like that, but it's in the attitude. You set off gaydar. I hope that doesn't make you mad."

"I don't mind."

Alex added, "He told me his Uncle Bradley called him the gayest straight boy he'd ever known."

"Yeah. See. Even your girlfriend agrees."

Alex liked it that it didn't ruffle Jim one little bit when someone said he set off their gaydar.

Jim continued: "So I sang, and Tommy loved it. I thought Barney did too, but he was hard to read. But what he did do that shocked me was he said, 'You're a good enough singer, sweetie, but we do drag shows here.' He thought I was a woman."

"I can believe it looking at that picture."

"I had to convince him I was a man."

"Did you have to show him your cock?"

"Not quite. I just showed him what was, or wasn't, on top. I opened my blouse and pulled my padded bra up enough to give him a peek of a flat chest underneath. The chest hair did it."

Harry said, "Wow. That's a great story. Can I write about that?"

"No you can't," Jim said. "You can't write anything about me."

But after a while he asked again. He said, "I'd really love to write about you. If you let me, I promise not to say anything you don't approve of."

Jim said he didn't want anything written. It wasn't that he was ashamed of his stint as a female impersonator. It was because of the riot and his suspicions about it and about the more recent killing spree that he still thought was connected. So he not only didn't want Harry writing about him, he started balking at letting him know anything else. Harry had to convince him all over again that he could be trusted. For a guy who was so socially awkward he couldn't flirt without appearing to be a stalker, Harry was amazingly skilled at convincing them to trust him. They could see why over the years he had been able to get quotes from cops and criminals no one else could get. Confessing secrets to him was like confessing to a combination wide-eyed kid and parish priest. Cautiously Jim continued answering his questions. Jim loved to spin a good yarn, so holding back had been excruciating. He was dying to blurt out his whole life as a cross dresser. Keeping it to himself all those years had gone against his nature.

He told Harry about how difficult it was to get dressed for a performance. He had to shave his legs and pluck his eyebrows and apply more makeup than most women ever wore. He didn't wear full body padding but he did wear falsies. "So the top I had covered, but the bottom was more of a problem. I couldn't use any kind of padding for my hips because of the striptease, so I went au naturel. It worked out pretty good because I've got a nice butt for a boy."

"I noticed," Harry quipped. Alex chimed in that she had too.

Jim had already mastered walking in heels, because he had been cross dressing long before he started performing in drag, but what he was not good at and what took a lot of practice was talking and singing like a woman without it sounding comically falsetto. "Tommy was great at that. In his Miss Tammy Tucker persona he sang the hit tunes of all the queens of country music and beautifully so. He sang country, but sounded more like, say, Peggy Lee than

Loretta Lynn. I wanted to be Miss Tammy's successor, and Tommy was ready to train a replacement. He was getting old. He agreed to help me perfect my act. We worked together on my voice and movement until I nailed it to the stage. Next I needed a hook to set my act apart. The movie *Gypsy* was playing at the Strand. Need I say more? I watched Natalie Wood in action, and that was that."

Harry said, "I know a lot of the performers got harassed. Some of the patrons too. My dad talked about that."

"Oh god yeah," Jim said. "You were taking your life in your hands just walking in here."

Harry said, "I know about that. I know about those cops called Walrus and Warthog. Brewster Crockett. He's still a sleazebag. And the one that got killed. I forget his name."

"Felts. Geez, how'd you know about them?"

"Like I said, my dad."

It turned out that Harry knew a lot about Walrus and Warthog and the police corruption back then. He knew about payoffs. He knew that they sometimes cornered queers in the alley behind the pub and beat the crap out of them. He even knew about the rape of George Newman, but not about the rape of Tom Rogers.

Harry said, "My dad had dreams of breaking a Pulitzer Prize-worthy exposé of the corruption in the force back then. And he wasn't alone in his investigation. He had a close friend who was a private detective who did some snooping around for him. Christopher Hatcher. He's retired now, but he's still around. Dad kept extensive notes. He never was able to find enough hard evidence or get anyone to go on record, so he was never able to break the story the way he would have liked. I've still got all his notes. Dad passed away a few years ago. Man, I'd give anything to be able to finish the story he never got to write."

That was enough to convince Jim that he could trust Harry. He told him about what happened to Tom, about how they'd raped him and how devastated he was afterwards, how he never came back to Barney's. And he told about the night of the riot, about how he had tried to sneak away and how the cops saw him but later didn't remember and never questioned him, and about hearing the shot that killed Fred Felts.

"Did you see who fired it?" Harry asked.

"No. I wish I had. I'm sure nobody did. That's the one thing I'm pretty sure they were telling the truth about. I mean, god, people were being rounded up and beaten with nightsticks and fists, and they were fighting back like mad, so it's no wonder that nobody saw who shot the cop."

Harry said, "The partner that survived, Crockett. I always suspected he was the one that shot him. It was his gun, after all. Man oh man, did he ever get off slick. And he socked away a lot of money too. They were getting payoffs from Barney and from drug dealers, and a few years after that Crockett and another dirty cop stole about forty-thousand dollars worth of illegal drugs from the police evidence locker." (Jim had said twenty thousand.) Crockett was working drug enforcement then. Hell's bells, everybody knew he stole the stuff, but he was never even a suspect. He quit the force not long after that. Started a property management business managing—or failing to manage, I should say—a bunch of rental properties. Bought out a... I forget what it was, some kind of retail store, and The Meat Market, and interest in Grant's. He even owns that espresso stand with the strippers. Obviously he used the money from the drug bust to get started."

"I know all of that," Jim said. But he was overjoyed to hear Harry say it.

Harry said, "Now he's pretty fucking wealthy, and pretty much untouchable too. He's got connections in high places and low places too that go back generations. Unless he has a sudden religious epiphany and decides to confess he'll never be caught."

At that point Alex stepped in. She said, "Whoa. This is going too far, and we're in a very public place."

Jim and Harry looked around as if they'd just awakened from a shared dream and didn't know where they were. It was after midnight. Alex said they should call it a night. "You can talk more later, preferably in a private place."

Jim said, "She's right. But we do need to continue this. I have some things to tell you that I think you'll find very interesting."

Alex said Harry could come to their apartment. "I'd love to. Thank you," Harry said.

They made a date for the next morning.

•

They went for their walk in the park early, and on their way home they stopped off at the bakery on the corner of Harvard and Broadway and got sweet rolls and Danish and then back home they put on a pot of coffee and changed out of their sweats. After enjoying a first helping of coffee and pastries with Harry, Jim got right down to business. He said, "You said you thought Crockett was the one who shot Felts. I think you're right. I'm practically a hundred percent sure. Not only that, I think he is the serial killer who has been murdering drag queens."

Harry said, "You're the anonymous caller to the police!"

"Uh huh."

"Makes sense. All right, I must say I wouldn't be surprised if you're right about Crockett, but what kind of evidence do you have and what possible motive would he have?"

"The evidence is clear," Jim said. "All of the victims, including two that haven't even been connected…"

"The car off the road on Mt. St. Helen's and the hiker on the Pacific Crest Trail."

"Exactly. Hey, you really are up on this stuff. So yeah, they were all performers who were there the night of the riot. Thank god Walrus didn't remember that I was there that night and never knew my true identity. Otherwise I'd be next."

"But what about a motive?" Harry asked. "I can get why he might have killed his partner, but why would he want to kill a bunch of old drag queens forty years later?"

"Motive schmotive. He doesn't need motive. He's doing it 'cause he's crazy."

"He is crazy all right. I know that. He's absolutely paranoid." As if the word paranoid had set off his own, Harry's volume dropped a notch and he glanced around like he thought somebody might be listening in. He even took a hard look at Alex's telephone and a table lamp—likely places where, in cop shows at least, bugs could be planted. He said, "He believes in conspiracy theories like about the Kennedy killings and that the whole Apollo moon mission was faked by the media and no telling what all. He thinks the FBI and the CIA are out to get him. He once reported to the police that one of his tenants in some cheap property was hired by the CIA to kill him. The guy he thought was after him was an elementary school teacher. No connections with anything. And just living in one of his shacks didn't give him access to Crockett anyway. So yeah, I'd say he's plenty paranoid and crazy, but still, I can't see why he'd want to kill off a bunch of harmless former drag queens. If he's afraid they'll tell something on him from way back when he was a beat cop, heck, he's pretty much free and clear on all that stuff. Nobody would take the word of some old queen over the word of a wealthy businessman no matter how crazy or corrupt he is. He's super rich. And like I said, untouchable."

Jim said, "But is he truly? More to the point, is he confident that he's untouchable? What I'm thinking is that he's thinking it would only take one cop that can't be bought off or one witness who is unafraid. What I think is he killed his partner on purpose. Maybe they'd fought over money or something. We know they were crooked as all get-out, and they probably had lots of dough stashed away."

"OK. Uh huh."

Alex started to speak up but couldn't think of what to say. Jim had told outlandish tales before, but to accuse someone of murder based on what she could only assume was a vivid imagination was beyond anything she'd yet heard from him.

Jim noticed that Alex was about to say something, paused for a moment, saw her reconsider and continued, "My guess is they had money hidden in the damn police station. Walrus coulda used the cover of the riot to knock him off and make off with the money. So. What if now, all these years later, he got to thinking one of those queens mighta seen him shoot his partner? It's been forty years. The surviving queens are either dead or scattered across the country. And if one of them saw Crockett pull the trigger and lied about it back then, maybe that's been eating at him all these years and he decides to tell the truth at last. Maybe he was scared to speak up before but now he's old and figures he doesn't have anything to lose but his life, and he ain't going to live much longer anyway. Besides, here's the other thing I'm thinking. I think Walrus has been feeling guilty for years, and he blames the queens for everything. In his mind he's been transferring his guilt to us. If it wasn't for us he wouldn't have shot his partner."

Onto the festering scab of rage and guilt Jim was sure had been building in Crockett for almost half a century he now projected another element—doubt about his manhood. If he and his partner raped men, wouldn't that mean in their pea-size brains that they were queer? Wouldn't that be a nagging possibility?

Alex pushed away from the table without excusing herself and started putting away dishes out of the dishwasher, pointedly ignoring their conversation while she clanged dishes like cymbals, scraped and rinsed the dirty ones and loaded them into the machine.

"If you're willing," Harry asked Jim, "I'd like for you to tell Hatcher what you've told me. He's the detective I told you about."

Jim's guard shot up again, but Harry convinced him that Hatcher could be trusted and before he left he said he would set up a meeting.

•

"You don't trust him, do you?" Jim said after Harry left.

"It's not him so much. It's you. You're cooking up wild theories. And yeah, I find it rather odd that you, Mister Skeptical, seem to trust him completely. Yesterday you thought he was out to get you, and I can't count the times you've said he's an idiot."

"What can I say? I was wrong. And he's a lot smarter than I thought."

"So you meet the guy and suddenly he goes from a joke of a reporter who can't get his facts straight to Mister Smarter Than You Think."

"Oh, aren't you having fun with this Mister This and Mister That. Look, I never said the guy was stupid. I just made fun of him because he reported on crimes like he was writing a humor column. He picked the weirdest of crimes to report on and made strange connections between disconnected events, but I realize now that was just his style."

"What about all the errors in his column?"

"Like what?" Give me an example."

The only one she could think of was one of Harry's columns they had discussed that first night they bumped into each other at Barney's. "How about this one?" she challenged, *"Transvestite murdered, no foul play involved. Only Harry could say there was no foul play in a murder."

"Yeah, but I don't think he wrote that. Reporters seldom write their own headlines. The copy editors do that."

She conceded that he might be right. Harry did seem to be more intelligent than she had thought. She just didn't like it that he and Jim were talking about crime investigation as if they were Lennie and Ed on "Law and Order."

A few days later Harry asked them to come over to his house to meet with his private eye, Christopher Hatcher. Harry lived in a modest bungalow not much larger than their tiny place, but a heck of a lot nicer. It was a two-bedroom built on a hill overlooking the West River in a neighborhood of much larger and more expensive homes. They climbed a short flight of stairs from the double car garage, which was closed and probably used for storage. Two cars were already parked in the driveway. "Looks like he's already here," Jim said.

Harry's front door looked like solid oak. His brass door clapper was a replica of Michelangelo's *David*. Jim rapped the knocker. Harry opened the door and invited them in. The main floor of the house featured a spacious dining and living area with hardwood floors and scattered rugs with Mideastern patterns. The whole west wall was glass and opened to a deck with a view of the river. It was not yet dark out. Sky and river were a uniform gray; trees on the farther shore were a slightly darker shade of gray and looked flat as if torn out of cardboard and pasted against the sky. Christopher Hatcher was standing on the deck with a cup of coffee in hand, smoking. He looked to be even older than Jim and Alex. She guessed in his mid seventies. A wavy shock of silver hair over his ears and curling around the collar of a wool plaid shirt, maybe five-foot-six and frail. She noticed skeletal fingers holding his coffee mug. It dawned on her that they were a bunch of senior citizens playing at cops and robbers investigating ancient crimes committed by equally ancient criminals. It's some kind of grotesque dream, she thought.

Hatcher flicked his cigarette over the deck rail to the rocky and driftwood-strewn beach far below, opened the door and stepped in.

Harry said, "This is Christopher Hatcher. Chris, this is Alex... I'm sorry, I forgot your last name."

"Martin."

"Right. And Jim Bright, formerly known as Amanda Darling."

"Hi. Nice to meet you." They shook hands all around. Hatcher reeked of tobacco smoke. Alex tried to not show her revulsion. She wondered how many people had been repelled by her smell over the many years she had smoked. Jim and Alex were wearing light windbreakers, Jim a baseball cap. They pulled their jackets off and looked around for a place to hang them. Hatcher pointed to an easy chair already piled with hats and coats. Alex handed hers to Jim and he added them to the pile. The place looked well lived in. Books and papers scattered haphazardly, plates with remnants of dried food cluttering the coffee table, a pile of newspapers in a corner, a blanket tossed over the back of a love seat.

Harry asked if they wanted coffee. Alex said she'd love some. Jim said, "Yeah, me too."

Soon they were all settled in a cozy conversation area in front of a giant TV that was tuned to CNN with the sound muted, Jim and Alex on the loveseat and the two of them in easy chairs.

Jim repeated all the stories he had told Harry. It took a good hour to go over it all, what with both of them constantly asking for clarification on one point or another. Harry made Alex nervous. He scooted to the edge of his chair, tapped his feet, leaned back and hiked his feet to the ottoman, ankles crossed, then both feet back on the floor. Hatcher sat at attention, back straight, feet planted, his eyes on Jim's lips. Alex thought he must have been aiding poor hearing with lip reading. Twice he interrupted to excuse himself and go out on the deck to smoke a cigarette. Harry used those breaks as opportunities to fetch refills on coffee, and Alex used the breaks to get up and stretch. She looked at the paintings on his walls. They were all abstract designs with dull colors. The work looked familiar. Probably some artist she'd seen in a local gallery.

Stepping back in, Hatcher said, "I think you're right about Crockett, but I don't see any way to prove any of it. It's just theory. There's not a stitch of solid evidence in anything you said. Not about the killing of his partner and not about the drag queen murders. Your testimony about the rapes and beatings forty years ago could bear some weight in a trial if there was ever enough evidence to bring him to trial and if it was allowed in, but it wouldn't be allowed. Hearsay. I think the only possible way to get anything on him, short of an eye witness, which you ain't got, would be to get him to confess, and that ain't likely to happen."

He'd been pondering it quite thoroughly while having his smoke.

Harry asked, "What if he found out that a surviving witness to the riot had been found?"

"You mean me?" Jim asked.

"Uh huh. If Crockett is really guilty, and he found out who you really are—I mean that you were Amanda Darling—wouldn't he want to question you, find out what you know?"

"Maybe," Hatcher said, "But even if he did there's no reason to think he'd give anything away. He's not going to come right out and say, 'by the way, I'm the one that killed all the other drag queens.'"

"He might," Jim said, "If I made him mad enough."

"Are you crazy?" Alex asked. She would have been less surprised if voices had started coming out of the paintings on the walls.

Harry said, "That's right. That might work."

That convinced her they were all crazy and furthermore, they didn't have the slightest concern for Jim's safety. But what really shocked her was that Jim seemed willing to go along. She knew he loved a good mystery. She knew he had a longstanding dislike of the rogue cop called Walrus. But she also knew Jim had never been particularly foolhardy. He might be brave enough to dive in a river to save a drowning man, because he was a strong swimmer. He'd feel confident enough for that. But he wouldn't rush into a raging fire to drag out a victim. At least she didn't think so. And surely he wouldn't have the guts to purposely enrage a killer in order to goad him into carelessly divulging his guilt. But Jim seemed oblivious to the danger. He said, "He hated us all. He hated that he had to patrol a gay bar. He hated that he probably harbored some homosexual yearnings himself that he was deadly ashamed of. He hated himself for killing his own partner, accidentally or not, and I don't think it was an accident. And if he really did shoot his partner, he probably blamed the performers at Barney's."

"That doesn't make any sense," Alex said.

Jim said, "Somehow in his twisted-up mind he probably thought we caused him to do it. So yeah, I think if I confronted him with all of that he very well might admit it. If I made him mad enough, I know just what he'd say. He'd say, 'Yeah, I did it, but you'll never prove it'."

"And then he'd kill you," Alex said. "There's no way you're going to do that."

She stood up and grabbed her coat. She said, "Come on. Let's go. We're not accomplishing anything here."

Her reaction was pure fear. Hatcher's was more logical. Ignoring her attempt to leave he said to Jim, "Even if you goaded him into confessing, it would be your word against his. You just said that he'd say you'll never prove it, and that's absolutely right."

Alex's head was reeling. She couldn't believe they were saying what they were saying. She couldn't believe they were plotting ways to get Jim killed. But she might as well have been mute and invisible. *Pay no attention to the hysterical woman.*

Harry said, "You could wear a wire. We could get it all on tape."

"Can you do that?" Jim asked. "Don't you have to be FBI or CIA or some shit like that to do that kind of stuff?"

Hatcher said, "All you need is a credit card and access to the Internet. If you know what you're doing, and I do, it's easy. The hard part, the way I see it, will be getting him to talk to you in the first place."

Harry said. "I can use my column in the Journal for bait."

Harry's column that appeared three days later was an almost completely fabricated story that linked Jim to the May Day Riot but with twists of facts concocted out of pure bedevilment by Jim and Harry.

Raindrops, the blog of the Daily Journal, Wetside, Washington, April 30, 2010

POLICE BLOTTER
By Harry Drews

The last survivor of the riot at Barney's Pub

Amanda Bright, a 68-year-old jazz singer, now retired, is the only living survivor of the riot of May 1, 1970, popularly known as the May Day Riot on the premises of Barney's Pub in downtown Wetside.

Miss Bright is a male-to-female transsexual woman, formerly known as Jim Bright, an advertising executive who has owned a marketing firm in Wetside since 1975. Until today, Miss Bright has kept her former identity as a drag performer secret. She has agreed to tell her story at long last and will appear as the guest of honor at the 40th anniversary of the May Day Riot at Barney's this Saturday.

Miss Bright had sex reassignment surgery last year but still conducts business (she is semi-retired) in the guise of a man and using her old name. "It's just easier that way," she said. "I was afraid I would lose some of my old customers if they knew. But now they will know. I'm tired of pretending to be something I'm not."

Like the legendary Stonewall riots in New York, the Barney's Pub riot pitted gay men, predominantly female impersonators, against police. Like Stonewall, the May Day Riot is remembered as the moment when homosexuals stood up and said we're not going to take it any more.

This year Barney's Pub will commemorate the 40th anniversary of the riot with a special concert featuring actors playing the parts of the female impersonators who performed in the pub at the time. The star of the show will be an actor impersonating Miss Darling, and Miss Darling will be in the audience and has been asked to talk about her experience at the time.

If you visit Barney's Pub you will see a framed newspaper clipping with an article about the riot and a picture of the drag queens who performed there in the late '60s. Among the drag queens in the photograph is a solitary woman, Miss Darling, who was billed as the only "real" woman to perform on the same stage as the female impersonators. Miss Darling's act was unique in that she only rarely revealed herself to be a man in drag, and no one, including audience members and people who worked at the pub, knew her when not in drag.

Reports of the riot at the time said Miss Darling left early on the night of the riot. Club owner Barney Pressman said he could not recall if Miss Darling performed at all that night, but a bartender at the time said she did her show but left before the riot started.

After the night of the riot there were no more drag shows at Barney's until they were reinstated in 1995. Miss Darling reappeared at Barney's in 2001, this time as a jazz singer and using her real last name, Bright. She performed there infrequently, not as a man in drag but as a woman. At the time she had already started hormone treatments but had not had sex reassignment surgery, and club patrons who saw her perform had no clue to her ambiguous gender. Few if any had seen her drag act. Indeed, most of the patrons at Barney's in 2001 had been young children at the time of the riot. Many were not yet born.

In her previous life as Jim Bright she had been responsible for a locally famous advertising campaign for Grant's Department Store, the famous Grant's Christmas ads which have been compared with the iconic Coca-Cola Christmas ads and to *Saturday Evening Post* cover illustrations by Norman Rockwell.

"It was no secret back in the day that Amanda Darling was really a man," Bright said. "In fact, the climax to my act was when I jerked off my wig to show the audience I was a man, usually to loud gasps of surprise and hearty applause. In the manner of all good actors, I never let my audience see Amanda out of character. Even I was not aware of my true self back then."

Bright said, "In those days there was a lot of corruption. The police who patrolled the area were bigoted and frequently harassed us. They got away with things they could never get away with now. Gay men were considered fair game. They could be arrested just for being gay and were routinely harassed and even subjected to violence. The police were as guilty as anyone else. Both uniformed police and undercover cops patrolled Barney's regularly. It was easy to spot the undercover cops. Their shoes were the first giveaway. They dressed like hippies, but somehow their outfits looked more like costumes. I can't describe it, but they were easy to recognize. We all knew who they were."

Bright said the police were just as responsible as the club patrons for starting the riot. "They used unnecessary force," Bright said. "The queens just fought back to protect themselves."

Bright added, "I could tell you stuff about those cops you'd never believe," but when pressed for details she refused to say any more.

With what I took to be a bit of pride, Bright said, "When they wrote up the riot and published that picture, they identified me as Amanda Darling, not as Jim Bright. The reporter thought I was a woman."

When asked if she witnessed the riot Bright said, "I was there to see it get started. I saw the police rush in swinging their billy clubs and I snuck out the back. It was scary, and I'm not a fighter."

Bright claims she is not and never has been homosexual. She was in a relationship with a woman before transitioning and is still with the same woman. "It wasn't until years after I performed in drag that I realized I had always thought of myself as a woman but had been in denial. At the time, I didn't think of myself as gay or transsexual. I was simply an entertainer. That's all. Amanda Darling was the greatest role I ever played."

Bright avoided a return to Barney's for many years. "By the time I did go back there was nobody left except Barney the owner and Randy Glass, who was the bouncer back then but is now the bartender and part owner. Imagine my surprise when I walked in and saw that picture on the wall with me in the middle surrounded by all the old queens. I talked Barney into letting me perform as Amanda without revealing my masculine identity. I wanted to see if I could make it as a jazz singer without the drag act. I think I did pretty well."

Miss Bright suffers from emphysema as a result of years of smoking, and has had two heart attacks in the past two years. She says she doesn't have long to live, which is why she decided to tell her story at last.

Chapter 15

"I can't believe you said that," Hatcher said.

"Said what?" Jim asked, as if he didn't know.

"That you were a goddamn woman. That you had a goddamn heart attack."

"And I can't believe Harry quoted it." Jim shot back. "I thought he knew I was kidding."

"Hey, we both agreed to tell it like that," Harry protested.

Alex said, "You have to know Jim. That was just one more of his many tall tales."

It was Friday night, one day till May Day, one day before the high school reunion, one day before Jim's big outing as Amanda Darling at Barney's.

"I can't help myself," Jim said. "A good story pops into my head and I blurt it out without thinking. I've always been like that."

To Harry he said, "I thought you understood that we were kidding around. I didn't think you'd write it."

Harry said, "You should never lie to a reporter."

Harry and Chris were deadly serious. Alex was enjoying their reaction. She said, "You should have heard what he said about his ex-wife." She told them about Manlow the chimpanzee, only she called him Manlove, and Jim didn't correct her.

Harry's column in the morning paper had created a small sensation. When Jim dialed in his office voice mail there were messages from former clients congratulating him on his courage in coming out as transsexual and inquiring about his heath. Everybody said they'd be at Barney's Saturday night to cheer him on. Randy from the bar called to say, "Man, you gotta see the poster we cooked up." There were multiple messages from Hatcher saying, "We've got to talk before Crockett calls. Meet me at Harry's at 7 p.m. Did you get my message or not? You better be here. Call me back."

When they met at Harry's again Hatcher said, "You got to be ready if Crockett calls. If he wants to meet with you, you got to find a neutral place to meet. I think the best thing would be to get him to come to your place."

"My place is pretty isolated," Jim said.

"I mean Alex's house. Her house would be perfect. We could bug the place ahead of time, and just to make sure, you could wear a wire, and we can listen to everything from her garage. The setup there is like here, Harry, with the living spaces above the garage. With the doors closed and cars parked in front nobody would ever suspect we were inside."

It was disturbing to Alex that he knew so much about her house. He had never been there. As far as she knew, nobody had even told him where she lived. She wasn't used to dealing with a private detective. It was creepy. She wondered what else he might know about her.

"What if he wants me to come to his office?" Jim asked.

Hatcher said, "Tell him you can't. We could use the heart condition and emphysema as excuses."

Harry brightened up. "Talk about serendipitous. Turns out it was a good thing I put that in the article after all. If he wants to set up a meeting you can tell him you're bedridden and he has to come to you."

"That might work," Hatcher said.

Harry asked, "Would you go as Jim or Amanda?"

"I don't know," Jim said.

Alex tried to tell them the whole scheme was dangerous and stupid, but they wouldn't listen to her. Boys playing cops and robbers, and Jim apparently totally oblivious to the danger. Finally she said, "If you insist on going through with this at least notify the police. Get some police backup so that, you know, when the son of a bitch pulls out a forty-four magnum to blow your brains out, maybe the real cops can burst in and save you."

But they all agreed that the cops couldn't be trusted to help. "They wouldn't get involved unless we had a lot more evidence, and if we had more evidence we wouldn't need to do this," Hatcher said. "If they knew what we were up to they'd probably bust in and arrest *us*."

"For what?" Alex asked.

Nobody acknowledged her question.

Hatcher stepped out on the deck for another smoke and Harry excused himself to use the bathroom, leaving Alex and Jim momentarily alone. Jim threw her a what's-the-matter look. She said, "This is crazy, Jim. We can't do it. *You* can't do it. You know you can't."

"I have to, I really do." He sounded miserable but determined.

"Well I don't get it. It's not at all like you. It's a crazy scheme and it's based on a hunch with nothing to substantiate it, so tell me why you insist on going through with it."

"Because the whole bunch of them from Anita to Bonnie Parker and Honey Jewel to Liza Jane and Miss Tammy Tucker were family to me. I can't just chalk it up as unsolvable. I can't let it go."

"Then I guess you'll have to do it without me."

"What does that mean?"

"It means I'm not going to put up with it. It means I'm not going to sit here and listen to the three of you plan some outlandish TV cop scheme that's sure to get you killed." She stood up. She said, "I'm going home. You can stay or you can come with me."

"But I'm the driver," he said.

She said, "I can walk."

She grabbed her sweater and marched out the door just as Hatcher came back in from the patio and Harry from the bathroom. "Where's she going?" Harry asked.

She shut the door behind her.

"She's going home," Jim said. "She, uh… She has some stuff to do at home."

"But you only have the one car," Harry said.

"I know. She likes to walk. It's nice out. She'll be fine."

It was a beautiful evening, not yet fully dark, with temperatures hovering in the sixties and a refreshing breeze. Alex saw other walkers and a few runners and bicyclists on the road. She tried to reconstruct everything leading up to the present situation as she walked through the sparsely populated neighborhoods along

West River Drive and then across to the City U campus, but all she could think of was that she hoped Crockett, if he was indeed the killer, hadn't read Harry's article.

What's up with these macho men playing cops and killers? Don't they understand that if the guy they called Walrus really is a mass murderer he will very likely kill Jim and anyone else who sticks his nose in his business?

Oh Jim, Jim, Jim, I don't want to have to bury you. I don't want to grow old alone.

She wondered if Jim's whole disconnect with reality, the wild stories he concocted and his apparent belief that he was invulnerable, had all started with the cross dressing. He pretended to be a woman, which despite his reasoned explanations she could never quite grasp, and then he spent the rest of his life in a make-believe world. Maybe it was his father's fault. Such unreal expectations the old man had. Maybe Jim had begun escaping into make believe as a child. But if that were so, Alex thought, then was his friendship with her false? Had it been false from the very beginning?

Best Friends – Jim and Alex's blog

Shoot 'em Up
by Alex Martin

My boyfriend loves cop shows on TV. I don't get it. Cop shows nowadays are dumb. Oh I know, people will argue that they're smarter than ever what with modern forensics and so forth, but from the standpoint of dramatic structure and insight into human nature they're hollow shoot 'em ups with lots of action and no substance.

Today's cops are not cool like Columbo. They're brutal. They try to be funny, at least some of them, but they're just vicious. They glorify violence and create the impression that breaking all the laws is permissible and even laughable if it means getting the bad guys in the end. Young boys and girls grow up watching that shit and want to be just like their heroes, so they become cops, and then we wonder why we keep seeing cops beating the crap out of people who may have done nothing worse than curse them. We see them on the news all the time, live videos of indisputable police brutality, and then they do a survey and discover that fifty-three percent of respondents or some such think the brutality is justified.

And we wonder why.

And character development? Forget it. These shows are all about chases and explosions and car crashes and gun battles that rage over half a city. And have you ever noticed that the bad guys have automatic rifles that can shoot five thousand rounds in two seconds, but they can never hit their target? Well guess what, folks. In real life the bad guys can kill you dead with a single shot from any old gun.

Like I said, I don't understand what my boyfriend sees in these shows.

Comments - 0

Chapter 16

Alex told him he had to leave.

"Just like that?" he asked. Just pack my stuff and hit the road?"

"Yes, just like that. Unless you call Harry and Hatcher right now and tell them you're going to tell the police what you know and then drop the whole thing."

"But..."

"No buts. No excuses."

He tried begging her to change her mind, but she refused to give in. So he packed the few possessions he had moved into her house and he went back home to Rock Creek where he stayed for two weeks, leaving the house only when he needed groceries or beer or cigarettes. Cigarettes! He had quit smoking more than a decade earlier, but the urge to smoke had never gone away. There was comfort in resuming old habits. The six pack of beer he bought the first day he was back home alone was the brand that had been his favorite before he met Alex and she tried to elevate his level of connoisseurship. He turned down jobs. His meals were frozen dinners heated up in the microwave. He skipped breakfast altogether. The grass outside said it was time to start mowing again, but he ignored it. He watched a lot of television, daytime soap operas and cop shows, and drank a lot of beer.

Alex continued her routines but without Jim. She continued her early morning walks and still worked part time at the bookstore, and at night she watched MSNBC and PBS. Like Jim, she ate mostly dinners that could be quickly heated up in the microwave. Over and over she picked up the phone to dial Jim's number and then set the receiver back in its cradle. Over and over she wrote emails to him that she closed without sending or saving.

Neither of them posted anything on their mutual blog.

Finally, Jim sent her a text message. It said: "It's over. Called Harry and Hatcher."

"I love you," she texted back. "CU soon?"

•

May in Western Washington is gorgeous. Days dawn gray and cool but gradually turn warm and bright. Everything is lush with a burst of color from flowering fruit trees and rhododendrons and, in front of Alex's apartment, a profusion of flowers given to her many years ago that neither Jim nor Alex could begin to name. On most days in spring the sun does not make an appearance until at least noon, but May Day dawned bright with sunlight streaming through their window to wake them before the alarm went off. Cast shadows from the wind chimes in their window danced against the wall. "Look, Jim," Alex said. "It's like a shadow puppet show. I think that's a favorable omen. "What do you think?"

"Puppets, yes. They're us, and they're dancing for joy."

It was their first morning to wake up together since their brief breakup. They stretched languorously. He rubbed her breast and her stomach and down. She scrunched down and rested her head on his chest. He messed with her hair. Eventually they got out of bed, washed faces and brushed teeth, and she made coffee.

"What happened to make you change your mind about Crockett?" she asked.

"I got to thinking about it, and I realize that you were right. It's too dangerous. Besides, I had a dream about it. In my dream Crockett pulled out a gun, but he didn't shoot me. He shot you."

It was the anniversary of the riot at Barney's and the day of their fiftieth class reunion—forty-nine years actually, but Mary Elizabeth Cockburn, nee Lucious (she married Lara Cockburn's brother) miscalculated and her fellow organizers didn't notice the mistake or wouldn't dare challenge her. By the time someone finally pointed it out invitations had already been mailed. For a month or so emails and phone calls had been exchanged by members of the class of '61 in an effort to contact classmates who had spread throughout the country, and even a few in other countries. (Reggie Sheffield was in Japan and Christine Rocker, who had divorced Smiley Russell, had recently gone to a village in Africa with a missionary group from her church.) The few who still lived in Wetside were hounded by Mary Elizabeth and Lara to help with preparations. Neither of them had spoken to Alex since their tenth reunion, but that didn't keep them from hounding her until she agreed to serve on the planning committee. She bitched and moaned to Jim. "It's like senior prom all over again. Decoration committees, invitations, line up a band, line up a caterer, line up all the men Mary Elizabeth has dumped over the years. OK, I made that last one up."

She agreed to sign up for an Internet classmate finder group and send out emails to everyone she could find, which was how she found out Christine Rocker was in Africa.

Jim hadn't wanted to go to the reunion, but Alex talked him into it. He agreed reluctantly at first, and then a mischievous grin lighted up his face and he announced, "If we've got to go to this shindig, let's make it fun."

She knew "making it fun" would likely involve some kind of elaborate hoax perpetrated on their classmates. "What sinister plot do you have in mind?" she asked.

What he had in mind was going in drag. Both of them, Alex in a tuxedo and Jim as Amanda Darling/Bright.

They went for their usual early morning walk in West River Park. There's a lovely five-mile trail, well shaded and with excellent views of the river. It was still fairly cool, but after a brisk mile they were sweating. Bands of dark forest green and a brilliant yellow-green swathed the ground as sun slanted between tall trees lush with foliage. At about the three-mile mark Jim took her hand. They'd never before walked holding hands. He started singing an old favorite song, "Truckin' like the doo-dah man…"

She tried to join in but neither of them could remember the words, so they threw in a lot of extra doo-dahs and broke down in laughter.

The reunion was to be at the country club, with dinner at eight and dancing after. Jim planned to spend the day in Rock Creek working on another campaign for Grant's and then get dressed before coming back home to pick Alex up. With each of them getting dressed separately, it seemed more like a date. The day before she had rented a tuxedo and a ruffled white shirt. Finding a tux with the right fit for a woman was not easy. She found hers at a theatrical costume shop. She had a ten o'clock appointment with the hairdresser. She got her hair cut short. She'd been threatening to chop it off for ages. Now she had a good reason. She told the hairdresser she was going for an androgynous look.

"Speaking of androgynous," she said, "Did you see that thing in the paper about the transvestite that was in the riot at Barney's?"

"Yes, I saw it." She had her head reared back with her hair in a sink full of warm water and her hands on the armrest of a chair. She tensed up, squeezing the armrest, steeling herself for the smartass remark she sensed was coming.

"I just don't understand." The hairdresser said. "Why would a man want to turn himself into a woman?"

Alex said, "It's called show business. You know, like the theater. Make believe."

"Yeah, but they said he had the operation." She went into a rant about how freaks of nature were upsetting the natural order and how that was a sign that the end times were coming. "And now they're celebrating the time they beat up and murdered policemen, the very men who were there to protect them. I just don't get it."

"It was just one policeman, and it was in self-defense, and the shooting was an accident," Alex said. She started to tell her the guy in the article was her boyfriend and that he was doing it as a lark and was not an actual transsexual. But then she'd have to tell her that Harry Drews had made up that stuff about Jim, now Amanda, living as a woman, and she didn't want to have to explain that.

The walk home from the hairdresser was just a few blocks, one of the nice benefits of living downtown. It was mid day. At Harvard and Market she saw a group of May Day celebrants marching in the street, blocking traffic, without a permit if they were being true to established tradition. Every year they picked different routes for their parade, all calculated to disrupt traffic flow—to interrupt for a moment the fat cats' ability to rip off the people, a demonstration that was practically ineffective but symbolically a monkey wrench thrown in the gears of the corporate/consumerist culture, pissing off exactly the people the protestors most wanted to piss off. The first year the police had arrested some of them, but after that they directed traffic and let them do their thing. Downtown merchants and shoppers always halted business to watch and cheer or jeer, depending. Some years the demonstrators got pretty rowdy. Once they broke a few windows and turned over trash receptacles. Mostly they were better behaved than that, and mostly the citizens of Wetside enjoyed the spectacle. A few people complained in letters to the editor. The letter writers assumed all the demonstrators were from City U., which some but not all were. Octogenarian Melody Sauer marched with them every year. That year they carried nonsensical signs such as "Protest Stuff" and "This is a Sign" and "I'm a better anarchist than you are." A lot of them carried blank signs.

Rather than turning down Harvard for home Alex continued on following the marchers until they passed Bev and Rhonda's, and then she stopped off for a latte and a sweet roll. It seemed like half of Wetside had the same idea. It took about fifteen minutes to place her order. Luckily someone vacated a seat just when she needed it so she sat and lingered over her latte and sweet roll.

For the rest of the day she had nothing to do. She puttered around the house, but how much house cleaning and organizing can you do in a 7,000-square-foot cottage? About five o'clock she took a bath and ate a cheese sandwich. She was hungry but didn't want to spoil her appetite before dinner. Her mother had taught her to avoid snacks for up to two hours before a meal. As soon as she bit into the sandwich she thought it was too heavy. She took two bites, and it seemed like it took forever to chew enough to swallow. She washed it down with tap water. Before getting dressed in the tux she wrapped her breasts with an Ace bandage in order to hide them. Not a good idea. It was so uncomfortable she decided to nix the whole idea of pretending to be a man. If she couldn't hide her boobs, she would go as a stylishly masculine woman. She'd seen an actress in some movie wear a tux and a man's hat, and she was extremely sexy. Maybe she could be like her. She figured that would knock Jim's socks off. Her options were to fool a bunch of their old classmates by presenting as a man or turn Jim on by appearing as a hottie in a tux. The choice was obvious.

By six o'clock she was ready to go, waiting nervously for Jim to arrive. Every five minutes she went to the full-length mirror in their bedroom to check out her appearance. *Should I wear lipstick or not? Yes, I should. What color? Something very dark. What about eye shadow? Eye liner? You bet. Also dark. Kind of an androgynous Goth look. Could I carry that off at my age? I think so.* She liked what she saw in the mirror. Then back to the front room to peek through the blinds. She hadn't been so nervous about a date since her first date with Leslie Grant, who turned out to be gay—not an auspicious beginning to her love life.

She was expecting Jim by seven. When he hadn't shown up by five after she started worrying. By a quarter after she was frantic. She called his home phone and his cell. Both went into voicemail. "Jim Bright advertising and graphics..." *OK, he's on his way. He can't answer his phone because he's driving.* Jim was a law abiding citizen, and Washington had recently passed a law against talking on a cell phone while driving. She fixed herself a drink. Just a light bourbon and soda to take the edge off. It was the tail end of rush hour. Maybe there had been an accident. That could tie up traffic for half an hour or more. But then he'd be stopped and could call her on his cell. At seven-thirty the doorbell rang. Jim would not ring the bell. He had a key. *Oh God! Has he been in an accident? Have Brewster Crockett and his goons caught up with him? Is this going to be the police telling me his body was found washed up on the banks of East River?*

Her hand was trembling when she reached for the doorknob. She stood for a moment, took a deep breath and pulled the door open. A beautiful woman stood at the door. It was Amanda Bright. Or Amanda Darling, older than in the newspaper clipping, a little grayer in her hair than when she sang at Barney's, but unmistakably the same woman, and inside her face beamed Jim Bright's proud smile.

"Oh my God!" they shouted in unison.

He said, "You look great."

She said, "Where the hell have you been? I was worried sick."

"It just took me a little longer to get ready than I thought. I didn't mean to worry you."

"It's all right."

He asked her how he looked. She said, "Fabulous."

"This dress is two sizes larger than the one Amanda wore in 1970." He turned his back and glanced over his shoulder and said "Does it make my butt look fat?" (Even for Jim that was a cheap jest.)

Stupefied, Alex was still standing with her hand on the doorknob as if talking to some stranger who rapped on her door, and Jim in his sleek yellow dress was still outside on the stoop as if waiting for her to invite him in. She said, "I just need to get my purse, and then we can go."

He said, "You can't carry a purse while wearing a tux."

"Why not?"

"Because men don't carry bags. If you're going as a man, you can't carry anything you can't stuff in your pockets."

"Oh, right. I didn't think about that. But I'm not going as a man so much as a…"

"As one helluva sexy broad."

"Oh yeah. OK. Wow Do you really think I look sexy?!" (The next day she would write on her blog: "I purt nigh pissed my pants. It's a wonder I didn't say gee wiz or aw shucks or something else kind of Obie Taylorish.") She fished her wallet and keys out of her purse and put them in her pocket, but that didn't feel right. *How do men put up with sitting on their wallets?* She handed them to Jim saying, "You've got a purse. You carry 'em."

On the way to the club Jim said, "Which name should I use?"

She said, "I don't think it matters. Amanda of course, but Bright or Darling. Hmmm. Bright I think. Everybody will recognize either name. Surely they all read Harry's column. The whole class is probably buzzing about you."

"Some, maybe. But half of them never read the paper."

She asked if he thought she should go with a man's name, and he said she should stick with her own name. "It's gender neutral. Besides, the invitation's in your name."

They were a handsome androgynous couple, Alex and Amanda. *Love the alliteration. We're looking good too. Going to knock their socks off.* After parking at the country club she took Jim's arm and they strolled in clinging to each other. She thought maybe they looked like young lovers or maybe like they were scared out of their wits. Maybe going in drag was the dumbest thing they'd ever done. Her anyway, for him it made sense. Inside were purple and gold party streamers (school colors), a disco ball, cloth draped tables with candles, everything sparkling; on the bandstand Van Cook's band the Vandoleers was playing lush music. It was the same band that had played for their high school prom but with only two of the original band members: Van, who had recently retired from the barber shop he took over from his father, on bass, and Greg Olson on piano. The original drummer had been killed in Vietnam, their guitar player died of lung cancer, and the original girl singer, Sheila True, lived in California and was not able to make the trip. To the right of the door leading into the ballroom was a bar, and by the door was a table where Lara and Mary Elizabeth sat taking invitations and instructing everyone to make name tags. "Be sure to include your maiden names," they told the women.

"Hi there," Lara said "Oooh, don't tell me. I know I know you. You're... I'm sorry, I guess I can't remember after all. It's been so long, and I'm afraid we've all grown older."

Alex slapped her name tag over her breast and said, "Alex Martin. The boy clothes probably threw you off."

"Oh yes, of course. Now I recognize you. My, my, you've hardly aged at all." She had not read Harry's article or heard that Jim was transsexual. Faced with a gender confused couple, one of whom turned out to be Alex Martin in boy clothes, she turned to the other one and said, "And you must be her... uh, partner. Is that the term they're using nowadays?"

Jim had written Amanda Bright on his name tag. Mary Elizabeth squinted to read it. Jim said, "I'm her wife. Amanda Bright."

"Bright? Oh my goodness, you must be Jim Bright's sister. We never really knew you, but..."

"No, my dear," Jim said with the smooth and conciliatory tone of someone explaining it to a child and a devilish gleam in his eye, "I'm not Jim Bright's sister. I used to *be* Jim Bright."

"I don't understand. Do you mean… Oh my god. Do you mean to tell me you had a… uh, a sex change?"

"Yes indeed, I certainly did," and to her horror and Alex's delight he elaborated: "First off I took loads of estrogen to grow myself a nice pair of tits. How do you like 'em (hefting them to demonstrate)? And then they took my penis and sliced that sucker and turned it inside out to make the prettiest little pussy you ever did see."

Flushed and stammering but nevertheless feeling obligated to comment, she said, "But it's nu-not uh, real, is it? Your, uh, you know."

"Oh yes," Jim said. "It's just as real as yours. And as you may recall, I was well acquainted with yours."

Mary Elizabeth looked like she was going to throw up. She pushed up from her chair and the color drained from her face. She clapped her hand over her mouth and mumbled, "Excuse me" and ran toward the ladies room. Lara, also blanched, sat in stunned silence. "It's so nice to be here," Jim said, and they glided into the ballroom. The lights were low. Four-person tables circled a dance floor, each covered with a purple and gold tablecloth (paper). Tented name plates had been placed on each table. Jim and Alex spent a good twenty minutes wandering around greeting people, renewing old acquaintances and looking for their table. It seemed that Mary Elizabeth was the only one there who hadn't read Harry's column. Everyone was congratulating him, calling him a sly dog for keeping his other identity secret all these years, asking whether to call him Jim or Amanda.

"Amanda by all means, my dear. Jim is history."

Some of Jim's other old teenage conquests were there. Now that Alex knew who they were she observed their figures and faces and was delighted to see that they looked much older than she. Or— the horrible thought hit her—could it be I can't truly see what I look like. *Could I possibly look like these crones?* Anna Shemper looked

251

like she had been washed and hung out to dry. Her skin was pale and her mouth puckered, lips like cracked red enamel. She greeted them coolly and told Jim she found the newspaper article about him "interesting." Betty Black had gained at least forty pounds and had her hair done up in the same beehive style she had sported at their senior prom. Alex wondered if Betty was purposefully being retro or if she actually thought that looked good. Betty gave them each a big hug and told Jim she loved the article. She said, "I'm so proud of you for coming out. That takes a special kind of courage." A porno picture flashed through Alex's mind. Jim at eighteen and Betty at sixty-seven wrestling in fleshy nakedness on the back seat of a '59 Impala. It was not a pretty picture.

Bill Barnes and Beverly Ryan were there together, married to each other now. Bobby Johnson was there alone. His wife of thirty-something years had recently passed away. Dudley Strong was there with a youngish looking wife, both looking as handsome and dignified as ever. Dudley was the boy that beat up Bubba Austin. He became a lawyer, served a term or two in the state legislature, and was now a circuit judge. Bubba Austin was not there. Neither was his brother Reggie. Johnny Delgado and Leslie Grant, both now openly gay, were there together, not as a couple but as friends.

Sharing their table were Rolly and Molly and Kimzey Williams, who appeared shell-shocked and frightened. "Damn if you ain't one good looking chick," Rolly said, standing up and making a show of pulling chairs out for Jim/Amanda, but not for Alex. "You're the guy," he quipped. "You can seat your own damn self."

"Yes I can, thank you very much." She hugged them all before sitting down. Jim said he was glad they had put them at the same table and Rolly informed them it had been at his request.

Kimzey smiled demurely, murmured something so softly no one could hear. As they conversed she looked first to Rolly as if for permission before speaking, and then she spoke politely and in a whisper. Alex could barely hear her and had to ask her to repeat herself. After a while she took to nodding and smiling and guessing what she said.

Rolly was in a jovial mood. He told Jim he made a beautiful woman and kidded Molly saying, "If he'd looked like this back in the day I might have married him instead of you."

A number of their classmates came up to their table and asked if they could take their pictures. Of course everyone was snapping pictures of everyone else, but they especially wanted pictures of Jim and Alex together because they were both in drag. They believed Jim was now Amanda, physically and psychologically. After all, hadn't Harry Drews said so in the paper? They stumbled to try and ascertain with delicate questions exactly what Amanda and Alex's relationship was. Were they a lesbian couple? Was Alex, who had always been quite the tomboy, transsexual too? The one thing that was clear was that most of them were totally accepting of whatever they may be. All but Mary Elizabeth and Lara.

Dinner was steak and baked potatoes with a tossed salad and asparagus. Iced tea and coffee were served, and chocolate pudding for dessert. After dinner the bar opened up, the band played, and couples got up to dance. Jim and Alex stayed for another hour. The band played all the old favorites from when they were in high school. Van was having a grand old time slapping the upright bass. The new guy on trumpet played a mean horn and jumped all over the stage in imitation of the late great Louis Prima, and the new girl singer joined him in a takeoff of Louie and Keely Smith.

The band played "Deep Purple." Jim asked Kimzey if she wanted to dance.

She said, "T-t-t-that would be nice," with a stammer she had not had as a youth. "If you don't mind dancing with a c-c-c-crazy woman. I was in the nu-nu-nut house, you know."

He said, "I know, and I don't care how crazy you are. I like you."

She said, "I like you too. I thought you were a nice boy, and now you're a nu-nu-nu-nice lady."

•

The reunion turned out to be more fun than they had expected. They loved freaking out Lara and Mary Elizabeth, and they enjoyed sharing a table with Rolly and Molly and Kay Kay. Jim was enraptured with Kay Kay. She was so sweet. Clearly she was damaged far beyond repair, but through years of suffering the likes of which they could only imagine she had dropped all pretension; she had erected walls, but when she opened them to the few people she felt safe with there was a welcoming glow inside. When she stepped out on the dance floor with Jim she squeezed his hand as if she were afraid she'd plummet into an abyss if she let go. Surely, he thought, she must be clinging with that same intensity to whatever shred of sanity remained. He remembered the stories about a sick sex cult and child molestation and was reminded that he and Alex had speculated about whether or not Kay Kay had been one of those children. Was there any truth to that? Such abuse could account for the kind of psychological damage she had suffered. What other children had been abused? What about Lara and Mary Elizabeth? Could they have been victims? Maybe that's why they still clung together.

She was so light in his arms it was a wonder she didn't float away. Her body felt like crinkled paper. He felt as if he were dancing with a pre-teen daughter at her first ball, and her watery, smiling eyes looking up at him made him feel as if she were proud to be in his arms.

Jim and Alex left the country club after ten and went to Barney's, which was really hopping. A drag queen in black was imitating Cher when they came in, lip syncing to "Gypsies, Tramps and Thieves." People in the audience were whooping it up and singing along loudly and out of tune. Barney met them near the door and escorted them to a table near the stage. Everyone spoke to Jim on the way, calling him Amanda and asking who his "fella" was, and telling Alex she looked marvelous.

As you enter Barney's there is a small bar to the left at the front. Six bar stools. From there you step down about six inches to the lounge and stage area. There's a rail separating the lounge from the bar, and after a few drinks most customers grabbed the bar to maintain balance before stepping down. Jim had consumed only one drink at the reunion. Nevertheless, he grabbed the rail for support, and just as he did he stopped dead still in shock at the sight of a man seated on the last bar stool. It was Walrus. Brewster Crockett. It was him. Over the past few days Jim had tried very hard to put him out of his mind. And yet here he was seated on the same barstool he had habitually occupied when intimidating the queens back in the day. It was shocking to see him not only for all the expected reasons, but because he did not look at all like Jim remembered, and yet he did. Memory can trick you that way. You picture in your mind someone you knew a long time ago and you never doubt that you remember what he looked like but you don't. The truth is, you've completely forgotten and have constructed a false image in your mind. And then if you see him again it comes flowing back and you recognize him immediately even if he's lost his hair and lost thirty pounds or grown a beard. That's why Jim had let himself think Harry Drews was Walrus when he was the mystery man he thought was stalking him. But Walrus—or Crockett rather, because he no longer looked like the remembered beast—was no longer a frightening presence on his customary barstool. He was a much older and less threatening version of the hated cop of memory-slash-imagination. A rough mental calculation told Jim that Crockett must have been close to eighty if not older. Back in 1969-70 when Jim was in his twenties he'd already been on the force for quite some time. Heavy back then, he was now all wrinkled skin hanging on brittle bones. He looked more like a turkey than a Walrus. A bony nose and chin, ears like something hung out to dry, a red nose, a few strands of white hair, and pale skin with liver spots. He lifted a finger in greeting and nodded his head their way. Jim nodded in return, uncomfortable with how pathetic he looked and feeling bad about wishing him ill, wondering what could have possibly drawn him out to the celebration of an event that surely held only tortured memories for him.

Harry Drews was there also, engaged in what appeared to be an intimate and animated conversation with a nice looking middle age man. Clearly he had finally figured out how to ask somebody out. And he didn't look so bad either. Harry, not his date. Jim decided that maybe he had seen him through a different prism before when he thought he was a stalker.

Barney helped them to their seats and told them their drinks were on the house. He asked, "Are you ready to see the new Amanda Darling?"

They were ready. Barney said they had delayed her appearance on stage awaiting the arrival of the original Amanda.

"Thanks, buddy. I would have hated to miss her act."

The actor that came out to do Amanda's act and sing her old songs looked astonishingly like Jim's Amanda. The face, the hair, the walk, even the way she looked from table to table and closed her eyes on the high notes, something she could never have seen Jim's Amanda do, was absolutely on target. The only difference was she might have been a few inches taller and slightly thinner. She sang two songs. During the second song Jim caught her eye enough to know she had spotted him. She pointed and winked.

"She's lip syncing," Alex whispered. It was not until halfway into the second song that she had realized.

"You're right. I hadn't even noticed," Jim whispered back. "She's pretty damn good, though."

The next song was a lush instrumental ballad. Amanda danced slowly, moving like a slithering snake, head held high, her long and shapely calves in white fishnet stockings, her gown similar to the one Jim had been wearing when the photo was taken, but white instead of yellow, with much deeper cleavage but not so low cut in back. She Pulled off elbow-length gloves and kicked off her shoes, turned her back to the audience and slid her gown down around her ankles and stepped out of it. Underneath she was wearing thong panties and a spaghetti strap bra. Compared to the bras and panties Jim had worn during his performances they were microscopic. *Could she possibly have male equipment hidden under that little strip of cloth?* Her next move, which the audience anticipated, would be to fling off her bra, spin around and reveal that she was a man.

But she wasn't a man, and she proved it. Topless and inarguably female, she bowed and walked off stage. Before the applause died down she came back with a robe draped around her and tied shut in front. She announced to the audience, "I'm sorry if I disappointed you, boys, but they couldn't find a male singer who could do justice to Amanda Darling's act, and I was honored to do it. And now boys and boys, girls and girls, and whomever or whatever you are, it is my great pleasure to introduce to you the real Amanda Darling."

She asked Jim to step up and say a few words. He thanked her, and thanked Barney and Randy, and spoke briefly about how much performing there had meant to him. He told them he was twenty-six years old and scared to death the first time he stepped on the stage at Barney's. He told them he had never performed anywhere else and had never even thought about it. Barney's was home to him. He asked how many people in the audience had seen him perform. Four or five hands shot up. Jim said, "I don't mean in the last decade. I mean at the time of the riot. Did you see me as Amanda Bright or as Amanda Darling? If you were here in 1970 raise your hand."

Only Barney, Randy and Crockett raised their hands.

The crowd shouted out for him to sing, but he declined.

Finally he said, "Confession time. I lied to Harry Drews. I made up all that stuff about being ill and about having a sex change. The original Amanda Darling was a man in drag, and that's what I am now."

Some of the men in the audience applauded wildly at that, but a few expressed their displeasure. They felt betrayed.

Later Crockett came over to their table. He stood quietly while waiting for Alex to finish what she was saying. He stood with hands clasped in front, bony fingers intertwined. He cleared his throat, "Ah hmmm," and said, "I think you might remember me."

"Yes, I do."

"I just wanted to tell you I enjoyed your singing very much in the old days, and I want to apologize for being who I was back then. I know I treated you badly, you and all the others. I was prejudiced then. I guess what you'd call homophobic. I could claim it was the times, that we didn't know any better, but that's bullshit and I'm deeply sorry, and I'd like to make it up to you."

Jim stammered that it wasn't necessary. He'd harbored hatred for the guy for such a long time, and now he was so frail and pathetic that Jim's heart went out to him as he watched his palsied hands grip the back of Alex's chair for support.

Crockett said, "I understand you're in advertising. I didn't know until I read Harry Drews' article, but now that I know who you are I remember that great Christmas ad you did for Grant's."

The Grant's Christmas ad was a ridiculous ad. It wasn't Jim's idea. Sam Grant thought it up. He practically hovered over Jim's shoulder all the way, which irritated the crap out of him because he didn't want anybody knowing that much about how he worked. Very little of Jim's artwork was original. His skill at drawing and painting had always been marginal, but he was pretty good at tracing and photocopying and otherwise reproducing pictures and changing them to suit his purposes, laboriously and stubbornly doing—even in the age of computers—what most graphic artists now do much easier in paint programs. The Grant's Christmas ad featured a Norman Rockwell style Santa in a doorway shaking hands with a small boy. The model for the boy was Sam's son, Sam Junior. Crockett asked Jim if he still had the original art and said he wanted to buy it as a present for Sam. He said, "Name your price."

Jim said he didn't have any idea what it was worth. Crockett offered a thousand dollars. Jim said that was more than enough.

"Bring it around to my office Monday afternoon."

"Yes sir," Jim said.

As soon as those words escaped his lips he knew he had made a big blunder. He didn't know why he said yes. It was a reflex, and he couldn't take it back. It put them right back where they'd been the day before with Alex fearful for Jim and Jim planning on meeting with Walrus, but this time not in the more easily protected place they'd planned on. He hoped he was right that he was a changed man and no longer dangerous.

He told Harry what had happened before they even left the pub, and he called Hatcher early the next day. "Are you calling from home?" Hatcher asked.

"Yes."

"Your house or Alex's?"

"Alex's."

"Stay right there. I'm grabbing Harry and we're coming over."

Twenty minutes later they were in Alex's place. "There's nothing we can do now but meet him on his turf or call off the whole thing," Hatcher said.

Alex said, "Then call it off."

Hatcher had brought a belt for Jim to wear. It was a web belt with a large military-style buckle. "It's a transmitter," he said. "It will record anything said within about ten feet, so be sure you stay in range. And resist the temptation to look down at it."

"Wait a minute," Jim said. "I'm not so sure I want to go through with this."

"You already told him you'd bring the painting to his office."

"No I mean going in with a wire. Yeah, I'll take him the painting. But trying to entrap him, I don't know. It seems like the anger I felt has all gone up in smoke. You should see him. He's just a frail old man."

"Yeah, yeah, I know. He's fucking pathetic," Hatcher said. "But look, if you're going to go to his office anyway, baring gifts and forgiving him all his past transgressions, then at least wear the fucking wire just in case. It won't hurt. And don't keep looking down at your belt. That's a dead giveaway. Me and Harry will be listening to everything that's said. We'll be in a truck parked outside his office building. We'll record it all."

The truck was a panel truck from something like 1980. Hand lettering on the side advertised *Harold's Handyman Service*.

Alex said, "You know, you could get UPS to deliver the damn painting, and he could mail you a check."

But Jim said, "No, I'll deliver the painting. I'll be careful. I'll give it to him and take his check and thank him, and get out as quickly as possible." He actually wanted to see Crockett again, perhaps, he thought, to prove to himself that he hadn't dreamed his change of heart.

He drove to Rock Creek to get the art. Finding it was not easy. It was stacked with other old pictures behind some boxes in a bedroom that hadn't been used for anything other than storage since Uncle Bradley passed away. It was sandwiched between two sheets of cardboard held together with duct tape. Jim sent up a cloud of dust getting it out. He wiped it down with a damp cloth and taped it back securely between the cardboard sheets. On the way back to town he played a Classic Queen CD.

Crockett's office was on Market half a block from Barney's. Jim took the elevator to the sixth floor, found the door to 620. A placard on the door read *Crockett Enterprises*. Jim pushed the door open expecting to see a receptionist seated at a desk, pictures on the wall, maybe even clients waiting for an appointment. There was a reception area of sorts—a single desk—but no one was seated at the desk. There were no pictures on the walls and no people in the two uncomfortable looking chairs. An inner door into Crockett's office stood ajar, and through that door he saw Crockett seated behind a large desk. He waved Jim in, saying "Shut the door behind you."

Stepping in Jim held up the picture and said, "Here's the picture," and started to pull the tape off.

Crockett said, "What, are you stupid? Do you think I really want that fucking picture?"

Suddenly he was Walrus again, older but still a menacing beast. His voice was scratchy but not as weak as it had sounded the night before. He clutched a lighted cigarette between bony fingers. The hands that had trembled so noticeably in Barney's showed only a slight tremor. His chin was scruffy with gray stubble. Watery eyes glared at Jim. He looked him over as if to assure himself he had the right guy, as he knew Amanda well but had never seen Jim as Jim.

For a moment Jim couldn't respond at all, and when he finally did he said, "Then what do you want?"

He said, "I want to know what you know about that little queer that called himself Miss Tammy, the one that did the country songs. And I want to know what you saw the night those queers attacked the police."

Jim's expression was that of some kind of poleaxed ape standing with mouth agape. He knew the Walrus was a crude and vicious bastard. Always had been. But Jim had fallen for the old man's pretend contrition. Crockett growled, "What about that big queer son of a bitch that claimed we raped him? The lying bastard. George was his name. He called himself Anita Dick or something like that. Like that was so freaking funny. Well I gave him a dick all right, right where he wanted it. And he thought he was so tough, the son of a bitch. I hear he's dead now, and I couldn't be happier. But we didn't do none a that shit they claimed. You know that, don't you? They was the queers, not me and Felts, rest his soul."

Jim couldn't follow his contradictory talk. Hadn't he just denied raping George and then bragged about doing it? Spit was spewing from his mouth. He crushed out his cigarette and wiped his mouth with the back of his hand.

Jim went ballistic. He hadn't planned on challenging the old man, but his tirade triggered a million hurts. All the memories of their snide remarks, their holier-than-thou attitude, the slaps upside the heads of half the queens he knew and loved, the pokes in the belly with their nightsticks. He could still hear the pain in Tom Rogers' voice when he told them about how they abused him. Jim said, "You son of a bitch. You raped 'em. You and your partner, you raped 'em both."

"You don't know that. How do you know that?"

"I know they wouldn't lie."

"So what if we did? They had it coming," he shot back.

"Why? What did they do to deserve it?"

"What'd they do? They didn't have to do nothing. They were queer, weren't they? That's all the reason we needed. Hell, they didn't have nothing to bitch about. They loved taking it up the ass. We just gave 'em what they wanted."

"You gave them what *you* wanted," he challenged. "You like it with guys, don't you?" He was so mad he didn't once think about the danger he might have been in. It was all visceral reaction on his part. He said, "You hypocrite. You're just as queer as they were, but you never had the guts to admit it."

"Don't you dare call me queer you transvestite dick sucker." He stood up behind his desk and Jim stood in front of it. Two old men squaring off like young bucks, each so mad they didn't know what they were saying. Crockett admitted the rapes of George Newman (Anita) and Miss Tammy, and he said it was George who shot his partner.

"How do you know that?"

"I seen him do it."

"You did not. If you'd seen it you would have testified at the trial. You said you didn't know who did it."

"Well I was mistaken then, but I know now. I remember it now."

"You remember what you want to remember, and you make the rest of it up."

Crockett moved around to the end of the desk, gripping for support, his balance unsteady. He picked up a paperweight as if to use it for a weapon. It was an eight ball.

"What are you going to do, hit me with that? You can barely pick it up."

Jim accused him of having sex with his ex partner and was shocked to hear him say, "So what if we did? It don't mean nothing. We were real men, not girly men like you and the other queers."

They circled his desk. Jim accused him of killing all the queens from Barney's Pub. He outlined his theory, telling him that he knew that all of the murder victims were men—or in some cases now, women, since some had transitioned—who had performed as female impersonators at Barney's. He said, "The police haven't been able to identify them all, but I can, and you know it."

Again he said, "So what?"

"I'm right, aren't I?"

"What if you are? You can't prove it. You can't prove a damn thing. And the cops, they don't even care. They never have. Besides, you're not going to live to tell about it."

And with that he reached into his desk and pulled out a pistol and pointed it at Jim, his hands now shaking so much Jim was afraid he'd trigger it whether he meant to or not.

Curbside in front of Bev and Rhonda's in the Harold's Handyman truck Harry Drews and Hatcher were listing to Jim and Crockett. They heard them shouting at each other but didn't know Crockett had pulled a gun.

"Shouldn't we do something?" Harry asked.

"Like what?" Hatcher said. "We're blocks away. By the time we get there and ride up six floors on the old elevator... well, I don't know. I mean... Hell, the guy is old and frail. I think Jim can handle him."

"That's it? You think Jim can handle it? What kind of detective are you?"

"Well if you got any bright ideas, let's hear 'em."

And five blocks to the south Alex paced the floor in her apartment anxiously waiting for the phone to ring or for Jim to come through the front door. Outside all was quiet and gray.

As if the world were responding to a theatrical cue, things began to happen all at once in Crockett's office. Sunlight suddenly broke through the clouds and knifed through the window casting long bars of shadow through the blinds, the thrum of a bass from a passing car radio shook the window panes, Crockett began to sweat profusely, and his face drained of color, and the door to his office was slammed open and half a dozen policemen burst in with guns drawn. Crockett tried to turn in their direction. He attempted to aim the pistol at them, but then he went limp. His pistol dropped to the floor and so did he. He crumpled. His chin hit the edge of his desk with a thunk and then banged against the floor. The cops holstered their guns, and one of them rushed around the desk and dropped to his knees and turned Crockett's limp body onto his back and began mouth-to-mouth resuscitation while another called for an ambulance. Crockett opened his eyes and then let them fall shut again. Again he opened his eyes. He lifted his head weakly. The cop who had been giving him mouth-to-mouth said, "Just lay still. Don't try to move."

263

When the emergency medical guys got there they said it looked like he was having a heart attack. They hooked him up to oxygen and put him on a gurney. There were three of them. They asked what happened. One of the medics questioned Jim while the others wheeled Crockett out. Once again Crockett opened his eyes. He said, "I guess you got me, boys."

Raindrops, the blog of the Daily Journal, Wetside, Washington, May 4, 2010

POLICE BLOTTER
By Harry Drews

End of an era: Queen killer and Melody Sauer die

Wetside police believe they have solved the recent serial killings dubbed the drag queen murders. Plus, they may have found the answer to a cold case going back forty years when the person allegedly responsible for all died of a heart attack while being confronted by the police. The alleged murderer did not confess to the police but did confess to a witness.

Jim Bright, whom I recently reported on as the last living survivor of the May Day riot at Barney's Pub in 1970, claims that local businessman Brewster Crockett, 82, confessed to the recent murders of five victims, all of whom were involved in the 1970 riot. Bright, also known as Amanda Darling, recorded Crockett's confession. Police officers have listened to the confession. What may happen next is not yet known since the alleged killer is dead and can't be tried and it is not known if the recording would be allowed in court.

Crockett owned several businesses and rental properties in Wetside, including the Grab-N-Go, recently featured in this column, and The Meat Market, a gay bar. Bright's girl friend, Alex Martin, phoned the police and reported a confrontation in Crockett office.

"She didn't really give us enough to act on, but the officer on duty had a hunch something serious was going down and he acted on that hunch," said police spokesman Snake Collins.

Bright was wired with a recording device and had questioned Crockett about the killings, and he allegedly confessed to them all. When the police broke into Crockett's office Crockett collapsed and dropped his gun. No shots were fired. He was rushed to Mercy

Hospital where he was pronounced dead from a heart attack at 8:36 p.m., May 3.

Collins said, "We may have saved Bright's life by bursting in when we did. Crockett had a gun on him but collapsed with a heart attack, likely due to the fright of being confronted by policemen with weapons drawn."

In other news, 86-year-old Melody Sauer of 1428 Mercer Street passed away during court proceedings yesterday. Miss Sauer died in the same manner and at almost the same time as Crockett. She succumbed to a heart attack in a moment of confrontation. She was defending herself on charges of disturbing the peace, resisting arrest and assaulting a police officer. Miss Sauer passed out while on the witness stand. A court officer attempted to revive her, but she never regained consciousness. Her last words were, "That's none of your damn bees wax" in response to the prosecutor's question, "Do you believe in God, Miss Sauer?"

Coroner J.B. Van confirmed the cause of death was a heart attack.

Sauer had been arrested for refusing to move off the sidewalk at the request of a police officer. She was protesting what she called police harassment of the bikini wearing baristas at Grab-N-Go.

Sauer lived life to the fullest. She was a notorious local character with a record of petty crimes and scrapes with the police going back to World War II when she performed as a striptease dancer in a local nightclub that catered to soldiers departing from the train station in Wetside en route to deployment first to bases in California and then to the theater of war in Europe and the Pacific. Repeatedly arrested during the war on charges of indecent exposure and prostitution, Miss Sauer was often quoted as saying, "I just like to give the boys a reason to come home."

The passing of Melody Sauer marks the end of an era, an era of corruption in which prostitution and other forms of vice were winked at and tacitly approved by a law enforcement establishment that was as dirty as the mean streets they failed to clean up. My father, Harold Drews, who wrote this column for thirty-six years before I inherited it, often wrote about Melody Sauer. He once wrote, "As goes Melody Sauer, so goes the city of Wetside."

And now I, too, shall be gone. This is my last column. Between my father and me this column has appeared in the *Wetside Journal* throughout most of the 20th century and the first decade of the 21st, but I am getting old now; it is time to retire. I will miss you, Wetside. In the words of my favorite rock band, what a long strange trip it's been.